Neverthorn

Neverthorn

Of Quirks and Curses, Book 1

SHANNON MAYER

MICHAEL  JOSEPH

PENGUIN MICHAEL JOSEPH

UK | USA | Canada | Ireland | Australia
India | New Zealand | South Africa

Penguin Michael Joseph is part of the Penguin Random House group of companies
whose addresses can be found at global.penguinrandomhouse.com.

Penguin Random House UK
One Embassy Gardens, 8 Viaduct Gardens, London s w 11 7 b w

penguin.co.uk

First published 2025
001

Set in 13.5/16pt Garamond MT Std
Typeset by Jouve (UK), Milton Keynes
Printed and bound in Great Britain by Clays Ltd, Elcograf S.p.A.

The authorized representative in the EEA is Penguin Random House Ireland,
Morrison Chambers, 32 Nassau Street, Dublin d02 yh68

A CIP catalogue record for this book is available from the British Library.

HARDBACK ISBN: 978–0–241–70183–6
TRADE PAPERBACK ISBN: 978–0–241–70184–3

Penguin Random House is committed to a sustainable future
for our business, our readers and our planet. This book is made from
Forest Stewardship Council® certified paper.

For the readers who are too old to get called
up to a magical school but know that they have magic
within just waiting to be let out, given the chance.

And . . . for the readers who want that magical
school to have more sexual tension than a pair
of giants making googly eyes at each other, but less
gratuitous scenes than an Only Fans account.
Neverthorn is more of a balance between those two.

Like a fine wine, ready to be chugged at the
end of a never-ending day.

I

I was just yards away from laying my hands on the crème de la crème of gemstones when I smelled trouble. Literally. The stench of rotten eggs that had me scrambling for cover in the tiny apartment. The foul odor was the hallmark of a particularly shady binding spell. It was cast by a half-assed Dwimmer who probably thought I was too dumb to know the difference between magic and a leaky stove.

Fool.

Moving slowly through the third-story apartment that was most certainly not my own, I kept low to the ground, flicking my fingers around my body, concealing myself in shadows.

Was this the right way of casting this particular spell?

No.

Effective as hell?

You bet.

As long as my luck held, and the spell didn't fizzle out on me.

Untraceable, too, which was rather handy seeing as it wasn't on the Thaumaturgy Senate's list of 'acceptable' spells.

Creeping along on my belly, I tucked myself under the ruffled bottom edge of a flowered couch cover that must have been manufactured in the seventies. Then I held my breath. This turned out to be a smart move, as I met the empty gaze of a leathery, mummified rat that had all but melded into the floorboards, right under my nose. I turned my head and grimaced, watching for feet to pass by the couch, wondering who the hell they might belong to.

The old witch who currently lived in this apartment was well known in magical circles as a collector with an odd way of living. Unlike most witches, who tended to settle in areas surrounded by our own – Salem, Asheville, or Triora, Italy – she moved around a lot, certain that someone was after her trash heap of 'treasures.' She took garbage bags full of junk with her everywhere she went, and regularly burned her homes down – insisting it was the only way to cleanse herself of the spirits that followed her.

Agatha Daisy Faganello was, in short, a weirdo among weirdos.

I had followed her here to Rio de Janeiro and had been casing her apartment for the last month, hoping to find the perfect time to slip in, nab what I came for, and get out. Keeping track of all her movements and habits, taking note of the wards she meticulously placed to protect her treasures before she left every night to collect more junk.

I felt like I knew her.

So, I wasn't totally surprised when the shoes that finally came into view weren't the fuzzy bunny slippers Aggie preferred. Nope, scuffed black boots that had to be size twelve or bigger were closing in on the couch.

A crackle of static from a short-wave walkie-talkie burst through the air, then a click of a button.

'No, boss, she isn't here.'

Native English speakers, and American, like me.

I ignored the little flutter in my chest as the boots went by again. Maybe some holier-than-thou Runecoat hoping to bust Aggie for practicing unsanctioned magic or some bullshit like that?

'The binding spell brushed up against someone, then . . . nothing. She must have left already,' Boots continued.

A second voice, male, a bit raspy, came through the walkie-talkie, and it tickled something at the very edge of my memory. Familiar but . . . not.

'She didn't fucking vanish into thin air; she doesn't have the skill. Find her.'

'Yes, boss.' Another *click* of the walkie-talkie as the static went silent. 'Bastard wizard thinks his shit don't stink,' he muttered under his breath.

As he made his way around the room, I slid further under the couch, past the rat, stopping at the pile of crumpled-up papers, with a stash of kindling and a packet of matches perched on top.

Aggie at her finest, prepped to burn and run. I settled next to the kindling and held still, straining to hear every movement.

My mind ticked through the possibilities. So, if Boots *was* a Runecoat, then who was the wizard? Or were the men not magical law enforcement at all. Maybe they were here for the same reason I was?

The Unicorn Diamond was a sweet little piece. Shaped like the eye of a unicorn, it looked purple but gave off every color of the rainbow when held to the light. Legend had it, the gem bestowed luck on its owner. So, while it was worth a cool million plus due to rarity and carat weight, it would command triple that from the right buyer, like the high-stakes poker player who had hired me.

I knew a few things about magical items, but there was magic, and then there were fairy tales.

One you read before bed for shits and giggles. The other could get you killed.

I scrunched up my face as the dust under the couch tickled at my nose.

Breath caught in my suddenly tight chest and my vision began to blur. Pulse pounding, I forced myself to focus on the items I could see and mentally cataloged them.

Dead rat.

Dust bunny.

Pen cap.

The black, scuffed boots came to a stop as the intruder sat down on the couch, the springs poking into my back, pinning me face down to the floor. Sweat slid down the sides of my face as my vision began to flicker, specks of light threatening to pull me under.

Keep it together, Harlow. You can do it. Slow breaths, in through your nose —

'Boss, she isn't here. I've checked everywhere, and the binding spell isn't latching onto anyone.'

'She's there. We watched her go in five minutes ago, Brick,' the other man said with a heavy sigh. 'Check all the rooms, the closets, anywhere she could hide.'

Again, that voice tugged at some long-buried memory, and they distracted me for a moment. Long enough to focus on the words being spoken.

They weren't after Aggie *or* the diamond.

They were after me.

Harlow Chandramallika Daygon. Neverthorn Academy dropout in the magical Dwimmer world at sixteen, black market valuables purveyor in the Unlit human world at twenty-nine. Sure, I was an amazing thief out here among the Dims – humans, that is. One of the best. But my work didn't exactly mark me as worthy of attention from magical types unless said attention came with a heavy dose of scorn.

So then, why were they after me?

The question made breathing impossible, and my upper lip broke out in beads of sweat. I had a minute, two tops, before all Carol-the-human-therapist's coping tools went straight out the window and I fully lost my shit.

'I've already been through the whole place . . .' Brick whined, breaking the ominous silence.

'Look again!'

'Roger that.' A short pause, followed by a muttered, 'Asshole.'

'I can still hear you, Brick.'

'Sorry, boss.'

He didn't sound sorry at all.

'Bring Ms. Daygon in, or don't bother coming back out.'

Brick stood, easing the springs off my back. I forced myself to stay still until his footsteps faded down the hall before sucking in a gulp of air. Then, I scuttled out from under the couch and swiped a hand over my clammy face.

I had to move fast. From what they'd said, it sounded like there were more men watching the building, and I needed to buy myself some time before they were called in.

Thieving 101: *Distractions work wonders.*

Grabbing the pile of kindling, some of the crumpled paper, and the matches, I crouched next to the velvet-covered couch and set my fire starters on the cushion. I didn't dare use a spell until I had to, in case they could trace it.

Striking a match, I lit the crumpled paper and used a single piece of kindling to poke at it, burning the tip to a quick char.

Ears tuned for Brick's footsteps, I flipped the raggedy crocheted blanket lying across the back of the sofa over the burning pile of wood. Then, I slid back along the linoleum floor. The crackle of flames was barely audible at first, but with the tinder-dry couch, it wouldn't take long to catch.

Gripping the last piece of kindling, I scooted into the kitchen and pressed my back to the small island.

There was no way I'd be able to get the Unicorn Diamond

out now. I frowned and glanced up at the peeling paint on the ceiling.

Unless . . .

Smoke was filling the room rapidly, filtering through the apartment.

'Ah shit,' Brick snarled at the fire, stumbling into view. He had his back to me as he used a spell to put the fire out, his focus entirely on the flames.

Moving light and silent, I leapt over the island onto his back, snaking my arm around his neck, and clamping down as fast and hard as I could.

'Lights out, big guy,' I whispered into his ear.

He only got out one grunt before he went to his knees, buckling under the speed at which I'd cut off the blood to his head. I held him until he was flat on the ground, then dropped him.

I'd have three to four minutes before he came around.

Which meant it was now or never.

'Brick, why is there smoke coming out the window?'

The question crackled over the walkie-talkie. I grabbed it up and, adjusting my voice as low as I could, I hit the button on the side and said, 'Looks like Agatha set a booby-trap.'

'Find Harlow; we're running out of time. The Runecoats will be here soon.'

So, these guys aren't the magical version of the FBI after all. Who the hell were they?

A new and inexplicable dread spread through me. Still gripping the last piece of kindling as if it were a weapon, I sprinted to the back bedroom where Agatha spent most of her time.

Should I have aborted my mission and just bolted out of there? Probably. But I wasn't leaving without the Unicorn Diamond now that I was this close. The bounty on the purple gem would pay for a house in a safe neighborhood and finally let me turn my temporary shelter for teen runaways into a proper one, with actual beds to sleep on instead of used couches with springs poking through. Better yet, it would be like a real home for me and my sister, Opie.

When was the last time either of us had that?

I flipped the mattress on Aggie's bed, feeling along the edges . . . and there it was. A tiny tear near where Agatha would lay her head, visible from the side window. Every night I'd seen her reach in and touch what I hoped would be tucked inside.

I stuffed my hand in and pulled out a black velvet pouch. A groan from the other room told me my time was up.

Using my forefinger and thumb, I made a swift pinching motion – my own spell, thank you very much, and again, untraceable – shrinking the velvet pouch and whatever was in it to the size of a marble before repeating the maneuver with my last piece of kindling. Who knew when I might need to light another fire?

When I was done, I tucked them into the pocket I had sewn into the inside collar of my jacket.

Another groan, static off the walkie-talkie. 'She got the drop on me. She's gone.'

No time to waste, I went straight for the window, slid out and climbed up, using the handholds I'd set into the stone the night before. Once on top of the building, I pulled my phone from my back pocket and hit redial.

'Josh, I'm out. I have it.'

'Good job!' my getaway driver and partner in crime said with a laugh of relief. 'Milkshakes on me.'

Just the thought of ice cream blended with strawberries, covered in thick whipped cream, made me feel a little better. I sprinted across the rooftop, the glitter of the night and the hum of the city spilling upward. 'I've got a tail, so meet me at the back-up site.'

'You got it. See you in five.' There was a hum from the engine of his bike, and then the line went dead.

Five minutes.

A crackle of energy spun me around and suddenly four cloaked figures stood on the building in front of me, each with their right hand extended in the classically trained dueling stance. They were prepping to cast Hecate knew how many spells at once.

'I wish I could stay, but I've got people to see and all . . .' With a grin, I leapt from the edge of the roof, spinning in mid-air so I could face them as I fell, both middle fingers extended.

Later suckers.

'She jumped, she jumped!'

Before I hit the ground, I wove a quick spell of air, cushioning my fall, praying it wouldn't fail me. My luck held – thank you, Unicorn Diamond.

I landed on the balls of my feet and was moving before the men on the roof had even taken a step in my direction. Of course, I should have wondered why it had been so easy to get away.

Four more figures were waiting for me on the ground and began flinging binding spells my way the second I rounded the corner. I dodged left, then right, but my feet flew out from under me as I felt a telltale slap at my ankles. A second later, I face-planted into the sidewalk.

So much for Unicorn Diamond luck.

2

Stars exploded behind my eyelids but there was no time to assess the damage. I sat up, fingers flicking as I frantically traced an escape rune into the air, freeing my ankles. Then I rolled to my feet just as another round of spells smashed into the building next to my head, shattering the brick and sending me spinning away. I took a narrow alley that ended in a fence and split the wire with a quick spell and the slash of my hand.

My clothes tore on the edges of the chain link, and my forehead throbbed even as blood stung my eyes, but none of that slowed me. Ahead, there was a crowd of people drinking, singing, and dancing along the street.

The perfect second diversion.

Thieving 102: *Lose yourself in the crowd.*

I dove into the melee, snagged a colorful shawl and used it to swipe the blood from my wound before wrapping it around my shoulders. Then, I whipped off a quick illusion rune to change the appearance of my hair to a chocolatey brown instead of its usual, almost white blonde. I forced my feet to dance along with the music, weaving between the other dancers, spinning and turning, trying to see if I was still being followed.

My phone rang and I picked it up.

'Josh?'

'I've got two cars on my tail now too, black SUVs like cops or something. I can't get to our second pickup. What do you want me to do?' There was more than a note of panic in his voice. He didn't do well under pressure.

Ice slid down my spine. 'Keep moving and just try to get there, okay?'

'I hope you've got some sort of magic up your sleeve, because this ain't looking good,' he said over the roar of his bike.

Yeah, so Josh was a Dim. Human. No magic for him. In fact, he didn't know witches and wizards existed at all, never mind that I was one. Dims tended to lose sight of their moral compass when faced with the possibilities of what magic could do for them. Hell, even us Dwimmers struggled with that temptation . . .

I knew every time I used a bastardized rune instead of just relying on my wits and stealth to do a job, I was taking a risk of being found and punished by the Senate for performing unsanctioned magic. But I'd gotten so good at shielding it. And, as terrified as I was at the thought of being magically shackled by them, I had mouths to feed. And I was sick and tired of piecing together small scores just to keep a roof over our heads. The quickest way to financial security for me and mine was through magic.

A fact I was sorely regretting now. I had to find a way to Josh; from there we would be in the clear.

I tapped my upper lip as I considered my options. 'Try to shake them. I'll keep circling back to the spot if I can. Either way, call me back in ten minutes. And stay safe,' I added. 'I want that milkshake later.'

I hung up first, tucking my cell away. This was bad. They were damned persistent, whoever they were, coming all the way from the States to find me. And with two cars following Josh and all the men on my tail, there were a lot of them. Surely more than would be warranted for a few bits and bobs of non-violent, unsanctioned magic?

Most concerning of all, though? I'd spent the thirteen years since I'd left Neverthorn blazing my own way, modifying traditional rune spells into my own shorthand version. While I did my best to save them for the direst of situations, as far as I knew, the ones I did use had been undetectable. Which begged the question . . .

How in Hecate's name had they found me?

There had to be at least one powerhouse Dwimmer behind this. A witch or wizard strong enough to sense even the tiniest sizzle of magic in the air. Smart enough to realize that there was more than one way to throw a rune.

But who?

Still moving with the crowd, I let the momentum take me all the way down to the market square and waved at strangers, who drunkenly waved back. I swayed and stumbled as I slipped away from the crowd and let myself into the first door that I found unlocked.

I didn't dare use my magic to change anything else about my appearance. It had been risky enough changing my hair color. Good thing I was prepared.

Pulling off my jacket, revealing a dark tank top underneath, I transferred my loot into the small pocket I had sewn into my bra. Girls love hidden pockets.

I tossed the jacket on the ground. Tearing the shawl into strips, I shimmied out of my pants and wrapped my hips in the bright material.

Knee-high boots, bright skirt, dark tank top. Making my way through the dim room, I found an empty vodka bottle and grabbed hold of it.

I let myself out, walking with a slight wobble, while I scanned the streets.

The first person I saw?

Frigging Brick.

He was not cloaked like the others, and I watched him do a slow turn of the courtyard we were in. 'Anything?'

He clicked his walkie-talkie, his eyes skimming past me. 'Nothing, boss.'

I couldn't resist pushing my luck, and bumped him as I stumbled past, and he scowled down at me.

'Get out of here, lady.' He shooed at me with his hands, and his magic pushed me back a few feet. I let the shove of magic hurry me along and smiled.

A kernel of hope blooming in my chest, I made my way to the pickup site, trying to keep my pace slow and easy.

The bus stop across from my meeting point was full of revelers headed home, the bench packed with drooping bodies, the smell of vomit and alcohol covering anything else.

The rumble of a familiar bike engine on the far side of the park called to me, and I started across the street, headed in that direction. Josh was the best getaway driver I'd known and meeting him had been a tidy bit of luck. It didn't hurt that he liked to bring me milkshakes and did whatever I told him to when it came to planning a heist.

I mean, for a Dim, that made him a slam dunk in my book.

I touched my fingers to the side of my bra where the Unicorn Diamond was tucked into my hidden pocket. 'Maybe you *are* lucky after all.'

Picking up my pace, I broke into a jog, a grin tugging at my lips.

Of course, that grin dropped a split second later as a body slammed into me, taking me to the ground with such force it knocked the wind out of me.

'Get off me,' I growled, then twisted and delivered an open-handed blow to my assailant's throat, crushing his windpipe. With a gurgle, he let me go. I was about to take off again, but I was hit with a full body binder from an unseen attacker that wrapped around me within a split second and cut my fury short, stealing my breath.

It felt as though a snake had slithered up and around my legs, pinning them together, then around my arms so that I stood like a soldier at attention. There were very few Dwimmers who could cast a spell that powerful, that complex, that fast.

I scanned the area in a panic and caught sight of Josh in my periphery. He was standing beside his bike twenty yards away, motionless, his jaw hanging open.

'Josh!' I screamed his name. But as three more figures advanced on me, I knew it was a lost cause. He must've known it too, because his eyes popped wide. Then he shook his head, leapt back on his bike, and gunned it.

Chickenshit.

'Give it up. It's done.'

There it was again. That damned *voice.*

He was behind me, and I couldn't turn to look, my head and neck locked in place.

'Look, you can have the diamond,' I began. 'I was just picking it up for a friend but –'

'There is no diamond.' He was close enough that I could smell him now. Leather and crisp air and dark magic, laced with wood smoke from a crackling fire, warm and tantalizing. The smell took me back to being sixteen in a blink, and then the person it was attached to stepped into my line of sight, obliterating all else.

He was a massive wall of a man, easily topping 6'5", with shoulders so broad they blocked out the moon. He'd filled out since I'd seen him all those years ago. I managed to zero in on his face and blinked. Deep-green eyes capped off with dark, slashing brows, the right one bisected by a scar that went from forehead to chin. I swayed in place, dizzy with shock as the other figures around me, including the guy I'd karate-chopped in the throat, seemed to melt away.

'Typhon Moreno?'

It wasn't really a question. Despite the added scar, the black hair that was now kissed at the temples with a premature hint of gray, and the face that had matured by more than a decade, Typhon Moreno wasn't a guy you forgot. Even now, the rib positioned directly over my heart throbbed with pain of the past.

Don't fall down that rabbit-hole again, dummy.

His gaze held mine as he tipped his head. 'It's Doyen Moreno now.'

One of my former peers from Neverthorn Academy a few years above me, Typhon, had been the only student plucked straight from graduation and set onto the path of professorship without ever leaving. He'd always been chilly and standoffish toward everyone, but once he'd started his training, he'd really cranked it up. In fact, he'd been instrumental in me leaving when he'd aimed his dislike directly at me, though I was never totally sure why.

Judging by the scowl on his face, nothing had changed.

His eyes drifted over my face. 'We've been looking for you for quite a while now. I was sent to . . . present you with a choice, Ms. Daygon,' he said. A movement on each side of him told me we were being flanked, and Brick came up behind him.

'What kind of choice? I mean, let's be honest. You have me all bound up in your magic, so my choices are pretty limited at the moment.'

He didn't so much as move, but I could feel the menace rolling off him, pressing on me. 'Harlow Daygon. You can come to Neverthorn of your own accord, or –'

'I'll take option number two,' I said without hesitation. It didn't matter what it was, there was no chance I was going back to Neverthorn for any reason. Not only was the place outright dangerous, being there would open the floodgates to so much trauma I wanted to forget. Just the thought of reliving it had me breaking out in a cold sweat despite the warmth of the night.

'*Or*,' he continued, his gaze growing impossibly colder, 'you can go back to your empty motel room over on Avenida Rio Branco.'

I cocked my head and stared at him, panic rising in my chest. 'W-why would my room be empty?'

'Because we have Ophelia. We picked her up a few hours ago, right after you left.'

My stomach dropped and it took a second to manage a tight smile and meet his gaze again. The second I let him see my terror, any shot at negotiating with him was out the window.

Damn it. I'd been so careful, for so long. But after a life on the run, I'd clearly gotten sloppy of late. And now Opie was paying the price.

A wave of sick rolled through me, and I had to swallow it back.

'Joke's on you,' I finally managed through numb lips. 'Do you have any idea how much that girl eats? Besides, we both know how much you love a chatterbox. She'll have you begging me to take her back inside a week.' I let out a laugh that sounded shriller than I'd intended, and Typhon cocked his head. He held out his hand and Brick set a folder into his palm. Typhon flipped it open and started reading.

'Ophelia Rose Baumgarten. Youngest daughter of Hecketa and Svenson Baumgarten. An illustrious family that goes back centuries and has produced some of the most accomplished Dwimmers in recorded history.' He looked up over the papers at me. 'They chose to cast little Ophelia aside without even sending her for schooling when they realized she would never be a great witch and possessed no Quirk to make her special.'

My chest tightened, but I couldn't find the words to deny what he was saying. Typhon handed the papers back to Brick. 'You should've seen her face earlier tonight when she learned that Tarquinius himself, Sage of Neverthorn Academy and the professor who trained her father, had sent for her. She wanted to make sure it was okay with you before she packed her bag, but once we were able to stage a phone call with "you" thanks to a truly excellent Mimic, she jumped right in the car.'

Bastards.

When I'd come across Opie on the streets three years ago, she'd been a skinny ten-year-old kid in desperate need of a kind word and a good meal. And unlike all the other kids – Dims and Dwimmers alike – who had passed through my little apartment for a hand up, she'd wound up staying. She thought of me as her big sister now, which was a serious upgrade, because her actual big sister was a piece of shit, just like her parents. The Baumgarten family could be as illustrious and wealthy as they wanted to be, but at the end of the day, they were ruthless elitists who mated solely based on bloodlines in an effort to build the perfect magical specimen with a rare and coveted Quirk – a singular magical trait that would set them apart from the rest.

Like horse breeders, only, you know, for people.

And they had over two centuries of Quirks to their credit. There was Opie's first cousin Malena, the only Switch known in Dwimmer history who could change her outward appearance to match someone else's so completely that their own mother wouldn't be able to tell the difference. There was her great-grandmother Prudence, one of only three known Creators ever born. The woman could literally defy the laws of physics and make matter from . . . well, nothing. There was her second Cousin Anya, who could see the immediate future, making her the best fighter ever born until she was poisoned by her own sister, and, most recently, there was Ophelia's own sister, Nilda, who could fly.

Then there was Opie.

She'd told me her story haltingly, in a broken voice. When they realized she was struggling to learn even the most basic spellcasting at home, they hadn't waited to see if she had a Quirk . . . hadn't given her a chance to go to Neverthorn and learn. In their eyes, she was a pox on the Baumgarten name, so they cut her off, like a rotten limb. Removed her from the family tree.

I still hadn't thought up a punishment harsh enough for those people yet, but when I did, I'd be the one doling it out.

I mentally added both Typhon and his boss, Sage Tarquinius, to the list of people I owed an ass-kicking on Opie's behalf as I held his gaze. Because I knew something they didn't.

Opie didn't just not have a Quirk – she had no magic at all. Being told she did, and then finding out she didn't? It would shatter her. Did they know that she had zero magic? Had her family told on her to the school?

'We know,' Typhon said, as if reading my mind. 'She has no magic.'

'Why?' I asked, shaking my head. 'What could possibly be so important to set her up to hope and believe in something we know isn't ever going to happen? I'm not worth it, Typhon. There is no reason to want me back.'

His eyes hardened. 'Once you agree to the terms, I can

brief you on the basics. At the school, Tarquinius will fill you in on any more information as needed.'

I tried to let that digest, but his non-answer only gave me heartburn.

'So, what's the play here? As long as I go with you, you guys are going to pretend to teach her magic and treat her well? Is that right?'

He inclined his head, his lips tight.

'And what assurances do I have that she won't get hurt? I've been there, Typhon. You can't bullshit me. Kids were encouraged to test out their own poorly mixed potions, pressured to attempt complex runes that backfired on them, asked to take on too much too soon . . . and that was years ago. You can't for one hot second make me believe it's better now. It's going to be worse than ever – especially for Opie.'

'No.' He shook his head. 'Not for Opie. If you come, we will keep her safe. You have my word on that.'

I resisted the urge to tell him exactly how little his word meant to me. 'And if I don't?'

'Then she'll be there all alone, wondering why you refused to join her as you promised in your call with her. Wondering how to navigate this new life without any guidance from someone who has been in her shoes . . . out of their depth, in a strange new place, not fitting in.' He lifted one broad shoulder as if it didn't matter to him either way. 'Eventually, assuming nothing truly awful befalls her, I imagine she'll get kicked out for having no magic at all and come home a broken shell of the girl she used to be. Only you won't be here to comfort her. You'll be busy serving a sentence for breaking a multitude of laws and she'll wonder why she's been abandoned, yet again.'

He could've used a sledgehammer instead of a razor.

'Is she still nearby? Let me talk to her.'

'That won't be necessary –'

'Let me talk to her right now, or we are done here. You can have me taken by the Runecoats or whatever you need to do, but I won't come to Neverthorn.'

It was a risky play, because in order for him to believe it, I had to mean it. And I did. But something told me that, for whatever reason, him returning to Neverthorn without me in tow wasn't an option – not if they'd sent him all the way to South America to find me. Not based on the way he'd spoken to Brick through the walkie-talkie.

So here we were, horns locked. Now to see who flinched first.

He stared me down long enough that I had to resist the urge to squirm, but then he let out a low growl. 'I'll need to mend the cut on your head. You're bleeding and she'll wonder why.'

'Fine.'

He rubbed his fingertips together and stepped closer, forcing me to crane my neck or have my face buried in his barrel-sized chest.

'Can you hurry up? You're suffocating me.' I winced as the mending rune began to knit my skin back together.

'You smell like vodka,' he growled. 'Are you drunk?'

His magic sank into my skin, tingling as the wound closed. 'I wish,' I muttered.

The second the cut was healed, he stepped back, tugged a walkie-talkie from his pocket and held it to his mouth.

'Bring the girl.'

He must've anticipated my demand because a sleek, black car pulled up less than two minutes later. Luckily, that was all the time I needed to plot my next move.

'Don't try anything stupid,' Typhon muttered through clenched teeth as he reached for the back door. Before he could pull the handle, the door flew open, and a tiny copper-haired whirlwind tumbled out. Opie launched herself my way, nearly knocking the wind out of me.

'I still can't believe it, Lo-lo. Tarquinius sent for me! They think I've got potential! They think I might be the best Dwimmer in the whole Baumgarten family, but I'm just a late bloomer. Tarquinius's letter said the best usually are, and it might take me another year or two, but . . .'

She pulled back and gazed up at me, her face lit with a joy I'd never seen.

'This was the wish I made at my past three birthdays, and now it's coming true. I guess I am magic after all, ha!'

I swallowed back the burning rush of bile, forcing a smile. 'I guess so,' I agreed with a nod. 'That's so cool.'

'Yeah, and Doyen Typhon says that he thinks I'm going to fit right in. I know I'm still behind in my training; once I'm at Neverthorn I'll catch up.'

I sucked in a breath and tugged her close to me again before bending low and pressing my lips to her ear.

'I need you to trust me, Opie. Hold tight, and don't let go.'

She would hate me for this. Maybe forever, but I had no choice. Better she hates me than go to Neverthorn and find out the truth.

I traced a rune in the air and instantly felt the wind rush and swirl around me, making me nearly sick with relief. I'd never dared even try a Spiriting spell before because I hadn't figured out a way to make it untraceable, but I was desperate.

As I started to fade away, though, I realized my arms were empty.

'Opie!'

'She's already signed her letter, Harlow.'

Fuck. Me.

Unless the school formally withdrew her admissions offer, she was bound by her acceptance. Opie had to go to Neverthorn.

But she doesn't have to stay, I reminded myself, looking for some silver lining here.

I pulled back the Spiriting rune and once again held tight to the kid in my arms as I turned to Typhon in defeat.

'Of course. I . . . just wanted to pop us home to pack some clothes before we left.'

Despite the despair and panic threatening to drag me under, I kept my tone light. We locked eyes and I willed him wordlessly to play along.

His gaze didn't soften, but he didn't call me out either.

'She's packed and her suitcases are in the car. One of my men will transport her to Neverthorn now while you and I get your things. We'll meet them there later.'

So Neverthorn it was.

'Perfect,' I snapped, gritting my teeth so hard it was a wonder I didn't chip a molar.

Opie gave me one last squeeze and beelined for the car.

'See you soon, Lo-lo. It's gonna be sooo awesome.'

'Yeah. So awesome,' I parroted. 'See you there.'

The car door closed behind her and Typhon stepped toward me, close enough that the smell of leather off his coat swirled up my nose again. For the first time, I realized how different he looked. At nineteen, he'd been good-looking in a dark, brooding way that had all the girls swooning. At thirty-two years old, life had clearly given him lemons and he'd taken a hard pass on the whole lemonade thing. In fact, I was pretty sure his insides were even more scarred than his outsides.

I hated him then for how he'd treated me.

And I hated him now for what he was forcing me to do.

'It was a necessary evil,' he said, as if reading my thoughts once more.

'Save it,' I shot back, refusing to give him the satisfaction of seeing just how shattered I was. 'Let's just get this shit-show on the road.'

He turned wordlessly and started walking. I trailed behind him, watching the car with Opie in it as it melted away into the night.

'Try to keep up,' he muttered over one broad shoulder.

'Can you at least tell me what's going on now? Seriously, Typhon . . . I haven't seen you in over a decade. Are you even a doyen for real, or just some half-assed Runecoat wannabe doing Tarquinius's bidding?' Honestly, I just couldn't imagine him being a teacher. He was such a dick.

He finally stopped and turned to face me, closing the space between us with a single step as he glowered down at me. 'I *am* a doyen at the school. And as for what's going on now, we are heading directly to Neverthorn. No need to actually go and pack your things. You can just grab what you need at the Nevershoppes when we pick up your uniform and books.'

My eyes popped wide. Either I'd misheard him, or I'd entered the ninth circle of hell.

'Say what again, now?'

He let out a long-suffering sigh. 'What is it that you aren't understanding, Harlow?'

'You think I'm *re-enrolling* at Neverthorn? I thought you just needed me there for like . . . a day or two!' I let out a crack of laughter as I shook my head furiously. 'Nope. No way. I said I would *come* to the school with you for Opie's sake. I never said anything about attending.'

Besides, Neverthorn Academy wouldn't allow someone my age back in . . . would they? Moreover, why the hell would they want me to attend?

'Your class attendance is part of the deal. Take it or leave it,' he said, producing an envelope from his coat pocket and holding it out. 'Here is your admissions letter. Sign it.'

'I need to know why,' I growled, staring at the oh-so-familiar missive like it was coated in acid. 'And I need to know now.'

Typhon's mouth went flat and his eyes hardened. There was a dangerous edge to him that hadn't been there before, when I'd been at Neverthorn the first time. How far could I push him?

'Sign the papers.'

I crumpled them in my fist and held his eyes despite wanting to look away. 'Tell me.'

He tapped his fingers against the paper and just slowly shook his head. 'Because right now, you're our only hope in saving the world.'

I was sure that I was hearing this wrong. That my ears were on vacation and had not just . . . that could not be right. He put his hand over mine and literally helped me sign the papers as I stood there, stunned.

Shock was too small a word. I'd thought I was in trouble for the spells I'd been using. That had been my best guess up to this point. But this? This couldn't be right.

'I'm sorry. What?' The single word question came out like a bleat. 'What? What? No, that can't be . . .'

Typhon let go of my hand, my signature clear as day. 'Heronius is . . . out of commission. He can no longer defend us against Nocta.'

Heronius Maximus – yes, his parents actually gave him that name – had been tasked with keeping Neverthorn and its European counterpart, Heathermoor, safe from Nocta.

Nocta's end goal, as I'd understood it, was to break through the weave that separated the Dwimmer world and the Everdark – a place where dark magic thrived – allowing the Dwellers who lived there to come to our side and take over the realm.

For decades now, Heronius Maximus, along with Sage Tarquinius, and the Thaumaturgy Senate – the gatekeepers of magic – had managed to keep Nocta from completely destroying the weave. But without Heronius leading the charge . . .

'W-what do you mean out of commission?'

'I mean he can no longer do the job. And, according to Tarquinius, our fate may very well lie in your hands. Harlow . . . we believe you might be the key to stopping Nocta.'

My palms went slick with sweat and blood rushed to my ears. The evilest being in all of the Dwimmer world. Disrupter of spells. Destroyer of lives. General of his own damn army.

And it was on *me* to stop him?

3

My brain buzzed like a nest of angry bees as I tromped through thigh-high brush in a heavily wooded forest.

It had been a dizzyingly long night. A private jet sent by the school picked us up in Brazil and flew us to Montreal, where Typhon had used a proper Spiriting rune to get us south to the St. Lawrence Seaway. Now, we were bushwhacking our way through the wilderness of the most remote of the Thousand Islands to get to the other side, where we would take a boat to our final destination: Neverthorn.

'Uhhh, remind me again why you didn't just Spirit us right to the water's edge instead of into the middle of frigging Jurassic Park?' I asked as I rushed to keep up, yet again. 'I know you're more than capable.'

Once I'd established there was no way of getting out of this mess, I'd had no choice but to go along with Typhon's plan. He'd always been a strong wizard, even when we were teenagers. He'd improved over the years, and while my magic was pretty nifty if unconventional, there was something to be said for a guy who worked as an instructor *teaching* it. Magic wasn't just his job – it was his whole life.

A life that now apparently included ruining mine.

One good thing; I was pretty sure my suffering would be brief as they'd quickly realize they'd got the wrong person. Brief but excruciating. The months I'd spent at Neverthorn Academy had been the worst of my life, and that was coming from an orphan who spent the latter half of her teen years basically homeless.

Typhon grunted and pushed aside a swath of ferns so big they could have fed a brontosaurus. His voice fell into a teacher's drone. 'A Spiriting spell can be used to transport ourselves from one Unlit location to another, but once we're this close to Neverthorn, it's illegal to use it, to keep people from just popping directly into the school. It's a safety precaution. Do I need to also remind you that Unlit means human realm? Hecate's ass, you should know all this stuff. What are you, thirty now?'

I let out a snort. 'Not even close. I'm twenty-nine.'

He shot an unamused look over his shoulder and continued hacking his way through the forest like some sort of goth Indiana Jones. He seemed surprisingly comfortable, given the brush was so thick we couldn't see more than a few feet in front of us.

'Are there any poisonous spiders in these parts?'

'Yes. And it's venomous, not poisonous. Venom is injected, poison is ingested,' he replied, continuing forward and letting a sapling branch snap back and hit me square in the chest.

Asshole.

'I've been meaning to ask . . . my friend Josh is going to be wondering where I went. He'll probably call 911 eventually. That would be sticky for you if the human police come looking for me.'

Josh most definitely wouldn't. That was some Thieving 103 shit: *Never call the cops.*

Ever.

But as furious as I was with him for leaving me behind, I knew Josh. He'd come back and look for me once he'd put a plan together. He was what you might call a slow thinker.

'I already sent him a text from your phone that you were okay but had to lay low for a while.'

'There are kids who need –'

'I also told him to shut down the apartment for the runaways. No one else will miss you.'

The thing was, Typhon wasn't wrong. There had been no kids except Opie for several weeks. And other than Josh . . . there was no one else. A few silent minutes passed, and I shivered in the cool air, choosing to believe it was the air and not sadness that made me shiver. 'Are we almost there?'

As soon as the words left my mouth, we stepped into a clearing. If I hadn't been so focused on searching the trees for black widows in hiding, I'd have heard the rushing of water.

'Hand me your pouch.'

'What pouch?' I wasn't about to give up the goods that easy.

He reached out, his fingers brushing against my neck once more, and that light shiver intensified. He hooked the collar of my shirt and gave it a tug.

'The one you hide your stuff in. I've been watching you while you were observing Agatha. Give me the pouch so I can check you for weapons. Now.'

Well, damn. He really had done his homework. I knocked his hand aside, then reached into the pocket sewn into my bra, tugging out the little bag in question. He waved his hand impatiently, and I tossed it to him.

'How did you do that?' he asked, frowning.

'Do what?'

'Make it so much smaller.'

Duh. I shrugged. 'Magic.'

'Obviously. Which you learned where?' he pressed.

He wasn't going to like my answer.

'I created the rune for it myself. I call it "nicking notions."'

The name was *adorable* if I did say so myself.

'Have you been doing that the whole time since you left Neverthorn?'

'Doing what?'

'Creating your own runes.'

Something in his face told me that 'yes' was the wrong answer.

'Not the *whole* time . . .'

'If I'd known that, I'd have –' A muscle ticked in Typhon's jaw as he broke off and glared at me. 'I told Tarquinius that this will never work. You have no discipline, and you leap before thinking it through. And creating your own runes . . . Do you understand how dangerous unsanctioned runes can be?'

He wasn't wrong, I'd had a few spells go sideways, but for the most part I'd been successful. Really, the big clue was that I was still alive . . . 'Seems like we're on the same page here, Typhon. So why don't you scoot across the river and grab Opie for me, then me and her can skedaddle,' I said, jerking a thumb over my shoulder in the direction of the forest. 'Just tell Tarquinius we got away or something. Surely you can make up a plausible story.'

'You honestly think he'd believe I wasn't able to catch you?'

This fucking guy . . . the ego on him surely hadn't dimmed since I'd seen him last, despite the new scars.

'I don't know what you want from me!' I snapped, coming to the end of my rope. 'You're no happier than I am about this, so let's put our heads together and solve the problem. Oh! I know!' I said, thrusting up a finger like the idea had just come to me. 'You can let me and Opie go.'

'With Heronius out of the picture, there are only a handful of Dwimmers with the *potential* to defeat Nocta, and we need all of your kind on deck. You're coming to Neverthorn, so get used to it.'

'"Your kind?" What the hell does that even mean?' I bellowed, anger and fear leaving me feeling like I was in some sort of nightmare. That had to be it. This was just a bad dream. Some sort of anxiety-induced hallucination.

He didn't answer my questions. Typhon just stood in front of me and traced an intricate pattern in the air as he held up my tiny bag, and it expanded back to its full size. He tugged out a jewelry box, flicking it open with his thumb.

'This was her coin collection,' Typhon said. Hers. Agatha's. Damn it.

There was no diamond, unicorn or otherwise, inside. I'd been baited and set up from the start.

I leaned in to see a familiar set of gold coins gleaming up at me. Hecate's symbol of the triple moon was pressed into one side. The other was the bust of a man with antlers. The Horned King. The two gods Dwimmers looked to, neither of whom could save me now.

There was no choice. I knew when I was done.

'Let's get this charade over with, then,' I said with a heavy sigh as I trailed after him toward the roiling waters.

In the Unlit world, it still looked to be a part of the St. Lawrence Seaway. But once we tossed the coins in the air, it would become the Dwimmerfolk version of the River Styx. Or, as I liked to refer to it, Shit's Creek.

I'd seen it during the day on my first trip to Neverthorn, and it *was* lovely. The crystal-clear water had looked like a pane of glass as technicolor fish swam and otters frolicked. The bottom was gilded in coins, it seemed like there were millions of them, and when the sun shone on them, it bathed the shores in a golden light. It was like something out of a Disney movie. But now, just before dawn, the churning water was a deep unfathomable black. Like it hid the darkest of secrets, the deadliest of sins . . . and probably a few bodies.

A sense of apprehension rolled over me, and I felt like that sixteen-year-old girl again, terrified to leave her mother. Wishing I could postpone school again, just one more year . . .

I shoved the thought away and sucked in a shaky breath as Typhon tossed the coins from my pouch high into the air. Before they could hit the water, a small, rickety row-boat appeared with a skeleton at the helm. His finger bones clacked together as he plucked the coins from the air and popped them into his empty eye sockets, both with the Horned King facing out.

Judging us.

I pitied the fool who tried to steal even one penny from the bottom of his river. I'd heard tales, none of which ended well for the would-be thieves. Even *I* wouldn't take that job.

'All aboard,' the skeleton, Charon, called, his voice creaky and crackling.

Typhon headed to the river's edge, not waiting to see if I followed, because he knew what I'd finally come to accept . . . for now. I belonged to those in charge at Neverthorn until I figured out what was happening and left with Opie.

''Sup, Bones,' I said as I stepped gingerly onto the boat, wincing as it rocked. 'Long time no . . . see.' I motioned at his coin eyes.

Charon ignored me, and Typhon and I took our seats. There were only us two this time, as opposed to my last visit, when dozens of students of varying ages were transported at a time.

'Where are the other students? The ones you said were like me . . . all full of *potential*,' I asked, swallowing back a rush of bile as Charon slipped his pole into the water and we lurched into motion, the waves rolling us side to side and only very slowly forward.

'They came yesterday. We wanted you all to start together, but by the time we located you and set up our . . . meeting, it was too late.'

Perfect. Not only was I a twenty-nine-year-old woman attending magic school with a bunch of thirteen- to nineteen-year-olds, but I was also the 'new kid.' Or 'new old lady,' to be more accurate.

I forced myself to ask the question I'd been avoiding for hours, even though I was pretty sure I wasn't going to like the answer one bit.

'So . . . what actually happened to Heronius, anyway?'

Typhon's green eyes were hard as he stared me down. 'Heronius is dead.'

My jaw dropped. I think I even spluttered. 'What? That . . . that can't be. He's . . . Heronius. He can't be dead.'

He gave a curt nod. 'He can and he is. He was killed defending Heathermoor from an attack.' His voice was low and steady, but there was something in his expression . . . Hurt? Anger? It was hard to tell. Especially since I was reeling at the news myself, despite knowing deep down all along that if they were bringing in *me* of all people, things were bad.

'How?'

'Tarquinius will debrief you all on that when he feels it's time.'

Dead.

Heronius, the strongest wizard to ever graduate – outside of Nocta – had been killed and, as it stood, there was no one to step up to take his place. And for some reason, they thought I – arguably the worst wizard to ever darken the doors of the Academy – might be a good replacement?

Tarquinius and the Senate had lost their fucking minds. It was the only answer.

I gripped the sides of the boat and bent my head between my knees, fighting the urge to yack as terror took hold. Frantically, I searched for items to mentally ground me, and I rattled them off in my head.

Water.

Gold coins.

The school in the distance.

Typhon's boots.

It wasn't working.

I sucked in a wheezing breath and squeezed my eyes shut. Typhon Moreno, my sworn enemy, would now get to witness my greatest shame, worse even than not finishing my schooling.

A full-blown panic attack.

Suddenly, warmth shot through me like a flame, starting in my belly and spreading outward, leaving a trail of tingles like fingers across bare skin. The sensation was gone almost as quickly as it had come, and I looked up with blessed relief to find Typhon staring back at me, one inky brow arched.

I narrowed my eyes at him, heart rate spiking at the thought of his magic *in me*. True healing was an ultra-rare Quirk, but a quick fix like this wasn't beyond a strong Dwimmer, which Typhon most definitely was.

I stood gingerly and retook my seat with my back to him, determined to ignore him the rest of the trip. My skin itched from his magic, and I fought not to rub at my arms and my chest. That spot where my rib had nearly pierced my heart all those years ago, when I'd been in school . . . to say it was still a sore spot was an understatement.

In short, I didn't like how his magic made me feel even if he'd stopped me from rocking in a fetal position at the bottom of the boat.

Vulnerable. Like I was sixteen again, staring at him across

the room as his rune slammed into me. I clenched my hands, until my fingernails dug into the wood of my seat, pushing the memories away.

Once we reached Neverthorn, I'd be mostly free of Typhon. There were loads of other doyens teaching at the school. Odds were, I'd only have to look at his miserable face once in a while after today.

Praise be to Hecate, let it be true.

Ten more minutes to sit here in silence and stew about what was to come . . .

I could suffer through just about anything for ten minutes.

'Why did they call it Neverthorn, anyway?' I blurted, approximately four minutes later.

Silence.

'Is Mrs. Wickersham still working in the kitchens?' I asked.

Long sigh.

'She's our head chef now.'

There it was. A sweet little silver lining.

The only, and I mean *only*, good part about attending Neverthorn had been the three meals a day plus snacks. The food was nothing short of amazing. The best of every type of cuisine, from every part of the globe. Buttery, shortcrust hand-pies nearly bursting at the seams with roasted meats and parsnips. Spiced chickpea curry with garlic naan to dunk. Fluffy pancakes dotted with toasted pecans, doused in warmed maple syrup. A full English roast with rich gravy, crispy roast potatoes, and Yorkshire puddings, all the handmade pasta you could eat with every kind of sauce imaginable . . . It almost made me forget the shame of being unable to read runes the way other kids could . . . for a little while.

There were nights – long after I'd left Neverthorn, and my mother died, before I'd bolstered my magic and loosened my morals and turned to thieving – that I'd have given my left pinky to eat the floor scraps from one of those meals. And Aida Wickersham was the genius behind the best of them; that she was still at the school . . . well, glory be to Mother Hecate.

I was so enthralled by my food fantasies that I lurched in surprise when the boat bumped shore again.

'Off,' Typhon said unnecessarily.

I didn't wait for him. I made my way off the rickety boat and took a right toward the hulking towers that peaked above the thick forest. Best to just get this over with, like ripping off a bandage.

'Stop,' Typhon called, bringing me to a halt.

What now?

'You missed orientation. You need to go to the Never-shoppes for supplies first.'

I closed my eyes and took a long breath. 'Seems a waste when I'm quite sure they'll realize their mistake before week's end.'

'One can hope,' he said. 'Until then, get your supplies.'

We locked eyes, but there was no point in arguing. Looked like I would be stuck with him for at least another hour.

Gods above and below, save me from this.

Five minutes later, we stood at the fountain that marked the entrance to the shops. Each of the squat little stores on the cobbled pathway could've been home to a hobbit. The structures were built from knotty pine, their stone chimneys cheerily puffed white smoke into the now early-morning sky. A few had moss-covered rooftops.

'You guys still haven't updated this place? I hope at least the student uniforms are a little trendier.' I shot a pointed glance toward his long, black cloak. Underneath it he wore dark pants and a long-sleeved dark shirt, finished off by, you guessed it, a black belt and matte black buckle.

He rolled his eyes and shot a glance at his wristwatch — also black. 'We have just over an hour until your first class starts.'

He strode ahead, his long-legged pace eating up the cobblestones beneath him.

I fell in behind. 'I can't help but wonder how you ended up being sent to wrangle me. Surely you didn't volunteer . . .'

His harsh laugh sounded hella-rusty. 'I drew the short straw,' he said as he shoved the door to Neverthorn Uniform Shoppe open.

I let out a groan as I scanned the offerings. Still the same crisp white shirts with the monogrammed cuffs, traditional black neckties that would change color to match your house once selected, black pants for the boys and knee-length skirts for the girls.

'You can't be serious with the skirt. It's the twenty-first century, for Hecate's sake.'

'You have the option to select pants if you prefer,' a stiff voice interjected. I turned to find a dark-haired, sour-faced woman staring down her too-narrow nose at me from beneath a pair of bifocals.

She cocked her head and studied me for a long moment.

'Wilhelmina Benjamin, shopkeeper,' she said through pursed lips. 'You must be Harlow Daygon. Your reputation precedes you. Let's get you fitted, shall we?'

She swept to the back of the empty store, and I forced myself to follow her. Typhon trailed behind us as he again glanced impatiently at the door.

Wilhelmina gestured to a circular stand in the center of the back room.

'Climb up so I can get your measurements.'

I stayed put. 'I'll save you the time. Thirty-six, twenty-three, thirty-five.'

She squinted hard at me and shook her head. 'I think not, dear. You're shaving a good two inches off that waist.'

I shot her a quelling glare. 'That's not my waist. That's a food baby from the carbonara I ate on the plane. It will be gone by lunch.'

Hey, sue me. It was a lot of carbonara, and it was *delicious* . . .

Speaking of which, that was the last time I'd eaten, and I was starving.

The shopkeeper headed back out to the main floor, toward the racks, and began gathering various items.

'Whoa. What the hell is that?' I blurted as my gaze caught on something the shopkeeper had collected.

Wilhelmina followed my gaze and shrugged. 'A satchel.'

I blinked and shook my head. 'No. No, it most certainly is not. That, madam, is a fanny pack, and unless I'm playing the role of a sixty-year-old American dad on an Italian holiday in the annual school play, I will not be wearing one of those, thank you very much.'

Apparently, the apparel had not changed for the better – it had gotten worse.

'Bag it all up.' Typhon growled the words, anger radiating off him.

I turned back toward him. Those nostrils flaring, that little muscle near his steel-cut jaw ticking. The way his green eyes spat fire.

That's what made other girls swoon. Not me.

Fuck that and fuck him.

'Where to next?' I snapped, reaching for the bag Wilhelmina held out.

Typhon stalked ahead of me, and I again had to jog to keep up as we exited the store. Again, I just couldn't keep my mouth shut. I had to dig at him.

'Weird . . . I remember what you did to *me*, but I'm not

sure exactly what I did to you that made you hate me so much.'

I wanted to snatch the words back the second they were out. Apparently, sixteen-year-old me still hadn't gotten over the intense feelings of rejection that came whenever I thought of Neverthorn in general, and those only increased tenfold when it came to Typhon.

He stopped short and turned to face me, his face a mask of impatience.

'It's not just you. It's your type.'

'Yeah, and what type is that?' Another question I didn't actually want answered, but I asked it anyway.

He stepped close enough that the tips of his boots touched my own, and I could almost feel the sparks shooting from his eyes as he towered over me. His magic radiated around him, cloaking him in shadows as his anger rose.

'Selfish. Cavalier. That type. *Your* type. This is all a game to you, but for some of us, it's everything.' He shook his head, clearly disgusted. 'The weave between worlds has been steadily thinning since Nocta's been at large. For more than fifty years, it's been held together with the magical equivalent of spit, glue, and elbow grease, but we're at the end of it now. A great wizard and good friend is dead, and we're one false move away from the whole thing unraveling.' He stepped back and shot me a look so full of scorn, I barely suppressed a shiver. 'So, no. I don't fucking care if you feel like being here or not, Harlow. In fact, I don't care about how you feel at all.'

That spot, right above my heart? It panged with such ferocity I could almost feel it as if the break was fresh and not thirteen years old.

What did I say to that? Nothing. Not a damn thing..

Without another word, he turned and made his way toward the bookshop.

For the next half hour, I stayed quiet as we gathered more supplies. It wasn't even hard, for once. I wasn't sure if I could've trusted my voice to speak even if I'd wanted to. Because as much as it was in my DNA to argue, to refute everything he'd said, he wasn't all the way wrong.

I *was* selfish. I had to be, because nobody else but Opie cared about me. Not here, not back home. So, if I had to choose between saving the world and saving the two of us?

I was going to choose me and her every time.

4

With multicolored cobblestones under my feet, the pathway lined with forest on one side and the lake in the distance on the other, you'd think it would have been a relaxing ten-minute stroll from the Nevershoppes to the wall surrounding the academy.

Ten minutes of excruciating silence that I felt bubbling up in my guts like indigestion gone sideways.

Back when I'd been at school, I'd walked on eggshells and prayed no one noticed me, even in my assigned house. The whole time, I'd struggled with my spells. Rune crafting was taught under the strictest guidelines. The skill required the user to trace a series of shapes in the air and then fill them with magic in the form of energy. The more pristine and precise the rune, the less magic it needed to power it, in the same way that a properly executed push-up resulted in stronger muscles over a poorly executed one. Hence why inexperienced witches and wizards invariably got caught if they tried to use unsanctioned, low-rent magic out in the Unlit human world. They didn't get it quite right. And I could hardly blame them. The runes they taught at Neverthorn had always wound up jumbled in my mind. Too many shapes for a single spell. I'd botch the order or get mixed up and forget to close a loop, so the magic would just trickle out, rendering the spell weak or completely useless, stinking up the entire class. Which was why I did magic my own way once I left this place. It had been so easy once I wasn't bound by *their* rules. And I'd gotten damned good at it, making most of my spells untraceable.

But I could still hear the giggles as I messed up the same rune over and over . . . could still see the scorn, or worse, pity in the teacher's eyes . . .

I blew a shallow breath out between my teeth.

'What are you hissing about now?' he growled at me.

'Hissing?' I tipped my head to the side as if to get a better look at him. 'You do know what humans sound like when they breathe, don't you? Or has it been that long since you've interacted with real people?' I shook my head and took a deep breath. 'I'm *stressed*. This place is my own private hell, overseen by you – my own personal nightmare.' I hitched my bags up farther on my back, my feet stilling as we came to the only entrance in or out of Neverthorn's grounds.

I swallowed hard as I looked at the thorns and brambles that made up the gate – thick and solid as if made of steel, dark-bronze discoloration that could have been rust but wasn't, and even spots that were peeled away. The gate was far stronger than steel, though. Tarquinius had created it to protect the students, imbuing it with all manner of protection wards.

A protection and a prison. At least in my estimation.

Arching a good twenty feet over our heads as well as twenty feet across, the opening was big enough that I wondered for the first time what it had been made to accommodate.

A giant?

No, they'd been gone for over a hundred years.

A dragon?

Also extinct.

Maybe a griffon, with the body of a lion and the head of an eagle. There were a few of those left, and they could get pretty big.

Typhon stopped and pointed at the gate. 'You know the

drill. You open the gate, and it will sense which house you belong to and set you in it.'

'I already have a house.' My tongue felt thick in my mouth. 'Felinita.'

Considered by many to be one of, if not *the*, weakest of the six houses, but also the smartest. When they beat out a stronger house it was always through strategy. I was not opposed to being put back into the smart house.

Felinita was what my first arm bracer had been marked with upon entering the gate. The crest was a small house cat with a delicate set of wings perched on her back.

I found myself glancing at Typhon, knowing a Draconell house crest wrapped around his forearm and down onto the back of his hand. The serpent's head was in an attack position, all fangs and flame across the top of his hand.

Top of his class, top of the houses. Draconell was the best of the best. They had the most power behind their rune casting, were generally the quickest at it, too, which made them lethal in battle. Unfortunately, they also tended to come from the most prestigious families. All of Opie's relatives had been House Draconell.

Add to that, the Senate, who pretty much made all the rules governing magic, was made up primarily of House Draconell.

Which made them top of the asshole heap, as far as I was concerned.

'Put on your new bracer. Things change.' Typhon tucked his hands behind his back. 'The gates have been set by Tarquinius to ensure you end up in the proper house.'

'Wait . . . and we weren't before?'

His mouth set in a grim line, and I knew I wasn't going to get an answer. But maybe his lack of answer was enough. Had things been rigged my first time around?

'Why would the school have wanted students to be sent to the wrong house?'

Silence.

I snorted and shook my head. Trying to talk to this man was an exercise in frustration. And still, I kept on, desperate for information. I circled back to an earlier question, hoping he'd give me something more.

'Tell me about the others. You said there were more people that could take the place of Heronius? How many? Is it going to be me and a bunch of kids?'

Crouching, I dug around in my bag as he spoke. The thing wasn't all that deep, but I'd shrunk my new supplies to fit into it and they were hard to find.

'Seven others. They are all from a different house originally too.'

That was good at least. I wouldn't be the only fish out of water.

'Of course, they all have their first house crest etched into their arms since they didn't give up half a semester in and quit when things got tough.'

Shots fired again, and this round hit home.

Rage shot through me, melting away my anxiety. 'After what you did to me, you have the nerve to act like I'm in the wrong for leaving? I got news for you –'

'As for age,' he continued as if I wasn't even talking, 'some are in their twenties. Most aren't quite as old as you. Now get the bracer on, let's get this done. I have a class to teach.' He jerked his chin toward the gate, as he stepped to the side.

Patience had never been his strong suit. Apparently, that hadn't changed.

The wind around us picked up, keening through the trees at the base of the wall that wrapped around the grounds.

Clouds drifted across the sky, dampening the light until it might as well have been early evening instead of morning.

Behind the wall but still out of view was Neverthorn Academy, and while I was mostly pissed about having to go back, there was a tiny part of me that couldn't help but wonder what might've been if things had gone differently.

If I'd started school with the others at the age of thirteen.

If I'd lived a life that didn't involve constantly being on the run.

If my mother had never gotten sick.

If I'd never left . . .

I still remembered the stories my mom had told me. How she had lived with her friends in the girls' dorm of Felinita. Of the fun they'd had and the magic they'd made. Of course, she'd been a pretty decent runecrafter, and popular to boot.

Everything I wasn't.

My throat tightened as I thought of the last time I'd seen her. I'd begged to stay with her instead of going to Neverthorn. How she forced me out the door, teary-eyed but determined . . .

'I've already held you back for too long. It will make you stronger. And stronger is safer, my heart.'

Nope, this was not the time to think about that memory, or her.

I stood and put the new leather bracer onto my right arm, sliding it up.

The bracers always went onto the dominant hand. Most Dwims were lefties. Not me. Had to be different, even in this.

The leather molded itself to my arm, slid around my thumb and sealed itself to me. It wouldn't come off now until the Sage announced that I had graduated. Not a dog collar, exactly, but it might as well have been, and I squashed the rising sense of panic, of being collared and chained to this place again.

'Who helped you get your first one off?' Typhon asked suddenly, motioning at my wrist.

I shrugged. 'A mixture of half-cooked spells and a sixteen-year-old's stubborn determination.' I squared my shoulders and started toward the massive gate that seemed to shiver on my approach. 'To be crystal clear, there was no one to help me with anything, ever, once I left Neverthorn, Typhon. I did it myself or it didn't happen.'

The weight of his gaze was heavy on me, but I refused to look at him. Refused to let him see the pain of the past in me.

I stood with my toes brushing the bottom edge of the gate. The thick vines flexed, like a snake constricting, sensing my presence. 'You know, this isn't any less terrifying than the first time.'

Typhon stepped up behind me, blocking my exit, the heat off his body flooding my back. 'Lift your hand and open the gate.'

I turned my head, and we were so close. I drew in a slow, subtle breath and wrinkled my nose. Damn, he smelled good.

Twisting back around, I reached out and set my hand over the thick Neverthorn crest that held the two halves of the gate together.

Staring at it, I took in details that I hadn't my first time through the gates. The round emblem was the size of a dinner plate, with spokes sliding out from the center of it. Seven of them, thick enough that there were details engraved into them. Details that made me think of the different houses on the other side of the gate.

Typhon pressed closer to me, his massive body pinning mine to the gate, taking my attention from the crest. The thrill that ran through me was all too familiar, and I hated it.

How I'd misinterpreted his darkness for sadness.

How I'd desperately wanted to heal him.

How I'd stupidly thought we might have something in common. Pain. And that his was buried under a layer of armor only I could penetrate.

It only took a literal killing blow aimed at my heart to dissuade me of that notion.

I catch on quick like that.

My rib started to ache again, and I leaned into the gate. 'Can you just give me a little fucking space please?' I muttered. 'I know what comes next. I won't move.'

'I'm making sure you don't try to run. The selection of houses is . . . not the way you remember it,' he said, his voice a low rumble that I felt through my whole body.

The gate rippled as I splayed my palm against the crest. Without warning, the thick brambles shot toward me, and I couldn't help but try to leap back.

'What the hell!' I yelped.

'I warned you.' His arms were around me like iron bands, holding me in place as I leaned back, into him. 'It knows the dangers we face, and the magic has reacted accordingly. There's no room for error. The gate must get the placements right.'

The breath whooshed out of me as my right arm was wrapped up, vise-like, in the vines. Then my legs, then my upper body. I was lifted off the ground, feet dangling.

'Shit! Typhon . . . I don't like this.'

He let me go, leaving a hand on my lower back. 'It won't kill you. I don't think . . .'

I whipped my head around to see his lips twitching. Was that almost a smile?

'Fucker.'

'Not lately,' I thought I heard him say.

45

Was he cracking his first joke while I was being lifted from the ground by a sentient gate made of what I was now assuming were man-eating, magic-made vines. The thick, snakelike cords tightened and pulsed around me, a heartbeat deep within the creation that had been made to keep students safe. To keep monsters out, and students in.

But I was no monster.

Even as I thought it, the vines eased their hold on me, allowing me a deeper breath. A single, thin vine crept toward my right arm and the bracer. The thorns dripped black, as though the vines were bleeding.

Or maybe crying?

This was nothing like my first time through the gate. Then it had been a single flare of magic. A single vine had reached out and, easy peasy, the Felinita crest had been etched into my armband. A very proper setting of the house among young ones entering their first year.

This was . . . feral, wild in the way that only nature and the most chaotic of magics and gods could be, like the magic of the Horned King.

Unpredictable. Dangerous.

The thorns struck at the leather armband, the tips of them driving through to my forearm as they etched an image. I jerked and yelped but really couldn't move much.

I saw the wings first and nodded to myself.

'Felinita,' I called over my shoulder. 'Just like I said.'

The vines tightened around my middle, cutting off my air.

I stayed still. Sometimes fighting wasn't worth it when it came to nature.

Only . . . the gate and its vines kept tightening. I glanced back at Typhon, who was frowning.

When the pressure on my ribs had me arching to get away, I'd had enough. I flexed my right hand, flicking my fingers one at a time, flames dancing off the tips. I needed enough heat to make the vines drop me. Only instead of loosening, they wrapped further around me until I was fully encased, to my neck. I tried to scream, panic hitting me hard. Why wasn't Typhon doing anything?

'Help,' I rasped.

There was a sudden sharp scent of flames burning green wood, and then the vines dropped me on the other side of the gate. I stumbled before catching my balance.

I gasped and spluttered. 'What was that about? Why did you wait so long to help me?'

Typhon walked through the gate to join me, calm as a summer's day, the vines pulling back for him as if nothing had happened.

'That . . . is the welcome that you and each of the other seven have received. Violent, and wild. And I didn't help you. The gate released you of its own accord.'

I swallowed hard. 'Why?'

He shook his head. 'The job was done. Your house crest made itself known.'

The bitter disappointment on his face told me that, until this very second, he had thought Tarquinius had made some sort of mistake with me. That I didn't belong back at Neverthorn at all.

'I thought you said this place was safer now,' I mumbled, rubbing at my sore ribcage.

'Don't twist my words.' His expression was grim. 'I said I would ensure *Opie*'s safety. Now that we've cleared that up, I suppose it's my duty to welcome you to your new house.' He motioned to the leather bracer, and I glanced down.

Wings, yes there were wings, but they weren't attached to a small cat. In fact, I'd never seen this crest before.

'I don't understand.'

I traced the design, feeling the heat of it where it had not only been etched but *burned* into the leather. The body of the creature was made of fire, the wings spread wide and wrapped around my forearm. It continued down over the top of my hand, ending in an open flame shooting from its mouth.

Impossible.

'House Phoenix. Reinstated out of pure necessity. Previously denounced and eliminated fifty years ago for dangerous and destructive behavior and an insatiable thirst for power. This is why it's especially unfortunate that we need one of *your* kind to stop Nocta and his army.'

Typhon brushed past me.

I stared at the gate a moment, then lifted both hands and flipped it off. The gate mimicked me back and that . . . well, shit, that made me laugh.

Magic was unpredictable, but at least it had a sense of humor. Unlike some people . . .

Typhon kept walking, obviously expecting me to follow.

'So, Phoenix was meant to be my house from the start? Is that what you're telling me?'

'Apparently.'

I shook my head, still catching my breath as I caught up to him. Hecate's hands, that would explain so much. Why I always felt out of place . . . why I'd never found a friend . . . maybe even . . .

'Is that why I couldn't learn the runes the way they wanted me to? Because I was in the wrong house, and –'

'Nope. I'm afraid that was all you.'

Alrighty, then.

'Your dorm room is on the seventh floor,' Typhon continued.

'Wait . . . there was no seventh floor when I was here.'

'There is now. You're one floor above Draconell. Neverthorn . . . re-adjusted . . . as the new House of Phoenix students arrived.'

The path we were on was as wide as the main gate, towering plinths on either side of us, like an oversized cattle chute made of river rock and cement. In between each plinth was a tree, no one tree the same as the next. But honestly, as familiar as it was, this was all tripping me out.

The gate. House Phoenix. On a floor *above* House Draconell?

Just being here was enough to make my brain hurt.

I reached up and pulled an apple off the tree closest to me and took a bite out of the fruit, so deep red it was almost purple. The flavor was a burst of freshness, tart and sweet at the same time, that had me moaning out loud.

'This is so fugging good.'

Typhon picked up his pace. 'Your first class starts in fifteen minutes. Go straight to the third level, room 308 for History of Magic. Doyenne Elmwood will be teaching you and the others from House Phoenix all morning. After that, you'll head to Politics, followed by Controlling the Weather with Doyenne Storm, finishing sometime after five.'

'Today? Like all day? I haven't even slept yet.' I swallowed the last of my apple and tossed the core.

'We're late, so make it work. You will have time to rest going forward. That said, you and your housemates will be on a unique schedule Monday through Saturday, which will change week to week as we assess your skills and needs.'

I blinked. 'Wait, why not two days off? You know, a normal weekend?'

He paused and let me catch up to him as he glanced down at me. 'Because we are preparing to fight a war.'

I swallowed hard.

Right.

That.

'What about my stuff, then? Take it with me?' I hitched my bag a little higher on my back.

He shook his head and picked up his pace again. 'Keep the satchel. You won't need your books yet. I'll have the staff take the rest to your room in your new dorm.'

I looked down at my clothes. I was most certainly not in uniform. Perfect.

We rounded a slight curve in the path and the front of Neverthorn Academy popped into view. The place was massive, a mixture between castle and prison, dark stone and blocky towers that peaked at the top of, yup, I did a quick count. Seven floors now. That's what I'd been seeing when I'd first gotten off the boat, my new dorm on the top floor. That was why the school had been visible this time at a distance.

For anyone human coming to visit Dark Island, they saw a rundown castle. For any Dwimmer who made the trek with ol' Bones . . . we saw it as it really was in our world. Here and there I saw a flicker of figures – humans visible on their side of the magically woven fabric that separated us from them. They looked like ghosts until they raised their cameras to take pictures.

The main door was to the left of the building, set into an arch that mimicked the front gate, just on a smaller scale. The wooden doors were studded with brambles, vines, and the Neverthorn crest in the middle, glimmering with deep magic.

Typhon made a quick motion with two fingers and the door opened inward on silent hinges.

'You know how to get to the third floor?' Typhon asked, his voice . . . different now. Calm. Serious. Professorly.

I snorted.

He raised an eyebrow. Faster than a striking snake, his hand was on my throat, holding me tight. I stared up at him as he all but dragged me close to him. 'Can't have you setting a bad example, can we?'

His fingers flexed one at a time – tracing the runes directly into my throat.

I blinked up at him as he let me go. 'What did you do?'

'Can't have you dropping the F-bomb every two minutes. Tarquinius has an issue with bad language.'

'Son of a boot licker!' My jaw dropped and I tried again. 'Kiss my asterisk! Fricky dicky doo da! You're such a donkeyhole!'

I was panting hard, filled with horror at this newest twist. They could have just asked me to tone it down. Instead, he'd stripped me of control. One more chain binding me, trapping me.

I hated it.

His eyes didn't so much as flicker as he held out his hand.

What was this now? An olive branch? With some serious trepidation I put my hand in his, and something flashed in his eyes as he jerked away like I'd burned him.

'Your *bag*, Ms. Daygon. Give me your bag.'

Ms. Daygon now? Okay . . .

'When do I get to see Opie?' I demanded as I handed over my bag.

'Tonight, at dinner,' he replied as he looked me over. 'You will need your uniform.'

Before I could ask for my bag back, his fingers flickered through a series of shapes glowing with magic and the material on my body shifted from street clothes to school uniform.

I shot a glance down at my uniform then gaped at him. Yet another violation.

'You swapped my clothes?'

'You could do a rune like that to swap your own clothes if you hadn't quit school,' he said, apparently taking my words as a compliment.

Bastard. At least he'd left me my knee-high boots.

The massive clock that hung on the octagonal brick wall of the main entrance hall ticked softly. One minute to the top of the hour. The floors were tiled, solid white marble, the walls were paneled in a deep, rich wood. Banners for each of the houses hung on the walls in an array of colors, except for the wall against which the clock stood. I couldn't help it, my eyes went straight to House Phoenix. The banner was new, and shiny, with gold and red embossing across the lettering.

One more soft tick, and the clock let out a boom as the hour struck. It rumbled like thunder as I stood there, and I found myself moving on instinct.

One second, I was alone. The next, a crush of students flooded the halls as they left their dorms and headed to class, but hardly anyone spared me a look. Well, that wasn't entirely true. I got a couple good side-eyes from some of the older kids. In particular there was a nice little gang of boys that all tried to stare me down, as if glaring at me would somehow scare me off.

A quick glance at their cuffs confirmed their behavior – Draconell.

'Fresh meat,' the biggest of the boys growled as he went by.

Apparently, despite my new house, school wasn't going to be any different than the first time around.

Great.

I made my way to the set of stairs to the left, the main set that branched off on each floor.

I stopped on the first floor. This was where a first year's classes would be. A first-year student like Opie. It had been only yesterday that I'd seen her, but my anxiety spiked. What if they'd used her as bait to get me to come and she wasn't even here? I needed to see her with my own eyes.

'I'll be late anyway,' I muttered to myself as I hurried down the hall to my left, pausing at each door until I found her.

'I was in Rio, with my sister.' Opie's voice filtered out through the doorway.

'Your sister Nilda?'

I swallowed hard and peeked into the classroom. Opie was turned away from me, facing two girls. One was smiling, the other had her head tipped to the side like she was inspecting a bug.

'No, Nilda doesn't . . . Nilda and I aren't close. I was with Harlow. My . . . I guess she's my adopted sister.' Her shoulders curled in, like a protective cloak.

There was a long pause, then the smiling girl shrugged. 'Cool, you want to sit with us?'

And just like that, Opie lit up, and followed the two girls to seats near the back of the room.

I lifted a hand to her back, a bittersweet sense of acceptance settling in my chest. We were here, and that wasn't likely to change in the immediate future.

I fingered the note in my pocket with a sigh. I'd written it for Opie on the plane ride over and had stuck it in my boot in the hopes of giving it to her as soon as I got here. Just a bunch of random thoughts about Neverthorn, the other houses, and how to keep your head above water in a place like this when you didn't belong. Clearly, it would have to wait.

'See you later, kiddo,' I whispered, turned and jogged toward my own class.

The third floor was nearly empty, with only a few students roving the halls. I hadn't been up this high during my first run at Neverthorn. All my classes and my House Felinita rooms had been on the first floor, near to the kitchens.

I sighed as I slowly made my way to room 308. A voice was echoing past the door, into the hallway.

I leaned against the wall to listen before I let myself in.

'There are eight of you now, but by the end of the year, several will have gone home, if not more. We are looking for the best of the best, the one who can take Heronius's place. Although I must admit, I can't imagine that person is here . . .'

That voice was vaguely familiar, though I didn't remember a Doyenne Elmwood.

'Agree,' a male voice chimed in. 'Heronius is dead, and *he* was supposed to be the best of the best. It seems like a suicide mission to me.'

'Luckily, no one asked for your opinion, Mr. Weatherby.' That voice . . .

Suddenly, a memory hit me so hard, I actually stumbled backward, my chest clenching.

'You hide your cruelty behind all that makeup, but I see you,' I snapped at Nikita. I knew I shouldn't have said anything, I knew I should have just kept my head down, but she was picking on one of the littles in the lunchroom again.

Her fake red hair swung to the side, and brilliant blue-green eyes narrowed as the bane of my existence wove a rune rapidly, sending me flying.

'And you have a lot of opinions for someone who can't do even half of what they should be able to by this point in the year. Why is that?' Her fingers flew through the runes again, and I was lifted from my chair and propelled toward the door, which I hit hard enough to knock the wind out of me.

Nikita stood over me, smirking. 'Is it because you didn't have a daddy to teach you? Or is it because every time something gets hard, you freak out, cover your ears, and start sweating like a racehorse? Maybe you should do us all a favor and use that bag they give you to breathe into and put it over your head instead.'

I shook off the memory, and shoved the door open, stepping into room 308.

I already knew what I'd see, but it was still a shock to my system.

'Ahhh . . . welcome, Ms. Daygon. Many thanks for gracing us with your presence today. I see you are one step behind the rest of the class, per usual.'

Nikita Pendergast, my former schoolmate and nemesis. She still looked the same, if a little older.

I forced a grin as I eyeballed her copper hair, and the fake smile painted on her crimson lips.

'And I see you're still a raging bully with a god complex and a bad dye job. Good to know that things haven't changed around here.'

And that's how I ended up with detention not fifteen minutes into my first day back in Neverthorn Academy.

5

Nikita Pendergast, now Elmwood. My childhood arch enemy was a doyenne teaching at Neverthorn. What were the odds?

'Pretty fricking good, the way the past twenty-four hours have been going,' I muttered to myself as I started down the long corridor.

Maybe I was actually dead, and I was suffering for all my sins.

It made a sort of twisted sense, except my version of hell definitely would've featured sharks.

Okay, so not hell. Just my life.

That tracked, too.

I trudged down the hall toward the library for my immediate detention, absently taking stock of the changes that had been made to the school. I had to admit, things had improved. The décor was still stuffy, with a nod to tradition that would've pleased the Senate when they did their inspections, but now there were also television screens peppered throughout the common areas.

Mind you, the screens were only showing proper rune casting, how to tie your tie, and correct usage of pea shoots in a potions class. Still, it was tech that hadn't been here last time.

As I approached the open doors of the library, I peered inside, noting the amount of space allotted for books and computers was about fifty/fifty. They must've known that even the lure of magic couldn't get kids to step away from their laptops and iPhones. According to signs plastered next to them, the electronics only worked within the magical space, but at least it was something. That was one of the bugaboos of technology here. Phones and such worked, but only within the magical Dwimmer world. You couldn't make a call to anyone in the Unlit world, or vice versa. Each network operated within its own realm.

I should've headed through the doors right then and checked in with the librarian like Nikita had told me to. Instead, I kept walking. I hadn't slept and was in the grips of a brutal caffeine-deprivation headache, to boot. Once I got some food and coffee in me, I'd go face the music.

The smell of bacon and yeasty bread lingered in the halls like an invitation, and I followed my nose. By the time I stepped into the main kitchen, I was literally drooling, and my belly was rumbling.

A bald guy with a short-cropped beard stood at a butcher's block in the corner of the massive room, eyes locked on the knife chopping onions on its own in front of him. 'Can I help you, ma'am?' he asked, his knife pausing in the air, floating in mid-chop.

Ma'am? He was like five years younger than me, tops.

'Um, I'm a new . . . ish student and just got in this morning, so I missed breakfast. Can I just grab a scone and a plate of bacon, maybe?'

I sent him my best, most charming smile, but it was wasted as he'd already gone back to slicing and dicing with only one finger using a repeating spell on the blade.

'Talk to Cook. We're not allowed to give the students food without her say-so.'

I swallowed a sigh, already sorely missing my lack of freedom.

'Can you point me her way . . . ?'

He jerked his head in the general direction of the rest of the warehouse-sized kitchen but didn't look up again.

'Perfect. Very helpful,' I muttered under my breath as I continued. Typhon had said that Mrs. Wickersham was the head chef nowadays, so I kept my eyes peeled for her auburn hair and stout form as I scanned the white-aproned staff.

I didn't know what was on the menu for lunch but judging by the smell of sizzling butter and herbs, it was going to be delicious. My stomach rumbled again, so loudly one of the cooks turned to face me as I passed, a concerned frown knitting her brow.

'Did you just growl at me?'

'No, erm, sorry, just hungry is all.'

Her forehead smoothed, and she pointed her whisk dripping with sauce straight ahead. 'Cook will get you straightened out; she's down that way.'

I followed her directions and, a few moments later, found myself face to face with the woman herself.

'Mrs. Wickersham! Do you remember me?'

The older woman looked up, the wooden spoon she'd been using magic to operate stopping mid-motion.

'Harlow "Shortbread" Daygon!' She stepped back and threw both hands in her air, letting out a delighted laugh. 'How could I forget you?' She studied me up and down and shook her head. 'I remember telling you all that food would catch up with you one day, but apparently, I was wrong. Some of us are built sturdier than others, ain't it true? My stars, you could put away the shortbread before it was even on the cooling racks!'

'Guilty as charged,' I agreed, surprised by the sudden rush of warmth I felt toward the woman. Mrs. Wickersham had always been kind. And back then, when it felt like everyone either hated me or disregarded me entirely, that had mattered.

A lot.

'I'd heard Tarquinius was bringing some students back

into the fold. I'll admit, I hadn't guessed that you'd be one of them.'

'You think *you're* surprised? Imagine how I feel. I was just minding my own business' – *trying to rob an old lady* – 'and Doyen Moreno and some goon came and grabbed me off the street. But what Tarquinius wants, Tarquinius gets.'

The Sage was pompous, but he was also known to be a great wizard who ruled with a firm yet fair hand. He also possessed the strongest defensive Quirk the world knew of – he could shield like a mofo. And he could expand that shield as wide as the school. Which was what made Neverthorn so safe. He was revered by most, worshiped by some, feared by a few . . .

For whatever reason, he'd never given me the warm and fuzzies. To be fair, I'd spent zero amount of time with him my first go-round at the school.

Mrs. Wickersham grinned, apparently taking my words as a joke, which was probably for the best. 'Yeah, well, I'm glad to have you back, Shortbread. You're the type that made me fall in love with cooking in the first place. You're a pleasure to feed.' She raised her brows and grinned. 'Am I safe in assuming that's why you're here?'

'Well, now that you mention it . . .'

She swiped her hands on her berry-stained apron and bustled away, only to return a minute later with a pillowy croissant slathered in orange marmalade, two fat, glistening sausages on a plate, and a little packet tied off with white baker's string.

'For now, and for later, a bit of shortbread,' she said with a wink as she handed them over.

'Bless you, Mrs. Wickersham,' I whispered. 'You are a saint. Now, if I could just beg a cup of coffee, I can get through whatever else these sadistic bass carps have in store for me.'

I winced and she squinted.

'Bass carps, huh?'

'Doyen Moreno's work. Apparently, he felt I had a potty mouth.'

'That man. Tough on the outside, but soft and gooey in the middle.' She grinned and shook her head as I stared at her like she'd grown a second one. 'Well, you'll be pleased to hear that we've got a fancy new coffee machine against the wall on your way out. Just pick your poison and press a button.'

Maybe I was going to like it here, after all.

I let Mrs. Wickersham get back to work and headed for the coffee station. Once I'd made myself a mocha latte, I settled myself in a little alcove under the stairs. The second I sat on the stone floor, memories flooded my brain.

How many times had I hidden in this very spot, sobbing my face off over a plate of food, wishing I could go home? Praying for some miracle that would get me out of this place . . . only to find that, when my miracle came, it would be in the form of my worst nightmare.

Tarquinius's long, wizened face loomed over me as he spoke . . .

'Ms. Daygon, I regret to inform you that your mother is dead.'

The rest had come in shattered phrases that I could barely comprehend through the haze of shock.

Blah blah blah, short sabbatical from school, blah blah blah, return to your studies after her funeral, blah blah blah, thoughts and prayers.

I forced myself back to the present and swiped at my face, surprised to feel dampness on my cheek. When was the last time I'd shed a tear for my mother or anyone else?

The day I buried her, that was when.

My short sabbatical turned into me never going back to Neverthorn and making sure they couldn't find me if they tried . . . which they hadn't. I'd made a life for myself. It wasn't great, but it was still better than this place. What I'd learned was that *not* crying was a lot more fun than crying. I'd be damned if I was about to start with the waterworks again now.

I lifted the croissant to my mouth and chomped down, groaning as the crisp pastry gave way to bittersweet marmalade. I folded my legs criss-cross under me and tucked into the rest of the food. When I'd eaten both sausages, downed half my coffee, and licked the last crumb of pastry from my fingers, I let out a sigh of contentment. *And* I still had a packet of food to put away for later. Shortbread no less.

I held my fingers an inch apart and pinched them together, shrinking the parcel to the size of a matchbook, and tucked it into my fanny pack. Then I stood and headed back down the hallway.

By the time I got to the library, I was feeling significantly better than the first time I'd approached those doors half an hour before. Still, I paused at the threshold – my mistake.

'Enter! And make haste about it,' a nasal voice bleated from somewhere to the left of me.

I stepped into the room and turned toward a hulking mahogany desk piled so high with books from end to end that it was impossible to see over them.

'Don't just stand there, come on, then, you're letting all the heat out!' the voice demanded.

I squinted, wondering if it was the books talking, or –

'My word, child, can you hear me or not?'

It was only then that I caught sight of the woman behind the books. Or some of her, at least. All that was currently visible was a mass of steel-gray curls, a pair of bespectacled eyes, and a short snub of a nose.

Doyenne Portencia. Miserable old – my throat tightened, and I could feel the word changing even as I thought it.

'Independent study or in-school detention?' she asked, not bothering to round the desk.

'Detention.'

'Which class?' She managed to look down her nose at me, even though she sat below me.

'Doyenne Elmwood sent me.'

Her eyes narrowed and I smiled serenely back at her as she motioned. 'Back room, farthest to the right. Sign in at the door. Your assignment is self-explanatory.'

I padded through the library, marveling at the seemingly endless shelves and banks of computers. While there were a few older students working independently, the space was mostly empty as the rest were likely in class.

All but you, big mouth.

I wanted to regret it. I really did. But all I regretted was not having time to come up with more cutting insults. If I had to be in detention, I might as well have earned it.

When I reached the assigned room, I pushed the door open with the toe of my boot and stepped inside but stopped short when a clipboard on the wall began to glow like a beacon.

'*Sign in at the door,*' Doyenne Portencia had said.

'Right,' I muttered, looking for a pen. There was none, so I traced my signature on the blank paper, and my name appeared a moment later. Glittering for a moment, it sank into the paper, black as night.

It *was* sort of neat being back in the magical world, but I wasn't about to admit it to anyone besides myself. And it certainly wasn't neat enough to offset the trauma of being here.

But there was still Opie, who was absolutely losing her sheet with happiness – her face that morning as the two girls included her was . . . was everything for her. She'd dreamed of being part of the magical Dwimmer world for so long. I sighed. I had to play ball.

At least for now.

I headed into the empty room and took a seat in the back. There was a laptop set up on each desk.

I opened the nearest laptop, which powered up instantly. For a second, I stared at it blankly. It looked like a standard interface, except there was no internet icon. In its place was a magic wand.

Could I send a message via the internet out of the Dwimmer realm after all? It was a long shot, but I had nothing to lose by trying. I tried to sign into my Gmail, but the site wouldn't even come up when I searched for it.

'Come on,' I whispered. Nothing. Apparently, it wasn't just the phones that worked on a local net. 'Son of a pixie beech.' I frowned 'Beech. Beech!' I slapped my hand on the table.

With nothing else for it, defeat rolling through me, I clicked on the wand after my failed search engine results. A flying wizard buzzed around the screen like a mini tornado, before the words *Choose an assignment* appeared with two clickable options beneath it.

— Write a 5,000-word paper on a dark Dwimmer and their inevitable defeat. Use the library resources and cite your work.
— Write an apology in the form of a sonnet to the doyen or doyenne you have disrespected that resulted in your detention.

'Oh, you've got to be kidding me.'

It wasn't my first detention, I'd had my share, but the punishments had apparently gotten even stupider over the years. I would literally rather lick one of Bones' empty eye-sockets than do either of the things offered to me. As I sat there, though, the text color of the choices shifted from black, to orange, then to red.

Select your assignment now!!! came slashing across the screen like a hollered warning before disappearing.

'Geez!'

With a sigh, I clicked on option B, which opened a new window that mimicked a luxurious piece of stationery with a flowery border. I glanced around the room, grabbed a chair from a few feet away, and dragged it up next to mine. Then I propped my feet up, cracked my knuckles, and began. If I couldn't say the words, at least I could type them . . .

> *There once was a bitch named Pendergast*
> *With a stick way too far up her narrow —*

The laptop snapped shut on my typing fingers like a toothless maw, and I let out a gasp of pain.

'Son of a biscuit!' I yanked my hands back and flexed my sore knuckles.

Clearly, the academy hadn't gotten the memo about corporal punishment being so twentieth century . . .

My knuckles were still smarting when the laptop opened again a minute or so later.

This time, there was only one choice remaining, and I let out a groan.

Looks like I'd have to spend my day researching some long-dead or imprisoned witch or wizard. But that didn't mean I had to start right now. I was nothing if not an expert at procrastination.

I shut the laptop and stared down at the toes of my boots. I'd probably feel a lot more like myself if I wasn't dressed like some prep-school version of a Stepford wife.

First things first . . .

I stood and unfastened the tie from around my neck,

already feeling better. I tied it loosely around my waist and dragged it lower, so it hung off my hips, and let the ends fall to the side. Next, I went for the fanny pack. With a few tugs on the adjustable straps, I was able to fit it diagonally, from my shoulder to the opposite hip, tight across my body.

Now it felt more like a place I could be packing heat instead of diapers and hand sanitizer.

I was just considering alterations on my pants, making the legs tighter so I could tuck them inside my boots, when a low voice called from the doorway.

'Hey there.'

I startled, and my hand lifted, a rune at the ready on the tip of my fingers. Old street habits died hard, and sneaking up on me was a good way to get a rune in the face. Or a fist.

A girl who appeared to be in her very early twenties with wavy brown hair and cat-eyeglasses stood there looking piti-ful as could be. I dropped my hand quickly, hoping she hadn't taken offense to my nearly spelling her.

'Is . . . is this detention?'

'Yeah,' I said with a half-smile of encouragement. 'Just make sure you sign in.'

She did, then tiptoed into the room.

'I can't believe I'm here. I don't . . .' Her pale throat worked as she shrugged helplessly. 'I've never gotten in trouble before.'

Seriously?

'Seriously?'

She'd *never* gotten in trouble? Ever?

'What are you in for?'

'I'm not sure.' She shrugged her slumped shoulders and sank into the seat next to mine. 'I just asked a few questions about the lesson. Doyenne Elmwood seemed irritated and asked what house I was in before. I told her Felinita. She said, "It figures," and I asked why, because I wasn't sure what she meant by that.' She paused and gnawed at her bottom lip. 'That was the wrong thing to say, I guess. Apparently, it's not for me to ask why and I needed to come down here and adjust my attitude.'

No surprise there. Nikita had been head mean girl back when we were kids, and if her minions didn't fall into line, they quickly became her enemies. The fact that she and the rest of House Kirinash always went head-to-head with Felinita probably didn't help.

She looked around and then shot me a confused frown. 'Where's Ross?'

'Who's Ross?'

'This guy who got sent here for trying to call Doyenne Elmwood' – she lowered her voice to a whisper – 'the b-word. We've all had the no-swearing gag put on us. Apparently one of our new housemates is a potty mouth.'

I cleared my throat. 'I haven't seen him.'

'Weird. She sent him down here right after she sent you.'

It seemed like I wasn't the only rebel at Neverthorn Academy this year. Either that, or Ross had written one hell of a sonnet in record time.

'He hasn't shown up yet, not that I've seen anyway, but I'm sure he will before anyone comes looking. What's your name, anyway?'

'Fable Delphinium O'Shanahan. And you're Ms. Daygon. First name?'

'Harlow. Nice to meet you, Fable.'

She sighed heavily as she settled into her chair. 'You too. Sorry I was being so weird. I just don't like to upset the apple-cart, as my mom used to always say. I'm a people-pleaser.'

'Ah, yes. I guess you might say I'm more of a bear-poker.'

Her lips tipped into a hint of a smile, and then she drew back in surprise.

'Oh! I just noticed your uniform. Cool way to wear your satchel.'

'Fanny pack,' I corrected with a nod. 'And yeah, looks much better this way.'

'Wow, she must be on a roll today,' a male voice said, interrupting our conversation a second before a tall guy in a student uniform walked in. His nearly hazel eyes were striking, surrounded with long dark lashes that I would have spent way too much money to achieve. His deep-brown skin, and tightly shorn black hair only accentuated his eyes further. 'Ross Elkson,' he said, approaching me, hand extended. 'I already met Fable here at orientation yesterday.'

'Harlow.' I gave him the obligatory shake and made to pull away, but he held on for another second, his hazel eyes locked on mine.

'Are your legs tired, beautiful? Because you've been running through my mind since I saw you earlier.'

'Blerf,' I muttered, faking a gag. 'Let's just save that for someone way younger and dumber than me, okay, Romeo?'

He shrugged and shot me an easy smile. 'Worth a shot.'

I was just about to ask him where he'd been for the last forty-five minutes when another voice chimed in, this one female.

'There's only five people left in her classroom now, and one of them is Phyllis!' A girl with curly black hair, and skin a few shades lighter than Ross's, was shaking her head in disbelief as she gravitated toward us. 'I don't remember Elmwood being a teacher when I went here the first time. And there is no way I am letting some chick who's *maybe* five years older than me talk to me like I'm a child now that I'm grown. It's just not going to happen, and I had to explain that to her.' She wiggled her fingers at me. 'Name's Marina.'

'Harlow,' I replied with a wave in return. 'Who's Phyllis?'

'Phyllis is the sixty-five-year-old lady that was sitting in the corner of the classroom,' Fable said, adjusting her glasses. 'Apparently, because House Phoenix was a late addition to this semester, they had no one available to oversee us. She'll be acting as our housemother but will also be coming to classes with the rest of us. To make sure we behave.'

Strange. All of it was so very strange.

'And who else is left?' I asked, my brain trying to follow this turn of events.

'There's Gary, the one with the bright red hair, two girls, one named Ellie and the other Caterina, and a guy named Zeed Sorn. He's super smart,' Marina said.

'Agree,' Fable chimed in with a nod. 'He was two years ahead of me, but we were friendly, and there's no question that he was one of the smartest kids at Neverthorn.'

'The rest of us are probably wasting our time,' Marina said.

'What makes you say that?'

Fable shot a glance at Ross and then Marina before shrugging.

'I did really well on all the book stuff . . . same as Zeed, but from what we've been able to gather it seems like none of us exactly graduated at the top of our classes as far as rune crafting is concerned . . . unless you did?' Fable asked, looking at me.

'Oh, god no,' I snorted. 'I wasn't even bottom of my class. I spent less than four months in this place, and my traditional rune-crafting skills are trash.'

The sudden hush that had fallen over the room was eerie, even for a library.

'If we all sucked then what the fruck are we doing here? Why us?' Marina murmured. 'Gods, I hate this gag!'

'No clue, but I agree with Marina,' Ross said with a slow nod. 'I bet Zeed's got this locked down. We should all just let him have the job and walk away.'

'No one has this job "locked down,"' a crusty female voice chimed in, 'as is evidenced by all you ingrates being in detention at once. Ellie, Caterina, and Gary are barely holding on in that class.'

I looked up to find an older woman entering the room. A frown deepened the already very deep lines in her face. She might have been sixty-five, but she'd clearly had a rough run of it. I noted with surprise that she was wearing what looked like all-black widow's weeds from the Victorian era.

Phyllis, if I was a guessing girl.

A tall, lean guy in his early twenties with the face of a Michelangelo painting, swept into the room behind her, mouth puckered like he'd just eaten a lemon. Green eyes, thick straight black hair . . . I wasn't sure but if I were to guess, I'd say he was of Asian descent.

Ross chuckled. 'Zeed, not you too, my man? What, was she upset that you're prettier than her?'

'Elmwood is loathsome. Positively loathsome. All I was trying to do was explain to her why her logic was flawed, and she kicked me out,' Zeed snapped, shooting Ross a dirty look.

'I'll not have you bad-mouthing the teachers here. She's under a great deal of stress, as are we all,' Phyllis said in her pack-a-day voice. 'You have the rest of Doyenne Elmwood's class period to utilize the library and finish your five-thousand-word reports.'

'Five thousand words . . . That's the only option?' Zeed asked, frowning.

'Apparently now it is. You can thank your classmate Harlow here for that since she tried the sonnet option and ruined it for the rest of you,' Phyllis said, shaking her head at me sternly. 'I'll be back at noon on the dot. Then we will go to Politics, followed by Weather Manipulation to close out the day.'

It was only when she tapped it hard on the stone floor that I realized she was carrying a walking cane.

'You can get on the right foot again if you just accept the fact that you're all back in school and need to behave as such. It's not because Tarquinius wants to be mean. It's because there's a chance that some of us . . . or you lot, at least, will be facing situations with life-or-death consequences. So, let's show our Sage that we can be good *and* obedient students this time 'round, shall we?'

She scanned the back of the room, locking eyes with each of us in turn, but seeming to linger on me the longest. She'd already clocked me as trouble. She might be older than the rest of us, but her mind was sharp as a tack. No wonder they'd put her in charge of us.

Okay, Phyll. I see you.

'Off you go!'

Hecate only knew why I cared if this lady was disappointed in me or not, but I found myself standing quickly to join the others.

As Marina, Zeed, and Ross exited the room as a group, all grumbling under their breath, Fable hung back, eyeing me in question.

'Want to work together? If you want to gather sources, I can start writing,' she said, her cheeks going pink. 'I know a fair bit about both Naomi Gonzalez and Artemis Norcroft already.'

I'd heard of both in passing, so I nodded.

'Plus, I'm great at research,' she added.

I doubted I'd be here long enough to make friends, but it beat trying to do this thing alone. Besides, she was House Felinita first too . . . we had that in common.

For the next hour, I scoured the library for everything I could find on the dark witch and wizard we'd selected.

Unsurprisingly, there was a lot. Four full biographies, two for each, and countless mentions of them in various Dwimmer encyclopedias and textbooks.

'Perfect,' Fable said with a delighted smile as I set yet another tome down on the table with a *thunk*. 'Now if you can check the microfilm and see if we can get something a little more personal about each of them. It was over a hundred years ago, so there won't be any video clips, but you might find some archived black and white photos from when they were kids or something like that. It adds a nice touch to see how they started out so innocent and then . . .' she curled her hands into claws and narrowed her eyes menacingly, 'went bad.'

I found the closest bank of laptops and took a seat. Fingers crossed, I clicked on the little wizard, and this time he took me to an intranet. It took some poking around, but eventually I found what Fable was looking for. Video clips of hundreds of witches and wizards, archived alphabetically.

I went for Naomi first, typing in her last name, and found three images. I clicked on the last, and a faded sepia-toned image opened on the screen. It featured a child holding a half-eaten wedge of watermelon, the other half of which she wore on her shirt and face.

Naomi was a real cutie, with a wide smile and chubby cheeks. She didn't look like she'd grow into the woman who had later started an underground movement to kill all the human Dims and create an entirely magical world.

Sounded familiar. It was like every dark wizard's greatest wish, to wipe out the Unlit world and everyone in it.

I scrolled to the previous image and opened it to find an engagement photo from an old newspaper. She was married in December of 1936, and the joy that had been brimming from her in the previous picture had drained away. She looked . . . defeated. Like someone had put a lampshade on her light. It made me feel weird and maudlin, so I exited out. The most recent image was dated a year after that, and I didn't bother to open it.

'Let's show them the good old days, before you went to the dark side, how about that, Naomi?' I murmured, sending the image to a nearby printer.

I scrolled to the Ns and found Norcroft next. Over a dozen images popped up. Figured. Men got all the glory back then.

I had just finished printing the last of three images I'd selected for old Arty and was about to shut down the wizard when I stopped myself.

It was probably a bad idea.

For all I knew, it might even send some alarm bells blaring.

Then again, no one had said I *couldn't* . . .

My fingers twitched as I scrolled upward.

Norcroft.

Nopler.

Nolan.

I froze as I stared at the name on the screen in front of me, which seemed somehow larger than all the others even though I knew it wasn't.

Nocta.

Did I really need to know more about him right now? Maybe I could scare myself even more sheetless another day, after I'd gotten over the shock of even being here.

To click or not to click. That was the –

Click.

A dozen image files appeared, newspaper clippings appeared, and I scanned the headlines.

Car Accident Kills Treasurer Wenton and Two Young Children. Found to Be the Work of Nocta.

Near Miss as Nocta Reaches the Shores of Dark Island Before Being Stopped by Heronius.

End of an Era . . . Heronius Slain, Nocta Declares Open War.

I sucked in a breath through my nose and let it out slowly.

Nope. I didn't need to read any of this sheet. Not right now. Not when I'd met the ragtag crew of second-rate runecrafters slated to defeat him.

Then again, to know thine enemy was to know thyself. Wasn't that the saying?

I just still wasn't sure whether Nocta was *my* enemy yet or not. The chances of *me* having to face him at all were slim to none. In fact, none of my new housemates exactly inspired confidence. I had to assume there was something we hadn't been told yet. Something that made Tarquinius think one of us was capable of more than just getting kicked out of class on day one.

What made House Phoenix different? That was maybe the real question here.

I was about to close the last of the clippings when I saw the link. A single video file at the bottom of the screen, dated just weeks ago. I tried to open it, but my hand seemed frozen. In fact, my whole body was suddenly icy with fear.

He's not going to leap through the screen, dummy.

I sucked in a deep breath and let it out through my nose, and then I opened it. A pretty newscaster with a megawatt smile popped up.

'And that's it for a list of this month's centenarian wizards and witches. May all of you make it to your bicentennial!'

Her smile dimmed, and a frown skated across her face as she held one finger to her nearly invisible earpiece.

'And this just in, a Dwimmercraft Digest exclusive. Witches and wizards . . . for the first time in nearly fifty years, we have what we believe is an image of Nicodemus Oliphant . . . otherwise known as the infamous wizard, Nocta.'

The woman disappeared and a picture materialized in her

place. I stared at it for a long moment as the cold fingers of dread trailed down the back of my neck.

The image was a screen grab of a video, so the pixelation was not great.

The man staring back at me had distinguished salt and pepper hair and an angular face that most would call handsome. But it was his eyes that held me captive. It had been decades since I'd seen those eyes, and it had been only the once, but they were just as I remembered. Full of rage, and pain, and a touch of madness. Purple, with silvery irises, just like mine.

'Who's that?' Fable whispered from over my shoulder.

But I couldn't even make my throat work to reply.

Because the man in that picture – Nocta, the greatest evil in our world. The big bad wolf lurking around every corner. The reason I was here at Neverthorn . . .

Was my father.

6

I barely managed to squeeze an excuse past my tightening throat before pushing past a confused-looking Fable and stumbling out of the library. The walls of the vast hallway seemed like they were closing in, and I knew there was no stopping the oncoming train.

'Excuse you!' a tight voice barked as I shoved the bathroom door open and nearly clotheslined the girl coming out.

You're okay. Deep breaths through your nose, out through your mouth.

But I wasn't okay. Less than five minutes ago, I'd been like millions of other people with an absentee father, a deadbeat, a guy I'd met once. The only name I'd known him by was Nic. A father I'd never thought to meet again.

Now, I was the daughter of the most hated, most dangerous wizard in the Dwimmer world.

I managed to make it into one of the stalls before all hell broke loose.

I latched the door behind me and dropped to my knees to press my head against the cool stone wall. My breaths came in short, frantic gasps, each one a desperate struggle for air. I could feel my heart pounding, an erratic drumbeat with an echo that seemed to reverberate through my entire body.

The metallic tang of fear coated my tongue, a bitter reminder of my helplessness. For all my rush to get here, now it was like the walls were closing in on me, suffocating me. My mind raced with a thousand fragmented thoughts, each one more terrifying than the last. The world outside the stall ceased to exist. It was just me, my terror, and the cold, unyielding floor.

Tears streamed down my face, and I let them, consumed by a force I couldn't see or touch but could feel in every fiber of my being. I lost all sense of time, but my knees were aching by the time the sound of running water from outside the stall penetrated my panic. Even then, it seemed like a movie playing in the background, disconnected from my reality.

Toilet.

Lock.

Tiles.

Spider.

It felt like an eternity, but eventually the panic began to ebb, like a storm running out of steam. The band around my chest loosened, and the pounding in my chest slowed.

Voices in the room kept me from spiralling.

'We just have to be nice to her.'

'Why again?'

'Because she's new and . . . Tarquinius asked us to. You know that's worth it.'

A heavy sigh. 'She can't do anything though! The others will laugh at us if we stay friends with a girl who can't even cast a basic rune, Phoebe.'

Sheet, they were talking about Opie.

With trembling hands, I reached for the latch and unlocked the stall door. As I stepped out, the cool air of the bathroom greeted me, a small but welcome relief, but the two girls were already gone. I couldn't deal with that right now, not when I could barely hold my own sanity together.

I straightened, shoulders and neck stiff from clenching. Then I sucked in a shuddering breath and blew it out slowly. The panic could come back tenfold if I wasn't careful. Right now, more than anything, what I needed was some space and fresh air.

I leaned against the sink. My face was wrecked, my lavender eyes red and swollen, my hair slicked with sweat. I splashed cold water on my cheeks and threw my pale blonde locks into a quick topknot. Then I made a beeline for the door and exited, keeping my face turned down and eyes glued to the floor.

I put one foot in front of the other and didn't stop moving until I busted out the front doors of the school.

The countless thoughts that had been so wild and scattered only moments before had been reduced to one.

Nocta was my father.

Blood pounded in my ears, and I knew I had to move, or it was another headlong dive into the maelstrom.

I strode toward the main gates that I'd passed through that morning. Strange, how in such a short time everything had changed.

My legs churned and I broke into a run, as if I could outpace the thoughts chasing me.

The gates peeled back, allowing me to exit as I bolted through, sprinting now. I pushed myself as hard as I could, arms and legs pumping.

I took the trail that led around the back of the Nevershoppes. The trees on either side of it blocked out the sun, but I didn't care that the darkness etched the world around me in shadows. I ran all the way down to the water's edge, then ran along the bank until my body and mind began to calm.

I finally caught myself on the flat top of a large rock and stared out across the river. Charon was there in the middle, his boat rocking lightly in the waves. His head turned my way, and I looked down at my toes, just there where the water met the land. I took a step back, putting distance between me and certain death as I lifted a hand to him.

'Sorry, didn't realize how close I was.'

He turned wordlessly away.

My belly snarled and I swiped a hand across my face, taking the worst of the sweat off.

Now that some of the initial shock and panic had faded, I had only one destination in mind. The Black Bear pub, at the far end of the street of Nevershoppes. Not open to minors, I'd never officially been inside, but I'd stolen enough from the back door of the kitchen that I knew how good the food was. Greasy and not at all at the high level of Neverthorn's chef-quality dishes. It was exactly what I needed right now . . . along with a pint of beer.

I made my way back to the trailhead and ducked through the bushes to the back of the pub. The door was cracked open to let the heat out, and by the sounds of things the lunch rush was in full swing.

Slipping up to the door, I spun a quick rune with my hand and held the spell lightly on the tip of my index finger. I flicked my finger and magic shot off, straight through the kitchen, hitting the tray of drinks that a waitress had balanced above her head.

The tray flipped and the beer crashed down around her as she let out a blood-curdling scream as if she'd been stabbed and not just soaked with drink. Every one of the kitchen staff ran out to see what the yowling was about, and I let myself in, grabbing the closest takeout bag, and a pint of something the color of amber that sat beside it, foam spilling over the top.

Working my way around the side of the pub, I found an overturned log and rolled it with another flick of my fingers to settle it against the wall. I took a seat and opened the takeout bag.

Score.

A double order of fish and chips, extra tartar sauce and . . .

I took a sip from the glass. Beergarita. Perfect. The sip turned into me downing half the glass, the buzz hitting me quickly. Double score for Dwimmer alcohol, it had a bigger punch than the stuff from the Unlit world.

I set the ice-cold drink down beside me and started in on the fish – perfectly flaky halibut, with actual dill in the batter. I almost didn't need the creamy tartar sauce.

Almost.

I let myself focus on the flavors of the meal, ignoring the whole reason I was out here eating my feelings and drinking like it was the last sip I'd ever have.

Ignoring the fact that I'd just found –

Nope.

Still eating. Still not going there.

'Nice move with that bag.' A figure stumbled toward me from around the corner.

The other shops were closed for lunch hour so I'd hoped I wouldn't be disturbed, and I let out a sigh.

'Thanks.'

'Imma use that trick next time I don't have money for –' The man bumped into the wall, slid down into a slump, and promptly began to snore.

Apparently, I wasn't the only one starting on the drink early today. I looked back to my food.

Eat it while it's hot, Harlow.

A rustle in the bushes a few yards away had me stopping short again, a bite of fish halfway to my mouth. A flash of movement, and then a small, waddling animal popped out. White body, black mask, and black rings around his tail, he wasn't a traditional-looking raccoon. But then, this was the Dwimmer world. Anything was possible.

The bushy little beggar squinted up at me, making a grabby motion with his tiny claws.

'No way man.' I stuffed the bite into my mouth and chewed. 'Go find your own meal, trash bandit. You have no idea what kind of a day I'm having.' Nope, not thinking about what I'd found on the computer. I shook my hand at him. 'I was forced to come back here. Frucking gagged!'

It was like . . . like they were trying to make me not me. To steal every part of me away from my identity to my actual voice. Emotions bubbled through me and my fingers tingled.

He waddled a little closer and made the grabby hands again, this time doing a soft chitter that was too damn cute to ignore. I sighed. I was a sucker for a sob story.

'Fine. Here.' I tossed him some of the fries.

He promptly scurried closer and grabbed them up, eating them one at a time, the bliss on his face obvious as he chewed, open-mouthed.

'They're good, I know.' I bobbed my head, reached in and found one of the extra tartar cups. I cracked it open and slid it across the ground to him. 'Dip them.'

He grabbed the cup and did just that, dipping his fries and then nibbling. A soft purr slid out of him, not all that different from a cat.

Talking to him was easy, and I finally let the words out, in a small whisper.

'How could I have known that he was my father? I couldn't have. No one here has even seen his face in . . . the news lady from the library clip said fifty years or something. He's been hiding from everyone.' I leaned back against the wall of the pub and dug in my bag for the second piece of fish.

My new friend continued chittering away as he ate, and I slid into memories that I'd tucked away, deep in my mind.

I couldn't even say how old I was that one time I'd met him. Seven maybe?

'*Belina.*'

He'd breathed her name, as if she were precious and beautiful, the way I knew her to be. He didn't see me peeking out of the closet through the slats, had no idea I was listening in on their conversation. 'You must *never* let her go to that school. They will destroy her, because she is mine. You know that.'

My mother turned away from him. 'You promised you wouldn't come back. That you'd . . . never meet her. You swore it, Nic!'

'I didn't come to *meet* her. I came to talk to you.' His voice was a calm baritone, resonating in me. But even within it, I could hear the anger growing. 'That school will be the death of her.'

'She's years away from even –'

'They would take her now if they knew. They would come, break down your doors, and snatch her away in a heartbeat. You're a fool if you believe otherwise.'

I scrunched up my face. I wasn't going to let anyone take me away, and my mama was no fool. I flung the closet doors open and stepped out.

'I'm not leaving, Mama.'

The man – my father – turned in surprise, his eyes, so like mine, widening. 'Hello, Harlow.'

I frowned up at him and repeated myself. 'No one is taking me from Mama.'

His smile was soft as he knelt in front of me. 'Ah, so fierce for one so young. You will protect your mother then?'

I gave him a serious nod. 'Yup.'

'And I will show you a new bit of magic to help you keep her safe.' He took my hand and folded my fingers gently.

Pressing my thumb over the tips of my ring and pinky finger at the same time, he then put my index and middle finger together, then flicked them apart. 'That is the motion. The rune is cal–'

'Nic, please don't,' my mom begged, her voice hitching. 'Please don't teach her anything.'

'One rune, Belina. To remember me by.' His eyes never left mine. Intense, they trapped me as if I were cornered with a mountain at my back and a lion crouched in front of me. But despite my tremors, I never looked away. Even now, I could see his face in my mind's eye, clear as day . . .

I blinked hard, staring at the exit of the Black Bear pub as my hand reflexively mimicked the shapes he'd shown me, wishing I had someone to talk to. Someone I could trust. Feeling so trapped here. As if they were trying to silence my voice . . . and everything else about me. The magic flowed off my hand, a flickering light that circled everything around me, passing over the man slumped against the wall then surrounding my new raccoon friend. He squeaked and danced on his back legs as the magic grabbed hold of him, yanking him upward.

'That's . . . weird.' I stood; the initial glow of magic-wielding already gone but leaving me feeling a bit revitalized. I turned to see my four-legged lunch partner staring up at me with wide dark eyes.

'What the hell was that?' he demanded in a raspy voice.

I stumbled back, momentarily struck dumb with shock.

'Have I lost my mind, or did you just talk?' I finally managed to stammer.

'Well, it sure ain't Disney, but yeah, I guess I can talk now. What was that smoke about?' He waddled toward me and grabbed at my pant leg, tugging me. 'For a minute there, I thought I was hallucinating again. Those forest

mushrooms are a doozy if you get them out of season.'
He shook his head.

'Can you just stop . . . Please don't say anything else.' I
held up a hand, my head thrumming. 'I just need to let this
sink in.'

I stared down at my hands, wondering if somehow the
mysterious rune taught to me by my father and buried in the
deepest part of my psyche had somehow given this creature a voice . . . which was when I noticed the smoke drifting
across my boots. No, not smoke, a thick fog that coated the
ground so heavily it looked as if I stood on clouds. It rolled
out of the forested back side of the Nevershoppes, crawling
through the trees like fingers, reaching for me.

I shook my head hard. Just my mind playing tricks. It had
been a long and trippy day. I needed to get back to Neverthorn, get my head together, and take a hot shower before
my next set of classes.

'I-I should go.' I got the feeling of a strange sense of
impending doom.

'Obviously,' the raccoon snorted. 'Surely, you're aware that
instant, all-consuming fog is never a good sign. Even I know
that, and I'm just a talking raccoon. You can call me Bandit.'

Heart hammering, I took a step back from the forest as
figures began to take shape, using the fog as cover, stalking
closer.

Not my imagination after all. Something was coming
for me.

Pressing myself against the wall of the pub, I slid along
it, moving toward the street. I passed by the man, and held
my finger to my lips, but he was out cold. The figures drew
closer still, and even though they were mostly camouflaged,
I could tell they were big.

Really frucking big.

And then my name . . . a whisper from the fog.

'*Harloooow.*'

Annnd, that was my cue to get the hell out of there. I spun to make a run for it, but the fog was everywhere now, enveloping the entire street. Cloaking the Nevershoppes in darkness, leaving me all alone. I took a step and ended up slammed back against the wall, a thick hand pinning me by my throat.

I grabbed at my assailant, clawing at their wrist, but barely scored a scratch. It was like their arm was covered by a hide more than by human skin. I squinted through the fog, gaze traveling over bunched muscles, a massive shoulder, to a short neck, finally landing on a head that was not human, but wolf-like, with tusks protruding from its muzzle and a single horn between its eyes. The other arm was scaled like a snake, the fingertips hissing, little fangs protruding from them as the creature lifted its hand to my face.

'Move and they'll bite,' he growled, his voice thick as if the vocal cords were not made for speaking.

The tiny serpents with their forked, flickering tongues were so close to my cheek that I didn't dare close my eyes.

'I think you've got the wrong –'

'Boys, we've got her, let's go,' he called over his shoulder as he tightened his grip on my neck and dragged me from the wall.

I was about to let out a scream when there was a flash of black and white, and a high-pitched howl rent the air. I looked down to see Bandit's jaws locked onto the creature's inner upper thigh. The distraction was enough.

Breaking away, I bolted into the cover of fog, spinning a rune as fast as I could, whipping my hand from shoulder to hip. An icy gust of wind blew down the street, taking the fog with it.

Fear and the threat of death had always been a good motivator for my runes to work.

Gasping for air, I turned to see my attacker and his cronies all clearly for the first time. There were half a dozen of them, and not one of them was human. Each of them looked . . . pieced together, and not well. They were made up of all sorts of animals, patched together on the frame of a human body. But some of the arms and legs didn't fit right, some of the heads seemed to be on sideways. And they all shared one thing in common. A bold N stitched into each of them somewhere on their skin.

N. For Nocta.

He'd sent them after me. They circled around. There was no way I could make a run for it. Fruck me.

I swallowed hard and cocked my head, my mouth running because my feet couldn't. 'You guys are a mess. What did he do, stick a whole bunch of critters in a blender and hit puree?' I kept my tone light as I settled back into a fighting stance.

The leader – the one who'd had me by the throat, let out a low snarl.

'Get her.'

Two of the creatures charged me at the same time. One with its head down, triple horns gnarled but sharp as he bent at the waist in an attempt to ram me. I leapt straight up, running along his back, snapping a rune down into him as I went. A rune I normally used for breaking down particularly stubborn doors.

It wasn't a total knockout, but it was enough, and he went down howling in pain, the sound of bones shattering loud enough to cleave the air.

The second creature was more sinewy than the others, and I realized at the last second that he had a long, dark-green, barbed tail.

He swung it toward me, and I pivoted out of its way, wincing as the barbs swept past my face. I landed in a crouch and frantically flung another rune. I'd created it on the fly when I'd had to dive into a river to escape an angry shopkeeper. Back then, it had allowed me to breathe underwater. This time, I was hoping it would do the opposite and make it impossible for *him* to breathe air.

The creature grabbed at his throat as he struggled, and I nearly crowed in triumph. My joy was short-lived though, as ropes whipped around me, finding purchase and dropping me to the ground. They grew tighter and tighter, until I could barely take a breath. Regular ropes yanked tight by monstrously strong creatures.

Not ideal.

'Bandit,' I managed to squeak out as I searched for him, finding him crouched on the edge of the pub's roof. 'School. Protect. Opie.'

'You can do that yourself.'

The raccoon let out a funny little bark as he leapt from the roof and landed on my middle, his teeth and claws tearing at the ropes.

That wasn't what saved me though.

A blast of magic slammed into my attackers, sending them flying through the air as Bandit fought to get me free. I wiggled my fingers and managed to get a rune of undoing flicked at the ropes. They fell off me just as I caught sight of another figure rushing toward me. A man I didn't recognize, wearing a long, dark coat . . .

'Back up, you ugly bastards!' The stranger paid me no mind, his attention fully on the creatures rising to their feet and heading back toward me. His coat flared out behind him like wings, an avenging angel as he spun runes faster than I'd ever seen before. Nocta's minions tried to flee, but his magic caught them one by one, tearing them limb from limb – undoing the magic that had bound the monstrosities together.

Black smoke spilled out from their bodies, flying straight up into the sky.

In the end, there wasn't much left but piles of animal pieces. A few snakes slithered away, a single bird took flight, and that was that.

I was on my knees, Bandit on all fours in front of me.

'You okay?' he whispered.

I nodded shakily. 'You?'

He bobbed his head, chittered, and skulked off toward the forest as a shadow enveloped me.

I tipped my head back, squinting into the now-visible sun to stare into the handsome face of my savior.

'I owe you my thanks . . .'

'Liam. Liam O'Connor. And I guess that's one way of looking at it. Although, it would've put a slight damper on my day to sit by and watch a woman get torn from limb to limb by those fuckers. So, it was sort of a selfish gesture on my part.'

Liam had an easy smile, eyes the color of melted chocolate, and sun-kissed brown curls that only added to the whole angel impression. As untrusting as I was as a rule, I could already feel the fight-or-flight tension slowly leaving my body as the adrenaline drained away.

The bravery of the beergarita was gone.

'Regardless, I appreciate you stepping in. A lot of people would've run the other way. I'm Harlow Daygon.'

His gaze flicked to my bracer before returning to my face. 'House Phoenix, hmm? I heard they were reinstating it.'

'That's what they tell me.'

'Well, Harlow Daygon, can I help you up?'

87

My legs felt like jelly, and everything hurt, so I shook my head. 'Actually, I think I'm gonna sit here for a minute and assess the damage before I try to stand, if you don't mind.'

'I don't mind one bit. In fact, I can sit right down beside you and –'

'What's going on here?' I turned toward the hard, clipped voice and found myself staring up into the face of a furious Typhon Moreno.

'Where are Nocta's men?' he demanded, the tension pulsing from him almost palpable.

Liam turned, a hint of dimple flashing. 'Well, aren't you a big fella?'

Typhon's dead-eyed glare would've intimidated most, but to Liam's credit, he held his ground and stared right back until I felt compelled to fill the tense silence.

'They're . . . gone. I was attacked, and Liam helped me. H-how did you know Nocta's men were here?'

'I saw the dark fog roll in out of nowhere. Nocta's trademark,' Typhon grunted, eyes never leaving Liam. 'I can take it from here.'

'Why don't we let the lady decide who's going to take it from where, hmm?' Liam's tone seemed light, but I could feel the threat underneath it. He wasn't backing down from Typhon.

The two of them stared each other down.

Fear still skittered along my spine. I'd been this close to being snatched by Nocta's men. I just wanted to go back to the school, as crazy as that sounded even to me.

'Hey! Hi, there,' I said as they both finally looked my way. 'Still on the ground and not sure if I have use of my limbs yet, so if you two are done measuring your ducks . . .' Damn that language gag!

Liam shook his head and smiled down at me with a wink.

'No need for that on my end, I've no insecurities about my duck size. I'm happy to be on my way so long as you've got a friend here and feel safe.'

I wouldn't go *that* far, but I could already tell Typhon was pissed and the charming stranger was only making it worse.

'I'll be fine. I don't think he's going to try and kill me . . . today, at least. But thanks again for stepping in. If I see you around, drinks are on me.'

'You'll see me around.' He lifted a hand and waved as he backed away. 'And I'll hold you to that offer.'

It wasn't until Liam headed into the pub, disappearing from sight, that Typhon turned his attention back to me.

'What the hell happened?'

'I'm fine, thanks for asking. Really appreciate your concern –'

'Tell me exactly what happened, Harlow. Now.'

I covered my face with my hands and then ran them over the back of my neck. 'I don't know. One minute I was sitting here eating my fish and chips, and the next the fog rolled in and Nocta's men were on me.'

He scowled again, staring off into the distance. 'I don't get why the protection wards didn't alert us to a breach . . .'

What did I know about what it took to breach Tarquinius's shielding spells? I shrugged and the motion made me wince.

Typhon frowned and reached out a hand. 'Can you stand?'

I nodded. 'Yeah, pretty sure.' I let him help me up, ignoring the pulse of energy that arced from his hand to mine. Before I could pull away, he drew me slowly along after him, up the street and back toward the school. I looked over my shoulder to see Bandit skulking along behind us, using the buildings for cover.

As if he blended in at all. And what did he think he was hiding from? Nocta's men were gone.

'Sit.' Typhon had us at the end of the street where the fountain gurgled. The mermaid in it reached for the sky, a horn to her lips, the water pouring out of the horn and sliding down her arms and face, back into the fountain. It was beautiful and sad, as if she were crying endless tears.

I sat on the edge of the fountain as Typhon tore the sleeve of his shirt off and dipped it into the water, then wiped the blood from my face. 'Any major pains?'

I stared up at him. 'Would it matter if there were?'

His eyes flashed. 'My job is to protect you and the other students.'

'If that's what's bothering you, don't worry, it was my choice to leave the school.'

'Are. You. Hurt?'

I glared at him and let out a sigh. 'Some tenderness in my ribs but, as you know from personal experience, I've had worse, so don't get your panties in a knot over that. And *don't* try to heal me, either. I've had enough of you messing with me.'

Something flickered in his face but was gone in an instant. 'I'm not a healer. I was just going to take some of the pain away . . .'

It *did* hurt like a son of a beech.

'Fine.'

He put a cloth in my hand and lifted it to my bleeding nose. 'Hold that.' He sat next to me and put his hands to either side of my torso. Fingers flicking along my ribs, his head bowed, I realized as his magic sank into me that he was checking me for breaks.

'Keep breathing, Harlow. I can't find cracks if you don't breathe.'

Except, I couldn't breathe. His hands were warm, and his dark hair right under my nose smelled . . . amazing. I couldn't pinpoint it, and I was clearly still addled from the brawl, which is why I will forever say that it was an accident that I took the cloth from my face and bent my head to smell his hair.

His head came up at the same time mine lowered, our noses brushing against each other as he leaned back, and for the space of a heartbeat we were so very, very close. I could feel his breath on my lips, see his eyes dip to my mouth. Knew that he could feel my breath too. It would take nothing to close the distance, to press my lips against his and –

Jesus, what the hell was I thinking?

He shot to his feet and glared at me.

'Sorry, just a little disoriented,' I blurted. 'No breaks, right? All good?'

He grunted in response.

'Right. Should we go tell someone about those creatures?' I coughed.

He nodded and took a step back. 'Yes, Tarquinius will want a full report.'

Right, that was the smart thing to do. Give a full report. Of course, I could have told him right there that I didn't *think* that Nocta's men were trying to kill me. That I thought they were trying to kidnap me, even if they had been rough as hell with me. What had they said? *Boys, we've got her, let's go.* But that would mean explaining who my father was.

There would be countless people at Neverthorn who wanted their revenge on him and would surely consider taking it out on me instead. Especially since, the very same day I returned to Neverthorn, Nocta's men mysteriously found a way to breach the wards and get in. If I didn't know the truth, even *I'd* have suspected me of being in league with the bad guys.

I could still hear his warning to my mother, all those many years before.

'You cannot let her go to that school. They will destroy her if they find out she is mine.'

I hated to agree with a psychotic villain but there was no doubt about it.

If Tarquinius or anyone at Neverthorn found out Nocta was my father, I would either wind up in prison or dead.

7

The meeting with Tarquinius went pretty much as expected. He chewed me out for twenty minutes about cutting out of detention and missing lunch and my next class. Then, he chewed me out some more for leaving the school and heading to the pub.

'Given your advanced age in comparison to your schoolmates, one would think you'd want to set an example for the other students, Ms. Daygon,' Tarquinius had said, his wiry eyebrows furrowing like a pair of silvery caterpillars. He was wiry across the board, his hair, his frame, his glasses. Like someone had taken pipe cleaners and created a stick figure out of them, and then draped it in a dark-blue curtain.

The color did nothing for his pale complexion, making him look like his head was detached from the rest of his body. As for how I felt after being scolded by him? Mostly just annoyed. He wasn't nearly as scary as I'd have thought a Sage should be.

I bowed my head in false contrition. I had no choice but to keep my mouth shut about my reasons for leaving Neverthorn.

Facts were facts, and he wasn't wrong. I'd broken more than one rule, which had caused this whole mess. What he didn't know was that I was pretty sure I'd unwittingly lured Nocta to me. In fact, the more I thought about it, I was almost certain of it. He'd taught me a rune he'd created for me when I was a child. One he could track. I'd all but flung the door open and put out the welcome mat for him and those creatures to find me.

I glared at the back of Typhon's head as he led me toward the large auditorium.

'Stop glaring at me. It's not my fault you don't know how to follow directions.'

'I don't get why you can't bring me to talk to Opie. Just for a little while.' What I'd overheard in the bathroom had me certain the girls she thought were friends were anything but. 'I need to see that she's alright with my own two eyes, then I promise to sit through your stupid assembly, quiet as a mouse.'

He stopped so fast, I nearly ran straight into his broad back before stopping short. The motion made my ribs ache.

'Ophelia will be at the assembly with her housemates. Talk to her then.' He paused and shot a look at me. 'While I encourage the silence of a mouse, I doubt you're capable.'

He turned away abruptly and continued down the hall, leaving me to hurry after him again.

I wasn't sure if it was just the shock of the day finally wearing off or the exhaustion from all that had happened, but the words struck a nerve, and hot tears sprang to my eyes.

I threw up my hands in frustration. 'I talk too much, I'm a magnet for trouble. It's super annoying . . . Which is why it's in everyone's best interest to let me leave.'

Why couldn't he see that? I'd grab Opie, we'd get off this godforsaken island, and head back home to my little bed and breakfast for runaways. I'd never do that stupid spell Nocta had shown me again, and we'd be safe. Just the two of us.

And this time, I'd actually appreciate it. No more taking the important things for granted.

We'd just reached the auditorium, where a handful of students still trickled in. Typhon turned to face me once more, his firm lips twisted into a frown.

'You can leave, but the girl stays. As always, your choice.'

I was about to lay into him when I felt a set of arms wrap around my middle in a vice-like grip that had my ribs groaning.

'Lo-lo! I'm so glad to see you!' Opie squealed, skirting around until we were face to face. Her cheeks were pink with delight and her eyes were bright with excitement. 'This place is ahhhmazing. A thousand times better than I'd ever imagined. I'm in House Unicorna. I love my classes so far, and I've already got some new friends, Krishna and Phoebe.'

She jerked her head toward the two girls standing a few yards behind her, whispering behind their hands, snickering as they watched us. As soon as they realized I was looking at them, they stopped talking and offered smiles and a wave.

Friends. The ones put in place to pretend to be her friends. But I couldn't say that to her. I lurched toward her and passed her the note I'd written during the plane ride over.

Sure, everyone knew that House Wolven was known for their prowess in physical combat. But she needed to know that they also acted as a unit, like a little army of their own. If you messed with one, you messed with them all.

And House Kelpish might go with the flow most days, like the harmless seahorse depicted on their crest, but I pitied the fool who didn't realize how stormy those seas could get when angry.

She needed to know that the kids in House Kirinash were pretty to look at, but that wasn't the only reason so many of them wound up becoming movie stars. They were almost as strong as the students in Draconell, but wily. The greatest of pretenders. They could fool you into believing almost anything.

I probably should've written more about Draconell. I'd told her how some had a mean streak a mile long, and how strong their leadership skills were, but I forgot to explain how that made them bad team players. Draconells might put up a good front, but at the end of the day, they had only one person's back.

Their own.

Something I needed to keep in mind myself when it came to Typhon.

'I'll catch you later on. Maybe at dinner?' Opie called as she backed away, tucking the note in her pocket without even glancing at it.

'Sure thing. We can eat together if you want. I have a few more things I want to t—'

But I was talking to myself, because she'd already rejoined Krishna and Phoebe, and the three were walking arm in arm to find empty seats next to one another.

Something else I should've mentioned. Students of House Unicorna were a tricky bunch. While some I'd met in my short stint here had been outwardly friendly, and they loathed confrontation, they could also be two-faced – and what I'd heard in the bathroom only confirmed that truth. She needed to keep her guard up . . .

'She wants to be here, Harlow. And if you interfere with her finding her place, it's only going to drive a wedge between you. Let her figure out the truth on her own.' Typhon's voice was right at my ear, low and serious.

I knew he was right, but I didn't have to like it.

'You do you, and I'm going to do me.'

Something about the way his gaze narrowed on my mouth again made my cheeks blaze, and I backed away. No more talk about anybody *doing* anybody else. It was time to get the hell away from Typhon. The more time I spent around him, the more space he seemed to take up.

I was still catching my breath when I sidled up next to

Fable, who was just about to take one of two empty seats next to Zeed and the rest of our house members.

'Hey,' I said, forcing a smile.

'Hey! Are you okay?' she demanded, looking me up and down. 'People are saying that we're here to talk about some sort of attack over at the Nevershoppes, and you were there? Is that true?'

The rumor mill still churned as efficiently as ever here, apparently. 'Yeah . . . I'm totally fine.'

Fable let out a squeak as she caught sight of Bandit, who had apparently snuck in behind me in stealth-mode.

'What is that?' Fable asked, eyes wide.

'That is Bandit,' I said, matter of factly. 'He's my . . .'

What was he? Not a pet, per se. I knew instinctively that he wasn't mine to command or 'keep'. But he had been as loyal as any retriever when my life was in danger. 'My new friend.'

'Right . . .' she said, cocking her head. 'You know you can have a familiar, but they're seriously old school. Totally out of style.' She cleared her throat. 'Usually it's a cat.'

'What can I say? I like to be different.'

I sat and he climbed up onto my lap and settled in without a word, so I didn't have to get into the whole talking-raccoon part, which was good. There'd already been enough excitement for the day.

His steady warmth gave me something to focus on, and the anxiety of being in a crowd this big, this packed, eased some with his presence. I laid my hand over his middle and he let out a low rumbling purr.

Calm, I just needed to stay calm.

As people trickled in, I took in my new housemates. I'd met Fable, Ross, Marina, Zeed, and, of course, Phyllis at the library.

A girl with short black hair in a stylish pixie cut leaned forward. Her light brown eyes were soft, like a deer's. 'I'm Ellie. I think we were in school together; you were a year ahead of me.'

I winced. 'Were we?'

'House Felinita. I was quiet . . . I don't think we ever spoke.' She bobbed her head.

Zeed tapped the table. 'We were all House Felinita, then. Why is that?' An excellent question. 'I mean, Felinita is known for their smarts and ability to strategize, but rune crafting . . .'

Our group cringed in unison at the reminder. 'Me and Fable, Ross and Caterina kind of overlapped in school,' said the only other guy at the table.

Caterina nodded toward him, her brilliant red hair wildly out of control. She reminded me of a Disney princess with the way it flowed around her. 'I didn't go when Gary was here, but yeah. There is overlap between most of us. Ellie and Marina and I were all in Felinita at the same time.'

Typhon hadn't said we'd all come from the *same* house. Surely, that was no coincidence, and it only made me trust him less.

Zeed's jaw tightened. 'There is something strange going on. We need to find out what it is. It doesn't make sense that we'd all be pulled from the same house.'

They all turned to me.

'What?' I demanded.

Marina tapped the table. 'You seem to have some street smarts. What do *you* think?'

I shrugged and let my mind tick through the possibilities. 'Off the cuff? I'm thinking they stuffed all the kids who were supposed to be in House Phoenix into House Felinita because they had nowhere else to put us. Who would look hard at kids in the weakest house? Nobody.'

A few mumbles of agreement, because we'd all been there on the lowest rung of the ladder, getting picked on because we were in House Felinita.

'Marina's right, Harlow. You seem like you know a lot about the world. What did you do for a living?' Ellie asked, her voice soft as her eyes. 'Before, I mean.'

I blew a raspberry as I scrambled for an answer. 'Odd jobs. You?'

Ellie blushed. 'I was in a Dim school training to be a nurse.'

'Firefighter,' Ross said.

'Photographer,' Caterina piped up.

'Engineer,' Zeed said, no surprise there.

'Police officer,' Marina added. 'Assuming I still have my job when I go back.'

'I work in a warehouse, stacking boxes at night,' Gary said.

We all looked to Fable. 'I'm in training to be a teacher. I like kids.'

What I took from this was that all of them were employed in the Unlit world, because none of them were strong enough to be considered for a job among the Dwimmer community.

'Okay, so what else?' I scrunched my face as I pondered. 'What about Quirks? Anybody got a good one?'

I scanned the forlorn faces in front of me and cleared my throat.

'Nobody?'

They all shook their heads.

'You?' Ross asked, eyeing me hopefully.

'Nope. Nada.' But there had to be some reason Tarquinius had chosen us . . . 'Okay, how about *potential* Quirks that haven't surfaced yet? Strong ones that come up in your families every generation or so? My great-aunt was a Clairvoyant. Maybe Tarquinius is hoping if they put us in our proper house, our Quirks will reveal themselves?'

They all exchanged looks and Zeed spoke first. 'My grandad had an uncommonly green thumb. He could make plants and trees grow super-fast. I think he was the only one, though.'

Neat. I tried to think how that might win us a war against Nocta but came up empty.

'Fable?'

She shrugged. 'My aunt and granny both have X-ray vision. They can see through solid structures . . . like walls and stuff.'

Again, cool, but surely not something that had made Tarquinius flag her as the potential chosen one.

'No necromancers or fire wielders?'

Marina was shaking her head and about to speak when Tarquinius stepped onto the stage at the front of the massive hall.

'Students of Neverthorn,' he said, voice booming over the microphone on the dais as the rest of the room went silent. 'Today, the school's defenses were tested by the Dwimmer world's most vile of evils. Nocta sent his emissaries to our hallowed grounds, as he did to our sister school, Heathermoor, last month. Needless to say, we passed that test.'

He held up a triumphant fist, opening his fingers, a burst of light rising from them. Fireworks flickered over everyone as the students erupted with applause, the sound of their cheers deafening the room before both faded away, as Tarquinius held up his hands for silence.

'Sir, I thought there were wards in place to protect the school from Nocta? That's what my parents told me,' a familiar male voice toward the front of the room called out. 'How did they get through them?'

That was one of the boys from this morning. A Draconell kid.

The Sage's lips twisted as he lowered his hands. 'There were and are, young Julius, many wards in place. Which is why we only saw the two very small, isolated attacks. One by the Nevershoppes, where the wards are less robust, and one here in the school's courtyard. No students were hurt, and Nocta himself did not and cannot set foot on school grounds. Fear not for your safety. We will always protect you.' Tarquinius continued to talk, but my heart stopped.

There had been *two* attacks?

'There was an attack in the courtyard?' I turned to Fable, heart pounding.

'Yes. Although calling it an attack is a stretch. Three creatures of some sort just appeared out of nowhere, apparently. A student passing by the entryway caught sight of them and called for help. Doyenne Storm was holding our lesson on Weather Defense in the gardens and rushed to the courtyard. I only caught the aftermath . . . it was over before it started. She mowed them down with a lightning rune, and that was that.'

Only three assailants, and again, no damage done to any students or professors. Strange . . . such weak attacks at the helm of such a strong wizard. Maybe he hadn't sent his men for battle. Maybe he'd sent them for information.

About me?

My fingers tightened on Bandit's fur, and he wriggled in protest.

'As you all know,' Tarquinius pressed on, 'we have the newly reinstated House Phoenix here. Soon enough, the threat of Nocta will be neutralized completely by them.'

Low whispers broke out, and some of the other students turned toward me and my group. I had to admit, they didn't look like they were exactly brimming with confidence, and I could hardly blame them. There would be upperclassmen who had been in school with several of my housemates and knew full well that we weren't exactly the cream of the crop.

Word traveled fast, after all. And the fact that most of us had spent the morning in detention probably didn't help our image.

'Seems dodgy. Some of those losers were in school with us, I'd bet they can't cast runes as well as my gran. Might as well have her take on Nocta,' Julius snorted. His housemates around him snickered and laughed.

At us.

At me.

Shame bit into me and Bandit squirmed on my lap until I realized I was clutching his thick coat. I breathed through my nose and fought to calm myself.

Tarquinius waited until the laughter faded, as he'd done with the applause.

'While your gran is a dear friend of mine, and a powerful witch in her own right, that won't be necessary, Julius,' Tarquinius drawled.

The headmaster waved his hand loosely in the air and a scroll of solid black paper appeared above his head, then slowly unfurled. If words were written, I couldn't see any. Tarquinius touched a finger to the paper and words that hadn't been there a moment before turned into bright white light that flew off the page and glowed above all our heads.

A voice that was not Tarquinius's, but a woman's, circled around the room.

> *In the darkest hour,*
> *In the darkest days,*
> *The child with the power*

Shall the darkness raze.
House Phoenix will rise
And save those lost,
The soul behind the eyes,
The cost beyond the cost.
In one hand the world will live,
In the other a death will give
Our world peace,
And the darkness will cease.

The words faded, the scroll went black and the words above our heads disappeared. In the silence you could have heard a mouse fart.

Tarquinius looked at our group, his deep brown eyes almost . . . sorrowful.

'That was the last prophecy of the Oracle of the Horned King, before she disappeared thirty years ago.' Gasps followed that little tidbit. 'While they might not seem like much to you right now, House Phoenix has been resurrected. They have been prophesied as the saviors of our world. And we will all help them become the best that they can be, to face their destiny, so one or perhaps more of them may save us all.'

No pressure there.

Every freaking chair seemed to creak as the entire auditorium turned to us. The others beside me squirmed. Well, there was the answer we'd been searching for.

A prophecy about our entire house . . . this was no small thing. You didn't mess with prophecies, and you sure as sheet didn't try to change them – even I knew that. Not when they came from the Horned King's Oracle.

Hell, I wished they had told us sooner. It would have helped make sense of why they brought us back. Then again, sharing it now with the whole school was smart – there would be fewer grumbles from the dissenters if they knew we were here because of a prophecy.

Tarquinius was a smart old codger.

Opie's face was all I saw though, shining with pride. She grinned and I saw her whisper to her friends, 'That's my sister.'

Gods, it was going to break her heart when I failed.

Tarquinius tapped his hand against the lectern.

'Now, as for the attacks today, I imagine Nocta got wind of the fact that we're looking for a replacement or replacements for Heronius but haven't yet found them. Until we do, I suspect he will continue to try to probe for weakness. But have no fear. We have several measures in place to increase protection, and we intend to prepare the House Phoenix students for the dark days ahead as quickly as possible. For the time being, we will move forward with caution until we're certain that we've done all we can to ensure the safety of all students here at Neverthorn. To meet that end, I hereby invoke the rule of two. Students will be matched up with one of their housemates as a pair. Whenever you leave Neverthorn, you will be with that person. No one . . . and I mean no one,' Tarquinius's gaze landed unerringly on me, 'is to leave this school alone. As for the members of House Phoenix in particular, we will need to take a different approach. If Nocta somehow got wind of one of you being the eventual replacement for Heronius, or if he has heard of the prophecy, you might already be on his radar. Therefore, you will be paired with your companion at all times outside your dorm rooms.'

There were more than a few grumbles around the room.

'Companions everywhere? What if we forget?' Zeed's voice rang out from a couple of seats down.

'Staff will be keeping an eye to ensure that doesn't happen.'

Tarquinius frowned again, his wrinkles gaining newer, deeper lines. 'If anyone is caught breaking the rules, your house will lose private-room privileges and be forced to stay together in a shared dorm room. You'll also miss out on the Solstice Games at mid-terms.'

Collective gasps spread around the room of 'he can't do that, can he?' and 'no way I'm missing the games.' I'd missed my own Solstice Games, what the kids affectionately called 'The Coliseum.'

I wondered if I'd make it to them this year.

Unlikely at the rate I was going, and it was just my first day.

'Maybe they'll let us be paired together,' Fable whispered as various doyens and staff members stepped to the front of the auditorium. I could see Nikita skirting around some of the other professors to stand next to Typhon. He glanced down at her, then away.

'House Felinita, make your way to join Doyenne Parunah for your pairings. House Draconell, to Doyen Moreno. House Phoenix to Doyenne Elmwood . . .' he droned on.

I tapped Bandit. 'Off you get, buddy.'

With a grumble, he leapt from my lap and waddled toward the exit as we all made our way to our respective lines.

When we got to our section, I made a concerted effort not to glance at Nikita, and even took a step away from Fable. If she knew we wanted to be paired together, it would be super on-brand for her to ensure we weren't.

Ellie stood next to me. 'It's weird, isn't it? Like Zeed said about all of us being from the same house, and all that? And the prophecy . . . I've never heard of anything like that relating to a house before.'

I nodded. 'Weird indeed.'

I tried to wrack my brain, thinking of anything else we might have in common.

'Did you . . . leave anyone behind? You know, like a partner?'

She blushed. 'No. I don't think any of us had a partner. Which also adds to the coincidences.'

'Well, maybe you'll find the love of your life here.' I flicked my eyes toward the students who'd grouped together, nodding toward a tall, handsome young man with a buzz cut. Ellie shook her head.

'Not really my flavor. Too much testosterone.'

'Ah, gotcha. There's this really nice –'

'I know you love being the center of attention, but I'm running the show here,' Nikita cut in.

I remembered my vow to fly under the radar and managed a smile.

'Roger that.'

Her nostrils flared but she didn't take it any further, instead, quickly rattling off the pairings. Zeed and Marina, Ross and Caterina, and then Gary and Ellie. It wasn't until there were three of us left – me, Phyllis, and Fable – that I knew for certain I was about to get frucked.

'Well, this is unfortunate,' Nikita said with a tight smile that suggested it was anything but. 'Seems like if we keep counting by twos right to left, it's Phyllis and Fable paired. Which leaves an odd man . . . or in this case, woman, out.'

I bared my teeth and shrugged, 'No skin off my asterisk.' Guh. Frigging Typhon and his stupid spell. 'I'm happy to fly solo and take the risk.'

'Oh, that won't do at all,' Nikita replied, stepping toward me, eyes shining. 'It looks like it's going to be me and you, Ms. Daygon. Just like old times.'

For whatever reason, she'd wanted it this way. Over my dead body was I going to willingly spend time with that . . . punt.

I coughed a word under my breath before I spoke. 'If my

choice is death by Nocta's franken-critters or spending one-on-one time with you for the better part of my day, I'll risk the monsters.'

'Be that as it may, my job here is to protect you students from doing anything stupid that might put you or your classmates in harm's way . . .' she raised a brow, 'for the second time today.'

I clenched my hands together, barely resisting the urge to whip off a rune that would temporarily seal her mouth shut.

A thought occurred to me then. She was clearly married, hence the change to Elmwood. Where was her husband? Maybe he'd faked his own death to escape her.

The pairs began to peel off and I had to go with her. I smiled and held out my hand, which she ignored. She gave me her back and snapped her fingers like she was summoning a poodle.

'Follow me.'

I'd been at Neverthorn for approximately half a day, and it was already the second worst of my life.

Fruck this place.

8

The day finally slid to an end, and with it came a dinner that soothed some of the ragged edges of my aching everything. Head, heart, body. A triple threat if ever there was one.

It was almost like Mrs. Wickersham knew what a sheet show the day had been and had prepared the meal accordingly. The spread across the main table looked like comfort food on steroids. Mac and cheese with lobster, deep dish pizza that looked like it had come out of a Chicago pizzeria, chicken and waffles smothered in a thick syrup, triple-decker grilled cheese next to a huge pot of steaming tomato soup, a plate of burritos that were the size of my arm, a whole section that looked like it had been pulled out of a Chinese buffet line. That didn't even include the dessert spread.

Our house was the last to arrive for dinner, having been held past the bell by Doyenne Storm. She wasn't unkind, but damn she was hard on us as she tried to teach us how to manipulate weather, as well as block it. My left shoulder ached from where I'd been thrown across the open courtyard when I couldn't block a bolt of lightning.

Yup. Lightning.

Straight at me.

I loaded up on lobster mac and cheese as I thought about the rune for blocking weather manipulation which was a grade three spell. I'd not gotten past grade one in school, so I had that excuse. But still, shame dug into me, making me feel like I was sixteen again. Alone, afraid, and unable to do even the basics. Not that my fellow housemates had done any better . . .

They were as bruised and battered as me, and by the looks of things, everyone else in the school already knew we'd sucked at our last class. Despite Tarquinius sharing the prophecy, and trying to buffer us some, I could feel the dubious stares as I filled my plate.

That prophecy was only going to carry us so far.

Once my bowl was heaped with cheesy goodness, I spared a glance around for Opie and found her deep in conversation with her two new friends. I couldn't help but wonder if she'd read my note yet.

With a sigh, I went and sat at the only open table.

'Maybe she should have given us umbrellas,' Zeed said with a wince as he took the seat across from me. 'We'd have had a better chance at stopping the rain at least.'

Fable sighed. 'I get why we have to learn it.'

'You do?'

I grunted a laugh, it was all I had energy for. I couldn't see any reason we'd need to learn weather defense. Maybe I was just slow. Or tired. Or hadn't had enough caffeine.

She sat next to Zeed. 'Brutal it might be, but what if Nocta or one of his generals whipped up a magical hurricane? We have to be able to deflect lightning that's thrown at us, like Doyenne Storm did. Or what if a blizzard eliminated visibility and we were ambushed? I don't have to like it, but I understand why.'

A snort from a table behind us, lilting, high cultured. House Kirinash. 'They have to explain why they need weather defense? Unbelievable. And *they're* going to save us.'

'We're all going to die.'

A long show of laughter and then the voices melted away and I made myself ignore the shame that burned in my belly, creating a new ulcer next to the one my anxiety had surely opened up.

'And just think, we get to do it all again in a few days, and again in a week, and again and again, until the Solstice Games.' I took my first bite of food, and the sweet, tender lobster melted in my mouth. I couldn't hold back the groan of pleasure that slid from my lips. Silver lining engaged.

Gary and Ross joined us next, and eventually the other girls from House Phoenix found their way over.

Phyllis was the last to join us, her worried eyes saying it all, as if we didn't already know.

We sucked. Big time.

'Mind if I sit with you guys?' I looked toward the head of the table to find none other than Liam O'Connor smiling down at us, his gaze finding mine. 'Harlow.'

'Hey?' My brain stuttered and went offline for a second. 'Um, guys, this is Liam. The guy who saved my bacon outside the pub.' I turned back to Liam. 'W-what are you doing here?'

He made his way down to the only empty seat, right next to me. His arm brushed mine, leaving it tingling as he lowered himself to the chair. 'It's a pretty boring story, actually.'

'Let's hear it,' Ross said. 'I could really go for some boredom after today, to be honest.'

Liam chuckled, his dark brown eyes sparking with good humor.

His gaze flickered over me, and I looked away. Nope. I did not need the distraction of a silver-tongued charmer, no matter how pretty his eyes might be.

'Well, I was a doyen teaching at Heathermoor, and our headmaster got an urgent message from Tarquinius requesting my presence to help with the reinstatement of House Phoenix. I caught the next flight over, a brutal red-eye that had more turbulence than I care to admit.' He shrugged. 'And here I am.'

'Last-minute urgent business ruining your day,' Marina

said, popping a piece of a roll in her mouth. 'I hope you at least got a big, fat check?'

'Not really,' he laughed. 'Honestly? I came for the food. Wickersham is a damn genius, and I've never found pizza that matches hers.'

I couldn't help the laugh, a little tension leaving me. 'Man, you are not wrong.' I lifted a spoonful of my mac and cheese and cheers'd it against his slice of pizza.

For the next half hour, Liam regaled the table with stories of student antics at Heathermoor, pulling in each of my housemates one at a time until he had them all laughing, and every other table in the dining hall looking our way. Even the reserved Phyllis cracked a smile, not once, but twice.

And those looking our way included Nikita and Typhon. The duo of doom. I laughed a little louder than I had to and let my eyes lock with Typhon's.

His stone face didn't so much as twitch, but by the way his eyes flicked to Liam, Typhon was *not* happy that he was here, even if it was to help with reinstating our House Phoenix.

Liam, whose thigh repeatedly brushed against my own, his shoulder bumping into mine as he talked. I chalked it up to tight quarters, but I wasn't wholly convinced. We sat there longer than anyone else, filling up on desserts – I downed at least four slices of shortbread, letting each piece melt on my tongue – Liam animated and seemingly at ease being the center of attention.

'Curfew in fifteen minutes.'

Typhon's voice cut through the story about Liam finding a pig locked in the closet of a student, only to figure out that he'd unlocked a Quirk that allowed the student to turn into various farm animals but didn't know how to turn himself back.

'I'll be gone before that.' Liam leaned back in his chair. 'Typhon,' he said with a nod by way of greeting.

'O'Connor. Don't you have to finish unpacking?'

Liam shrugged. 'Already done.'

Typhon didn't back down. Just tucked his hands behind his back and widened his stance a little.

'Make sure you don't keep them here past curfew. They need to be on point, at the top of their games, each and every day.'

Liam nodded. 'You got it, boss.'

Fourteen minutes and fifty seconds later, with Typhon staring daggers through him, Liam finally stood and stretched.

'Time to hit the hay. I don't need the grumpy professor adding me to his naughty list.'

We all stood to join him, and Liam pressed closer to me. I felt a poke on my arm and a moment later, he was pushing something into my hand.

Instinctively, I accepted it and tucked it under the sleeve of my shirt.

A rolled-up sheet of paper.

A note?

What was *this* about?

With one last wave he left, without another word.

Typhon watched Liam leave, his eyes narrowing as if he could see right through him.

His eyes drifted over to me as he made his way back over. 'Ms. Daygon. A word before you leave.'

A word.

Fable, Zeed and the others all gave me sympathetic looks as the two of us headed out of the dining room.

'How long has Pendergast been teaching here?' I asked, as much to control the topic of discussion as out of curiosity.

Typhon stared hard at me, and I wasn't sure he was going to answer at first. 'She married and moved to Scotland to teach at Heathermoor. Her husband was a doyen there. He was killed a couple years back when Nocta and his creatures took out a whole tower at Heathermoor. This is only her second year teaching at Neverthorn.'

My mouth went dry, and my stomach turned. No one deserved that.

He held out his hand and I held out mine with a quizzical glance.

'What, you wanna play patty cake?'

His frown was instant, the scowl darkening his face. 'Give me what O'Connor slipped you.'

'I don't know what you're talking about.'

I was backing up, step by step, and he followed, stalking me like a jungle cat. By the gods he was a big man, his shadow enveloped me.

He snapped his fingers at me. 'Give it to me. Now.'

'You might be large and grumpy, but you don't scare me, Typhon Moreno. I'm not giving you sheet.'

I bolted, racing for the stairs and catching up to the rest of my housemates before they'd reached the third floor. I was breathing hard and almost giddy that I hadn't gotten blasted in the back by a binding rune.

I let out a sigh of exhaustion.

'You in trouble?' Marina asked quietly.

'Nope.'

I stepped into my dorm room a couple minutes later, stunned to find Bandit curled at the foot of my bed, fast asleep. He must have sniffed my room out and made himself at home. Apparently, he thought he could come and go as he pleased.

It wasn't until I changed into my pajamas and was snuggled up under the covers that I took out the tiny, rolled piece of paper Liam had handed me . . .

9

The next morning, I woke up with a knot in my stomach. Bandit must've sensed it, because as I got ready for the day, he kept nudging my ankle with his nose like he was trying to comfort me. By the time I got dressed and buckled on my fanny pack, I was already muttering affirmations under my breath.

You're strong, you're smart, you're resilient. You've got this. You're a bad beech. Kick all the asterisks.

'I mean, after yesterday, how much worse can today be, right?'

'Who says that out loud?' Bandit replied with a shake of his fluffy head. 'It's like you're asking for trouble.'

I winced. 'Good point.'

'I'm a literal fountain of wisdom. I'm going to the woods for the day. Enjoy your classes.'

'Enjoy them? How?' I called after him as he waddled from the room.

I had to admit, it was sort of not terrible having Bandit around. He was gone most of the day hunting and whatever else raccoons did, but at night it was like having a stuffed animal that snuggled me back.

To my surprise, Nikita was oddly quiet as she led me down the stairs and through the hallways to breakfast. I risked a glance and noted the dark shadows under her eyes and a faraway expression.

'If you walk any slower, I'm bringing a cattle prod next time,' she snapped, interrupting my thoughts.

My pity dried up like a grape in the sun.

'Bring the cattle prod and see where I put it,' I shot back.

She scowled and lifted her hand. For a second, I wondered if she was going to hit me with a rune, but then she lowered her arm.

'One of these days, Harlow, someone is going to shut that smart mouth of yours permanently, and I hope I'm there to see it.'

We made the rest of the walk to Typhon's class in silence, but I was already dreading having to see her a couple hours later.

Top of my list of things to do:

Get a new companion, stat.

When I stepped into the classroom, I found Typhon standing over his desk. Fable was seated in the second row and waved me over, pointing to the empty seat beside her. I headed toward her, feeling Typhon's disapproving glare on me every step of the way.

'Now that everyone's finally here, we can begin,' he grumbled, thrusting a knife into the apple he'd been halfway through eating and then setting it on the desk.

Blocked by Typhon's frame, I hadn't seen the second teacher.

Liam stepped out to the side, winked and smiled at me from behind Typhon and I lifted a hand in a tiny wave, wondering if I looked as confused as I felt.

What the hell was going on? Why was he here?

My cheeks flushed as I thought back to his note. Four little words is all it had said. Nothing more. No date. No time.

We need to talk.

'House Phoenix students,' Typhon said, moving to the center of the room and derailing my thoughts. 'We have a special guest here for the next few weeks, who will be stepping in to oversee some of your classes this semester. This is Liam O'Connor, who you met last night at dinner. He's a former graduate from Heathermoor Academy, and a current doyen there. He's also a gifted wizard whose own Quirk is to identify and find latent Quirks in other wizards. The Senate felt it was important that we delve deep to determine whether or not there are members of House Phoenix with powers yet untapped.'

Interesting. Maybe that was what Liam wanted to talk to me about? But then why just me?

My stomach did a little flip, and I shoved the thought aside.

Typhon continued, sweeping a hand in Liam's direction. 'I'm delighted to turn the classroom over to your *temporary* Doyen O'Connor. Please give him your undivided attention as his assistance could be invaluable.'

I had to bite back a smile because, despite his words, Typhon looked anything but delighted. In fact, he looked like he wanted to throw hands. If Liam noticed, though, he didn't show it.

'Thank you so much, Doyen Moreno, for trusting me with your pupils today. I'm really hoping I can help.'

Typhon cleared his throat and continued. 'Also joining us in class today is Julius Rendimion.' He gestured to a tall, sour-looking guy with red hair and poison-green eyes.

I'd seen him at the assembly. It wasn't a face you'd forget. Like the Baumgartens, the Rendimions had carefully selected spouses exclusively for magical power, and the children were casting runes before they were able to read.

'Julius is a fifth-year student from House Draconell and will be shadowing me for this class as he works to become a doyen,' Typhon drawled.

Julius offered a half-hearted wave but there was no disguising the sneer beneath his fake smile.

Typhon seemed to melt into the background, taking a seat in the far corner as Liam prowled the front of the room and began to talk animatedly.

'First of all, I want to start by saying that Quirks are no more special than you, or you, or you.'

He pointed at Zeed, Fable, and then me. His dark eyes turned solemn as Julius let out a snort. 'I mean it. It's no different than being born with orange hair or green eyes. It's something innate, not something that you've earned, so it's not something that someone should take pride in.'

Subtle jab at Julius, which had the boy narrowing his eyes suspiciously.

Let's go, Liam.

'That said, it *is* something one should honor and treat with reverence, and appreciation. It's not something to be lorded over someone else or boasted about. By the same token, if you do not have a Quirk, you can still be just as special. Think of all the human Dims who have no magic at all but have changed the world. Scientists, civil rights leaders, poets, artists. If, by the time the semester is over, you've discovered that you don't have a Quirk after all, don't ever stop digging deep for your latent talents and your purpose here on this earth, magical or otherwise. Is that understood?'

I thought of Opie and how special she was, and the joy she brought to my life, with no magic to speak of. I thought of my own mother, who was a middling witch with no Quirk, but gave so much love and good energy to the world before she'd died; volunteering at the local homeless shelter, shoveling our elderly neighbor's driveway, and working tirelessly to make sure that I didn't miss having a father.

Liam was right.

But I'd still rather find out I had a Quirk. Though I suspected most of us were on the old side for discovering a latent ability, the fact that they were even trying made me think Tarquinius was hoping there was more than met the eye when it came to the students of House Phoenix.

I hated that I was pretty sure we were about to disappoint him . . .

Then again, there *was* the prophecy.

Liam continued and I tried to tune back in. If there *was* a way to shake a stuck Quirk loose, I wanted to know about it.

'It's important to remember that there are as many kinds of Quirks as there are different people. Sometimes a new Quirk pops up, say like Tarquinius being able not only to shield himself, but being able to shield an area the size of Neverthorn. Doyenne Parunah has an interesting Quirk. She is able to make things,' he paused as if looking for the right word, 'damp.'

Ross frowned up at him. 'Damp?'

'Condensation.' Liam nodded. 'Which in the right situation, could be very useful.'

I hated to think poorly of someone with a Quirk when I didn't have one, but making things damp did not sound even slightly useful.

'Slowing time, a Stall, is a less commonly known Quirk,' Typhon added. 'A Shift who can take the form of certain animals. A Mimic is another. A witch or wizard who can emulate the voice of another person perfectly.'

Liam nodded, his back to Typhon. 'Some Quirks are far more dangerous than others for obvious reasons. Death Touch, Syphons and Firebreathers among them.'

'Whoa, whoa, whoa.' Ross held up both hands. 'Those aren't real. You're making sheet up.'

Liam huffed a sad laugh. 'I wish I were.'

I couldn't help but notice the thundercloud on Typhon's face as Liam spoke. 'Tell us about them,' I asked.

'Well,' Liam shrugged. 'There isn't much known —'

'Because they don't exist,' Typhon said, his voice icy. 'We train in absolutes, O'Connor, not fairy tales.'

Liam spread his hands wide, palms facing us. 'They are real. I've met all three of those Quirks in my life. I would not like to do it again. The Death Touch is exactly what it sounds like. A single touch and poof, your opponent is dead. That being said, the Dwimmer who had that Quirk couldn't control it. As hard as he tried not to, anyone he touched died. Even those he loved.'

Something in me constricted, horror crawling up my throat. But I couldn't look away as Liam went on, his eyes sad.

'The Firebreather was a similar case. Could breathe fire but struggled to control it. Made it so she went into hiding, until her death.'

Yeah, okay, so if this little talk was supposed to make us want a Quirk, I wasn't sure I was the person for the job.

'And the Syphon?' Caterina asked.

'A Dwimmer of incredible power, who can steal other people's magic to use however they wish.'

I swallowed hard. Awful.

'But the issue with all three was training. Control. If one of you should have a Quirk of that nature, we will work together to make sure that you have the upper hand, at all times.'

Typhon's face was a serious thundercloud, but he said nothing. The others in the class seemed to take a breath, sighing in relief. Me . . . not so much.

Liam headed to the blackboard at the front of the room and picked up a piece of chalk.

'But that's enough about Quirk possibilities. We could talk all day about them. I'm going to explain the process of triggering latent Quirks so that you all understand what we're going to be doing in this class. We have a small group, which should make things easier, but I need you all to swear to me that anything that happens here stays within this group. We're going to have a circle of trust between us. In order to find latent Quirks, especially later in life, we need to delve deep. It's not always going to be comfortable; it's not always going to be fun. Sometimes it's going to hurt. But it's what must be done in order to uncover the truth. If you all agree that this classroom is a safe space, raise two fingers and say, "I will."'

We glanced around the room at one another and, as a unit, raised our fingers.

'I will,' we said in unison.

Liam whipped off a rune as we did, and our promises flew from our fingers to his like fireflies. He gathered them and tucked them in his coat pocket, then nodded. 'Let's begin. Who would like to go first?'

Zeed's hand shot up, with Marina as a quick second, Fable, Ross, Gary, and Caterina all following suit. Phyllis remained quiet in the back, and Ellie made a big show of inspecting her fingernails as I settled deeper into my seat.

Liam nodded toward Zeed. 'Okay, Zeed, why don't you come on up and take a seat?'

Zeed hurried to the chair beside Typhon's desk.

He was almost vibrating as he glanced at Fable, who offered an encouraging smile and thumbs-up.

'I'm ready. Whatever I need to do . . .'

Liam laid a hand on his shoulder and nodded. 'You can start by closing your eyes.'

Zeed snapped his eyes shut and sat stock-still as Liam placed his palm on Zeed's forehead.

'Have you ever tried meditating, Zeed?'

'No, not really.'

'Okay, so let's start by having you clear your mind as best you can. Any lingering worries, thoughts of failing, thoughts of home, wondering whether a certain special person thinks you're a nerd or not, I want you to let it all go.'

This got a chuckle from some of the others, and I had to admit, if the goal was to make a person feel as comfortable as possible, he was doing a hell of a job. Liam had an easy charm about him that it was hard not to appreciate. It was why his stories were all so easy to believe. He was as smooth as whipped cream.

I risked a glance at Typhon, whose scowl had only deepened as he crossed his arms over his chest.

Apparently, the doyen was immune to Liam's charm, which was no surprise. He probably hated ice cream and puppies too. Then again, there was some serious rivalry between Heathermoor and Neverthorn — there had been for years. Like the rivalry between the Hatfields and McCoys, I had no idea how it really started. Maybe that was enough?

'Let your muscles relax, starting from the top. Let your jaw go slack. Release your neck, and let your head loll forward. Shoulders next.'

Liam's voice dropped to something near a whisper.

'Feel the tension draining from your body.'

Liam began sweeping his hand over Zeed's head and face, not touching him, but grazing past, as if he was swiping cobwebs away.

After a few moments, Zeed visibly slumped, the worry lines in his face disappearing.

I caught Fable's eyes and raised my brows as we both leaned forward in our seats. Waving away the anxiety in a situation like this was a feat in itself.

Liam curled his fingers inward, leaving only his index finger extended, as he pressed it to the center of Zeed's forehead, physically touching him now. His fingertip began to glow, sparks of magic skittering off Zeed's face.

'What do you love most in this world, Zeed?'

His throat worked as he mustered a reply. 'M-my mom, I guess?'

A snicker sounded from the wall beside him and Zeed's cheeks went crimson, but by the time I looked, Julius's expression was unreadable.

Donkeyhole.

'Ignore everything but the sound of my voice, son. It's your mom you love the most. Same goes for me. She's an amazing woman and makes the best chicken and dumplings you ever tasted.'

The words seemed to settle Zeed again, and he nodded slowly.

'Yeah. Uh, mine is just really supportive. She never makes me feel pressure or anything even though –' he broke off, but Liam encouraged him to continue. 'Even though I'm not where I want to be as far as my magic skills yet.'

'That's really important. You're so lucky to have her.'

He had no idea how lucky, and I hated how my throat tightened at the thought of my own mom.

'And can you tell me, Zeed, what do you fear most?'

'Letting people down, I guess?'

'What people, specifically? Your housemates? Your professors? Family?'

'My dad, mostly.'

Fable pressed a fist to her lips and blinked hard, her eyes suspiciously glassy. He was older than her, and they'd known each other their first time around at Neverthorn, but I was starting to wonder if there was a connection there . . .

'You feel compelled to impress him?'

'I feel compelled to be better than him,' Zeed shot back,

fists clenching at his sides. 'He . . . let's just say he isn't as supportive as my mom and let's leave it at that.'

'Alright. This next part isn't fun, but it's necessary. Everything we are doing today is part of the process. If I could
make it easier on you, I would.'

Zeed tensed but he nodded.

'Bring it on.'

'I need you to cast your memory back to the time in your
life that you felt the most powerless. Don't just think of it.
Actually picture it in your mind. Remember the feelings. Let
them envelop you.'

My guts churned as I looked on, glad I wasn't in the hot
seat, but unable to look away. I wanted this to work for him
because if it could work for Zeed . . . maybe it could work
for all of us.

You got this, Zeed.

'Are you there now? Can you picture it clearly?'

Zeed opened his mouth and then snapped it shut, nodding instead.

'Embrace it. Let that shame and anger and fear spread
inside you. Let it build, and spread, and consume you. Do
you feel it?'

Zeed gritted his teeth and ground out a 'yes'.

Liam's face was a mask of concentration as the light from
his fingertip grew impossibly bright.

'There is a rope beside you now. Do you see it? Reach for
it, Zeed. Reach for the rope and pull.'

Zeed lifted a hand in the air, grasping for something only
he could see. 'It's there, but it's out of reach. I can't . . .'

He reached further, and further still, before lunging from
his chair and stumbling. Liam grabbed him, catching him
before he fell.

'Okay, you're alright. I got you.'

Zeed's lashes fluttered and then he opened his eyes.

'What . . . what happened? Why did we stop?'

He was coated in sweat, his skin sickly pale, hands trembling as he stared at Liam.

'It wasn't meant to be today, son.'

'Did . . . did you see a Quirk inside me, at least?' he croaked, tipping his head in question.

Liam pursed his lips and shook his head slowly. 'No. But that doesn't mean it's not there, alright? We're not going to give up hope, we're just getting started. It can be a process. Taking hold of that rope you saw, that's the first step.'

Zeed nodded but the devastation was plain on his face, and if I was a hugger, I'd have given him one right then.

Liam helped him as he shakily made his way back to his seat. Then, the visiting doyen scanned the room. His eyes locked on me, and for a second, I wished I could nicking notions myself into being so small that he couldn't see me. If *that* was just getting started, I wanted no part of –

'Harlow, would you like to come up?'

10

Liam stared at me. 'Harlow?'

I held up a hand. 'Oh, wow, yeah. Honored, truly. But I actually have to head out early today. I have some razor blades I'd rather be eating, if it's all the same to you.'

Liam's eyes sparkled with a flicker of humor, but he kept a straight face.

'I see where I went wrong. I posed it as a question. Harlow, it's your turn now. Come on up.'

Dread clawed at my insides as I forced my feet to move toward the front of the classroom. He gestured for me to sit, and I did.

'Close your eyes.'

I let my eyes drift shut and hated it immediately. I could feel everyone's attention on me.

'I really feel like today isn't a good day for me. I'm feeling bloated, and my sciatica is acting up –'

'Harlow,' Typhon murmured, just my name and it was enough to still me.

'Okay, let's go. Relax my muscles, think happy thoughts. Who do I love most? My sister Opie. What do I fear most? Undercooked pork products.'

And getting too close to Typhon Moreno.

I could sense rather than feel Liam's fingers sweeping away the cobwebs in my mind and was surprised to find it weirdly calming. My body relaxed a little, the low-level headache that had been a near-constant companion since the streets of Rio faded, and I let out a sigh.

'That's it. Good,' he murmured, his voice soft and silky.

I could almost feel the press of his thigh against mine, the warmth flowing back and forth between us. And I wasn't sure I didn't like it.

'Think of the time in your life when you felt most powerless,' he whispered. 'When everything inside you railed against the injustice of it all, and your fondest wish was that you were stronger. Strong enough to get out of the situation and change your lot in life.'

'Does right now count?' I whispered back, half-hypnotized into doing his bidding, and half-wanting to fight every step of the way because I knew it was going to hurt once we got into the meat of this little project of his.

'You know it doesn't.'

I wet my lips as he pressed his finger to my forehead. The magic slid through me, warm and sparkling like champagne in my blood. But then a darkness came, hot on its heels, luring me toward it.

A younger, teenage me, crouched outside the open door of my mother's bedroom as she spoke to a man in a white coat on a Skype call.

'*We can start treatments ASAP, although there are no guarantees. Your family needs to understand, we'll do everything we can, but it's spread to your liver and –*'

'*I understand. Let me tell my daughter first. Please . . .*'

'I'm there,' I croaked, desperate for it to be over. Desperate for a way out . . . *any* way out.

'There is a lever, a little way down the hall. Walk toward it, Harlow. Reach for it and lift it up.'

How he knew it was a lever rather than a rope was beyond me.

But I saw it, just a few yards away, like a lifeboat in the

midst of the stormiest sea. It was like moving through molasses to get there, but eventually, I did.

'I've got it. I think I've got it,' I muttered, reaching, feeling the smooth metal of the lever, lifting slowly, inch by inch.

Waiting for the sensation when it finally snapped into place –

'It – it's right there. I've almost got it. It feels like a sneeze, you know? Like it's tickling my nose and about to come out but then I can't quite –'

A rattling boom had my eyes flying open. The door to the classroom was flung open, bouncing off the stone wall behind it. I jerked back in my seat and my eyes shot wide as a chorus of gasps exploded around me. Tarquinius stormed in a second later, a brittle smile on his lips.

'Doyen Moreno, Doyen O'Connor, can I speak to you both in my office? Class, you're dismissed,' he added without glancing our way. With that, he swept from the room, leaving behind a silence so tense it was deafening.

Typhon's brows caved into a scowl even as Liam flashed one dimple in a reassuring smile. My legs were still quaking from the emotional rollercoaster I'd just gotten off, and it did little to help.

'Well, it seems as if we're closing shop thirty minutes early today, class. Why not take advantage and head out to the courtyard for some fresh air while it's still warm enough that you can't see your breath?' Liam turned to Typhon. 'Doyen Moreno?'

Typhon tipped his head in a clipped nod and stood, heading for the door.

'If you aren't with your rule-of-two partner, stick with the group until your next class starts.' He shot me a pointed look. 'No exceptions.'

The two of them exited the room together, leaving the

rest of us staring after them. I was still so shaken; I could barely process what had just happened.

'Holy crow. What do you think that was about?' Ellie asked, tucking a strand of inky hair behind one ear on repeat, until she seemed to realize what she was doing.

'I don't know but I have a pretty good guess,' Julius said with a chuckle, drawing all eyes to him. 'Maybe he finally realized that you guys are useless, and they've put their money behind a team of donkeys when they have a whole stable of thoroughbreds waiting in the wings.'

He casually whipped off a double rune and juggled a pair of fireballs in one hand and a trio of snowballs in the other, a smug smile perched on his lips.

Lovely. A true blue donkeyhole, and a Quirk, to boot. Casting two separate runes at once was a highly coveted specialty. Twice the weapons, twice the power. Something a guy like Julius most certainly didn't deserve.

'Wow, impressive,' Marina said with a low whistle. 'You should join the traveling circus. Maybe they will even get you a unicycle and a red nose that honks. Won't that be exciting!'

Rage flashed in his eyes, and he wheeled on her and lifted his hand, but he wasn't expecting me, and I was on him before he could execute his attack.

'You might want to rethink that if you plan to carry on that illustrious family name, Julius.'

The knife that had been sticking out of Typhon's apple was now clutched in my hand and pressed against his groin.

Was he a kid? Not in my mind. At nineteen, he knew better and was old enough that I didn't feel bad about putting him in his place.

He lowered both hands slowly, the balls of snow and fire disappearing as he swallowed loud enough for me to hear it.

'Must be tough on the ego to have to rely on Dim bar

fight tactics to protect yourselves. You'd better watch it, or I'll set Mortan on you. He's as crazy as they come and loves to inflict pain,' he mused, playing it off as coolly as he could.

'I'm actually good with it,' Marina said. The others chimed in quickly, agreeing.

'Yeah, whatever works,' Zeed added with a shrug. 'Survival is the key. Not fancy moves.'

Julius elbowed me in the stomach, shoving me off him.

'Make your jokes. But you lot are the clowns of this school, prophecy or not, and soon enough, everyone will see it, including Tarquinius. You'll get sent back to the Unlit world so you can live your unremarkable lives while me and *my* house restore order here the way it should've been from the start. Then we'll see who's laughing.'

He stalked out of the room and slammed the door behind him.

'Oof. Seems like somebody's mommy didn't love him,' Marina said, shaking her head slowly.

'Maybe he missed breakfast and he's hangry?' Ross added.

Fable shook her head in wonder, still staring at the door. 'I just can't imagine being that mad all the time. Must be exhausting.'

But the chatter stopped as quickly as it started, and the weight of Julius's words laid over us like a wet blanket. So far, there was nothing except a thirty-year-old prophecy to suggest that he was wrong. And as much as I didn't want to be back at Neverthorn, I wanted to leave on my own terms. Not because they sent me packing.

I jabbed the knife back into the apple and forced a bright smile. 'Let's grab some snacks from the kitchen and get that fresh air before they toss us in another class.'

I needed a plan.

And I needed it soon, before this place chewed me and Opie up and spit us *both* out.

'So, what was it like?' While the others were sprawled out on various pieces of furniture dotting the Phoenix House common area, Fable had dragged a chair directly in front of mine and was staring at me intently. And even though she'd already peppered me with questions about it as the day progressed, this was the first time it seemed like she really wasn't going to take a shrug for an answer.

'I don't know,' I said, stalling for time. 'It was . . . stressful, mostly. Especially at first.'

Having my deepest thoughts probed had made me feel a little like a beetle on its back, and part of me was thrilled when Tarquinius had interrupted the session, because I wondered how much Liam could see in my head. But the other part couldn't help but wonder what might have happened if I'd gotten the chance to finish the job . . .

No. It was definitely better this way. I was already feeling squidgy about Liam poking around in there. It had taken everything I had not to even let Nocta cross my mind just in case Liam could read my thoughts. If he didn't know Nocta was my father already, I certainly didn't want to fill him in, unwittingly or not.

'Did you get any sense at all of what might happen when you pulled the lever?' Fable pressed.

'Uh, not really.'

'Not even an inkling?'

'Should we switch to Spanish, because this is starting to feel like the Inquisition.'

She pulled back and pressed a hand over her heart, cheeks going pink. 'Oh my gosh, Harlow. I'm so sorry. I can get a little intense when I sense a mystery afoot. I would be *obsessed* if I was in your shoes. How could you think of anything else other than that frigging lever?'

'Same,' Marina said from her perch on the love seat in the corner. 'It would drive me bananas.'

'I will say this,' I continued. 'When I was about to pull the lever, I didn't feel afraid. I felt . . . hopeful. Like it was a way out of the intense situation I was in.'

Fable blew an amber curl from one eye as she nodded. 'Okay. So, a positive vibe from it, then. Well, that's something at least. After this afternoon, I'll take even a shred of potentially decent news.'

Rune-crafting class had gone . . . not excellent. My expectations had been pretty low, but it was even worse than that. Each and every one of us had botched some aspect of almost every single rune we tried. It was almost like we'd all gotten even worse at the skill than when we'd been at Neverthorn the first time around.

If I'd been permitted to do them my way instead of theirs, I could've shown them, but every time I tried to broach the subject, Doyen Eryn shot me down, his eyes hard.

'Magic needs to be three things, Miss Daygon.' He'd held up a hand and ticked them off. 'Teachable. Repeatable. And traceable. What do you think would happen if a bunch of poorly trained wizards were out there just slinging home-crafted runes around like it's the Wild West?'

I wanted to tell him that they might be pretty good cat burglars, but he'd smacked a hand on my desk and lowered his head to glare at me, jowls trembling with outrage. 'I'll tell you what! Somebody would get hurt. You would be no better than Nocta!'

131

I couldn't help the flinch. No better than my father . . . but I didn't believe that. A rune could be used for good or bad, it was a tool, nothing else.

I wish I'd stopped by his desk at the end of class and told him how much the two hours we'd spent there doing it his way had hurt us all. By the time it was over, any lingering good feelings we'd taken from Doyen O'Connor had been shattered, leaving our whole house feeling small and defeated if the hung heads and rounded shoulders said anything.

'I'm not sure I would want to pull the lever at all,' Ellie murmured from her spot cross-legged on the floor, pulling me from my thoughts. 'What if it was one of those Pandora's box type deals? What if I found something I couldn't stuff back away again? Something really bad.'

Zeed tossed a kernel of popcorn in his mouth and shrugged. 'I think we have to try to trust the process, like Doyen O'Connor said. He's supposedly the expert in this field. If he can shake loose a Quirk that might help us face off against Nocta, I'll pull whatever he wants me to.'

Ross let out a crack of laughter. 'That's what she said —' he broke off with a squeak when a pillow launched by Marina hit him square in the chops.

I looked around the room at the glum faces.

'With the prophecy being what it is, we've all got to move forward with the assumption that we have some bad-asterisk latent Quirks. We just need to have a little patience. We just got here, guys.'

'And if Harlow is right, I for one can't wait to find out what they are,' Gary announced, pushing himself off one of the sofas. 'But I'm fried. This day has been plenty long enough for me and my brain is like mush. Anybody want to eat junk food and watch a mindless sitcom until bedtime?'

Everyone raised their hands, and I stood. 'Always. And I

just happen to have charmed a dozen snickerdoodles from Wickersham at lunchtime for emergencies. I definitely think this qualifies. Be right back.'

Fable pushed her chair back to give me space to pass, and I made a beeline for my room just a little way down the hall. My footsteps echoed in the empty space, and I was just about to open the door to my room when a hand closed over my shoulder.

'Jiminy Crickets, what the fruck!?' I demanded, heart hammering as I spun round.

'Are you supposed to be alone?' Liam asked, his dark brows knitted with concern.

'I'm not alone.'

He cocked his head and made a point to search the surrounding area before eyeballing me again. 'Is that so?'

I ignored the heat creeping up my neck and pushed my door open. 'What I mean is that all my housemates besides Phyllis are literally ten yards away. I'm pretty sure that doesn't count as being alone.'

'Given that I just snuck up behind you and could've sealed your mouth and nose shut with a suffocating rune long before you managed to execute . . . whatever,' he mimicked my karate hands, '*that* was supposed to be.'

'You okay out there, Harlow?' Bandit's sleepy voice called from inside my room.

Liam frowned. 'Aren't raccoons supposed to be nocturnal?'

I held up my hands helplessly.

'Yeah. And they're also not supposed to talk. He's having an existential crisis, I guess. Look,' I lowered my voice and leaned closer, 'Your cryptic little note has been hanging over my head all day. Do you want to tell me what that's about or did you need to lecture me more about why I'm out here alone?'

133

He hung his head for a second and then met my gaze, his deep-brown eyes full of apology. 'I'm sorry for the note. I didn't want to say too much in case it was intercepted.'

I didn't admit that it very nearly had been.

'And while I worry about your safety after the other day, I know you've got plenty of people lecturing you already. As long as you take the threat of Nocta seriously, I'll lay off, yeah?'

'Believe me, no one is taking it more seriously than me.'

He searched my face for a long moment and then nodded. 'Excellent. So do you have a few minutes to talk now?'

'I'm on a cookie run. Let me just drop some snickerdoodles off for the others. I'll be right there,' I pointed at my door, 'and then back here.'

Liam gave a solemn nod, as if I weren't poking fun at the distance I was technically alone.

My legs felt a little like jelly as I delivered the goods to my housemates, and begged off the TV marathon, citing a headache.

When I stepped out of the common room, I found Liam waiting by the stairs up the hall.

I headed toward him and tried not to let my imagination run wild. What if he was just being nice to get me off his scent? What if he took me to the rooftop, told me he knew I was Nocta's daughter, and then tossed me over? There was no reason for him to know it, but I couldn't help wondering.

I'd always had a good imagination, and I was a champion of playing the 'what if' game.

'Where are we going?' I asked as we entered the stairwell. 'Like you said, I'm not really supposed to be wandering around alone.'

'You're not alone,' he corrected gently.

'I mean, without my companion.'

'You're with me . . . one of your teachers. Surely, that

doesn't conflict with the spirit of the rule of two. I'll take the heat for it if there is any. Deal?'

I nodded but a minute later, as we continued upward, I realized he still hadn't answered my question.

'Where are we going?' I asked, a little more forcefully this time.

'To the roof where we have some privacy.'

My skin prickled and I clenched my jaw to keep my teeth from chattering. 'We can just sit right here. Plenty of privacy here . . .'

'I also have something I wanted to show you.'

We'd reached the end of the stairs and the heavy door leading out to the rooftop squealed open with a motion of his hand.

'Harlow?'

'Yeah, I'm just thinking for a sec.'

Weighing my options, really. If I walked outside with him, any real chance of getting away *if* he meant me harm would drop to something near zero. But he'd shown no inclination to hurt me, just the opposite. He'd saved me from Nocta's men. He'd tried to help me find a Quirk. He was a teacher.

You're being stupid, Harlow. He's here to help you.

Besides, if you don't go with him, you'll never know what he wanted to tell you.

Curiosity got the better of me once again. 'Okay, let's go.'

I followed him out into the cool night air, suddenly glad that I'd donned a House Phoenix sweatshirt after dinner. I realized as we moved toward the edge, we were at the very top of the northwest wing's turret. And it was way higher from up here. I gripped the railing in front of me and swayed a little on my feet as I looked down.

'No, no, if you've a fear of heights, don't look down, look up. Over there,' he said, pointing to my far right.

I turned and let out a low gasp.

The night sky to the north was lit in a riot of pulsating colors. Blue, yellow, green, and even a hint of red.

'The Northern Lights,' I murmured, my throat feeling oddly thick. Every once in a while, the beauty of earth did that to me. It was almost as if the shock of our violent, selfish, often ugly planet co-existing with something as amazing as this reminded me that there was good in everything.

And everyone.

'I've never seen them before. It's . . .' I trailed off, embarrassed at the crack in my voice.

'Beautiful, I know.'

For a few minutes, we just stood there watching the show, the lights undulating like lazy fat serpents swimming through thick black water. But soon enough, I became aware of the heat of Liam's body next to mine. And of his smell. Vanilla, but not like a cookie. More like a warm, masculine scent that made me want to lean in –

'I appreciate the light show, but how about you tell me what we're doing out here,' I said, scooting subtly to the side, giving myself a little room.

I looked up and met his gaze, trying not to be taken by his boyish good looks.

'Initially, I wanted to talk to you about the other day outside the pub. But then after class this morning, it turned into more than that . . .'

My throat worked as I tried not to let my thoughts run wild. He didn't look mad. In fact, he looked . . . concerned more than anything.

Time to bite the bullet. 'Let's start with the first bit.'

'The raccoon.'

'Bandit?' I shrugged. 'What about him?'

'Did you bring him to the school with you?'

'No. He was there, behind the pub when all that stuff happened.'

'And could he talk the whole time?'

'Nope.'

His eyes narrowed in concentration. 'At what point, exactly, did he first speak to you?'

I thought back. 'After I did a . . . um, my mom taught me this rune when I was a kid. She went here, Neverthorn. She was in Felinita, and –' I broke off when I realized I was rambling. Nothing like too much information to mark a lie. I swallowed hard and started again. 'Anyway, yeah. I just did a little rune in the air.'

'Show it to me.'

I closed my eyes, and pictured Nocta's motions, and repeated them. Before it was complete, Liam's big, warm hand closed over mine.

He let out a low hiss. 'That's a pretty strong bit of magic for a woman to teach her child.'

'What is it? What does it do?'

'It can rob another of their senses to disarm them for an attack. Harlow . . . I think you may have stolen the voice of someone outside the pub and given it to Bandit.'

I blinked up at him as my vision blurred.

Stay calm. Count backwards from ten.

I thought about the man who'd passed out drunk not ten feet from where I'd cast the rune, and where Bandit had gained his voice.

'I-I – that can't be. I would never do something like that.'

'Of course not. Not on purpose. Maybe you misremembered the rune? Maybe you missed a motion in the sequence or something?'

I nodded. 'Yes. Yes, I must've. My mother was such a good person. She'd never have taught me something as dark as that.' I stared up at him, guilt stabbing at my insides. 'What do I do? Liam, I can't have that on my conscience. I've got to fix it.'

'There's no reversing a rune like this. I'll take care of it. I'll go down tomorrow and see if I can find him – whoever it is that Bandit's voice first belonged to. See if I can give him a new voice. It might not be his, but it's better than nothing.'

'Most of that area was pretty empty because the shops were closed for lunch and the rest were inside eating. But I did see a man,' I said, forcing the words out through numb lips. 'He was drunk and had stumbled out the side door and sort of passed out . . .'

'Did you get a good look at him?'

'No.'

I was too caught up in my own sheet.

'There can't have been more than one person to lose their voice at the pub so I'm sure I'll track him down. It's going to be alright, Harlow. You have my word on that.'

I nodded, acid still roiling in my gut.

'And directly after that, the fog rolled in?' he continued.

'I wouldn't say directly,' I hedged.

'Pretty soon after?'

'I guess.'

'So, is it possible something about the spell lured Nocta here to Neverthorn?'

Nope, I couldn't have him going down that path. I tried to play it casual as I shook my head.

'I don't see how. Seems more likely he was lurking around and maybe had spent time weakening the wards.'

Liam frowned. 'I suppose.'

'What was the other thing you wanted to talk about?'

I was desperate to move away from this line of question-ing, even though I had a feeling the second part was going to be even worse than the first. Now I just wanted to get it over with so I could go to my dorm room and have a nervous breakdown in private.

'Latent Quirks.'

I blinked at him.

'Why me?' I asked, thoroughly confused. 'Why not invite all of us out here, then?'

'You're special.'

I let out a low laugh. 'Funny, I don't feel special. And we've known each other for two days. How could you possibly –'

'Because I sensed it. Inside you. Something I've never felt before, Harlow. Something so powerful, it dwarfs even this.' He lifted a hand to the sky, his gaze so sincere it was hard not to believe him . . . or at least believe that *he* believed him. 'I need you to commit to the process. It's buried deep, but I feel like if we can get through some of the debris, there is a real chance you could be The One.'

For a second, I wondered if getting hurled off this turret wouldn't be so bad after all . . . he was saying I could be the one to stop Nocta. The one to kill my father.

I turned away from him to stare at the lights. Anything to avoid looking him in the eyes. 'Look, I am willing to try. But I don't have the same confidence you do. There's a chance that I don't have a Quirk at all. That it's something else you're feeling inside me.' Latent, genetic evil, maybe? I thought with a shiver. 'Plus, I'm not sure if you realize this, but I've got a lot of baggage. It might take all year just to get through it.'

His lips went tight, and he shook his head. 'That's the thing of it. We don't have all year, Harlow.'

I wrapped my arms around my waist as his words sank in. 'What do you mean?'

'The Northern Lights.' He gestured to the sky. 'Beautiful

and terrifying all at once, like so many of Mother Nature's creations. Harlow . . . they're early. We shouldn't be able to see them this time of year. And moreover, they certainly shouldn't contain red.'

I stared at him, nonplussed.

He spoke slowly.

'There is another prophecy, one that I brought with me from Heathermoor.

> *'When the sky spits yellow, blue and red*
> *And all the colors but the last are dead*
> *Only four more full moons remain*
> *Before the Phoenix must rise again.'*

'Holy sheet.' The blood rushed in my ears, and I gripped the edge of the turret once more for balance. 'How long?'

'Three and a half months. Maybe a little less.' That must have been what the other prophecy had been referring to . . .

In the darkest hour, in the darkest days.

The winter solstice.

Only a hundred days between now and then, give or take.

One hundred days to prepare one of us to save the Dwimmer world from Nocta, or all would be lost. He'd rip a hole between us and the Everdark and that . . . that would be it for everyone.

'I've got to go. The others might come check on me.' I wheeled around and all but sprinted back to the stairwell. Liam had to take the stairs two at a time to catch up with me just as I reached my floor.

He grabbed my arm and tugged me around to face him.

'It's going to be okay. Do you trust me?' he asked, his solemn brown eyes searching mine.

'I'm sorry, but I don't trust anyone.'

He gave me a grim smile. 'That's alright. I'm going to

change that. And when I do, we're going to figure this out. Together.'

He released my arm, and I stepped through the door, directly into the rock-hard chest of Typhon Moreno.

'O'Connor. Ms. Daygon, might I ask why you're roaming the school without your companion?'

I opened my mouth to reply, but Liam cut in before I could.

'I thought it was best to speak with her one on one about the methodology of triggering a latent Quirk. She's a little more . . . worldly and therefore less trusting than some of the other students. I wanted to reassure her that she's in the safest of hands so that she can move forward and dig deep for that Quirk without fear.'

Not the whole truth, but close.

Typhon cocked his head and studied the other man intently. 'And is she?'

Liam's eyes narrowed, darkening. 'Is she what?'

Typhon didn't blink, a muscle ticking in his jaw as he replied. 'Is she in the safest of hands alone with you?'

Liam's hands flexed at his side for a split second. A moment later, though, the easy smile was firmly back in place.

'Absolutely. I would guard her with my life.'

Typhon nodded slowly as he backed away. 'I'll hold you to that.'

He headed back down the hall, and I let out a pent-up breath.

'Does he scare you?' Liam asked.

I pondered that for a hot second before answering. 'I don't think scare is the right word. More like he makes me feel unsettled. What about you?' I asked, eager to turn the conversation away from my feelings about Typhon. 'Does he scare you?'

Liam chuckled and leaned against the wall to peer down at me. 'He irritates me, but the feeling is more than mutual. And our ideas of what makes a good professor are very different. We're like oil and water. We're never going to mix, so it's best if I keep my distance.'

Same. But somehow, I couldn't seem to manage that, even if I tried.

'Thing is, though . . . I *don't* trust him,' Liam said.

'Is that right?'

'I just have the sense that he's hiding something. Something important.'

I shifted from foot to foot and turned my head away so he couldn't see the sudden color in my cheeks. I was hiding something important. Who was I to judge?

But I couldn't deny that Liam's words left me unsettled.

'I'll let you go. But think about what I said, yeah?'

I nodded and made my way toward my room.

In fact, I'd probably spend my whole night thinking about it.

He thought I had a Quirk.

That I would be the one strong enough to face Nocta.

12

As much as I wished I could forget all I'd learned from Liam that night, the next few days only added to my confusion. He'd wanted me to work with him to find my Quirk . . . had asked me to trust him. And then? He disappeared. When we'd returned to Typhon's class the next day, Liam wasn't there, and no mention of him, either. When Fable asked when he would be coming back to class, Typhon had told her that he had other matters to attend to. But as luck would have it, Julius was still very much with us. Although he tried to act decent when we were in class, he and his boy gang had taken to lobbing spitballs at us in the dining hall and making sure to let everyone he spoke to know that, as far as wizarding went, we all sucked.

Not to mention that whatever had been ailing Nikita making her seem so distracted had clearly worn off because she'd decided to take her position as my companion a lot more seriously. She was up my asterisk twenty-four/seven. Walking me to the showers, to my classes, and she was there waiting for me when I walked out of any room. She all but tucked me into bed at night, and I wasn't sure I wouldn't find her sitting outside my door, waiting for me to wake up.

Through it all, I had to listen to her berate me and put down the rest of House Phoenix.

By the end of day four, my ability to compartmentalize was fading rapidly as her digs continued to ramp up. Worse, I couldn't stop staring out the window, waiting for the next full moon, knowing it was now part of a countdown.

The last ten minutes of our History of Magic class were spent on historical places that Nocta might try to use to gain power, or as a strategic holding point for his army. 'Places where power is inherent,' Nikita said, tapping the map on the wall behind her. 'Name one.'

Zeed leaned back in his chair. 'Hidden places, like the old Welsh Dragon lairs, or the Waters of Pain near Heathermoor.'

Nikita gave him a begrudging nod. 'Correct. Places where great power once resided will leave a lingering residue. But even something as simple as a wishing well can hold power in the Dwimmer world, because it takes on the wishes thrown carelessly into it. Words have power, even those cast without caution.'

Fable scribbled down notes as Nikita went on to talk about how most places of power were well hidden from plain sight, to keep people from using them. 'But Nocta will be looking, you can count on that. He's cunning, and he knows that any advantage he can find will help him win this war.' The gong sounded, announcing the end of classes for the day. Time for dinner, and no more need to actually interact with Nikita.

If I didn't count her hovering nearby at dinner.

Waiting for me outside of the bathroom.

Stalking my bedroom door.

I blew out a sigh.

The other students filtered out in their groups of two. Ellie and Zeed both gave me a pitying glance. I shot Fable a wink and mouthed a thank you. She smiled, ducked her head, and then they were gone, leaving just me and my shadow.

'Really, it's a wonder any of you even bothered to come back to Neverthorn.' She bent over her desk, taking her time to tidy the books, papers and the like littered across it. There was no point in reminding her that it hadn't been my choice.

'Nocta is the strongest Dwimmer our world has seen in a

thousand years. And they think one of you middling wizards has a chance to even get close to him? Not a Quirk among you thus far.'

I leaned against the wall, knowing better than to argue. I'd heard worse in my life, and as much as I disliked her, I *did* have the ability to just ignore her – or pretend to ignore her. That seemed to bother her more than when I fought with her.

'What are you grinning about?'

I pressed my hands flat to the wall behind me. 'Just thinking of how a fight would go between us if we weren't inside these walls with all their pesky rules.'

One brow rose and she shot me back a smile of her own. 'You're kidding, right? You think you could best me? At rune casting?'

'Nope.' She started to nod, and I pressed on, 'I *know* I could.'

'You trained for less than four months before quitting. I've been *teaching* magic for longer than that. Your confidence borders on delusional.'

'You've practiced magic in a vacuum, protected by your position. I've used it to survive all these years. I promise you, Nikita, there is a difference.'

She turned away, but not before I saw the fury tighten her lips.

'You don't know anything about me, Harlow. You come back with your tough-girl boots and bad attitude like you're doing us a favor.' She let out a hollow chuckle as she turned back to face me. 'Tarquinius is compelled by the prophecy and needs to do his due diligence, but I promise you, no one wants you here. You're nothing but a thorn in our collective side.'

Hot embarrassment raced through me, because I knew she was right on all counts.

'And, honestly, it's sort of embarrassing watching you moon over Typhon. He'll toe the line because Tarquinius asked him to, but you were nothing to him when you came here the first time around, and you're nothing to him now. We're both just waiting for everyone else to realize it so we can send you packing.'

Just hearing her use the term 'we' for her and Typhon was enough to turn embarrassment into fury. I spun the rune before I thought better of it, the same one I'd used on the creature that had attacked me in the Nevershoppes. One for breaking down doors.

Nikita's eyes widened and she dove to the side an instant before a satisfying crack filled the air and the stone wall behind her splintered.

She stared at me, wide-eyed, and shook her head.

'By Hecate's heart, you're a menace. Lucky thing your half-assed little rune didn't hit its mark.'

I didn't bother to tell her that if I'd actually wanted to hit her, she'd be on the ground.

'Yeah, I'm a wildcard. I could've killed you. I think we can both agree it'd be best for everyone involved if I got a new partner for this rule of two thing.'

'Tarquinius is the one who assigned me to you, and he's not going to change his mind.' She let out a weary sigh as she motioned to the notebook on her desk. 'So do us both a favor, Harlow, and wish us the hell out of this.'

She turned on her heel and stormed from the room.

Still buzzing with adrenaline, I glanced down at the page she'd flipped to.

Wishing Wells in the Northern Hemisphere
While there are arguments that no true wishing wells exist any longer in the southern hemisphere, that does not hold true for the north.

Three wells are known to be in existence, though hidden from Dwimmers and Dims alike, for their power is unlike that of any other artifact or place of power.

The first of the wishing wells is hidden on an island on the west coast of the continent. Known as the well of rain, it has been cloaked from sight for years. The last known wish was that the region be inundated with rain after a particularly bad drought, hence the name.

The second of the wishing wells has been masked effectively, and resides in Greece, not far from the ruins of Troy. This second wishing well is known to be particularly specific and so the language used when making your wish must be exact. This well was used to help Achilles achieve his strength, but he forgot to mention not having any weakness.

I almost stopped reading but pressed on when one word caught my attention.

Neverthorn.

The final well known to be in existence is within the grounds of Neverthorn itself. An island hidden from all, and protected by the strongest of Dwimmers, it would be the well that is best protected. Legend has it that Tarquinius himself cast a hiding rune on the well after a student wished their nemesis away, and they were never found again.

I turned the page with a trembling finger. The top line had been erased, but the next was all I needed.

The use of a wishing well is simple. A valuable offering must be made, then your desire spoken both in mind and by mouth. If the offering is acceptable, then the wish will be granted.

It didn't say anything else, not about the exact location of the well, or how I could find it. But . . . Nikita had just given me a way out. Not just out of our bond, but out of this place.

Forever.

Words I'd thought would never come out of me were whispered over that simple notebook. 'Thank you, Nikita Elmwood.'

If I found the well, I could literally wish me and Opie anywhere in the world, never to be found again. I could get us away from Nocta. Away from Nikita.

Away from Typhon . . .

Brushing my fingers across the page, I knew in my heart that it was for the best for me but especially for Opie. I had to get her out of here before she realized the truth.

I could do this. I knew I could.

Because if there was one thing I was good at, it was finding things that were meant to stay hidden.

13

I waited until after midnight and prayed everyone was asleep. I had a small bag on my back, and I was in my own clothes. Sure as sheet I wasn't leaving this place wearing a uniform or a frucking fanny pack. Bandit snorted and let out a little grumble in his sleep. He was curled up tight on my pillow, and I tucked my blanket around him. He was better off here. Maybe he'd find a kid to connect with once I was gone.

Slipping out of the main door to our dorm, I looked up and down the shadowed hallway. No Nikita. Most likely she was asleep by now, but even if she wasn't, she wouldn't come looking for me. She'd all but sent me on this mission, as eager to be rid of me as I was of her.

The halls of the school felt . . . weird late at night. As if the echoes of everyone who'd walked there for all the years of its existence still lay embedded in the stone. A shiver rolled over me and I shimmied my shoulders, trying to ignore the distinct sensation that I was being watched.

A tug on the cuff of my jeans had me spinning around and biting back a squeal.

'Where do you think you're going?' Bandit squinted up at me and yawned. 'And why would you think you're going without me?'

Heart hammering, I bent and ran a hand over his head. 'Right, sorry about that. Come on then, we need to get Opie.'

He ran ahead of me, silent on his paws. 'I'll get her. Where do you want us to meet you?'

'The kitchen.' I was willing to bet there would be some

leftovers of the pecan chocolate muffins that were more than worth taking with us. If we were really lucky, there'd be a few jammy dodgers – jam-filled cookies – left too.

In the kitchen I found everything I was hoping for, along with some scones and peanut-butter-filled truffles. I stuffed all the goodies into some containers I found, then used my nicking notions shrinking spell, pinching my fingers over them all, and packed them into my bag. I also snagged a large sterling silver spoon, whispering an apology to Mrs. Wicker-sham under my breath.

'Harlow?' Opie's sleepy voice turned me around. 'What's going on? Is this raccoon actually talking, or am I having a dream?'

I held my hand out to her and pulled her into a hug, ignoring the twinge in my ribs as relief flooded through me. I'd hardly seen her since we'd gotten here, and I hadn't let myself think about how scared I was for her while we were apart.

I kissed the top of her head. 'Yes, Bandit talks, but it's our secret, okay?'

She blinked. 'Okay . . .'

'Not freaking out about a talking raccoon?'

She shot me a sleepy smile. 'We are living in a magical school, Lo-lo, you think anything surprises me? But you didn't tell me what we're doing.'

I tugged on her hand. 'Come on, we're going on a bit of an adventure.'

'What kind of an adventure?'

'We have to find a wishing well,' I said softly as I led her through the kitchens and out the back door. I paused, stepped back into the kitchen and looked at the lintel above the door. A bottle had been laid sideways, hidden from most eyes.

Red wine.

I reached up and grabbed it, shrunk it down and stuffed

it into my bag along with my other goodies. Best I could do when I had no idea what kind of offering the wishing well would accept. The fancy spoon and the wine sure beat the nickels I used to throw into wishing wells back in the day . . .

'A wishing well? Is that for real?' Opie asked quietly as we stepped out into the night. The air was crisp, with just a hint of the oncoming autumn weather.

'I guess we'll find out.' I flashed her a grin. 'What would you wish for?'

'Nothing.' She grinned up at me. 'I have everything I ever wanted now that I'm here. I didn't do so hot at spell casting today, but the teacher, Doyen Eryn, was super nice. I really feel like it's going to be so great, Lo-lo.'

Fruuuuck.

My stomach flipped at the thought of how sad she'd be when I took her away. But sometimes you had to be the heavy and make the hard choices when you had someone relying on you. Nocta was coming . . . even sooner than I'd ever expected. As it stood, we had zero chance of defeating him. How could I protect Opie when I couldn't even throw a proper rune? And even if we did survive Nocta, it was only a matter of time before Opie realized that one of these things was not like the other. She didn't belong at Neverthorn, or any other magic school. The pain of that truth would only be more intense the longer it went on – when she realized she was being fooled.

I'd tell her when we got away from here. I'd be gentle, explain to her that . . . that she had no magic. But not until we got settled somewhere far away, somewhere safe.

I tightened my hold on her hand, giving her another gentle squeeze. 'Right. Well, I'm hoping to find the wishing well anyway.'

Opie nodded. 'Okay, sure.'

So trusting. Because she had no reason to believe that I would betray that trust.

Gritting my teeth, I lifted my right hand, fingers flicking through a rune I liked to call 'Finders Keepers.' I scrunched my fingers up so the tips all touched my palm, flicked them all out at once, made a fist, and then a half circle with my pinky. All while thinking of the wishing well. That was what I wanted to find. That was what I *needed* to find.

The magic flared into something else. Just the faintest of glimmers, iridescent wings, gossamer, almost like a tiny –

'Is it a butterfly?' she whispered.

I smiled, thinking of my mom. 'Yes.'

'Cool. Can you show me that rune?'

I cleared my aching throat. 'Third-year access only,' I lied.

'Nuts. Okay.'

I hung onto her as we followed the butterfly away from the main part of the school, toward the western edge where the thorn forest grew, towering over us. The butterfly flitted to the edge of the forest and waited, then wove its way into the tangled mess.

I scrunched up my nose and flicked another rune at the thorn bush. The rune fizzled out before it hit.

Awesome, it was spelled with something to deflect runes.

Guess I was going to have to do this the human way and bushwhack. I pulled my knife from my backpack and unshrunk it. My blade made quick work of the brambles, and thanks to all the gods, the well wasn't that far within the forest.

'Wow, is that it?' Opie breathed. I held onto her, literally holding her back as she tried to lurch forward.

'I think that's it, but don't get any closer. I'll take a look at it first.' I made sure she stayed well away from the rim.

'This is so awesome. Phoebe is going to freak when I tell her about this!' Opie said gleefully. 'Can we show her tomorrow?'

I didn't answer her as I made my way carefully around the well.

Bandit on the other hand waddled right up along with me. 'What's the plan?'

I crouched and put a hand to the light-colored stones – creams and light grays – that had been mudded together with a gritty white paste. Three feet high, the well didn't have an arch over it, nor were there any runes or markings indicating that this was indeed a wishing well. But I had no doubt. I could feel the magic humming under my fingertips.

This was our way out.

I pulled my bag around to the front of my body and dug around until I found the spoon and wine I'd nabbed from the kitchens. 'Maybe both?'

Bandit nodded. 'Seems reasonable. Better the offer, the better the odds.'

I stood and held the two items over the well and dropped them in. There was no clunk of them hitting hard ground, no plop of them hitting water.

I leaned over the edge of the well, the wish on my lips. I'd thought endlessly about the precise way to word it.

'Ohhhh . . . great well-dweller,' I called, 'please grant my wish that the three of us were transport–'

Water shot up around me, wrapped around my upper body like a fist and yanked me into the well.

Opie screamed, Bandit screamed, and I fought to cling to the edge, desperately clawing at the stone.

'Bandit, get her out of here!' I yelled as my fingers slid. The water rushed around me, even though I was clinging to the edge of the well. I struggled to breathe. Opie couldn't save me, and I didn't want her to see me die.

As the water enveloped me, I knew the truth of it. This had all been a trap, one that Nikita had set so expertly that I hadn't even picked up on it. I knew she wanted to get rid of me, but I hadn't realized just having me gone from Neverthorn forever wasn't enough for her.

She wanted me dead.

It shouldn't have surprised me. She wasn't the first person to try to kill me. Hell, she wasn't even the only doyen here to try. I had been so easily led. Somehow, my desire to leave had overridden my common sense.

Those thoughts faded to black. The water was so heavy on me, it yanked me down. I wove one last desperate rune, the one for breathing underwater.

I gulped as I went down, the water like air, the darkness around me absolute.

'Well, well, what do we have here?'

The voice was silky and smooth, curling around me. I floated in the darkness, trying to orient myself. There was no way to know what was up or down, but I could sense the belly of the well was impossibly vast. Far bigger than the entrance aboveground.

'I'm Harlow Daygon of Brooklyn,' I managed, surprised that my voice didn't just come out in a series of bubbles.

An impossibly fiery cauldron came into view beneath me. But before I could panic about that, a large, shadowed form swam over it. Every muscle in my body tightened. I squinted into the darkness and gasped as the figure drifted closer.

Tail fin and all, I knew a mermaid when I saw one.

'You aren't dead yet. Interesting.' She slowed to a stop in front of me. 'But you will be.'

I tried to swim, tried to move, but the water held me firmly in place.

'My name is Calypso.' Her hair was lit from below, dark green strands moving in the water all around her, covering her face except for her eyes that flashed yellow. 'You know,

154

Harlow Daygon, there was a time I might have granted your wish, if the price was right. However, I am a wishing well no more. For years now, I have been the well of death . . .'

I grimaced, doing my best to not freak out.

'If I'd known about your rebranding campaign, I probably wouldn't have stuck my head in here. Someone steered me seriously wrong.'

Her eyes narrowed. 'Ah, so someone tricked you into coming to see me? Diabolical. And proof to my point that Dwimmers and humans alike are terrible. I was tricked into this well, too, you know.'

'So you get it, then. We're a lot alike, you and me.'

I knew it was a misstep as soon as I said it.

'Alike?' Her laughter sent an icy finger of dread down my spine. 'Do you have any idea what I've been through?' She moved closer and I could see the grief and madness swirling in her eyes as the waters around us began to churn and bubble.

'I'm sorry. I –'

'Someone must pay for the wrongs done to me. And unfortunately for you, you're the only one here. Goodbye, Harlow Daygon.'

The rune that had kept me alive so far fizzled away, and suddenly, the air in my lungs was gone.

The panic was instant as I kicked and twisted and tried to scream. All that did was fill my mouth and lungs with water to hasten my demise. I caught her gaze as she looked on. A hint of melancholy in those strange eyes.

'Please,' I mouthed, my lungs burning even as my eyes began to blur.

But she didn't move.

This was it. I'd played the game without a net . . . Rolled the dice one too many times. And now I would pay the ultimate price.

My biggest regret?

That Opie would pay a steep price, too.

I love you, kiddo. And I'm so sorry.

My limbs stopped working. My vision went dark. Then, all of a sudden, I was in motion, like a rocket was driving me from the bottom of the well to the top. I struggled to open my eyes just as I broke through the surface, gagging and choking as I did.

Someone was in the water, splashing toward me, hands on my face. 'Harlow!'

Typhon.

He turned me on my side and sent a sharp blow between my shoulder blades. A hot gush of water spewed from my lungs, and I sucked in a rattling breath. It was agony, but also bone-deep relief.

He clutched me tight to his chest, like I was something precious, for just an instant before he pulled back to stare down at me. I sucked in lungs full of cool night air, my pulse racing. Was that fear in his eyes?

For me?

Not possible. But I didn't have time to think on it as he snaked a muscular arm around my waist and dragged us both from the well.

As soon as my feet hit solid ground, the yelling started. Typhon released me and stepped back as Doyenne Storm and Doyenne Parunah closed in on us, hollering over one another to be heard. Nikita was a few yards away, cheeks chalk white.

She was probably terrified I would tell on her, but who would believe me over Nikita? She was a teacher, and I was a student with a bad reputation.

No one would believe she set me up. Not even Typhon, and I knew it.

As my pulse slowed from the recent near-death experience and my brain reengaged, a whole other fear set in.

'Where is Opie?' I demanded, turning a circle as I looked for her. She stood behind Doyenne Parunah, pale and clearly shaken. She was okay.

'Why?' Typhon ignored my question, a muscle in his jaw ticking, his scar standing out in bold relief as he glared at me. 'This place has been hidden from students for decades for a reason . . . Ophelia was sure you were dead and came in screaming for help. Why would you do this, Harlow?'

I tried to conjure a plausible-sounding story but came up empty. I was too heartsick and exhausted for more lies.

'I thought . . . I could wish us away from here.'

Opie's gasp cut through me like a blade.

'I don't understand,' Opie cut in, moving to stare up at me, shaking her head in confusion. 'You know I love it here. Why would you do that to me?'

I swallowed past the knot in my throat and reached for her, but she pulled away. If I wasn't already wet and freezing, her expression would've chilled me to the bone.

'Because nothing is as it seems, Opie. This place will suck your soul dry. The only reason they took you here is because they want to control me. They will use you to get what they want, and then when they don't need you anymore, they will toss you aside and forget all about you.'

I didn't know who flinched harder, me or her.

'I don't know why you're making all this stuff up about Neverthorn, but I will never forgive you for this.' Opie's eyes were full of tears, and she swiped at them furiously. 'No one likes you here, so you want to leave. You don't care that I'm happier than I've ever been in my whole life. My friends were right about you, you don't belong here. I *hate* you.'

She spun and ran as the words hung in the air between us.

'You and me both, kid,' I whispered. 'You and me both.'

14

When I woke up the next morning, for just a few, blissful seconds, I thought it was all just a dream. But I wasn't so lucky.

I covered my face with a pillow and groaned as every little detail of the night before came back in a crystal-clear rush that made me want to vomit.

One of the teachers at Neverthorn had basically tried to kill me, the person I loved most in the world hated my guts.

Once Tarquinius had been apprised of the situation, he'd decreed that, starting tonight, we would all be moved into one massive dorm room, since *'Harlow can't be trusted not to sneak out.'*

Like my situation hadn't been bad enough before. I'd managed to take things from pretty frucking awful to ten times worse.

'Sorry, buddy. Last night was pretty brutal,' Bandit murmured, his husky voice barely audible through the down feather pillow I had my head buried in. 'But there's no point in dwelling.'

He scrabbled his claws against the pillow until I tossed it aside and met his gaze.

'You know, one time, in my youth, I had a terrible crush on this sow. She was fluffy, and cute, and had this amazing stripe down her tail. I was sure we were going to mate for life. Turned out she was a skunk, and since I had a nose, it didn't work out.' He shrugged. 'It was a bad time, I was heartbroken, but that didn't stop me from getting out there and trying again.'

I blinked up at him and cocked my head. 'Do you have a mate now?'

'Nope.'

He opened his little mouth to speak and then snapped it shut and shrugged. 'Okay, maybe I'm not the best at pep talks. Let's go eat. Food makes everything seem less terrible.'

I couldn't disagree with him there, so I rolled off the side of the bed and stood, grunting as my muscles quivered in protest. But the truth was, he wasn't entirely wrong. I had to dust myself off and try again.

For Opie, if for no one else.

'Why does my whole body hurt?' I demanded as I padded toward the bathroom to brush my teeth.

'Could've been toppling down a well and nearly getting murdered by a sea witch.'

I turned on the light and stared at my reflection in the mirror. A picture was worth exactly two words in this case:

Hammered sheet.

My hair stuck out in all directions and my skin was as pale as the underbelly of a flounder. Once Typhon had deposited me outside my room with a growled warning not to leave until morning, I'd taken a long, hot shower, but had forgotten to braid or dry my hair, and had gone to bed with it wet. Add that to a horrible night's sleep and the results were less than stellar.

I made quick work of stuffing my hair into a ponytail and had finished getting ready when there was a sharp rap on my dormitory door.

'Let's go, Daygon!'

Nikita.

'I don't have time for your dilly-dallying today,' she called.

'Be right out.'

Part of me wondered if she was going to pretend to be

apologetic after what she'd put me through, but when I opened the door, she didn't even spare me a glance.

'Tarquinius has suspended House Phoenix's regular class schedule for this morning. He wants to see you in the armory.'

I winced. Me? Or all of us?

'Excellent.'

In silence, she led me to a massive room in the basement and I found myself surrounded by the rest of my house-mates, who seemed as anxious as I did.

'I thought we had hand-to-hand combat this morning?'

So far that had been my favorite class.

'What's going on?' I looked around the room at the others from my house. But it was Doyen Bob – our only human teacher – who spoke up.

'We have new information that leads us to believe Nocta will be waging war on Neverthorn sooner rather than later.' I tried to look as surprised as the others. Liam hadn't been wrong then. All that stuff about the moons, he'd been on the mark.

Doyen Bob shook his head. 'We need to beef up your skillset faster if we can. Because of this . . .'

Doyen Bob pulled a remote control out of his back pocket and pressed a button. A section of the wall slid to the right and an oversized screen was revealed.

He clicked the remote again, and the screen blinked to life.

At first, I wasn't sure what we were looking at. A drone image maybe? Yes, that was it. A drone was capturing foot-age of what could only be described as a war zone from maybe fifty feet above the chaos.

'That's Central Park,' Fable whispered.

I blinked and sucked in a sharp breath. She was right, it was Central Park . . . just blocks from my own home in the city.

And it was on fire.

The camera zoomed in on franken-creatures that looked all too familiar.

'What are they doing there?' I had barely asked the question when a cloaked figure stepped into view.

Everyone in the room gasped as Nocta strode, almost casually, forward. As if he were there, in the park, on recreation. He lifted his right hand, and I could see the rune he cast so clearly, it was as if it were imprinted on my brain. A tornado ripped from his hands, causing a massive explosion to his right.

Explosion, though, was too tame a word. The earth ripped upward, trees were flung hundreds of feet, a crack ran north and south from the epicenter of the blow and he just . . . kept walking. Like it was nothing to him.

'Chaos for the sake of chaos,' Doyen Bob said. 'Central Park burned to the ground.'

I took a step closer to the screen, lifted my hand to do what, I didn't know. I shook my head. I wasn't even there, and I felt traumatized by the attack of my hometown.

'Can . . . can the Dims see them?'

In the far corners of the frame, people ran from the flames, like scurrying ants.

'No. He's working between worlds so that my kind are shielded, but the destruction is very visible.'

I turned to see everyone's faces pale, almost in tandem.

'Why? Why is he attacking the Unlit world now?' He'd never done it before. Fable reached over and grabbed my hand, gripping me hard.

'Heronius is gone, the Dwimmer defenses are weakened without him, and the prophecy is in play. I imagine he's setting the stage for the end game. Taking control of the Unlit world, the Dwimmer world, and Everdark, and claiming ultimate power over all three.'

Tarquinius strode into the room, his aura one of determination. He shot me a long, hard look. I was too shaken by what I'd just seen to feel ashamed, though.

Doyen Bob clicked his remote and the wall panel closed over the screen.

Tarquinius came to a halt where the TV had been. 'First things first, after your classes this evening, we'll be moving you all into one dormitory room for your own safety. The threat level has been raised for several reasons that I will not be disclosing at this time.'

I kept my eyes pinned on the floor.

'There will also be some changes to the schedule. As you can see, today's class will be held here, in the armory,' he boomed, waving us closer to where he stood in the center of the room. 'Doyen Bob has kindly agreed to allow me to stand in for this special demonstration.' He gestured to the short, stocky instructor in the corner, who nodded affably. 'But before I begin, I'd like to caution you to keep these lessons to yourselves. This training is specifically designed for students in House Phoenix. As you can see by the drone report, Nocta is only ramping up his campaign of terror. We all need you to be ready to face him.' He drew his wiry brows together in a warning frown as he paced in front of us. 'While today's lesson is rather tame, as the weeks go by, they will get much more intense. We'll begin to employ weapons training and prepare you for the battles to come. What you learn here is for your eyes only. In unskilled hands, this information could prove deadly.'

'Getting pretty real, huh?' Fable murmured just loud enough for me to hear.

It was. And thanks to Liam, I knew why. But apparently, Tarquinius and the powers that be were keeping that terrifying truth under wraps – that we had a deadline that was tied to the full moons.

'The true key to battle magic is speed,' the Sage continued. His hand was nothing but a blur and, an instant later, swords that had previously been stored in a wooden barrel in the corner leapt from their sheaths and flew across the room. Each found a different destination – one for every student – and each stopped just an inch short of plunging into our hearts.

It was a powerful display of speed and mastery that had the others gasping in a mix of shock and fear. Was it really necessary to scare the crap out of your students in order for them to learn something?

Weren't we on edge enough after seeing Central Park get destroyed?

The swords hummed in the air for another moment and then swooped off, returning to their sheaths without drawing a drop of blood. Thank the goddess for small favors, I figured.

Tarquinius took a deep bow and then straightened as a few of the others clapped half-heartedly. Hard to work up the will to applaud when you'd just nearly been skewered, but Tarquinius was clearly not as skilled at reading the room as he was at throwing runes.

'Today, we're going to start with the propelling rune, which we use to shove our opponents back. Easy enough, even for a group with questionable crafting skills. I'm sure you all probably remember from your first time around here at Neverthorn . . . with the exception of you of course, Ms. Daygon.'

I didn't respond to the dig, because fruck him.

'At times, buying yourself that extra moment or a little

163

space to craft something more nefarious means the differ-ence between life and death. The goal today is to do it so swiftly, so that it can't be detected by the naked eye, giving us the element of surprise. Line up in pairs and one of you practice propelling while the other blocks. Ms. Daygon, come join me so I can show you how to throw the propelling rune.'

'No need,' I shot back with a tight smile. 'It was one of the few things I actually learned here at Neverthorn.' He raised his eyebrows expectantly. I choked out a final word. 'Sir.'

He frowned, but didn't press, instead turning to Phyllis.

'You and I can practice together, then.'

Based on the sudden flare of annoyance in her eyes that fled as quickly as it had come, I could tell the older woman wasn't any happier than I had been to be paired with him. She was just much better at hiding her irritation.

I should take a few lessons from Phyllis. She wasn't just wise, she had clearly learned the art of restraint over the years, something I was sorely lacking.

'Can you be my partner?' Fable asked, biting her lip as she leaned toward me. 'I know exactly what to do, but when I do it, it's almost like there's no . . . oomph behind it.'

I totally knew what she meant but hadn't been able to put my finger on it, or why it only seemed to feel that way when I was doing the runes their way, particularly here back in school. Honestly, I chalked a huge part of it up to the stress of being here. Because when I did things my own way, I felt . . . well . . .

Magical.

'I feel that way, too,' I said, 'but what's worse is that I don't even think I'm doing the runes right. It's like, I can picture them exactly in my mind, but then things get jumbled, and I can't quite get the order right. Let's go over to that corner and try to practice.'

Away from Tarquinius's prying eyes. Eyes that would make even the most adept wizard nervous.

For the next hour and a half, we worked, throwing rune after rune, exactly the way we'd been taught. One would think that all the repetition would've done us good. Instead, though, we all seemed to be getting slower and my head ached with the effort of trying to decipher the shapes and patterns in my mind.

Hell, even my fingers were cramping.

And Fable and I weren't the only ones struggling. Ross, Ellie, Marina, Caterina, Gary and Zeed stood a short distance away from us in pairs, frustrated and exhausted.

'My turn again,' Zeed demanded through gritted teeth. His skin was sickly pale, sweat beading on his brow.

Marina nodded and set her legs apart in a fighting stance.

He threw the rune her way, but she blocked it easily, even though they only stood a few yards apart.

'This is brutal,' Fable whispered. She was bleary-eyed as she stared at Zeed with a sad shake of her head. So far, she hadn't managed to block or hit me, even once, and I knew she was getting frustrated and feeling bad for our housemates. With a groan, she fired off another propelling rune, and this time, I didn't try to stop her. It was a weak attack, and I skittered a few feet back, shooting her a grin.

'There you go! Good job.'

'Don't patronize me, Harlow. I know you let me hit you. Please . . . it's only going to make it worse for me in the long run if I don't get past this.'

Guilt pricked me hard, and I knew she was right, but what could I do?

You can teach her your way.

I spared a glance toward Marina and Zeed, who both looked like they wanted to spit nails, and then back at Fable.

Fruck it. Either these donkeyholes wanted my help trying to save the Dwimmer world or they didn't. I was tired of doing things the hard way.

I motioned at the two pairs closest to me. 'Come here you guys.'

Zeed, Marina, Ross, Caterina, and Fable formed a semi-circle around me, and I lowered my voice to a murmur.

'We're all doing these spells like they showed us in school. What if there was an easier way? Think of it like shorthand. I can show you, but I can't promise Tarquinius is gonna like it . . .'

Zeed let out a short laugh. 'I would beg, borrow, or steal to be able to throw faster right now. Show me.'

'Same,' Marina said, nodding furiously.

I raised a brow in Fable's direction, and she gave me a thumbs-up.

'Seriously? It's kind of breaking the rules, which I know you're not a big fan of.'

'Please.' She snort-laughed. 'That was yesterday Fable. Today Fable has come to grips with the fact that something needs to change. Nocta is getting closer. We need to be ready.' She cracked her knuckles and tipped her head in a curt nod. 'Let's do this.'

I grinned. 'Okay, instead of doing these four separate motions,' I said, sweeping my index finger in a clumsy imitation of the series that Tarquinius had shown us, 'If you skip all that and make it into one, fluid motion, it looks like this.' I moved my fingers in a flourish that sent a stunned Zeed reeling back.

'Holy crap.' His eyes were wide as he rushed back toward me. 'That was amazing. Do it again!'

Within five minutes, all of them had gotten off at least one spell that actually did what it was supposed to, and they'd passed it on to the others too. I showed them a blocking rune too, because now we really needed it.

They picked the shorthand up like it was nothing to them, and for the first time, our runes were kicking asterisk.

'So good, Fable,' I crowed, pumping my fist as she blocked a real haymaker from Marina. 'Awesome!'

I had my hand in the air for a high five one second, and was frozen in place the next, completely paralyzed, unable to move. It only took a second to realize those closest to me were in the same boat.

'That is not the rune you were taught,' Tarquinius said, maintaining his hold on all of us long enough that panic started to creep up the back of my neck and radiate outward.

There was nothing I hated more than being controlled against my will. Not even raisins hidden in cookies in place of chocolate chips could compete.

This was right up there with stealing my ability to swear. Making me wear a stupid uniform. Taking away my ability to move . . . he was just proving how little freedom we actually had.

'There is a reason we have rules in magic. Without them, it would be impossible to track, and chaos would reign. The Senate strictly forbids it, and the last thing we need is them coming down on the school and poking their noses around. We're lucky they didn't come already after last night.'

I could feel the weight of my housemates' stares and my throat began to close. Was he going to tell them? That I'd been more than ready to abandon them all, not knowing whether I was the chosen one? Not knowing if they had what it took to defeat Nocta without me?

Tarquinius continued, his voice gentling. 'If you just open your mind to doing things the way you were taught, the way it's always been done, maybe it will come easier.'

The breath that had been suspended in my lungs suddenly released, coming out in a whoosh, and I yanked my hand down to hide my trembling.

Ten.

Nine.

Eight.

'I understand that's the way it's been done in the past. But this way is so much faster, and we seem to be having trouble –' I managed, relieved that my voice wasn't choked.

'We can't go changing everything just because your class-mates are struggling. It's up to them to figure out how to do it . . . the correct way.' He sighed heavily. 'As difficult as it is, we need you to keep pushing through the difficulties. You all need to put more effort in.'

Effort. As if we weren't sweating and not-cursing every time we had to cast a rune that didn't work?

I wasn't backing down. What was he going to do, kick me out?

In my dreams.

'This is literally our first lesson trying to go faster, and if the goal is speed, then surely, we need to explore every option, even if it means breaking the rules. Because as far as I can tell, Nocta's not following the rules . . . Central Park is gone because everyone follows the rules except him,' I shrugged. 'We're all just out here trying our best. Sir.'

He stared at me for a long moment and then nodded as if he'd come to some sort of decision then and there. 'And you seem to think your best is better than mine . . . is that it, Ms. Daygon? Your shoddy street magic can top centuries of tradition and practice?' He swept his gaze around the room, and he smiled before turning his eyes back on me. 'Let's see it, then. Spar with me.'

Bad idea. Terrible id–

'Sure. What the hell?'

His lips twitching into a smile as he waved me toward him and I steeled myself, already on guard.

But apparently not on guard enough.

His gnarled fingers twitched almost imperceptibly, and my legs shot out from under me as I went sailing across the room. Luckily, depending on whether you were me or Doyen Bob, I bounced off the combat instructor and managed to stay on my feet instead of hitting the wall. Still, the contact knocked the wind out of me. A second strike hammered me from behind, sweeping my legs out from under me. I hit the ground like a sack of stones and let out a grunt.

'Strength is important, Harlow, but the faster wizard will typically prevail.'

I stood again to face him. And, this time, when he lifted a hand, I was ready for his crusty asterisk. He thought he could just pin us down, when if he would let us do things our way, we could truly soar, maybe we'd even have a chance at facing down Nocta.

If only we could be *free* of the confines they'd placed on us! The anger burned in my gut, the knowledge that we were better than all this driving me on.

He flung a spell my way, and I whipped off a speedy block rune just in time to send his attack skittering away in a spray of sparks, harmlessly falling to the ground at my feet. Granted, he surely wasn't going full power, but I couldn't deny. It felt good.

A hush fell over the room as Tarquinius cocked his head and studied me like I was an insect he'd caught beneath a glass. I felt the weight of a second set of eyes on me and looked to see Typhon's hulking form against the wall by the door.

When had he come in? And more importantly, what was he doing here?

As I examined him closer, I realized he looked utterly exhausted. Dark shadows under his eyes, hair mussed.

I tugged my gaze away, cheeks burning as I tried to pretend I hadn't even seen him. Given that my pulse was suddenly pounding like I'd run fifty laps, and my palms were sweating, it definitely wasn't working.

If I got through this day without winding up dead or in a fetal position on the floor of my shower, it would be a miracle. But in for a penny . . .

'I don't get it. I heard you won't let Doyen O'Connor help find our Quirks anymore, you won't let me do magic my own way.' I crossed my arms over my chest with a bravado I definitely didn't feel. 'How are we supposed to help defeat Nocta if you won't even let us see what we're truly capable of?'

Energy crackled in the air between me and Tarquinius, and I tried to read the expressions that flitted across his face. Anger, to be sure. Irritation by the bucket-loads. And just maybe a hint of something like respect?

'The day I start running this place on the advice of a former student is the day I resign. Because you had the audacity . . . and character . . . to stand up for your fellow classmates, I'll let you off with a warning, Ms. Daygon. Next time you defy me, detention will seem like a fantasy.' He sliced a hand through the air. 'Class dismissed.'

Dismissed early again? Just where did he have to be that was more important than teaching the supposed saviors of the Dwimmer world?

With that, the Sage swept from the room, Typhon falling into step beside him.

'You were awesome out there,' Fable whispered, eyes wide.

'Amazing,' Zeed said, nodding as he shouldered his bag.

Marina squeezed my shoulder and offered me a grateful smile. 'Thanks for having our backs, Harlow.'

It was those words I tried to hold close to my chest to get me through the rest of the day, but by the time I climbed into bed that night, I felt like I'd been through the wringer and back again. Too many terrible days strung together and I was holding on by a thread. Bandit climbed up and settled on top of my head, like a slightly musty 'coon-tailed hat. I thought about shaking him off, but then realized I wanted him there. I buried my face in his fur and let the tears finally leak out.

When we failed – and we would, at this rate – everyone in this school would be in mortal danger. Including Opie. As guilty as I felt about leaving my new friends behind, I had to be the family that Opie deserved but never had. The one to put her first.

'I don't care if she hates me forever. I need to figure out how to get the fruck out of this hellscape of a place before it's too late.'

I 5

I tossed and turned all night, replaying not only the drone images through my head, but my sparring with Tarquinius. Something had gone wrong at the end, and he'd left so quickly, even though we easily had another forty minutes left in class.

None of this helped my anxiety and I couldn't stop sweating even though the room was cool. Every time I thought I was finally going to drift off, another wave tightened around my chest and my heart beat out of control as I stared up into the darkness.

Bandit grumbled under his breath. 'You're like a tornado tonight.'

'Sorry.' I threw my arm over my eyes. It was the first night in the dorms with everyone, and between my own thoughts racing, and the sounds of seven other people, there was no chance of sleep for me.

I gave up around five in the morning, swung my legs over the side of the bed and sat there a minute, contemplating my choices, which weren't many. I didn't want to wake everyone else up, but with us all smashed in here, I'd have to sit in bed staring at the ceiling to avoid making a noise.

The only good thing was that today was our day off. Our one day off a week, and I was about to take full advantage of it. 'Go back to sleep,' I whispered to Bandit. 'I'm going to get a coffee.'

He grumbled and burrowed deep into the covers.

I scooped my shoes in my hands and crept toward the door. I didn't want to wake anyone else up, except . . .

I found myself grinning. Yeah, this was going to be good.

Closing the door with a soft click behind me, I made my way to the fifth floor where I knew Nikita had her room. Walking the halls was forbidden, but I was going to get my companion right now. Like a good, obedient student.

She was going to love seeing me at five in the morning. At her door I stopped and snapped my knuckles against the door.

Nothing. I frowned and banged my fist against her door again. 'Nikita. I can't be out here without you, and I need a coffee.'

The door next to hers opened and a head poked out. Eyes beady with sleep and irritation, hair in a tangled mess, the girl yawned.

'She's not there. She left after dinner last night.'

I frowned. 'How do you know?'

Another yawn. 'She asked me to take her cat overnight because she wasn't going to be back till breakfast.'

Interesting.

Well, I tried. 'Thanks.'

I turned and started back down the length of the hall that went to the stairs. I considered going and waking up Opie but decided against it. She needed time away from me.

My footsteps were silent, which is why when I reached the fourth floor the sound of boots *right* behind me had me tensing.

A hand clamped onto my arm, and I was *yoinked* sideways, into a closet.

I threw a punch, caught my attacker on the side of the head, and had my knee driving for the groin before he spoke.

'Harlow, it's me, Liam!'

I slumped against the wall behind me, the semi-darkness

hiding his face from me, but the soft Irish lilt was unmistakable. 'What the fruck, man? What are you doing?'

'You ... you didn't see Tarquinius ahead of you?' He groaned and rubbed at his temple. 'If he'd seen you out by yourself *again* —'

'I went to Nikita's room to get her, but she isn't there.' I laid my palms flat against the wall behind me. 'I could have killed you!'

He grunted. 'With that right hook, you nearly did.'

A breath slid out of me. 'Where have you been?'

Light bloomed between us, a tiny glowing light over the palm of his hand. 'Tarquinius ... he doesn't agree with my methods of finding your Quirks. He wants to do it his way.'

'Are you serious? Why wouldn't he want both ways to be used if we are in such dire straits?'

'My argument too, and luckily, the Senate agrees with us.'

He'd mentioned not wanting them poking around ...

'Which is why I'm back now,' Liam continued. His eyes searched my face. 'Are you okay? Something happened while I was gone?'

I tipped my head back and banged it lightly on the wall behind me. 'Yeah, you could say something happened.'

Haltingly, I told him about the wishing well, Nikita's part in it, about being yanked in, about Opie, about being confined now to one big dorm room, and then the back and forth with Tarquinius the day before.

Liam was silent long enough that I was tempted to poke him to get a response.

'You really are chaos.'

Ouch. 'Fruck you too, Liam,' I snapped and made to push past him.

He caught my arm. 'I don't mean it like that, it's just ... House Phoenix is *known* for this sort of ... maelstrom around

174

them. The stronger the Dwim is, the more,' he shrugged, 'you know, trouble.'

I snorted. 'That's an easy out.'

He drew me closer. 'No, it's not. Between what you bring to this place, and whatever else is going on –'

'What else is going on?' We were so close now, almost nose to nose.

His throat bobbed. 'I'm not sure . . . what I know is that Tarquinius is pushing to keep me out of here. Turns out he wasn't the one who requested my presence, it was the Senate. So, even with the Senate's backing, he's still trying to have me removed. Maybe it's just about the Quirks, but I don't think so. Typhon . . . something is off with him too. Promise me you'll be careful around him, at least until I can figure out what's going on with him.'

Hecate's heart. I was so close to him and his words were so nice, so sweet and honestly, how long had it been since I'd kissed someone?

No. Bad Harlow. No kissing your teachers. I cleared my throat, and the door was yanked open.

Typhon stood there, his hair mussed, his shirt undone to the middle like he'd just chucked it on in a mad scramble and damned if that wasn't a tattoo peeking out, and . . . bare feet.

Why was he barefoot?

I blinked up at him, tried to find my voice because my emotions were pinging all over the place. 'Morning.'

'What the fuck is going on?'

Liam shrugged. 'We were having a private conversation.'

'Teachers don't have private conversations with students in closets.' Typhon hadn't moved but somehow his utter stillness made him look ever scarier.

'Liam was just taking me to get a coffee.'

'At five twenty in the morning.' Typhon turned slowly.

'Yes.' I smiled and nodded. 'Nikita wasn't available, so Liam it is.'

'Tarquinius wants to speak to you.' Typhon barely glanced at Liam. 'I'll take her to get her coffee.'

Sheet. What I'd wanted was a little more time to pick Liam's brain. He at least seemed to want to help us –

Truly help us.

Liam didn't have much choice. We both knew Typhon outranked him. He gave Typhon a jaunty salute. 'On it. I'll see you around, Harlow. Just think on what I said.'

Typhon waited until Liam disappeared around the corner. 'Let's go.'

I thought he would try to drag me back to my dorm, but he led the way, barefoot, down toward the kitchens.

Once I had an extra-large mocha in hand, along with a satchel of food from Wickersham, we started toward the dining hall.

'Typhon.'

'What?'

'How did you know we were in that closet? Because I'm pretty sure that you didn't see us go in, we were talking for like ten minutes before you showed up.'

He didn't slow his pace, and he didn't answer me.

I grabbed his forearm, forcing him to stop and look at me while I balanced my coffee and food in the other hand. 'How did you know?'

His muscles tensed under my hand. 'It's my job to know where you are at all times.'

'The whole of House Phoenix, or just me?'

Typhon's eyes . . . the Horned King could not have looked sadder. Why was he sad? 'Just you, Harlow. Because Tarquinius knew you'd be a problem from the start of this. And he was right, wasn't he?'

He pulled his arm away from my hand and motioned for me to sit down at the table closest to us. 'Eat your breakfast. I'll walk you back to your dorm after.'

It was the most open he'd been with me . . . well, ever. And even though I was the pain in the asterisk that everyone had had enough of . . . I wanted to talk to him more. It was a different pull than what I had with Liam.

I stuffed a bit of apple fritter into my mouth and chewed thoughtfully, trying to think of how to get him to be even more forthcoming.

'Why do you help the runaways?'

I choked on my bite of apple fritter, surprised by the random question. 'What?'

'What do you get out of it?' He sat beside me, a coffee in his hand. I'd been surprised when he'd put in two sugars, and two creams. I would have taken him for a straight-up black coffee kind of guy.

'They need someone who's been in their shoes.' I swirled my mug and stared into the chocolatey depths. 'I know what it's like to be alone, afraid, hungry. It's a beech when you're a grown-up but as a kid . . . it's terrifying.'

I didn't look at him, but I could feel his eyes on me, a weight that I wasn't sure I liked. 'And you get what out of it?'

'What do you mean?'

'Like a government grant, money, something.'

Fruck, he really thought I was a terrible person. I tried not to let him see how much that hurt as I twisted in my seat to look at him. Part of me wanted to get up and walk away because fruck him. The other part wanted to set him straight.

Latter half of me won out.

'I get the satisfaction of knowing that they won't suffer the way I did, Typhon. That they won't be alone, that they know they always have someone who will look out for them. I get that doesn't mean anything to you, really, but to me . . . it's why I will do everything I can to protect Opie. Why getting her out of here before she finds out . . .' I shook my head, my throat tight. 'You think I'm selfish, because I want out. I just want to save her from the pain that's coming. Both from the truth of what she is, and from Nocta, because he's not going to go easy on anyone. He'll kill us all. I saw the drone footage.'

Maybe it was too much all at once. Because he didn't speak to me again, not even to tell me he was taking me back to the dorm. He just stood, and I followed, hating the prickle of tears around my eyes.

He hated me. I got that, I really did.

So why did I keep trying to make him see that I wasn't the person he thought I was?

16

The thing with going to school six days a week is, it doesn't leave a lot of time to beg forgiveness from anyone. Not that Opie was giving me a chance to beg for anything. It had been nearly two weeks, and every time I so much as caught a glimpse of her in the halls of Neverthorn, she hurried away.

'What do you think, Harlow?'

I rolled onto my side to look at Fable. Other than Phyllis, who had her own quarters as an elder who had never left the school for reasons I still hadn't yet sussed out, we were still all in one big, stupid dorm room until further notice. So, we all got to listen to Zeed muttering in his sleep, Marina snoring, and Gary down at the far end constantly letting out noxious emissions in the middle of the night.

'What do I think about what exactly?' I yawned. 'And why are you asking me questions so early on a morning we don't have to be up yet?'

'One, I want to know how you really think we all are doing. And two, no point in getting used to sleeping in once a week, is there? Don't forget we have remedial runes with Doyen Moreno tomorrow. Just you and me, remember? He told us yesterday he wanted to see us in pairs for extra help whether we want it or not. Marina and Gary have to go today.'

I groaned and stuffed my head under the pillow as if that would be enough to block Typhon from my mind. I could still feel his fingers on my face when we were in the well. Could still feel the brush of his skin on mine when he'd wiped the blood from my face so gently after Nocta's creatures had attacked. Could still see the way his eyes had looked so sad.

Did I know that he had zero interest in me?

More now than ever after hearing what he thought of me and my runaways and my ulterior motives.

Did that stop my heart from beating a little faster every time he was near? Of course not. Because I was, if nothing else, consistent in my attraction to sheet men.

Why couldn't I be thinking about Liam instead?

Although, that happened sometimes too. At least that made some sense. He was kind, and sexy, and, you know, nice to me, despite no longer teaching us for the time being. I still saw him around the school, but he seemed to have a constant shadow now.

Doyenne Parunah was always with him, as if she were his companion now.

'She's apparently trying to get her Quirk to be . . . better.' Liam had managed to speak to me for all of thirty seconds, just outside the dining hall while I waited for Nikita. 'And she's not taking no for an answer. Not that I wouldn't help her, but I don't think it can be done.'

I couldn't help it, it was a little funny watching him try to dodge the old doyenne. And I couldn't really blame her, I would be trying to improve my Quirk too, if all I could manage was condensation on windows.

Nikita was the one who'd informed us of the current situation in our Monday History of Magic session. 'Tarquinius feels that, until House Phoenix can get a real handle on rune casting, it's a waste of precious time to search for latent Quirks, which none of you would even have the skills to use effectively. Obviously.'

According to my whispered talks with Liam, though, the Senate, on the other hand, wanted us firing on all cylinders to prepare for whatever battles were to come. In the end, they'd agreed to have him stay and assist with various classes, on call and at the ready until our rune-making improved.

If our rune-making improved.

I still got to see him in the dining hall on occasion, though, and whenever I did, I always wound up smiling.

For a little while, at least.

Then, that hint of pity would appear in his eyes, and I knew that he'd seen it too. Not just the lever or whatever was meant to trigger the Quirk, if I had one. But the whole scene that he'd been privy to. My mother. The doctor.

Me . . .

The creak of beds and a shuffle of bodies curbed my wayward thoughts. House Phoenix was waking up and it seemed everyone wanted to hear my answer. I'd survived in ways that most of them hadn't ever had to – none of them had been on the streets. I sat up and rubbed a hand over my right arm, feeling the textures of the cuff . . . tracing the phoenix. Underneath it was the faintest of lines that had been the start of my House Felinita mark. What I wouldn't give to have been in that house right now, without the weight of the world on my chest.

I wondered if the others felt the same.

'I want to know what you think, too.' Zeed shuffled over and sat next to Fable. 'At first, it seemed like people looked up to us,' his cheeks flushed. 'And I thought that they would be happy we were here, you know? Here to stop Nocta, especially after Tarquinius read the prophecy at the assembly. But it was like, once they realized that none of us were Quirks and word got around that we weren't exactly killing it on the whole rune-casting front, everything just went downhill.'

'Yeah, seems like even the few kids who didn't doubt us before won't make eye contact unless they're looking down their noses at me.' Marina sat down with a heavy sigh. She'd added a streak of jade green to the lock of springy curls bobbing over one eye, and it made her look like a bad asterisk.

'Same,' Ross groaned. He was in his early twenties, like most of us he'd been out of school for at least a couple years. 'I don't remember it being this hard last time.'

Each one of my fellow House of Phoenix peers had something to say about their re-induction to Neverthorn. None of it good.

'How in the sheet-balls are we supposed to fight Nocta when we all suck so badly?' Caterina braided her long red hair off to one side as she spoke. 'I mean, in all seriousness, I'm beginning to think this is someone's sick idea of a joke. I can't cast a simple blocking rune – I could manage it before though! How can I fight an army?'

A chorus of agreement rumbled through the room. But still, all eyes were on me. I wished Phyllis were here. As the eldest, everyone looked to her, but in her absence . . . yours truly was it. The questions they were asking were valid. What changed between the first time they were here, and now? If anything, we all should have gotten better at rune casting.

Not worse.

I stared at the floor between my feet. 'They'd have gotten rid of us by now if it was a joke,' I replied.

The others laughed at that, and I lifted my head, grinning. 'Look, I don't think any of you suck. We just . . . we just don't learn the way that they want us to.' Even as I said the words, I felt them in my bones as truth.

'It's like the propelling rune. The powers that be *say* it's only correct their way.' I flashed my fingers around me, using the rune that I'd developed and shoved the entire lot of them back a solid three feet. 'Other ways work too.'

'But Tarquinius won't let us use the . . . wrong runes,'

Marina said, holding up her hand to stop the murmurs. 'I'm not saying he's right, but how do we work around that?'

I grimaced, remembering the headache I'd woken up with the day after he'd sent me flying when I showed it to them the first time. He'd kept a tight rein on our 'special classes' since, and it had been nothing short of demoralizing.

What would it take to get him to loosen the training? Another attack on Heathermoor? Another attack on Neverthorn? Two more full moons?

'I don't know,' I admitted with a helpless shrug.

Fable twisted to face me, jaw set, eyes gleaming. 'We have to keep trying, practicing what we are told to practice. My brother was killed by Nocta's men last year. I won't stop trying.'

I stared at her, horror and grief flooding me. She'd not mentioned anything about her brother, but it made sense now that she said it. Her drive to succeed, to be good enough to take on Nocta and his army . . . it was about vengeance.

How would she feel if she found out that Nocta was my father?

I put a hand on hers. 'I am so, so sorry, Fable. More than I can say.'

She squeezed my fingers. 'I know.'

'Nocta's men killed my dad,' Zeed said quietly. Horror flashed through me, his desire to be better than his father made sense. He wanted to survive when his father hadn't.

'He killed my cousin. She was at Heathermoor two years ago when the tower was blown up,' Caterina chimed in.

Gary leaned against his headboard. 'He killed my great-uncle, in one of his attacks on the Senate.'

Each of the others in the room added to the casualty list, one by one.

The soft-spoken, near-reverent words of my classmates

rolled through me, tightening my chest until I couldn't breathe. Every single person in the room had reason to want Nocta's death. Because he'd killed someone close to them. Here they were, sharing in one another's losses and I felt like a damn traitor. A spy in the midst of those who had no idea who I really was. Because even though I had nothing to do with Nocta, it wouldn't matter. Blood was blood.

None of my friends . . . none of them could ever know.

Which is why I kept to myself more than ever after their confessions. Struggled with every class, even with Doyen Bob, because I could not unsee the grief on my friends' faces. I could not unhear the pain in their voices as they spoke of those they loved and lost to Nocta.

People who'd been killed by my father.

Later that night, unable to sleep, in the wee hours, I got out of bed and slipped out of the dorm. Maybe there was one thing I could fix, maybe one thing I could make right.

The usual noises fluttered through, but even with everyone in the same room, it wasn't hard to go unnoticed.

Except for Bandit who joined me in the hall. 'What we doing now? Tell me there is food involved.'

I folded up the piece of paper I had in my hand and gave it to him. 'Can you slip into Opie's room and give her this?'

'Yeah, but is there food involved if I do?'

I managed a tired smile. 'I am asking her to meet me in the kitchens, so yes to the food. I'll be there waiting.'

He leapt up and grabbed the note out of my hand and waddled his little butt down the hall before I could so much as blink.

I made my way to the kitchen, thinking Wickersham might already be there getting an early start on breakfast. Luck was on my side, and I found it empty. I made a beeline for the pantry, digging around for the ingredients to Opie's favorite breakfast treat. It was one of the only things I learned to bake from my mom before . . .

Bandit shot into the room, skidding to a halt. 'Mission accomplished. Don't eat without me!'

I snorted. 'I haven't even started making anything yet.'

'Wait, you can cook? You've been holding out on me.'

'No,' I pulled the pan I was looking for out of a pile of them. 'I can bake. I just don't have a large repertoire – I have like three things I can make. And really, am I going to bake something in my room?'

Bandit climbed up to sit on the counter. 'Is it going to be any good?'

'Unlike my rune work, this is pretty steady, but really, I should have thought to start it last night. This particular recipe is better if it's left to sit. And yes, it's going to make your stomach sing with how good it is.' I paused and looked over at him. 'Did it seem like she was going to come down?'

He shrugged. 'She was still half asleep, but she didn't say no.'

It was a start.

Nerves jiggled in my belly as I tried to focus on the task at hand. I mixed the flour and other dry ingredients first, then added the warm water. Kneading the dough on the floured surface of the counter, Bandit kept my mind occupied with chatter as I worked.

The dough was ready. I focused on my baking, rolling the dough into small round buns before I dropped them into a bundt pan. Melted butter, a package of dry vanilla pudding mix, copious amounts of brown sugar, and a hefty dose of cinnamon all went on top of the pile of buns.

Bandit watched me, his eyes widening. 'That's a damn sugar bomb.'

'Yes.'

'I love it.' He made grabby hands at the bundt pan.

I tucked the pan into the oven, then sat and waited.

A scuffle of footsteps on the stairs leading down into the kitchen snapped my head up. A second later, Opie poked her head into the kitchen, her eyes wary, her face still full of sleep.

'I got your note.'

I smiled. 'I'm making sleepy buns.'

'They are not sleepy buns,' Bandit laughed. 'That's not what you call something with that much sugar in them.'

Opie gave him a half smile. 'It's because you make them at night and cook them in the morning.'

I drew a breath. 'I'm sorry, Opie. I'm sorry that I hurt your trust in me. I'm sorry –'

'You almost died.' Her soft voice cut through me. 'What would I do if you died, Harlow? You're the only family I have left.'

I closed my eyes and gripped the counter. I wanted so badly to blame Nikita for all this. And while a part of me knew that yes, she had been a part of the disaster, ultimately it had been my decision to go to the well. My decision and no one else's.

I also knew that if I went up against Nocta and his army there was a chance I would die there on the front lines. I opened my eyes and looked at her, still seeing the little girl I'd scooped off the streets, the one crying for her mama and papa. Did I tell her that I was on a collision course with death no matter which way things went? No, I couldn't bring myself to shatter what was left of her childlike faith. I cleared my throat. 'I didn't know, Opie. If I had, I would never have tried to use the well.'

'I don't want to leave. I love it here. I have friends.' Opie frowned as I winced, thinking of how they'd spoken about her in the bathroom. 'They are good friends, Harlow. And I'm learning to do runes. And I'm actually pretty good at some of them. They're not quite working yet, but all my teachers think it's only a matter of time.'

I turned my face away from her as the oven pinged softly. I couldn't look her in the face when I knew what she was saying was not true.

'My parents were wrong. I have magic, I'm just a late bloomer. That's what Doyenne Parunah said.'

I pulled the pan of sleepy buns out of the oven and slid them across to her, unable to counter her even though I knew the truth.

Opie didn't have a lick of magic. I knew it, Typhon knew it, Tarquinius knew it. The only person who mattered – Opie – was also the only one still trying to believe.

Emotion clogged my throat, and I cleared it softly. 'They're hot.'

Smiling, she and Bandit dug into the buns. I went to her side and pulled her into a hug. She stiffened at first, then slowly relaxed into my hold. 'You aren't fully forgiven.'

'That's fair.' I pressed my cheek to the top of her head, breathing her in. 'Everything I do, I do to protect you, Opie. Just know that, okay?'

Her arms hung at her sides for a long moment before she wrapped them around me with a sigh. 'I love you, Lo-lo, but sometimes I wonder if it isn't you who needs protecting.'

17

Opie stayed with me for almost an hour, and just being in her presence made me feel better . . . but her words continued to haunt me after she went back to her room.

I put the pan in the sink and filled it with hot water and soap. Wickersham would not be happy if I left a mess.

Bandit let out a little chuff. 'Um, not alone.'

I didn't look over my shoulder. 'Sorry, I'm just cleaning up my mess, Mrs. W.!'

A hand dropped onto my forearm, spinning me around so that I was nose to nose with Typhon.

'What the hell are you doing?'

I smiled up at him, trying to play it off like my heart wasn't pounding out of my chest. 'Baking.'

The answer was not what he was expecting. His eyes shot to the pan in the sink, and the scattered remains of my efforts across the counter.

'What?'

'Opie was still mad at me, I needed to talk to her, make things better.'

I realized my mistake as soon as the words left my lips.

'You . . . convinced Opie to leave her dorm in the middle of the night, too? Fuck, Harlow.' His hand tightened and he snapped me close to him so that I was staring up into his face. 'We have you in your dorms at night for a reason. Especially now.'

I blinked up at him, his dark-green eyes framed with thick, dark lashes that I couldn't help but envy.

'But what *is* the reason you want us all locked in exactly? And how did you know where I was?'

Same question as before. One that he hadn't answered when he'd found me with Liam in the closet.

His eyes narrowed. 'You're predictable. I followed the food. But you aren't supposed to be wandering this place without Doyenne Elmwood.'

I shrugged, doing my best to ignore his close proximity. 'Here's the thing, I'm *pretty sure* Nikita is trying to kill me. So . . . I don't really want to be around her. You know, avoiding getting murdered, it's high on my list of things to do this week.'

His hand slid up my arm to my neck, fingers wrapping around so that his thumb sat in the hollow of my throat. 'Then you give me no choice.'

The heat of his hand was . . . too much, I tried to pull back, pressed my hand against his chest, right where his shirt was open.

Warm, his skin shivered under my touch, but he didn't pull away, if anything, he pressed closer.

He hung onto me, his fingers tensing one by one, not all that different from when he'd put the gag on me. But I was too addled by his touch to realize he was casting a rune directly into my skin. I could *feel* the intent of it, wrapping around me. A rune of bonding that went far beyond the rule of two.

I gasped as his magic sank hard into me, sliding under my skin and racing through my limbs. Before he could pull away, I mimicked the rune out of some sort of instinct. I wasn't sure he even noticed what I was doing, hell, I wasn't sure even I knew what I was doing.

My runes settled into his skin.

'What the fruck?' I meant the words to come out hard, angry, but they were . . . barely breathed.

'If you won't obey Doyenne Elmwood,' Typhon didn't let me go, just dragged me closer to his face, his eyes dilating as he stared down at me, like he was the hunter and I was the prey, 'Then you will obey *me*.'

Typhon let me go slowly, each of his fingers seemingly dragged from touching me. I withdrew my hand, though it felt like I was still attached to him, with long, thin spider silk. Unseen, but far stronger than it seemed to be.

Our magic had bound us together. Him on purpose and me . . . me kinda by accident.

With one last look, he turned, his long coat snapping out behind him, and then he was gone.

I swallowed hard, the pulse in my throat pounding from his touch. I fumbled for the pan and scrubbed it fast, keeping my hands busy as I tried to figure out how I felt –

'Was it just me, or was that seriously hot?' Bandit squeaked.

I leaned against the sink and let out a groan. 'Please don't say anything.'

'Yeah, that was definitely steamy.' Bandit leapt up onto the counter next to me, ignoring my plea. 'I mean, I don't know what it's like with humans, but a good bite on the neck is some serious foreplay in the nocturnal mammal world.'

I closed my eyes and leaned harder against the counter because the image of Typhon biting me on the neck was instant and the physical reaction it drew out of me was ludicrous. I clamped my legs tight, tried to think of anything but his touch.

Baseball.

Mud.

Stock market.

'I'm being stupid.'

'Nope, you're in the clear, Shortbread. You cleaned up,' Mrs. Wickersham stepped into the kitchen, 'which, if you're going to sneak into my kitchen and bake, is essential.'

I forced a smile to my lips as I struggled to relax my legs from being clamped tight. I had to get Typhon out of my head. He . . . he was a teacher, a donkeyhole . . . a fracking hot donkeyhole, but still. And now I was well and truly stuck with him – even now, I could sense him, and the rune I'd sunk into his skin meant I could find him, too.

One floor up and moving fast, away from me.

It was both a major annoyance and an inconvenience. I had things to do, and not a lot of time to do them. This bonding spell was going to make that all twice as hard.

'Thanks.' I slipped out of the kitchen and headed straight to the closest bathroom where I slapped some cold water over my face.

The woman in the mirror looking back at me was haggard at best. Horrified at worst. I shook my head, then fashioned my messy hair into a quick ponytail. As much as I hated the idea of bending to Typhon's will and rushing to class, I had to admit, the thought of him coming to find me and what might happen was far more terrifying.

Bandit followed me as I hurried to the room where Typhon taught runes.

'I'm going to watch today, in case you need me to run some interference between you two. Assuming that's what you'd want?'

'Yes,' I bit out. 'Exactly.'

When I stepped into the classroom, Fable was already there – it was just the two of us today with Typhon. She waved to me, and I went and sat down next to her. She started chattering, but her voice flowed in and around me, and I barely heard her. I was looking inward. Finding the new little bond that Typhon and I had. Whether he wanted to or not, the bond went both ways. He'd be entering the class-room in *three, two, one.*

The door banged open on cue.

'Basic rune work today, ladies. Pick one you struggle with and show me,' he said, all business as he headed to the front of the room without a glance in my direction.

That didn't stop my mind from going back to how his hand had felt on my neck, and how frucking hard and warm his chest had been under my fingers.

Fable went first, choosing a rune that would light a fire — one of the most basic in our world. She made the bursting motion with her fingers, over and over again. Barely a flicker slid over her fingers. Next, she tried a water rune, again, basic. One that would fill a glass with water pulled from the air.

Nothing.

'I don't understand!' She finally broke when she tried a basic earth rune that would soften the ground. 'Why is it so hard again now? I mean, maybe I wasn't amazing, but I could do basic rune work!'

'It's got to be the pressure.' I leaned back in my chair, fatigue hitting me hard after the long night and the burst of adrenaline with Typhon. I half closed my eyes. A nap would be most welcome right then.

Typhon's eyes finally slid to me. 'Which of the runes are you struggling with most?'

'I can make them all work,' I said with a tight smile. 'Just not the way Tarquinius wants me to do them.'

Typhon leaned against the desk and jerked his chin in a curt nod. 'Go. Show me the correct rune for propelling.'

I wove the rune for shoving a person back, the one that Tarquinius had us working on. I did it first the way that was *proper*. I threw it at the chair to my left, and it moved about a half an inch. 'It's better if I do it my way.'

'No!' Typhon said.

But I was already moving. I whipped my hands through

the version of the rune that worked for me, and hurled the chair across the room, smashing it against the wall.

'See? It's not that I can't.' I folded my arms.

Typhon studied me for a long moment, then he looked to Fable. 'Are you good at research?'

Her big amber eyes went wider yet. 'One of my best skillsets.'

'Go to the library. See what you can find out about people changing houses, and what putting them in the wrong bracer could do to their ability to cast runes. Is there a precedent for that causing issues with throwing runes or with magic in general? Could it stunt a potential Quirk from manifesting?' He frowned and rubbed a spot in the middle of his forehead, speaking for all the world as if we weren't there. 'Could be why they all could do better rune casting at home, once the bracer was off . . . but it doesn't explain the issue now. What has caused this?' He mumbled a last word that I didn't catch, but it seemed to spark something in him. He turned and looked at us, a new light in his eyes.

He'd figured something out.

Interesting. I hadn't even considered it, but if we had all been destined for House Phoenix and wound up being shoved in other houses, that would explain why we all struggled in school the first time around. And then the switcheroo into Phoenix so late in the process . . . could be what was causing all sorts of mayhem. Magic was a fickle beast, after all.

Fable was up and moving toward the door in a flash. 'I'll be back as fast as I can!'

He rolled his shoulders.

'I want you to show me some of your other runes. The ones you've . . . created. No one else from House Phoenix can throw runes like that. I'm trying to figure out why. Just don't cast them. Show me what they look like.'

I flicked a quick rune in the air without filling it with energy. 'That's one for making the lights go out.'

He nodded and watched me through hooded eyes as I showed him a few more.

I frowned, lowering my hands. 'So, you really think the problem we're having has something to do with us being in other houses previously?'

He shrugged. 'I don't know. This is uncharted territory. Tarquinius feels strongly about obeying the rules and using only proper, sanctioned magic, as do I. That's not going to change. So, whatever is blocking you all, that's what we need to work on.'

He pushed off the desk and strode toward me. The urge to back up was strong, but I stood my ground, craning my neck to meet his gaze head on.

'Going to try and choke me again, are you?'

Something flickered in his eyes and his voice went low and silky. 'Not unless you say please.'

I sucked in a sharp breath as he took my hand, folding my fingers so that I was ready to cast.

'Go again. Cast a rune of fire,' he said.

I tried to move my fingers the way I wanted, and he held them in the correct position. I frowned and the magic stuttered through me, like . . .

'It's like it's being dragged through mud.'

For the next thirty minutes, I tried to do the runes exactly as he'd shown me. Each was more disappointing than the last.

'I feel like I'm doing exactly what you are,' I muttered, feeling defeated already.

He took my other hand and brought the two together as if I were praying, in position to cast the first rune most children learned. Extending pressed-together hands outward and then snatching them back in allowed the caster to draw something toward them. So, pulling cups off counters or pots off of the stove became a real issue for young Dwimmers.

Typhon stared at my hands as he flexed them through the basic rune, over and over, his brows furrowed so hard it pulled at the scar across the one side of his face. 'I can't even feel the magic. Damn it.'

He didn't ask me to do it my way.

I just did.

I simply crossed my thumbs before I opened my palms. The spell latched onto Typhon and dragged him close enough to me that his chest pressed tight against me, our hands tangled up just below our faces.

'Try to break it,' I said.

His eyes were locked on my fingers. 'I can see your magic when you use the rune your way.'

I looked at him. 'The bonding spell?'

He nodded, though I saw the flicker of uncertainty in his eyes. He was lying to me. About what?

My breath caught. 'What does it look like?'

'Beautiful.' His eyes lifted to mine and the air between us charged as if I'd thrown a rune of lightning. His fingers slid over mine, ever so slightly, and I couldn't think of anything but how his eyes bored into my own. Neither of us looked away, but it wasn't a battle of wills. At least not in the way it had been when I first arrived.

This was a battle of temptation, one that I knew I shouldn't . . . I couldn't cross.

His throat bobbed and he drew a breath. 'You're right not to trust Nikita.'

Relief rocked me back on my heels. 'You see it too?'

The door banged open, and Fable stumbled back in, short of breath. 'I found a book!'

I turned to face her, half glad she was back and half wishing she would leave again.

'Awesome. Do you think it will help?'

Her grin faltered. 'Are you okay? You look flushed.'

'Working hard.' I shrugged and cleared my throat.

Typhon brushed past me and crooked a finger for the book, which Fable handed over. 'I'll have a look through this. See what I can find. Good job, both of you. We will pick this up tomorrow.'

He left without another word, and I couldn't help but wonder what would have happened if Fable hadn't arrived.

18

I kicked the blankets off my sweaty legs and let out a loud sigh.

'If you keep doing that, you're going to wake Fable,' Bandit murmured with a yawn.

'I can't help it. Why is it so freaking hot in here?'

But the little bugger was already sleeping again so all I got was silence. I couldn't even be mad at him. I was just jealous. After waking up in the middle of the night to bake for Opie and then spending the rest of my day feeling Typhon's presence . . . well, everywhere, I'd fallen into bed exhausted.

The bond to Typhon, though, made it impossible to sleep. I was going to blame him for my second sleepless night in a row. Every time I thought about the bond, and how his hand had felt on my neck, how his heart had beat under my palm . . . I started to sweat, and an ache started up between my legs.

I risked a glance at the clock at my bedside and groaned.

Two a.m. Even if I fell asleep in the next five minutes, I was going to be useless the next day. I closed my eyes and tried to meditate, clearing my mind of everything.

You're in a meadow, with a brook trickling softly nearby.

Brook.

Water.

Death.

Nope.

The spots where his fingertips had pressed the rune into me tingled. This time, though, instead of stopping there, the sensation traveled across to my shoulder, down into my chest and spread, filling me with a neediness that had me sucking in a breath.

What the hell?

My legs swung over the side of the bed, almost of their own accord. The next thing I knew, I was yanking a cotton robe over my shorts and camisole and padding silently out of the room. My brain had no clue where I was headed, but my body knew.

More accurately, the bond knew that I needed to move.

Typhon, something inside me whispered as I made my way down the stairs toward the entrance of the school on autopilot. When I got to the front door and saw him standing there, waiting expectantly, it was like something unfurled inside me.

Relief.

Anticipation.

It wasn't until we'd walked through the courtyard and out of the front gates that I found my voice.

'Where are you taking me?'

The question was pointless. I knew it didn't matter. The pull was that strong. He could be dragging me to the river to drown me, and I'd have gone with him still.

I shook my head to clear it and stopped short.

'Where are you taking me?' I said again, more firmly this time. Just in case he *did* want to drown me.

'On a field trip. We need to test a theory,' he replied.

'Yeah, well, I don't appreciate the whole vampire, mind-control bullsheet. It's a total violation —'

'Enough, Harlow!' He wheeled around in a flash of black robes and held me in place with an icy stare, eyes glittering. 'The reason I had to bond us together so tightly is so I could stop you from doing something stupid. Not just to keep you safe but also to keep your fellow housemates and Opie safe. You will get her, and them, killed if you aren't careful!'

I winced.

'I'd have loved to request your consent. We both know you'd never have given it, so what would you have me do? Let you roam around until you fell into another well and broke your neck? Or maybe you'd rather I let you stick with Nikita, and she can give you a little kick into one, instead? You left me no choice, Harlow.'

It was a bitter pill to swallow, but he was right.

'It still doesn't make you the boss of me.' I kept moving until the gravel beneath my feet became soft, cool grass and then I slowed, realizing that I had no clue which direction to head.

'If you stop running, I can show you where we're going.'

Thankful for the cover of darkness as my cheeks burned, I let him pass me. We continued in silence until the river came into view.

I paused, the first real prickle of fear skittering down my neck.

'Are . . . are you going to drown me?'

He didn't even bother to turn around. 'Keep it moving, Ms. Daygon.' So much for 'Harlow' . . . that had been short-lived, 'I'd like to actually get some sleep tonight.'

Interesting. I couldn't help but wonder if he'd been awake, all hot and achy like I had been. Would serve him right.

We didn't stop until we reached the water's edge. Then he paused and gestured downward.

'This is technically Charon's territory, but so long as we stay in the shallows where it's just sand and rock and don't venture deeper, he won't bother us.'

'If you say so . . .' I clearly remembered the look Charon had given me, just for dipping my toes in.

I'd been hot in bed, and the crisp, early autumn air felt good on my skin, but I wasn't exactly chomping at the bit to go wading either, though.

'Remind me one more time why we're getting in the water?'

'To test my theory.' His expression was thoughtful as he moved to stand closer, his hand going to my bracer. 'We need to go beyond the borders of Neverthorn, where you aren't being monitored. The water's edge marks the end of the school's territory. In order to retain their longevity and remain robust, any wards or spells that are cast from the school stop right here.' He tapped the tip of his boot on the bank of the river and slipped my bracer off.

Bugger, it had taken me three weeks to get my first bracer off on my own.

Part of me felt like I *should* trust him, but only the gods knew why. Liam didn't trust him, and I trusted Liam. I should believe what he said about Typhon.

Shouldn't I?

On the outside, it seemed like nothing had changed. At that moment, a dull ache reverberated through my ribs, as if I needed another reminder of the kind of damage Typhon could do.

He shrugged his annoyingly broad shoulders. 'We both know, if I wanted you dead, I could've killed you a dozen times by now. And if I wanted to force you into the water, it would take nothing but the wave of my hand. I know this is hard for you to believe, but I'm actually trying to help you here. Work with me, Harlow.'

So now I was Harlow again.

I hated the fact that hearing it from his lips made my pulse stutter, every time.

'Fine,' I muttered. 'What do I have to do?'

'The way it's going, you'll be killed the second Nocta lays

eyes on you, and where will that leave Opie? Where will that leave –' He broke off and stepped back, jerking a finger toward the river. 'Just get in the water.'

I yanked off my robe and got in the frucking water. Ignoring the chill, with Opie at the forefront of my mind, I turned my back on Typhon and lifted my hand, poised to whip off a simple rune.

'No! Not shorthand, Harlow.'

I squeezed my eyes closed, trying not to let hot tears of frustration leak out. 'Why are you so against it? Tarquinius, I get. He's old school. Traditions and all that. But you . . . why are you so against me doing things my way? I know what you think of me, but it's not just me trying to be difficult. I genuinely struggle to –' I let out a growl of frustration, not even realizing he'd closed the gap between us until he took my hand in his.

'Go ahead. Do it your way one last time and I'm going to show you why it can't continue.'

I chewed at my bottom lip, trying not to let the warmth of his finger laced with mine distract me. Then, with our fingers interlocked, I threw a rune meant to illuminate the space around us. It worked, albeit barely. It took me a second to realize Typhon was muting my spell with one of his own.

'Dang it, I'm tired of you people doing this . . .' I trailed off as the circle of dim light I'd created flickered and changed into a distorted image that slowly came into focus as Typhon pulled his hand from mine and manipulated it with his fingertips.

'Do you see it?' he whispered.

I squinted, trying to make out what I was looking at.

'It's . . . is it a cellar or a dungeon? And I'm not sure . . . a huge spiderweb?'

Only it was moving. Pulsing and rippling, some of the tiny, silky strands snapping, before it finally went still again.

'That's the weave, Harlow. The only thing separating us and the black magic of Everdark.'

I shivered. Everdark where all the evil and the monsters of the Dwimmer world had been locked away.

'Why was it pulsating like that?' Almost as if it were alive.

The image he'd shown me flickered and disappeared as he lowered his hand and met my gaze. 'Because of you, Harlow.'

I blinked at him as the words sank in.

'The way you throw runes is similar to Everdark magic. The weave can sense it . . . the chaos, the darkness . . . and it reacts. Every time you do it, there is a ripple in the weave. The more energy you give the rune, and the closer you are to the weave, the stronger the response. If it tears, and we aren't able to repair it quickly enough . . .'

A sense of dread closed over me. 'So, whenever I throw an unsanctioned rune, I'm putting my friends –' *and Opie*, 'in danger?'

His mouth was set in a grim line as he nodded. 'Yes.'

I bit my lip, trying not to think about what could've been.

'Why didn't you just tell me that? I would've stopped sooner.'

'We didn't think you were strong enough to truly hurt anything, until . . . well, until we realized you were. You have to understand, while we want you all to be prepared for what's to come, we also can't have our students using Everdark magic. It's a lot to take in, and you all have enough to deal with getting ready to face Nocta. The details about the weave are need-to-know. I realized tonight that you needed to know.'

I'd given him no choice. Because, Hecate forbid, I just do what I was asked for once without fighting back.

I blew out an unsteady breath as I tried not to think about

what was on the other side of that weave. What might have been released into our world . . . our school, if I'd been left to my own foolish devices.

'Beating yourself up about what might have happened is a waste of energy. I need you here and focused, Harlow. Stay with me, alright?'

I forced myself to shove the shame aside and turn my attention to Typhon.

'Let's start again, from the top. I need you to throw one of the runes you actually know how to do the correct way. Ready?'

'Ready.'

At first, my fingers felt clumsy like always as I tried to replicate a rune I'd been taught during my first, short stint at Neverthorn. But I pushed through and tried again. And again. And again.

'Look at my fingers, and try again,' Typhon urged, a sharp edge to his voice this time.

I turned to face him. 'I don't know what to say. I'm doing my best. Maybe it's just going to take a little time.'

'We don't have time!' he growled.

I shot him a glance, suddenly full of apprehension as I glanced at the sky again. The moon that had been hidden behind the clouds was now visible, and very, very full. The first of three before the prophesied attack.

'You aren't wrong,' I muttered.

'Someone told you, then?' Typhon said, eyes locked on me as I tugged my gaze from the sky. 'About the full moons and the solstice? Liam, was it?'

'I know you're trying to protect us or whatever, but not knowing is way worse, Typhon.'

'The pressure is already almost insurmountable, Harlow. Some of you would crumble under more.'

He wasn't wrong. But weeks had passed, and we were still moving at a snail's pace. The solstice was inching closer. Something had to give . . .

Ignoring the gentle tug of the river at my ankles. Ignoring the heavy weight of Typhon's stare. Ignoring everything inside me that said I was going to fail once again, I tried again. For Typhon. For Opie. For myself.

This was life or death. I had to do this. I poured my energy into what I was doing, holding nothing back for maybe . . . maybe the first time in my life.

There had always been something holding me back. Fear at the top of the list.

But this time, the runes and the magic felt different.

I let the fear go and cast a proper rune for manipulating water.

The result was instantaneous. A tiny droplet of water rose from the river, shimmering in the moonlight as it floated a few feet in front of my face. I let it fall and lifted another, then another. Soon, I was plucking drops out so quickly that my fingers were a blur, and the sound of the drops falling was like a symphony.

Drip.

Drip.

Dripdripdripdripdrip.

Bigger droplets rose and fell like gems glittering in the night sky, faster and faster. Joy spread through me as the magic shimmered from my fingers in a crimson flash and seemed to well up inside me in a rush. I embraced the feeling and lifted my hand higher, going on instinct, without fear, as I flung the runes in controlled abandon. The droplets fell as the river itself crested before me, a massive wave, tall as a two-story building. So much water that some of the rocky bottom of the river came into view, littered by the wreckage of an ill-fated rowboat, some of Charon's treasure, and a few wide-eyed fish.

It was only when I heard Typhon gasp behind me that I let my hand fall to my side.

'Harlow!'

The massive wave crested over me just as Typhon gripped my wrist and yanked. I pitched forward, letting out a squeal as we both toppled over, him into the ground, me onto him. I sucked in a breath, shocked from the chilly water. I shuddered as I realized that, without Typhon there, the wave could've hit me and dragged me into the river when it retreated, setting Charon off on a murderous path.

Then I realized I was fully sprawled on top of Typhon. Both of us soaked through, pressed together, chest to chest, hip to hip.

I stared down at him, so full of all the feels that I could barely form the words to explain it.

'It was so beautiful,' I whispered, knowing I should be embarrassed of the tears stinging my eyes, but weirdly not caring. 'Typhon, it was unlike anything I've ever experienced. I wasn't doing magic. I . . . I *was* magic.'

He released my wrist and lifted his hand to my face, gently brushing a damp lock of hair from my cheek.

'That was perfect.'

For a second, we just stared at each other. Then he rolled me off him and stood, pulling me to my feet.

He stepped back and dropped my hand, his expression blank again.

'I should've stopped you sooner, but I wanted to see just how good you could be, and you were . . .' He shook his head and then cleared his throat. 'Mission accomplished.'

This. This was what it was supposed to feel like all along when we were casting runes. I'd felt a hint of it when I managed to create a rune that actually worked properly, and the promise of it when I'd been trying to activate some latent Quirk. In the Unlit world, I'd always had to be careful, holding back just in case, and I mostly used my own runes, not something that was sanctioned. But even then, it hadn't quite clicked, and I thought I knew why.

I'd always been afraid of just what could happen. Of being found out.

Of having everything taken away from me, again.

And now that I'd had a taste of what the magic was meant to be, without the fear, surely nothing else would do.

So, I was thrilled with Typhon's next words.

'I'll be setting up another covert field trip. Be prepared to lose some more sleep.'

'When?' I asked, wrapping my arms around myself and shivering.

He absently whipped off a quick rune that had us both dry in an instant, then held my bracer out to me, and slid it back onto my arm. It latched on smoothly, as if it had never been taken off. 'As soon as I can arrange it. The two of us were easy enough to conceal. The next time, I want all of you . . . the whole of House Phoenix, to join. It's going to take some doing.'

My heart sank a little. Something about it being just the two of us, a shared experience that was like no other, had made it even more special. I shoved those feelings aside in a rush as I realized that Fable, Zeed, Marina . . . all of my friends would finally get to experience what magic should truly be and hadn't been for any of us.

I frowned as some of the euphoria faded.

'Wait . . . why?' I shook my head. 'Why did I have to be away from Neverthorn for that to happen?'

He looked off into the distance, and I could almost hear his mental gears grinding.

'Trying to decide how much to tell me, huh?'

His lips twitched and I knew I'd hit the nail on the head. When he faced me again, it was with no hint of a smile.

'I think that the powers that be – Tarquinius or the Senate . . . maybe both – intentionally dulled your magic. All of you in House Phoenix.'

His words were like a gut punch, and I weaved on my feet.

'That doesn't make sense,' I whispered. 'They brought us here to prepare for Nocta. How can we –'

'Not now,' he cut in quickly. 'When you were all here the first time around. They were afraid of your power after Nocta's attack on his fellow students all those years ago, and they placed muting spells on anyone destined for House Phoenix – I think they would have been imbued in your bracers.'

That made a wicked sort of sense. The bracers went on our dominant hand, the one for casting runes. A perfect place for a muting spell. And it made even more sense when I thought about how not just me, but all of House Phoenix had the same experience. Not great in school, better once they graduated, and now, sheety again.

'They were designed to bring you down to the level of the other students, both for their safety and yours. But some worked better than others, and after a few mishaps, they erred on the side of over . . . overcorrecting.'

The fact that he looked sick himself saying it didn't make me any less furious.

'*Overcorrecting?*' I demanded, nauseous at the thought of what had been kept from me. 'I thought I was useless. My classmates treated me like worthless trash. My life here was a living hell, and you brought me . . . *all* of us, back for more of the same?'

'I approached Tarquinius about it yesterday after something I read in the book Fable found. It all but confirmed my theory. He insisted that they'd removed the spells when you came back. He swore to me that was over and done with. And, to your point about Nocta, it only makes sense that it's the truth. Why wouldn't they want you at your strongest? My guess is that there is something else going on. I think that this could be something Tarquinius is doing, to try and force your Quirks out. But it would explain why neither you nor Zeed could quite trigger your Quirk.'

'Wait a second, we don't even know if we have one –'

'And we might never know until we leave school grounds, where Tarquinius can't see what we're doing. Where we can take off your bracers.'

Which was why he brought me here. By the river. So no one could sense that my bracer was off.

My head was spinning. To go from the highest high, crashing to the lowest of lows, had left me feeling raw and hollow inside.

I'd had to hide my magic except under the most controlled circumstances in the Unlit world so I couldn't be tracked. I was muted here because they wanted to dull my powers. I've literally never gotten to truly explore my potential.

Until tonight. And like it or not, Typhon had given me that.

'Did you truly not know until now?' I asked, trying to pretend that his answer didn't matter.

To his credit, he didn't play stupid.

'No. And as for Nikita . . .' he paused and raked an agitated hand over his face. 'I had an inkling she had it out for you pretty quickly as she hasn't changed since school, she's still a bully. But I have no proof. Nothing that I can bring to Tarquinius. But I'm working on it. She knows I suspected she led you to the wishing well, so she has to tread lightly, and now that you and I are bonded, you should be safe.'

I let his words marinate and then nodded. I might be a fool, but I believed him. The vise grip on my chest loosened just a little as I turned away.

'Alright then. I'm sure I'll have a thousand more questions once all this sinks in, but we should get back before I'm missed.'

And before I burst into exhausted, confused tears.

I trudged back toward the school, brain buzzing with a thousand thoughts as I tried to process everything that had happened.

What did this mean for me? For all of us in House Phoenix? My goal from the start had been to get out of this place as soon as possible. But the future that had seemed like the most precious jewel, sparkling just out of reach, suddenly dimmed. Once we left, I'd never be able to do it again. They wouldn't allow me to do magic like that out in the Unlit world. I'd never be able to let go like that. Be free.

Be magic.

And the thought made me want to vomit.

We made the rest of the walk in silence. When Typhon left me at my dorm, he touched my hand briefly, making the bond between us flare.

'One other thing, Harlow. Tarquinius has his eye on one of you, but he won't say which. He thinks . . . he thinks he knows who is going to be the one to take Heronius's place.'

I wasn't sure what he wanted me to say to that. 'Won't be me. I think we can both agree on that. I'm too unpredictable, remember?'

Typhon's eyes darkened. 'Zeed and the others, they look to you. I'm sure I don't have to tell you this, but don't do anything like what you did tonight without me there. Is that clear?'

I swallowed the knot in my throat and nodded.

'Crystal.'

Because even though he'd given me my first taste of freedom, nothing had changed. He was my warden, and I was his prisoner. No matter how attracted to him I was, no matter how much I stupidly wanted him, I couldn't let myself forget that.

Not ever.

19

I let myself back into the dorm room as silently as I could, closing the door behind me in an effort not to wake anyone up. So, when I turned to find Fable standing there, her face three inches from mine, I nearly sheet myself.

'What the fruck!' I hissed.

'I could ask you the same,' she whispered back. 'Now come on, follow me.'

She led me past the beds of our housemates into a little sitting room where we sometimes congregated and played board games. There was a wicker bowl filled with goodies sitting on the table and I let out a low groan. Sticky buns, donuts, glazed scones, muffins.

'Bless you,' I said, hurrying to sit on the comfy couch.

'I heard you leave earlier, and I almost followed you, but I figured if you'd wanted me to come along, you wouldn't have been sneaking out in the first place. So, I took a page out of your book and hit up the kitchens for when you came back,' she said, taking a seat beside me and curling her feet beneath her.

'Sorry about that. It wasn't really up to me,' I explained gently.

Fable picked up a silver carafe and filled two mugs with coffee, adding a healthy dose of cream and sugar to mine. I didn't realize how hungry I was until I actually had the food in my sights. I stuffed a chocolate-covered donut into my mouth and chewed with a blissful moan.

Fable poured herself some coffee and took a drink. Black, she liked it black.

I spoke around the donut. 'Typhon took me on a *private field trip.*'

'You had *sex* with him?' Fable gasped, the motion making her coffee slosh over the sides of the mug and making her let out a low yelp. 'I thought that was a good afterglow on you but . . .'

I nearly choked on the donut. 'Field trip is not a euphemism for sex, Fable. It was rune casting. He took me outside the bounds of Neverthorn –'

'Wait . . . what? He can't do that.' Fable shook her head. 'What was he thinking? He could get you both in trouble! I don't want you to get thrown out, you're like . . . my best friend, Harlow.'

A stupid warm glow wrapped around me. I could have pushed it away, but I clung to it a little.

I told her about going down to the water, about Typhon taking the bracer off. How hard it was to get the runes right, but how amazing it was once I did.

'It was the freest I've ever felt. Like for the first time my magic was mine and it was actually listening to me, and the rune was working. A rune that I hadn't tampered with or created. I've never . . . I've never felt connected to my magic and the runes like that before. Not in my whole life. And . . .' Did I break the promise that Typhon had extracted from me? Did I tell her and give her hope? Yeah, yeah I did. 'He wants to take us all out next time. But we gotta keep this between us. He doesn't want everyone knowing.'

Fable stared at me, her eyes glittering with unshed tears. 'That sounds . . . awesome. Do you think he'll really take us all?'

I nodded. 'Yeah. I actually do. He has to find a way to do it when Tarquinius isn't around.'

'That frucker.' She grabbed a scone and tore it in half.

'How dare he keep us from our magic! Why is he doing it this time? If he wants us to be strong, this doesn't make sense.'

I nodded and, for the first time since Typhon had taken me with him to the edge of the water, I let myself look at what had been done to not only me, but the whole House of Phoenix. 'They caged our magic because they were afraid of us, and now that they need us, they have to uncage us. But either it's not working, or they don't actually want to,' I snorted. 'Tarquinius claims they stopped muting us, but obviously that's not the case since taking my bracer off allowed me to cast like I've never been able to before. Typhon thinks it has to do with our Quirks and making them show up, which makes zero sense.' I rubbed at my arm cuff, feeling a flare of warmth there.

Fable took a shuddering breath. 'They set us up to fail. From the beginning. They clipped our wings.'

I reached over and put a hand on her arm, feeling her shake and tremble. 'But not now, Fable. Not now. We know the truth. We'll find a way to be connected to our magic again, and they won't be able to take it away from us. Ever.'

Her hand covered mine and she gave a fierce nod. 'Agreed. I even understand why they did it – to a point. They don't need another Nocta rising up, flinging power everywhere, killing people just because they can. I get that part of it.'

I flinched, guilt chewing at my insides. Guilt that I was his daughter? No, guilt that I could never tell her, because I knew how it worked. Guilty by association wasn't a saying for nothing. It was why you had to be careful who you worked with on the street. Reputation could be destroyed with a single wrong association.

Fable patted my hand. 'Look, this is good news. Even though it sucks what they did to us, blocking us. We know

now, and that means we can find a way around it. That's what Typhon is doing, isn't it?'

I nodded. 'I think so.'

'So, let's do our part. We are going to fight Nocta. To know your enemy is to know how to defeat them. Despite what Elmwood has been teaching us, I don't think it's the whole picture. I mean, all she keeps saying is that he's the strongest Dwimmer ever. That's not helpful, right?'

I shook my head. He *was* the strongest. And I was his daughter.

'I bet we can find out more,' Fable continued. 'More about him. About his weakness. Maybe he has a wife? Or a family? Maybe we could use them to find him on our terms. Bring the fight to him.'

My guts turned over and the only thing I could do was nod. I struggled to swallow and pushed the basket of food away.

'Sorry, I'm just . . . tired suddenly. Doing the runes that way was super draining. I need to get some sleep.'

By the time I crawled into bed a few minutes later, Bandit was under the covers, and he curled into the crook of my body. 'Rough night?'

'Yes.' I breathed the words. 'The best and worst.'

'Sleep.' Bandit rumbled and his soft purring body soothed some of the cold that had crept into me.

I didn't think I'd be able to sleep. Not after the magic with Typhon. Not after the pain with Fable. But I'd had too many restless nights and the second my eyes shut; I was out cold.

Only to find myself in a nightmare.

Following Opie across an open expanse of a field, a wall of thorns and brambles rose high above her head. She was with her two friends, they were dragging her along.

She didn't want to go. I tried to call out to her, but the words wouldn't come out.

I knew they were up to no good. I knew they weren't really her friends.

I hurried, running barefoot through the field, barely feeling the stones and hard ground. All that mattered was Opie.

The dream twisted around, and we were through the thorn bushes and a ramshackle house was in front of them. I couldn't hear anything, but I could see Opie's mouth open, and she was surely screaming as her 'friends' dragged her up to the door. The place looked . . . haunted.

Tears streamed down Opie's face; I saw her hands flash runes at the other girls but of course . . . nothing happened. My heart broke as I saw her realize the truth of it. That someone had been fooling her all along. That she didn't have the magic that the teachers and Neverthorn had been telling her she had.

I reached for her and then I stood at the door and the other two girls were running away. I didn't hesitate. I threw myself at the door and fell through, spinning through darkness, tumbling down what felt like a hundred feet before I hit the bottom.

A puff of dirt and dust rolled up around me. I lifted my head. Opie lay beside me, as if sleeping, I reached for her, and she sat up.

The space we were in was lit from above, a fiery red gemstone floated far, far above our heads. Opie pointed, her mouth moving. No words.

I took her hand and stood.

The space was dirty, but not empty. Dwimmers sat all around the edges of the room, on their knees. They wore black, their mouths were bound with thick leather straps, but none of them were trying to get the gags off. Their hands flashed the same rune over and over again, one I didn't recognize, their eyes never leaving the walls they sat in front of.

Opie pushed against me, her terror infectious. I dragged her backward, looking for a way out. But nightmares don't work like that. The only way out is to wake up.

A Dwimmer dressed all in dark gray, their face wrapped up so that only the eyes were exposed, approached us, finger pointed at Opie. I stuffed her behind me. Tried to yell, but nothing came out.

Typhon. I needed Typhon.

I spun with Opie and ran from the figures cloaked in the shadows, ran until my lungs were bursting. Hands grabbed at us, yanking us apart. I tried to scream for her, panic filling me.

I jerked awake, gasping. 'Opie.'

The room around me was silent, everyone was still sound asleep, and it looked like I'd only been out cold for an hour at best.

It had seemed so real . . .

Panic crept up the back of my neck, but I forced it down . . . made myself remember how it had felt out there by the river.

I was still stuck here in this sheet storm, but now I knew something I hadn't known before. I wasn't helpless. I had rune magic that was as strong as any Dwimmer out there. Nocta and his men would be coming with the solstice. If I could help the others in House Phoenix access their true potential before the big battle to come, that was all for the better. Because someone had to stop Nocta.

Even if I knew in my heart it wouldn't be me, no matter what Liam said. No matter how much Typhon praised me. I knew that they would never trust Nocta's daughter to face him.

But I could help the others. I could find a way to keep my friends and Opie safe. I had to believe it.

It was the only hope I had left.

20

For the whole rest of the day, it was hard to focus on anything but the nightmare that had left me full of dread. I was so distracted that I got my asterisk kicked in hand-to-hand combat, and Nikita had made me look like a fool yet again in History, no doubt pissed that she could no longer lord it over me that we were paired up. No point when Typhon had bonded himself to me.

To wrap the day up, when Doyenne Hanover asked me to perform a healing rune on the injured foot of a chicken named Maude, she'd ended up buck naked.

Maude, not Doyenne Hanover, thank the gods.

Yep. Instead of fixing the poor bird, my magic had skittered uselessly over her body and ended in an explosion of feathers. I don't know who was more embarrassed, me or Maude.

Now, we were sitting in the last class of the day, and it was somehow even worse than the ones before it.

Blocking runes with Typhon. It was bad enough that I'd had to see him between every class when he came to escort me around like some sort of giant secret service agent. He'd barely even looked at me, clearly distracted himself. And when I'd made an attempt to pick his brain about my strange and disturbing dream, he'd shut me down cold.

'I've got a lot on my plate today, Harlow. Save the therapy session for Fable or Marina.'

So much for our little bonding session by the river.

It was for the best, I reminded myself bleakly. When I

ticked off all the items on my to-do list, I knew I had to just keep going. Learn the runes. Help my friends. Protect Opie.

Nothing else mattered.

'Harlow?'

I looked up to see Fable leaning toward me, her amber eyes wide in question. Trusting me.

Even while I kept a dark secret from her.

'Sorry, what did you say?' I asked, guilt making my stomach roil. Fable mattered. In fact, after only a short time stuck in the same dorm room, the whole House of Phoenix was starting to matter.

Even Gassy Gary.

'I was asking if you wanted to try to block my cat got your tongue rune.'

I glanced around to see the others practicing some blocking spells as Typhon sat facing the wall, head bowed in either sleep or thought.

I shrugged. 'Sure. Let's do it.'

She grinned and tucked a lock of hair behind one ear. Then she took a deep breath and let it out in a rush. Her hands moved swiftly, sending up a light smattering of golden sparks.

I threw up the block rune – the proper way – and a second later, felt my throat close.

Sheet.

Fable blinked at me and leaned close.

'Did it work?' she demanded, hope blazing in her eyes.

I tried to speak, but knew it was futile. When nothing but a husky croak came out, she grinned and clapped her hands together.

'I did it! Yesss!'

'Not sure what you're celebrating, Ms. O'Shanahan.' We both craned our necks to see Typhon towering over us. 'This is Nullifractions class. You're learning how to *block* magic, which neither of you did. Try again.'

He swept back to his desk as Julius shook his head and held up two thumbs as he mouthed a mocking '*Well done . . .*' before following Typhon like the little suck-up he was.

Fable let out a low sigh. 'Doyen Moreno is right. I tried to block a couple runes against Zeed before and couldn't do it. I don't know how we're supposed to succeed in taking down Nocta when we're set up to fail from the very start. Cat got your tongue is great, but it won't save me in a fight.'

The tight sensation in my throat faded and I let out a sigh of relief.

'Let me talk to him. Maybe I can convince him that sooner is better on the whole getting us all out of here and seeing what we can do thing.'

I couldn't just sit back and wait. The sooner I was able to access my full power . . . test its true limits, make sure the others could do the same . . . the sooner we would all be safer from Nocta.

I pushed myself up and marched past my trying-but-frustrated classmates and stopped in front of Typhon's desk, where he sat, facing the wall again.

I kept my tone low, for his ears only. 'I know you said you have a lot going on, but I really think getting us up to speed to fight Nocta ASAP should be priority number one. Especially if you have your eye on someone.' He turned and started to talk but I shushed him before he could even speak. 'Don't brush me off again, Typhon. This is about giving us a fighting chance when Nocta comes knocking. He's already tested the waters. You said it yourself. Time is ticking. We've got to show them what they're capable of. They need to believe in themselves.'

He lifted one dark brow. 'You done?'

I nodded.

'Tonight. Right after dinner.'

I frowned at him suspiciously. 'Seriously?'

'Yes. That's what's been on my plate, Harlow. I needed to come up with a good reason to take you all on a field trip at night because there's no way to hide that you've all left the school at the same time.'

'And you've managed to do that somehow?'

The excitement that roared through me was almost dizzying. Just the thought of all that magic flowing, like electricity only more elemental . . . intoxicating but also necessary. Like water. Like air. Having tasted it now, my whole body pulsed with the need to taste it again. I stared down into Typhon's eyes and tried to focus.

He was speaking. I needed to listen.

'I'll tell Tarquinius I'm taking you all out to do manual labor along with extra instruction that you all desperately need. If he thinks it's a punishment, he won't push back.'

Yeah, perfect. Just what you wanted in the person tasked with the care of hundreds of young people. Ruthlessness with a smidge of cruelty for good measure.

I held my tongue on that and focused on the important thing. We were going to get to leave the Neverthorn wards again and do magic. Real magic.

It was enough to make me forget about yet another awful day and the even more awful dream.

By the time dinner was done, though, I was starting to wonder if Tarquinius hadn't been as amenable as Typhon had hoped. The doyen had been MIA throughout the meal, and the kitchen staff were already collecting the food trays.

'Do you think he changed his mind?' Fable whispered, her face lined with worry.

'No . . .' I poked at a leftover green bean and frowned.

'No, I think he really wants this for us. But he isn't the one in charge here, so who knows what might've happened?'

The words were no sooner out of my mouth than Typhon came striding up to our table, his face a mask of irritation.

'House of Phoenix, toss your trash and meet me at the entrance.'

Fable grinned at me as we both stood.

'Are we in trouble?' Zeed asked, shooting me a nervous glance. 'I really tried in class today. I was even able to block a couple runes, albeit not for long . . .'

I'd risked telling Fable and Bandit but had made them promise to keep the news from the others.

When we got to the front doors of the school a few minutes later, Typhon was waiting.

'Where are we going?' Marina asked, her eyes narrowed suspiciously. 'We're not getting kicked out, are we? Because my grandad will flip out. He was so proud that I was one of the chosen few to get the call back . . .'

'Yeah,' Gary chimed in. 'I think my dad's turned my bedroom into a man cave already.'

'Save the questions and follow me,' Typhon said.

He led the way through the doors and into the cool night air. The Northern Lights weren't on display with the cloud cover, and the full moon had waned, leaving us cloaked in eerie shadows. For about five minutes, we walked in silence. Everyone but Fable and, oddly enough, Phyllis, looked like they were on a march to their death. I wanted to reassure them that everything was okay, but clearly Typhon wanted to keep up the ruse until we were off school grounds in case he was being watched. Phyllis, despite her age, had been keeping up close to the front of the pack from the start, but had slowly wound up toward the back, near us.

'If this is what I think it is, there's nothing to be nervous about. In fact, it's a long time coming. They had no choice back then, but –'

She broke off, pulling the black shawl more closely around her shoulders, and I stared at her.

'But what?'

'Nothing. Just the ramblings of an old lady.'

'You know something.'

It wasn't a question. It was clear, and for the life of me, I couldn't figure out why I hadn't seen it before. A woman in her sixties who had come to Neverthorn as a child and never left. If there were things to know, mysteries to be revealed, who would have more intel on them than Phyllis?

And here I'd been trying to find some alone time so I could head back to the library . . .

'Phyllis. Please. It could help so much if we had all the information. I'm flying blind here . . .'

She took a look around as if to see if anyone else was close enough to hear. 'We haven't been failing, Harlow. I think we've been hamstrung. Intentionally, in the beginning. I think Doyen Moreno is going to help us stop –'

'Students,' Typhon called, bringing our merry band of misfits and Phyllis's admission to a halt. 'Entering the woods, we need to be aware of several things. First and foremost, there are creatures residing within that have the potential to do us harm. If you listen to me, you will be safe. Got it?'

We all mumbled a yes, but Zeed started fidgeting, shifting from foot to foot. Typhon leaned around Zeed to make direct eye contact with me. 'If you listen to me, you will be safe,' he repeated just for me, his voice lower. Softer. More lethal.

'I said okay,' I shot back, narrowing my eyes.

'Not to question you, sir, but are we sure this is a good idea?' Zeed asked. 'With all the Nocta stuff, shouldn't we stay closer to the school?'

Typhon stared him down until Zeed looked like he'd shrunk five inches. 'The rule of two is still being observed as you are all here with your partners. Not to mention, you are with me on what will be an instructional field trip.'

Zeed's Adam's apple bobbed. 'Yes, of course, sir.'

'Any other questions?'

His query was met with silence. We might not have the whole rune-making thing down yet, but we weren't stup—

'I did have one more question, sir,' Zeed said. 'Is this . . . is this the Dark Wood?'

Typhon didn't bother trying to hide his impatience. 'It is.'

The other students gasped and started murmuring to each other as I turned to Fable.

'What's the Dark Wood?'

She shook her head, suddenly looking really nervous.

'It's where the shadow creatures hide. I know you weren't at Neverthorn for very long, but I can promise you, this wasn't here when I was going to school the first time around. We all thought it was a myth. Like some old lady's house in an Unlit neighborhood that everyone thought was haunted, you know?'

'Like other areas of the island, it's kept shielded from your view as a way to keep nosy students from exploring where they shouldn't,' Typhon explained. 'I'm allowing you to see it now as it suits our needs. All done with the questions?'

But he didn't wait for responses as he led the way into the thickest part of the treeline, and we all followed. Like good little lambs, hopefully not to slaughter.

The second we stepped into the woods, the thicket of trees choked out most of the waning daylight and the temperature seemed to drop ten degrees. The croaking of toads, leaves that had fallen to the ground crackling under the footsteps of creatures I didn't even want to consider, were the only noises.

'Gotta admit, I used to live in the woods, and this is a

little creepy, even for me,' Bandit said, pressing closer to my calves.

Ahead, a dim light flickered as Typhon lit the way with an illuminating rune.

'Not far now, just a couple hundred yards.'

It felt like way further as we pushed through the thick vegetation, just waiting for . . . something to leap out and grab one of us like a snack off a conveyor belt.

By the time we all stepped into the clearing, I was light-headed from lack of oxygen, and I realized I'd been holding my breath the last few feet.

Typhon tossed the light he had created into the center of the space and stood beside it. 'We are here because this is one of the few places that the school's protective wards cannot reach.'

Zeed's eyes went wide, and Marina stepped closer to give his shoulder a supportive squeeze.

'To this point, I've had you all wrapped in a protective rune of my own. In order to show you why I brought you all here, though, I need to let it fall away. I will be within view of you at all times and you have my solemn vow that there is nothing in these woods bigger or badder than me.'

Despite my nerves, something in his tone sent an ache deep in my belly as I tried not to think about just how big . . . just how bad he could be.

Goddess, I was on a path of self-destruction if I kept up that line of thought.

'If you're sure you can protect us all . . .' Ellie said, joining Marina in giving Zeed a pat of reassurance.

Typhon didn't bother to answer.

We formed a loose circle around him, and he fashioned a quick rune with his left hand. There was a ripple through the air, a feeling like wings brushing over my face, and then it was gone.

'Hold your bracer arms out.' Typhon said.

Everyone did, and he went around the circle, whipping off a rune over each one, until each of the bracers was on the ground. Mine included.

No one said anything, but more than one set of eyes widened.

'Now I can explain what we're doing here. Actually, maybe it would be quicker just to show you.' He turned to me and cocked his head, something like a smile playing at his firm lips. 'Harlow?'

Butterfly wings beat against my chest as I stepped forward to join him.

'Just . . . anything?'

'Anything you've been taught to do the proper way,' he said.

I chewed on the inside of my cheek as I thought of some of the runes we had been working on over the past couple of weeks. A firefly flitted past, and I lifted my hand, settling on a gathering and duplicating spell. I let my breath out in a whoosh and forced my fingers to make the shapes required. A slash. A circular flourish. A pinching of my first two fingers and my thumb.

Nothing.

'You've got the first two backward,' Typhon called. 'Flip them around and try again.'

I bit my lower lip, frowning in concentration. Then I repeated the rune, following Typhon's directives. Suddenly tiny lights flickered toward me. First a few, then a few dozen. I could hear the gasps of my housemates around me as the tiny creatures illuminated the night like fairy lights on a Christmas tree.

'Holy crap, Harlow. That's awesome . . .' a low voice whispered.

I was too focused on the magic to reply. Watching as the metallic crimson sparks skittered off my fingertips. Feeling the power down to my bones.

All the confusion and clumsiness that I felt in class was nowhere to be found. Just like the night with Typhon at the river, I was *free*.

Typhon spoke softly behind me. 'There were some spells that were put on the House of Phoenix students due to events of the past. They were supposed to have been removed, but my theory is that they weren't. Not fully, at least.'

'I knew it,' Phyllis muttered.

'With your bracers removed, the spell used to mute your skills is off. At least as best as I can tell,' Typhon continued. 'So far, we've only got Harlow as proof of my theory. Who wants to go next?'

Every hand shot up with the exception of Phyllis's. Typhon beckoned Fable toward us first, and she rushed to join us.

'Go on. Any rune you're sure you know the proper movements for, even if you've failed at it in the past.'

She scrunched her eyes tight and then lifted her hands. Within a few short movements, I wanted to let out a whoop. It wasn't just me. It was working for Fable, too. The magic burst from her fingers and an instant later, the fireflies gathered in front of us began to move in sync. Left to right, then forward and back, then in a wild and dizzying dance.

'Awesome, Fable!'

'How does it feel?' Gary called softly.

'It's . . . amazing.' Fable's throat was clogged with unshed tears, and I almost leaned in to hug her.

Typhon waved the others forward, encouraging them to try their hand at it. By the time Zeed stepped up, it was like some sort of nerdy, magical rave. Fable and I handled the light show while Marina's magic had the trees waving their branches like arms, conducting Gary's orchestra of crunching leaves and whistling blades of grass, and Ellie's tiny little tornadoes that whipped around us. Caterina had the night birds swooping around us, singing. As for Phyllis, she tapped her toe, grinning like a fool, though she used no magic that I could see.

'Oh no,' Fable whispered, pulling my attention from the matriarch of our little group.

'What's the matter?'

She jerked her chin toward Zeed, who stood a little off to the side, his fingers flying as he tried to join in. Like most of our magic before we had our bracers off, it was nothing but a smattering of sparks. Enough for a short burst or a quick parlor trick before fizzling out.

I was about to go over to Zeed, but Typhon was already heading toward him. He was only a few feet away when he stopped short and wheeled around, hands high. The music, the lightshow, the dancing fireflies . . .

It all stopped as an inky darkness closed over us and my heart stuttered to a halt.

'Don't move,' he hissed.

I wondered briefly if peeing my pants would be considered moving but decided to keep the question to myself.

He whipped off a shielding rune and let out a breath. 'We're fine. It's alright.'

But even as he spoke, the sound of footsteps on leaves . . . big footsteps, had me shivering.

'What was that?' Fable asked, moving closer to press against my side.

'Wolf,' Bandit said, lifting onto all fours and sniffing the air.

The noise grew louder and a pair of glittering, red eyes came into view just a few yards from where we stood.

Wolf my ass. It was frucking massive. The size of a Chevy, its teeth bared and gleaming.

'What should we do?' Zeed demanded through gritted teeth.

'We're doing it,' Typhon said. 'He smells us on the wind, but he can't see or hear us anymore. Once he's satisfied his curiosity, he'll go away.'

I trusted Typhon's word on that, but there was no denying that all of us, including him, let out massive sighs of relief when the animal finally loped off in search of easier prey.

'Alright, then. I think I've made my point. You are all far stronger than you've been led to believe. Including you, Zeed. I think nerves got the best of you tonight, and if not for our visitor, you'd have come through. We'll try again another time.'

Wow. That was . . . nice? I almost asked him who he was and what he'd done with the real Typhon.

He turned to the rest of us. 'As for my theory about the muting wards, I'm still working out what to do with that knowledge. For the time being, let's keep it between us.'

Meaning he didn't know who could be trusted here at Neverthorn.

'What I'd like to do for now so you can at least start to really get down to work is put a charm on your bracers. You'll still be wearing them, so no one should be the wiser. I just want to loosen them enough to get them away from your skin . . . create like a magical barrier so you can access your magic better. Everyone okay with that?'

We all nodded as one. Reluctance in every move, we each put the bracers back on, and stuck our arms out a second time.

Typhon started with Zeed and moved down the line, throwing a quick and elegant rune to loosen our bracers. He spoke as he did, not missing a beat.

'I also need to approach O'Connor and see how something like this might have affected your potential Quirks.

Maybe next time, he can join us. But at least we've got a starting point.'

I was last to go, and I couldn't deny it. Even though the change was subtle on a physical level, mentally, I felt . . . freed when the leather came away from my skin. Like I was born again.

Typhon held my gaze, and I knew he could sense how I felt. I couldn't help but wonder if I'd imagined the graze of his thumb against my wrist as he pulled away . . .

'Let's head back and get a good night's sleep.'

Now that the danger of being eviscerated by the world's biggest carnivore had passed, everyone began chatting about their newfound skills. For the rest of the walk back to the school, they talked about runes they wanted to try next time. Zeed kept to himself and as much as I wanted to give him another pep talk, I knew if I'd been in his position, that would be the last thing I wanted.

We stepped through the front doors a short while later, exhausted but most of us giddy with our newfound knowledge, and I set my sights on Phyllis as she headed off toward her quarters alone.

I'd learned more than just some new magic tonight. I'd also realized that Phyllis was the key to a lot of things. She'd figured out exactly what had been happening with the blocks put on House Phoenix before Typhon had spilled the beans, and I couldn't imagine that was all she knew. It was time to spend some one-on-one time with Phyllis and get to know more about her . . .

And more about the secrets that were hiding here at Neverthorn Academy.

21

It took all of my willpower to stop myself from stalking poor Phyllis night and day once I'd gotten it in my head to talk to her about Neverthorn's secrets. I'd asked her more than once if we could meet and have a chat, but she put me off each time, promising she'd let me know when her schedule opened up.

I was giving her three days before I cracked open her schedule all on my own.

By dinner on the second day, I was almost coming out of my skin with impatience.

Fable, Ellie and Caterina sat to my right, reading over advanced rune-casting charts. Since the night in the Dark Wood, everyone in House Phoenix had re-dedicated themselves, throwing every effort at getting better. Faster.

Even though the runes weren't working like they did in the woods, they were *working*. Aside from Zeed, we were actually making magic, even if it was weak. And, as Typhon pointed out, it was building muscle memory.

'Learn it now, get fast at it, and when the moment comes, your magic and the runes won't fail you.'

Gary, Zeed and Ross were on the other side of the table, working on battle strategy, taking a look at old skirmishes between Nocta and Heronius, doing what they could to find a better strategy.

'Here.' Zeed stuck his finger into the paper. 'That's where I would stay. If Heronius had shored up his defenses, Nocta would not have been able to get through.'

I leaned over the table. Zeed had a point. But the images on the paper were continuing to move. Battle Strategy was actually a pretty interesting class – and I wasn't half bad at it. We were given blank sheets and a sheet of what looked like stickers of little Heronius, Nocta and army characters. We placed them on the paper and tapped the upper right corner. The battle played out then, based on where we thought the strategy was best. Each sheet was numbered so Doyenne Storm would know how many tries it took us to get it right.

Before Zeed had even hit go, I could see the hole in his plan. I almost felt guilty pointing it out, given his struggles with rune making, but pretending wasn't going to help him improve.

'Actually, with the way Nocta attacks from unexpected directions, I think your little Heronius is going to get it up the asterisk.'

Sure enough, within a few skirmishes, the Heronius sticker had been slashed up, the Nocta sticker waved his little hands in victory, and the paper burned to a crisp with a flash.

Zeed groaned. 'Doyenne Storm wants an unburnt battle strategy by tomorrow.'

Ross and Gary were in the same boat. They'd settled in, following Zeed's lead. Not a terrible idea, he was a smart dude – if he could allow himself to not be so tied up by what he thought he should do, and rather just do what he had to do.

I shrugged. 'Keep trying. Just . . . don't be so rigid, Zeed. I get that you have an engineer brain, and it's brilliant. But you gotta think outside the box. Nocta doesn't do things . . . normal.'

He frowned at me. 'Wait. You're done?'

I shrugged. I didn't want to rub it in that I had the assignment done on my first pass.

Zeed made a gimme motion with his hand. 'Let me see.'

I sighed and pulled the battle sheet out. My sheet had Heronius standing in the middle of the battlefield, fists in the air with his victory. I thought it more than a little gruesome that they were still using the dead hero as a moving sticker.

Zeed took the sheet from me. 'Holy sheet. You got it on the first try?'

Everyone at the table turned to me. 'Well . . . lucky strike I guess.'

His eyes narrowed. 'Harlow. That isn't a thing with battle strategy. How did you do it?'

I squirmed a little in my seat. 'I just tried to think about what Nocta might do, you know, if I was him. How would I attack, how would I set up my army. Then I built in Heronius's attack off that.'

Caterina leaned closer. 'You tried to think like an evil wizard? And you figured it out?'

Gods. This was uncomfortable. 'I want that perfect score in at least one class.' I tried to laugh it off.

Caterina took my paper and looked it over. 'That's brilliant, Harlow. Honest. Freaky, but brilliant.'

'Lo-lo!' Opie saved me as she ran over.

I wrapped an arm around her. She shot a look across at Zeed and a quick blush settled over her cheeks.

He grinned. 'Hey Opie, you haven't come to visit our table lately. Getting too cool for us?'

'Oh! No, of course not!' Her blush deepened.

He was way too old for more than a puppy-love crush, but she could have worse taste in boys. Zeed was one of the good ones. He motioned for Opie to put her hand out.

'Here. I remembered that you said you were collecting rocks of all colors, right?'

Opie's eyes widened as he dropped a solid, smooth black stone into her hand. 'Wow, where did you get that?'

'Picked it up when I was out for a walk in the courtyard.' He gave her a wink and she all but swooned. Damn, he could turn on the charm when he wanted. But also, damn, it was sweet. He earned some serious points with me for that move.

'Thank you,' Opie whispered, and then she was gone, whatever reason she'd come over melted away under the heat of her raging hormones.

Fable reached over and touched Zeed's hand. 'That was incredibly sweet.'

He shrugged, two spots of color blooming on his cheekbones. 'I'd bring you a rock too, if you wanted.'

They were staring at each other and damned if I couldn't almost see the sparks between them, as if they were their own kind of magic.

'Um. Yeah.' I scooped up my stuff. 'Time to go.'

Fable and Zeed remained, but the rest of us were gone and headed up to the dorm. As we walked, I saw two Rune-coats coming from the Sage's office.

Interesting. Were they checking in on him, or checking in on their man, Liam?

Marina echoed my thoughts. 'Do you think Liam will be coming back any time soon? I want to try and find my Quirk.'

Murmurs of agreement filtered through our group as Ross opened the door to the dorm and let us all in.

As I was about to step into the room, something whipped by my head, hit the stone wall and shattered. I dropped to a crouch and flung a rune in the direction the airborne missile had come from. One of my own runes, cast on instinct. I felt a twinge of despair and hoped it didn't damage the weave.

My rune slammed into the corner of the hall. Before I

thought better, I was running after whoever had thrown the . . . rock? What was it?

Didn't matter. The others were right behind me.

'What the hell was that?' Ross snarled as we raced around the corner and down the stairs that led to the sixth level.

Draconell's domain.

I caught a glimpse of a bulky body and shaved head on the stairwell below me. Julius's sheety Draconell buddy.

'Mortan, I know it was you!'

His laugh reached back to us, and all that did was speed me up. I hit their floor and Mortan wasn't quite inside his dorm.

I spun a rune faster than I think I'd ever done inside the school. Simple, but if it worked . . . so effective.

Gary, Ross, Marina, and Caterina slid to a stop just behind me. No doubt Ellie had stayed behind, she'd made it clear she would only fight if she had to.

Mortan cast a rune, the same one that Tarquinius had been throwing at us, only it was laced with something more. A fair bit of flame set to slam into us.

The five of us moved almost as one, casting a rune of blocking at the exact same time. Our collective magic filled the space, the runes slamming together and coalescing into one in sparks of red, gold, yellow, orange, and green. The runes we'd spun, and our magic, seemed to catch hold of one another, and expanded to fill the hallways, blocking the shove Mortan had sent, sure. But also . . . pressing on the walls of the hallway until the brick and mortar began to fall.

'Sheet,' Gary muttered. 'Time to go.'

We ran back the way we had come, as the walls and hallways seemed to explode at the seams.

Back up on the seventh floor, we kept running until we hit the dorm, and all but scrambled to get inside. Neverthorn had all sorts of spells set into the stone, it would repair itself, so I wasn't worried about Draconell losing their dorms. Then again, it would serve them right if they had to sleep down in the mess hall for a night or two.

Adrenaline was coursing, and it was Marina that started it. Giggling. 'Did you see the look on his face? That was frucking brilliant, Harlow!'

'What happened?' Ellie asked. 'What did I miss?'

We filled her in quickly until she was crying with laughter. 'Oh, gods, I wish I'd seen that!'

Marina fist bumped me, and I started to laugh. 'Did you see the rune though? How it grabbed hold of all our castings at once?'

Caterina nodded. 'I've never heard of anything like that. But the magic . . . it connected us. It was almost as good as the Dark Wood. I felt . . . like I found my home.'

'I'm sorry I missed it,' Ellie pouted a little. 'I'll have to come running next time.'

The others went still, even though I could see we were all still vibrating. Grinning, we looked at each other. 'We tell Zeed and Fable, but no one else,' I said.

'What about Phyllis?' Gary asked. 'Should we tell her?'

I shook my head. 'I don't know. Maybe. Let's sit on it for now.'

Because as much as I wanted to believe that Phyllis was one of us, I wasn't sure. She had all this knowledge – the trip to the Dark Wood showed me that – and she'd kept it to herself.

Did it mean she was against us? I didn't think that was the case. But to be fair. I didn't really know what to think.

Almost as if we'd called her, the door banged open and Phyllis stood there, hands on her hips. 'Please tell me you fools weren't on the sixth floor?'

Which set us all into fits of laughter.

Tears streaked my face, I was laughing so hard, hell, I could barely breathe. Phyllis rolled her eyes and slammed the door in our faces.

Every time I thought we'd gotten the laughter out of us; it started up again. The thing was, I don't think any of us wanted it to end. For the first time since I didn't know when, I truly felt like I was with family.

This was how being with your house in Neverthorn should have been. Laughter. Having each other's backs. Friends that were so much more.

Suddenly my tears of laughter shifted, and I was sobbing. A split second later, Marina, Caterina, and Ellie had wrapped me up in their arms and I was hugging them back.

'What just happened?' Ross whispered. 'I thought we were having a good time.'

But then he and Gary joined in on the group hug. And when Zeed and Fable opened the door a few minutes later, we dragged them in too.

And for just a little while, the world was good. It was right. And I was exactly where I needed to be.

22

'Ms. Daygon.'

I heard the words, the voice, but didn't register that they were talking to me. Until –

'Harlow.'

The growl of my name drew me up short. That and the hand on my elbow. I looked up to the owner of the hand. Typhon stood behind me, eyes narrowed. 'What are you up to?'

'I'm not always up to something, you know.'

He did not let go of me. 'Where are you going? Your dorms are the other direction, up the stairs.' He started to tug me in the opposite direction of Phyllis's quarters, but I planted my feet.

'Not all from the House of Phoenix are in the dorm, Typhon.'

'So, you're going to see Phyllis. Why?'

'I want to spend some time with her.'

'Nope. I don't buy it.'

I sighed and put my hands on my hips, finally freeing my arm from his hold. 'Maybe it's for help with remedial runes.'

'Bullshit.'

Fruck me. I shrugged. 'You want to sit outside her room and wait for me, that's on you.'

I turned away and started down the long corridor, Typhon falling into step beside me. A few students were still out, wandering the halls. But by eight, everyone had to be in their dorms. As if the whole rule of two wasn't bad enough. I was starting to wonder if this was a school or a daycare . . .

'When are they going to lift that ban on being out past eight, anyway? Isn't this supposed to be a safe place?' I trailed a hand along the ancient wall, feeling the nicks and grooves of centuries past.

'I'm not able to discuss it.'

'Of course you're not.'

His hand brushed my arm a second time. 'Not *able* to, Harlow.'

My feet slowed and I looked sideways at him. 'Rune gagged?'

He didn't nod, but he didn't shake his head either. A non-response from him was as good as a yes in my book.

Well sheet.

'But trust that there is a reason you need to stay in your dorm tonight, even more than any other night before.'

Tonight. So, did that mean the threat would be over tomorrow? And . . .

'Why isn't it a problem during the day?'

He just stared at me and my head spun with all the possibilities and my heart clenched.

'Is Opie safe?'

'In her room tonight, yes.' He motioned for me to continue onward down the hall. 'Not with you pulling her out at every damn opportunity.'

Two more turns and we were at Phyllis's room. 'Are you really going to sit out here and wait for me?'

He stepped back as he gave me a curt nod, his long coat swirling out and around him. 'You have thirty minutes before I come in and drag you out.'

Thirty minutes.

I knocked on the door, and Phyllis called out for me to enter. I opened the door and stepped through, fully expecting a dorm like the one we were in. Bare, with just the necessities. Maybe a few clothes hanging up.

Her room was nothing like ours. There was a thick, deep purple rug covering the stone floor, and I immediately kicked my boots off so I could let my feet sink into the plushness. Like standing on a cloud. The luxury didn't stop there. A small kitchen was to my left, with an old-fashioned wood-burning stove, and a fridge that looked brand new if the gleam on it was any indication.

The room itself spilled open to a fireplace that was crackling merrily. There were books and knickknacks scattered all over the living area: statues, stones, a pile of feathers, a bundle of rope, layers of material, a few sharp-looking . . .

'Is that a sword?' I pointed at the handle that was sticking out from under some of the material. Ornate, gold and set with blue and black jewels. Had to be worth at least a million on the black market. I couldn't help it; I might have reached for it.

'None of your business.' Phyllis flicked a hand, and the material smoothed over the very-distinct-pretty-sure-it's-a-sword handle. She narrowed her eyes at me, tugging the black robe she wore more tightly around her waist. 'What are you doing here, Harlow?'

I blinked and looked away from the pile of material. 'I've been wanting to talk to you and –'

'And I've been busy,' she reminded me with a frown.

'I know. And I'm sorry, but I just really need to talk to you.'

She must've sensed my desperation because her expression softened.

'You're here now, so talk.'

'I came to ask you about . . . rune work,' I managed. 'I've thought on it since –'

'Since the glade in the Dark Wood.' She bobbed her head with a sigh. 'Come on, then. Have a sit down. I saw you watching me.'

I followed her into the sitting area, near the fire. The warmth sank into me. I hadn't realized just how cold I was. The rain and temperature dip had gotten deep into my bones. I rubbed my arms and sunk into the plush chair. 'You got some good digs here.'

She waved a hand through the air, as if waving off a bad smell. 'Comes with seniority.'

'I guess being here for so long has its perks.' No point in dancing around the subject. I dove right in. 'You weren't surprised, in the Dark Wood, when our magic started working . . .'

She fussed at her silver hair, which was still pulled into a tight bun.

'Nope. Not surprised,' she admitted finally.

'You knew that we were being muted?' I asked. Not accusing, just curious.

'Rune gagged. Are you familiar with it?'

I nodded. 'Typhon is rune gagged as well. There is something going on he can't speak about. A threat . . .'

Her eyebrows shot up. 'On a first-name basis, huh?'

I let the comment slide by without a response.

'House of Phoenix has to stop Nocta, Phyllis. You've been around a long time. You've seen what he's capable of. Do we have any chance?'

She flashed a rune of gathering and a teacup floated to her from across the way, off the table. 'Well, I think at least one of us does.'

Her eyes shot to me, and I snorted.

'Whoa, I'm no one's hero, Phyllis. I will do what I can to help. After that, I will leave, take Opie with me and get gone from this place —'

'Fool yourself all you want. I see you helping Fable, Marina *and* Zeed. Even Gary, Ross and the other two that are joined at the hip.' Her smile wasn't soft. But it was knowing. 'They look up to you.'

I thought about the day before, how the magic had drawn us all together, how *right* it had felt.

'But it's you who we should be looking to for guidance. You've been here longer than almost everyone except Tarquinius and Doyenne Parunah.'

I looked at the clock that sat above her fireplace, knowing Typhon would be busting his way in to drag me out before I knew it.

'Did you . . . did you go to school when Nocta . . . was here?'

Her face absolutely drained of color, and I thought she wouldn't answer me.

'Yes. Yes, I did.'

My face felt hot, but I forced myself to continue. 'Did you know him at all? I mean, I'm not saying were you friends, but anything you know could help –'

Phyllis stood up. 'I think it's time you go.'

'I'm sorry, Phyll, I didn't –'

'Don't call me that,' she muttered, cheeks going chalk white. 'My name is Phyllis. Now please, I'm very tired and I need to rest.'

I turned to go, but in my rush to leave, I bumped into a pile of shoeboxes in front of the door. The one on top teetered and toppled over, spilling black and white photos all over the floor.

'I'm so sorry,' I murmured, flushed with guilt at upsetting her and then making a mess. 'I'll pick them up –'

'No! Just go!'

I was already bending over. 'It will just take me a sec.'

But I froze in place as my fingers hovered above an image. A group of teenagers, arms draped around one another's shoulders, wide grins on their faces. At the front of the pack?

A young Phyllis tucked tight beneath the arm of none other than my father. Nicodemus Oliphant.

I searched the floor and caught sight of several more. One of Phyllis and four other girls, another of the group again, and one of just the two of them. Phyllis and Nicodemus.

They looked so young. Carefree. Happy.

'Y-you knew him? You were friends with Nocta?'

'I thought we were . . .' Tears filled her eyes as she grabbed my elbow and pulled me up. 'But he killed the boy I loved. Good night, Harlow.'

Phyllis all but shoved me out of the room, slamming the door behind me.

'Fifteen minutes? Pissed her off too, did you?' Typhon gave a grim shake of his head. 'You have a talent for it.'

I didn't answer him, I couldn't. I just had to get out of there before my brain exploded and I said something I shouldn't.

'No running away,' Typhon said, his hands grabbing both my forearms before I could bolt. 'No running, Harlow. What's going on?'

I didn't know what to say – so I just shook my head.

'Fuck.' He all but dragged me along, through the halls and up a set of stairs. Through a door and then I was in a room I didn't recognize. Draped in deep blues and grays, it was a masculine space and smelled like Typhon. A moment later a glass was being shoved into my hand, and I tipped the whiskey up and straight down my throat. It burned and I coughed, but it helped. Like a slap to the face, it snapped me out of the shock.

'What did you say to her?'

'I-I asked a question.' I clutched the glass. 'And the answer was unexpected.'

The question that remained? Was what Phyllis told me *true*? Or was she lying? Were she and Nocta still friends? Could she be his mole here on the inside?

'No.' I whispered to myself and turned my back on him. 'I don't know if I can tell you.'

'You don't trust me.'

'Can I have some more whiskey?'

He came over with the bottle and poured it for me. 'That bad?'

'It could be. Or it could be something that . . . that doesn't matter now. I don't want to give up a secret that isn't mine.'

Especially given my own secret. How hypocritical would it be for me to throw Phyllis under the bus for being friends with Nocta fifty years ago when he was my frucking *father*?

'Ask yourself this, Harlow.' Typhon swirled his glass, the amber liquid rippling. 'Will it keep Opie safe to keep the secret, or to spill it?'

I glared at him. 'That's dirty pool.'

He shrugged, his eyes locked on mine, holding me in place. 'It's my job to protect everyone here, as much as I possibly can – a fact that I've repeated multiple times. And that means digging out secrets at times.'

What would I do for Opie? Because if Phyllis was working for Nocta, as a mole, then she might have helped him get into Neverthorn. Opie could very well be in danger of being hurt, or even killed.

The answer was simple. Anything. Even break the trust of someone who I liked.

'Don't tell Tarquinius,' I said.

'I can't promise you that.'

I shook my head. 'Then I can't tell you. Take me back to my room.'

He closed the distance between us, and I backed up. He followed, physically driving me all the way across the room until my back hit the far wall.

I was trapped.

He leaned in closer. 'If the secret is enough to make you need help overcoming the shock, then you know that you need to tell me. Why are you being stubborn with something that is obviously important?'

'Because she is my housemate. And I like her. And some secrets should be kept, especially if they don't matter anymore.'

Especially if they weren't your fault.

His eyes blazing, he leaned impossibly close. 'But if that secret is something that will hurt people, then I need to know.'

'Prove to me I can trust you then!' I snapped, the whiskey hitting me and making my eyes do stupid things like get watery. 'Promise me you won't tell Tarquinius!' I was pinned to the wall, his hands on either side of me as we yelled at each other. I swallowed hard and tried again, more softly this time. 'Promise.'

His body pinned mine in place so I could feel his every breath, see every emotion flicker through his eyes.

'Then you will give me something in return, to prove I can trust *you*,' he said. 'A trade.'

'I have nothing –'

'Promise me you won't try to sneak out any longer. And I'll keep Phyllis's secret no matter what it is.'

Now that was a sheety deal.

The smell of whiskey was all that was between us. 'Is it a deal?'

I should have said no. He stepped back and I blew out a breath as he twisted his hands into a rune that I didn't know.

The spell floated between us.

'I promise not to speak the secret that belongs to Phyllis.' His words came to life and were spun into the spell that hovered between us.

Thinking fast . . . I started to speak. 'I promise not to sneak out . . . unless one of our lives depends on it.'

244

He growled.

The spell broke like a glass shattering, digging little flecks into my skin across my clavicle; it felt as if a shooting star had left behind its trail on my skin. I reached up and touched the small indents even as they began to smooth.

Typhon had the same mark across his chest. 'Satisfied?'

'What happens if one of us breaks the vow?'

'The other will know.' He shrugged. 'Tell me what Phyllis said.'

'It wasn't what she said.' I rubbed a hand over the smattering of stars on my skin, wanting stupidly to see if his marks felt the same. 'It's what I saw.'

He waited, I drew a breath and still even with the promise I wasn't sure.

'They were friends,' I blurted out. 'And based on the pictures in her room, maybe even best friends.'

Typhon speared a hand through his dark hair and let out a low hiss. He was silent as he walked over to the small bar and poured a third drink.

'Harlow, if that's the truth, she could be working for Nocta. Or at the very least possibly giving him information if they are in contact.'

'I know!'

Typhon looked over his shoulder at me. 'This is . . . you have to release me from the vow. I have to tell Tarquinius.'

'He was the Sage of the school when they were in class together. Surely, he already knows about their connection.' I shook my head. 'And besides, she hates Nocta now. He killed someone she loved, just like almost everyone else in my house.'

'That's what she tells you. What if she's the one that let Nocta's men in? What if she's trying to set up the House of Phoenix to die? What if she is the enemy?'

I shook my head. 'I don't think she is.'

'You don't know that.'

What I did know was that I wasn't about to accuse a woman of treachery without knowing for sure. How would I have felt if Fable or Zeed, or even worse, Typhon, did the same to me because I shared the same blood as Nocta?

All I could do was shake my head and curse my whiskey-soaked mind that I'd spilled the beans in the first place.

'I won't release you from your promise. Not without proof that she's actually done something wrong.'

He threw the glass at the wall, and it shattered, like the spell across my skin. Only this time there was nothing but an indent where he smashed it.

I spun and was out the door, headed straight for my own dorm. I could feel him behind me, but I didn't slow my pace as I bolted for the stairs, climbing them two and three at a time. It had been a long, emotional day, and I just needed some time alone. A luxury that was becoming rarer and rarer these days.

'Harlow!' he called sharply from a few yards behind me as I reached the House of Phoenix door.

But I just pushed my way inside and slammed it shut behind me.

23

I leaned against the door to my dorm for a long moment to catch my breath. Why was it that every time I was around that man for more than a few minutes, he found a way to steal it, one way or another?

'Geez,' Fable said, letting the book she'd been reading fall to her side as she sat up. 'Did you get chased by a ghost or something?'

I shot a glance to my other housemates, who were all gathered around Gary's bunk with a pile of playing cards between them, paying us no mind. Caterina threw her cards into the pile. 'I win!' They all groaned and started dealing out again.

'Nope. I'm . . . I'm fine. Just really tired.' I shook my head and made a beeline for my own bed, where Bandit lay curled up tight. For someone who hated lying to people I cared about, I sure was getting a lot of practice lately. But there was no point in telling Fable about my suspicions. After all, they were nothing more than that. Suspicions.

'Where were you? They made an announcement right after you left dinner that we had to be back in our quarters by dark. Some safety drill or something. I was actually starting to get worried about you.'

'I had to talk to Ty—' I broke off and swallowed hard, 'Doyen Moreno about something.'

Her eyes lit up and she leaned closer. 'Is he planning another field trip for us?'

It had been all my roommates had been able to talk about since the other night. Everyone except Zeed, who had been uncharacteristically quiet and withdrawn. I peered over at him to find that hadn't changed. While the others laughed and carried on about their game of Uno, he seemed to be in his own world. There in body, but somewhere else in spirit.

I made a mental note to talk to Typhon about it in private.

'Why do you smell weird?' Bandit mumbled with a yawn.

My skin prickled as Fable stared at me. 'Harlow Daygon . . . have you been drinking?'

It was like someone had cut the speakers off at the exact right moment, because the entire room went silent.

'Holy sheet,' Marina blurted, tossing her cards on Zeed's bed as she faced me and Fable. 'Did you manage to smuggle booze into this place?'

'Please say yes,' Zeed added, suddenly much more engaged than I'd seen him in days. 'The stress is literally killing me. I could drink a whole bottle of . . . anything right now.'

'No!' I shot back, suddenly panicked as I tried to think of another lie. *What a tangled web we weave . . .* 'Mrs. Wickersham had a bottle out for the brandy cream sauce she made tonight, and I took a couple swigs. Medicinal, of course,' I added with what I hoped was a convincing grin followed by a wink.

Marina frowned. 'Bummer.' A few seconds later, her face lit with fresh hope as she eyed me speculatively. 'I overheard Elmwood talking to Tarquinius. She was saying that, since all has been quiet since the whole Nocta attack, it would be best to get back to normal. They are going to end the rule of two and move on, business as usual. Tarquinius said there was one more thing they had to deal with, and we'd be in the clear. They aren't worried about Nocta as he's been spotted near Heathermoor again. Samhain is next weekend.' She unfolded her long legs and rose to stand. 'I'm sick of being cooped up. My brother told me there's this fairy circle hidden somewhere on the island. That if you find it, they might even come out and play. You snag a bottle of that brandy, and we sneak out for some fun.'

With nearly a dozen pairs of hopeful eyes on me, I was loath to say no. Especially when it would be so out of character.

'A couple of you are underage. I don't want to break the law.'

Ellie, who was the quietest of the bunch, even piped in. 'Weren't you literally a professional cat burglar?'

Initially, I'd told them I'd done odd jobs, but as we grew closer, I'd come clean. Now I wanted to bite my tongue off for ever sharing that with them. But luckily, I was armed and ready. Using a line I'd used a dozen times with my runaways, I shrugged. 'I'm not a role model. I'm a cautionary tale. Do as I say, not as I do. Besides, what if something happens to one of you? That's on me.'

'Well, we're going whether you join us or not,' Zeed shot back as he crossed his arms over his chest.

The others nodded in agreement, and Marina grinned. 'Yeah. How bad would you feel if we went without you, and one of us got hurt?'

'How bad would *you* feel if I ratted you out right now, and instead of doing something fun, you were all on lockdown for Samhain?' I countered.

A bluff.

And damn them, they knew it.

'Didn't you once tell me that the only thing lower than a buddy frucker was a snitch?' Fable asked, eyes narrowed.

Et tu, Fable?

They'd backed me into a corner.

'Fine. I'll make you a deal. If the rule of two has been revoked, and there are no other incidents between now and Samhain, we can sneak out to find the fairy circle.' The room erupted into cheers.

Marina headed over to my bunk and held out a pinky.

'Deal.'

For the next couple of hours, I tried to read beside Fable while the others talked and played their game. But when the clock struck midnight, another hour after that, I was still wide awake. Tossing. Turning. Thinking.

Which was why I was the only one who heard the soft, pitiful voice calling outside our door.

'Help. Please . . . help me.'

I stared at the door for a long moment, straining to hear over the sounds of snoring all around me.

And there it was again. A second, weak cry.

'Please . . . help. Someone.'

Sheet.

I scuttled to the edge of the bed, careful not to disturb a drooling Bandit, and rolled off the edge of my mattress.

This is not your problem Harlow, a tiny inner voice chimed in. But because I'm myself, I shut that sheet down immediately.

I reached for the bond with Typhon, just checking to see where he was. Somewhere below me on the sixth floor. Asleep or on watch? I couldn't tell.

Besides, I was just going to peek my head out there and see what was what. For all I knew, a student from another house had just had a run-in with whatever nightwalker was stalking our school and needed my help.

I crept across the room, stopping to snatch a heavy candlestick from the dresser as I approached the door.

'This is fine,' I whispered under my breath, laying a hand on the knob and turning slowly. 'No big deal.' But the second the door released, I snatched my hand back and fashioned a quick blocking rune to have at the ready. I was still considering backing out when the low voice moaned again.

'Someone . . . anyone?'

So much pain. No . . . agony and fear filled that voice.

Fruck it.

I opened the door the rest of the way and gasped as a figure appeared directly in front of me. A young woman with white-blonde hair in a tangled mess around her too-pale face. She was wearing what looked like a formless black sheet. For a second, I couldn't move, and that was all the time she needed to wedge her foot between the door and the jam before I could slam it shut.

'Don't go! They're going to get me and take me back! I just need someone to help me!' she begged, her voice barely more than a weakened whisper as she clutched at my wrists with clawed fingers. Her fingernails were long and ragged, as if she'd used her hands to climb up the side of a rock face . . .

Or from the bottom of a grave.

'I'm sorry,' I whispered, shaking free of her grasp and pushing her backward. 'I can't help you!'

Even though I hadn't pushed hard, she was so slight – so frail – that she went flying across the corridor to crash against the opposite wall. Then she let out a strangled gasp and fell to the floor in a heap.

I dropped the candlestick and let my dorm room door close behind me as I ran to her side.

'Sheet,' I murmured, casting a sputtering, poorly working illumination rune to see her more clearly as I knelt beside her. In the light, it was clear as day. She couldn't have been more than nineteen or twenty and was in a weakened state, her gaze almost feverish as she tried to sit up. Most likely a student I didn't recognize, in need of help. I would never forgive myself if I'd truly injured her.

Frucking Typhon with his cryptic, useless warning.

'I'm so sorry . . . I thought you were . . . I didn't realize you were a student. Are you okay?' I took hold of her bony upper

251

arm and gently helped her to stand. Thank the rune goddess, she was able to stay on her feet, albeit a little unsteadily. 'Where does it hurt?'

Her teeth chattered violently as she latched onto me again with both hands. 'Everywhere. I'm empty and they keep taking and taking.'

Her eyes were a blue so milky and pale they looked like they belonged to a woman eighty years older than she.

'Please. I'm starting to forget who I was, and soon I'll be gone forever. You have to hide me somewhere before he finds out I'm gone.'

Her panic was so all-consuming that it became my own.

'Slow down,' I whispered, patting her tangled hair as soothingly as I could manage with my own trembling hand. 'You're alright now. Just slow down and tell me what happened from the beginning.'

'There's no time. Please!'

'Move away, Harlow!'

Illuminated by his own magic, I looked up to see Typhon standing a few yards away, blood running in rivulets down one arm, nostrils flaring. His face was pale, and he was shirtless, his chest covered in sweat.

'Typhon? What —'

'Harlow Daygon! Step back from the wraith immediately!' another voice bellowed from further down the long, dark hallway. The lights flicked on, and I squinted against the blinding brightness.

'Noooo!' the girl howled, covering her head as Tarquinius, Typhon, and Nikita slowly moved closer, hands raised like a trio of gunslingers.

What the actual fruck —

Unsure of what to do, I went with my gut and turned my back on him, covering the girl's slight form with my own. If she was a wraith — whatever the fruck that was — there was no way she could hurt me in this state.

Or, at least, that's what I was betting my life on.

'Talk to them. Help them understand, you're not here to do anyone harm,' I murmured, tucking her closer to my chest. 'It's going to be okay.'

'I can't go back.' She pulled away, tipping her tear-stained face to mine. The wildness had faded from her eyes, leaving behind only sorrow and an acceptance that physically hurt me to witness.

'My name is Lucy. My parents are . . .' she trailed off and shook her head slowly, letting out a bitter laugh, 'I don't remember their names anymore. I thank you for your kindness, Harlow Daygon.'

I could sense Typhon, so close now, but before I could turn and beg for mercy on her behalf, Lucy yanked herself away from me. I watched in stunned horror as she took half a dozen steps and hurled herself through the glass pane of the window at the end of the hall.

We were on the seventh floor. My heart plummeted as her scream rent the air. I lunged for her, as if I could stop what was happening.

Everything after that was a blur. Typhon grabbed me and pulled me close as he whispered soothing words I couldn't quite make out beyond the buzzing in my ears.

'Are you hurt?' he murmured. 'Harlow, talk to me, *are you hurt?*'

I clung to him, his warmth drawing me in, driving away the sudden cold. I didn't answer him. Couldn't. That girl . . . she was only a few years older than Opie.

'She was too young.'

His hands moved over me, checking for wounds. I started shivering, bare legs and arms covered in goosebumps as the shock set in.

The only thing anchoring me in that moment was Typhon. The rest of the world seemed to have faded. 'Who was she?' I whispered up at him.

The pain in his eyes was reflected down the bond connecting us, and again, his mouth didn't move. If I'd been unsure whether he was rune gagged, I now knew for certain he was.

Tarquinius grabbed my arm, tugging me from that bubble of safety and grounding that Typhon held me in. 'Back to your room.'

My roommates, awakened by the shattering of glass, piled out of our room, freaked out, asking if I was alright, their voices filling the space. Ellie caught my arm first, her hands gentle as she tugged me forward.

'Come back in, Harlow, we need to get you warmed up. You're in shock.'

Tarquinius shifted his focus from me to Nikita. 'Go check if the wraith survived.'

Nikita all but saluted him before she turned and ran for the stairs.

As if 'the wraith' could have survived the seven-story fall. She was no wraith, just a little girl.

And I'd failed her, spectacularly.

By the time I was safely tucked back into bed an hour later, I could almost convince myself that, like my dream about Opie the week before, it had all been a figment of my imagination. A terrible night terror that I would forget about come morning.

But deep in my heart of hearts, I knew the truth. The girl wraith called Lucy had plunged to her death right in front of me.

And her screams on the way down would haunt me for the rest of my life.

24

I'd barely slept for a few minutes before I jerked awake, hearing Lucy's scream, feeling it echo through my chest. Gasping, I sat up and looked around the dorm. No one else was moving.

I ran a hand over my face, the tremble of my fingers, the shaking of my breath . . . I needed to get a hold of myself.

I gathered some clean clothes and went to the oversized washroom that was for the girls. Multiple showers, tubs, and toilets all set behind screens. Still trembling, I could feel the build-up of an oncoming attack, could feel the sweat sliding down my spine and the sudden struggle to breathe.

'Fruck me sideways,' I muttered as I hurried to the closest shower, my vision darkening at the edges. I couldn't go running, couldn't dive into the moat around the castle, so a cold shower it was going to have to be.

I stepped behind the screen and flicked the lever all the way to the right, leaning against the tiles as a shudder wracked me. I wasn't cold, I was burning up. The spray of the cold water hit my toes as I stripped out of my pajamas.

My chest twisted and knotted, and the shakes in my hands had worked their way through to my whole body as Lucy's terrified face refused to leave me. And her face kept morphing into Opie's. Lucy had said something about being used up. About being empty. I thought of my recent dream, so real . . . so terrifying. Did Lucy mean she had no magic, like Opie?

I couldn't stop seeing the connections, real or imagined. That's what panic did. It magnified all my fears tenfold.

What if what happened to Lucy could happen to Opie? And how could I stop it when I had no idea what *it* was? Where had Lucy come from? And why had Typhon and the others been so intent on putting her back there?

The spiral pulled on the muscles around my chest until I couldn't breathe.

A sharp snap of air escaped my lips as I stepped into the streaming cold, the icy droplets cutting through the heat of my skin, cutting the lines of the anxiety as it tried to take control of me.

I bowed my head and stepped fully under the stream, hands out to the side to steady myself on the walls. Cold, so cold that it made my head ache with the temperature, but it knocked out the building heat of the attack until I was shivering for a completely logical reason.

'You are zero help to anyone if you fall apart, woman,' I muttered under my breath.

Five minutes turned to ten, and then ten to twenty before I finally felt in control enough to turn the water off. Shakily I dried myself off and slid into some dry clothes, my limbs icy like I'd just stepped out of a meat locker, skin still pebbled hard from the cold water.

Marina and Ellie stepped into the washroom as I opened the door to leave. Marina's keen eyes slid over me. 'You okay?'

'Better now.'

I knew she wasn't convinced, hell, I wasn't convinced. But I made my way out to the main room where my housemates were slowly waking.

They hadn't seen Lucy; they'd only heard the aftermath of her escape. The broken glass, the long scream, Tarquinius saying there was a wraith. My barely coherent, shock-laden explanation.

'Harlow . . .'

'I really appreciate your concern, but I just need to put a pin in this for now. I'm –' I broke off to meet Marina's sympathetic gaze and went with the truth. 'I'm not okay, but I also can't face this head on right now. Can we just pretend things are normal for today? Please?'

Ellie laid a gentle hand on my arm and nodded. 'Of course.'

'This just came, from Elmwood,' Zeed said, holding a piece of stationery as he rubbed the sleep from his eyes. 'Apparently, the rule of two has been revoked.'

What the fruck?

I held my hand out for the paper, glad to see the shakes were nearly gone. 'That can't be right. Not after last night.'

Why now?

Zeed's eyes flicked from me to the others. 'Do . . . do you think she might have survived the fall?'

I shook my head. 'No.' My throat was too tight to elaborate. As small and weak as she'd been . . . a fall like that. I blinked back hot tears.

'Mother Hecate bless her,' Ellie whispered, crossing herself. I wasn't sure the mixing of theologies would work, but maybe it would help Lucy, wherever she was.

'This doesn't make sense.' Ross took the paper from Zeed. 'From what you said, Lucy was just scared. Not a threat. But they were afraid enough of her to lock us all down? How long do you think she was wandering Neverthorn for?'

'She doesn't want to talk about it, Ross,' Fable said, tugging on a fuzzy robe as she stepped between us and scowled at him.

I gave her shoulder a pat. 'It's okay. I know we're all upset. It's just, I don't have any answers right now. All I have are questions myself. But the Senate and Tarquinius need us to defeat Nocta. We know that much is true. So, despite all the lies, I have to assume that our safety is their number one priority. If they say we can walk the school freely, I'm going to assume that's the truth. And until I see Opie and make sure she's safe, I can't concentrate on anything, never mind solving this mystery.'

'I can go with you?' Fable murmured, worry etched onto her pretty face.

'No, I need to talk to her alone. But thanks.'

I made my way down the stairs, toward the third floor. It was too early for breakfast, but hopefully she was awake. The Unicorna crest was etched into each of the doorways, a rearing unicorn, surrounded with white and purple runes. Opie's room was halfway down the hall, and I knocked once.

No answer.

I knocked a second time.

Third.

The fourth time I banged my fist against the door, panic finding its way back to me in double time. 'Ophelia! Open this door!'

The door flew open, and Opie stood there, her eyes wide and only half a braid in her hair. 'What!? What's the matter?!'

I reached out and grabbed her by the shoulders and dragged her into a hug, crushing her to my chest as I tried not to sob. 'I was just . . . you didn't answer the door right away.'

'I had music on while I was braiding my hair,' she mumbled against me, tipping her head to the side. 'Lo-lo, are you okay?'

'Yeah. Yup, I'm fine.'

'Then why are you squeezing me like I'm the last bit of toothpaste in the tube?'

I huffed a laugh and forced my arms to relax. 'Right, well . . . just one of those mornings where I don't know my own strength, you know?'

Her blue eyes squinted up at me, no doubt seeing more

than I wanted her to. 'Right. But you're okay? Because you scared the heck out of me.'

'I'm fine.'

Her hands went to the other side of her head, braiding the remaining half of her hair. 'You know what fine can stand for?' she glanced around and lowered her voice to a whisper. 'Frucked up, insecure, neurotic, emotional.'

'I should never have told you that,' I forced a smile. 'I'm good, Opie. I just feel like I hardly see you.'

'Because we're in different classes.'

'I know that. But even at meals.'

Her smile was genuine. 'We have different friends.'

'Right. Well, maybe you could sit with me for a meal today.'

She finished her braid. 'Sure. Breakfast then? Krishna and Phoebe like to sleep in anyway.'

'Okay, breakfast it is. Thirty minutes?'

She backed me toward the door and rolled her eyes. 'Perfect. That's how long it will take for my heartbeat to go back to normal after you scared the crap out of me with all that banging.'

She shut the door in my face, and I shook my head. A familiar voice tugged at my ears, and I turned to follow it. His voice drew me forward, the Irish lilt a soothing drawl I could use right then.

Liam.

He might know what happened with Lucy. If they found her broken body . . . or if she'd disappeared . . .

Hurrying, I caught up to him, grabbed him by the arm and yanked him sideways into a small classroom. He spun as he fell through the door, his fingers flashing into a rune, wrapping me in a body bind.

My arms and legs locked together, but with a quick jerk of my arms and legs, I busted free of it.

'Shit, Harlow!' Liam reached for me, helping to steady me. 'I'm so sorry!'

'No, it's okay.' I ran a hand over my face. 'With everything that's been going on, I get it. That was foolish of me to sneak up on you like that.'

He cocked his head to the side. 'What do you mean everything that's been going on?'

I didn't think he would lie to me, but was it possible he didn't know about Lucy?

'Harlow, whatever it is, you can trust me. I will do everything I can to help you.' His deep-brown eyes were sincere.

I hoped I was reading him right.

'You don't know about Lucy?' I leaned against a table and crossed my arms, holding myself tight.

He frowned. 'Lucy who?'

I took a deep breath and let it all out in a rush. 'Lucy is a girl who died last night. She was outside my room, looking for help. I tried to help but then Tarquinius, Nikita, and Typhon showed up, Typhon was covered in blood, and the girl was terrified and she . . . she asked me about her parents and then she threw herself out the window of the seventh floor. Tarquinius called her a wraith, but she felt just like a normal girl to me.'

I sucked in a breath and stared at Liam, watching him. Emotions rippled across his face, shock at the front followed by anger.

'No one has said anything to me.'

'It was awful. She was so distraught. She said they used her up. That she was empty.' If I thought Liam looked angry before, it was nothing to the shadow of fury that rippled over his features. 'Liam?'

'That's . . . fruck, Tarquinius sent me to the village, to guard the far edge last night. Said he thought Nocta might send another spy, or an attack —'

'Wait, what do you mean, another spy?'

He shook his head. 'Slip of the tongue. He wanted me on guard, so that I wasn't here. They had to have known that Lucy was going to show up in the school. But how is that possible if . . .' He paced in front of me, one hand on top of his head, the other tapping against his leg, keeping time with his steps. 'Do you think they could have known?'

His question caught me off guard. 'I . . . I don't know? They were looking for her, they showed up right after she did. Liam, what happened to her? What did she mean by she was empty?'

His shoulders slumped. 'I don't know how much I can tell you, Harlow. I don't want to put you in more danger. I don't want to see you hurt. You or your friends. Or Opie.'

I swallowed hard, seeing that connection between Opie and Lucy again, as crazy as it was. 'Why would you think Opie is in danger? Could she somehow end up like Lucy? Out of her mind, forgetting everyone?'

'I don't know, Harlow,' he said, his voice gentle. Kind. But it did nothing to the terror that his words had sparked in my heart.

If what happened to Lucy could happen to Opie . . . whatever control I'd had over myself was gone in a wash of fear so all-consuming that the world blacked out. My vision faded and I fell forward. I might have hit the floor, I don't know. I just couldn't breathe. I couldn't see.

And then I could see, and everything was moving too fast, I was too hot, someone was talking to me, trying to soothe me.

Liam cast a rune against my skin, the same one he'd used to calm us when digging around for a Quirk, but it did nothing. If anything, it seemed to skitter off my skin in a shower of sparks.

I pushed away from him, across the floor until I was under the table, my head against my knees as I fought to find some semblance of control.

Table.

Floor.

Liam's voice.

Fingernails dug into my palm.

'Breathe, Harlow. Just breathe.'

I ignored him, not because he was wrong, but because I almost had it. And I was frucking embarrassed. 'I'm meeting Opie for breakfast.' I spoke, but my words were slurred like I'd been drinking.

I wobbled to the door and was out before he could say anything else.

The dining hall wasn't packed, and I managed to get a plate full of food by labeling everything in my head.

Toast.

Eggs.

Bacon.

Fruit.

Jam.

Orange juice. Last thing I needed was a hit of caffeine when I was this far into an attack.

I slid into a seat next to Opie. She grinned at me, and I focused on the fact that she was okay. That she was safe as long as I was sitting next to her. It eased the bands that had wrapped themselves around my chest a little.

But it was only when a particular teacher strode into the hall, his black cloak billowing out behind him that I took my first full breath. Because as much as I wasn't sure of a lot of things. I knew one for sure.

Typhon would protect Opie.

And as stupid as I felt admitting it, after all he'd done . . .

despite Lucy . . . despite the thirteen-year-long ache in my chest caused by him . . .

I knew he'd protect me too. As if his life depended on it.

Which meant if I ever wanted to be able to move freely around Neverthorn and get to the bottom of the mystery wrapped around Lucy, I had no choice but to break the bond between us.

No matter what it took.

25

The next day, I still couldn't stop picturing Lucy's tortured face every time I closed my eyes. If she hadn't been a wraith in life, she'd become one in death, and she was haunting me. I couldn't sleep, I couldn't pay attention in class. I was a total wreck. I'd tried to get Typhon alone, to get some answers, but he seemed to be as wrapped up in his own sheet as I was, and he seemed to look right through me, as haunted as me.

'Harlow?'

I blinked my gritty eyes and looked up to find Doyenne Parunah gazing down at me with a frown.

'Are you feeling unwell?'

I almost said I was fine, but it would've been a lie. I'd reached the end of my rope. I needed a mental health day before the thin veneer holding the cracks together gave, and I finally shattered for real.

'Actually, my head is pounding, and my throat is scratchy.'

Her lips pursed as she laid a clammy hand on my forehead. 'A bit warm, maybe. Head up to the infirmary and remind the nurse that you're bunking with all your housemates. If you're contagious it might be better to keep you quarantined for the next few days. You'll miss the Samhain festivities this evening, but it is what it is. We don't need the lot of you sick.'

I'd forgotten all about Samhain.

The others exchanged worried glances and Fable raised a questioning brow my way. I forced a smile as I wiggled my fingers at her. 'I'll be okay,' I mouthed before passing her on the way out.

She knew I'd been struggling, and in truth, this was probably better for all of them. With the exception of Zeed, since our field trip with Typhon in the Dark Wood, they'd all been making great strides with their runes. And, because they hadn't seen what I'd seen with Lucy, they'd largely moved past it. Having me hanging over the group like a black cloud certainly wasn't going to help our freshly boosted morale. Until I could get a handle on the swirling grief and helplessness I'd felt in the wake of the girl's death, I was nothing but an unnecessary distraction.

I stopped at my dorm to drop off my books, and then made a beeline toward the kitchen. Although my appetite had taken an unprecedented nose-dive since the other night, I felt a little panicked at the thought of being quarantined with only clear soup and dry crackers at my disposal. I was no doctor, but it was common knowledge that true healing required chocolate, and going to the infirmary without a stash just in case seemed foolish.

A harried Mrs. Wickersham looked up from the bread she'd been kneading as I walked in, her shrewd eyes narrowing as she studied my face. 'You're looking rough around the edges there, Shortbread. I'd think you'd be on cloud nine about the feast tonight. What gives?'

I looked around and realized with a start that the kitchen was bustling even more than usual. It was only then that the sweet, heavenly scent of chocolate penetrated my daze, and I inhaled deeply.

'Just stressed and overtired.'

Mrs. Wickersham gave the smooth ball of dough one last slap before swiping her hands on her apron. 'I've got just the thing.'

She led me to a tray full of fat spirals of puffed, flaky pastry layered with thick ribbons of semi-sweet chocolate.

'Pain au chocolat . . . my favorite,' I murmured, throat tight that she remembered.

'You realize you say that about at least fifty percent of the things that come out of this kitchen, right?' she asked as she began plucking some from the tray and stuffing them into a white paper bag.

But her words didn't dull my joy as I bit into one.

'You're a goddess,' I mumbled, bending into a deep bow.

'Wait until you see the spread for the party tonight. Sweet potato and pumpkin pies, candied apples and caramel corn.'

And then Lucy's face floated back to the forefront of my mind.

'Thanks again, Mrs. Wickersham,' I managed, stuffing the rest of my pain au chocolat into the bag with the others.

I was just down the hall from the infirmary when the bell rang for the changing of classes.

'Excuse me!' a low voice snapped just as a shoulder jostled mine.

I looked around to see *Nikita* bent over to retrieve the book I'd unwittingly knocked from her hands.

'Maybe if you watched wh–' the rest died on my lips as she straightened. Nikita might be a horrid witch, but she always – always – looked beautiful. Not today. Her red curls stuck out every which way, and her eyes seemed so sunken in and hollow, she could've passed for a ghoul.

Maybe she'd caught whatever Lucy had been afflicted with . . .

'Nikita . . . Are you okay?'

She stared at my mouth for a long time, almost as if she didn't understand what I was saying, and then she finally nodded.

'I'm fine.'

Looked like Nikita Pendergast and I finally had something in common. We were both . . .

Fine.

Maybe now was the time to bury the hatchet. Extend the olive branch. And find out a little more about Lucy, if possible . . .

'Look, I get it. I think I'm feeling the same way you are. What happened the other night was one of the worst things I've –'

'I'm fine, Daygon. If I'm having a rough morning, it has nothing to do with the other night. That girl's presence put every one of us in danger. We will all sleep better now that she's been . . . neutralized. If I look distracted, it's only because Typhon and Tarquinius are headed to a meeting at the Senate, and I'm stuck here on Samhain Eve making sure you and your reject friends don't do anything stupid.'

I should've said something snarky back, true to form. Instead, it was all I could do not to weep with relief. No rule of two. No Typhon or Tarquinius. I'd spend my day in the infirmary and then, when the festivities started, I could head straight to the library and try to figure out who Lucy was, and why they were all so afraid of her.

The rest of my day didn't go quite as smoothly as I'd planned, though. Instead of being left alone to get some rest, the nurse had put me in a room with a girl from House Kirinash who had the same symptoms as me.

'Must be a bug going around,' she'd said.

Which would've been well and good, except my new roomie talked the entire time. Not a lot of the time. Not most of the time.

The. Whole. Time.

'And that's how I wound up staying at my Auntie Belinda's house every summer shearing sheep,' she was saying.

I had tuned out at the halfway point, but she clearly expected some sort of reaction, so I nodded.

'Yeah, wow. That's a crazy story.'

'You think that's crazy? Wait until I tell you about my Uncle Cameron and his one-teated goat!'

'Um, hey . . .' Lisa? Or was it, Laura? There had been so many words between the time she'd introduced herself and now, I couldn't recall.

'Gloria,' she supplied helpfully.

'Gloria. Look, my head is really hurting so I'm just going to close my eyes for a few, okay?'

She shrugged. 'Sure thing. I have to talk to the nurse about some stuff anyway. Sleep tight!'

She rolled out of her bed, and I let my eyes slide shut with a groan as she tottered out of the room.

Peace and quiet. Thank the gods above.

I started to nod off, and by the time a low voice woke me, the room was dark.

'You awake?'

I blinked to find Fable standing over me, face so close to mine our noses nearly touched.

'Geez, woman. Can you give me a little space?'

'Sorry. You didn't answer the first couple times.'

I pushed myself up to a seated position as my eyes adjusted to the darkness. 'So, what, you thought I was dead?'

'Goddess, no. You were snoring like a sailor.'

I swiped at a little drop of drool on my chin and wrinkled my nose. 'I guess I was really knocked out. What time is it?'

'Eight-thirty.'

'Holy sheet!' I'd slept for nearly four hours. I turned to see an untouched tray of coagulated soup and crackers on a table beside me and frowned. 'I missed dinner and everything.'

'You clearly needed the sleep. Which is why I hate to do this to you . . .' Fable paused to chew on her thumbnail.

'Do what?'

'We've got trouble, Harlow.'

I blew out a sigh and shook my head. 'Yeah, okay. That tracks. It has been like forty-eight hours, so . . .' I waved a hand. 'Spill it.'

'You remember how Marina and Ross and the others all wanted to go out for Samhain. Maybe try to find that fairy circle?'

I blinked up at her.

'Right. But that was just talk. You know, *before* a young woman hurled herself out the frucking window of the school.'

Fable lowered herself to the edge of the bed. 'They're stressed, Harlow. They're nervous, and the pressure is mounting every day we're here. I think they just really needed to let off some steam.'

'And what about you? You didn't need to let off any steam?'

'I really wanted to go. Especially since . . .' her cheeks flushed, and she looked away.

Especially since Zeed was going to be there.

'But I knew you wouldn't like it,' she continued on in a rush, 'and you're my best friend. So, even though snitches get stitches, I had to follow my conscience. If you're still not feeling well, I can go talk to Doyenne Elmwood, no problem.'

'Nope. No way.' I kicked off the blankets and stood. 'I'm feeling much better now that I got some sleep. How long ago did they leave?'

'Maybe fifteen minutes. They were going to see if they could sneak some brandy from the kitchens first, so they aren't too far ahead I would guess.' She stood and steadied me with one hand as I yanked on my sheet kickers. 'Harlow . . . can you maybe not tell them that I –'

'Of course I won't,' I said, almost offended at the very idea. 'I'll just say I was feeling better, went down to the party, and then got suspicious when they weren't there.'

'Cool.'

Cool was exactly right, I realized a short while later as we stepped out into the brisk autumn air. 'I should've brought my jacket.'

Bandit had tagged along and was ambling beside me.

'And they said this place is where, again?' I murmured. Even though I knew Typhon wasn't here at Neverthorn, I couldn't seem to stop casting nervous glances all around as we walked.

'Zeed said it was in the same direction as all the other hidden places on the island. Past the entrance to the Dark Wood, and then due west.'

I nearly skidded to a stop.

'Did . . . did he say how far from there?'

Fable hadn't realized I'd slowed my pace and continued on. 'About half a mile.'

Bandit shot me a glance. 'Okay, so looks like we're going to have to pass the wishing well. You think it's going to be a problem? That sea hag is probably still pretty pissed that you got away.'

That had Fable pulling up short as she turned around to face me.

'Sea hag? Harlow, what is he talking about?'

I cleared my throat and started moving again.

'So, um, yeah. About that . . .'

'Harlow and I took Opie to a wishing well so she could wish the two of them out of here, but there was this mermaid witch lady at the bottom of the well. She tried to kill Harlow, but Typhon saved her,' Bandit supplied as he took the lead, his chunky bottom wobbling as he walked.

I'd hoped to ease into that discussion with a little more finesse, but he wasn't wrong, so I stayed silent.

'You were going to leave us? Without even saying goodbye?'

Fable's face crumpled and she looked like she was about to cry.

Sheet.

'No, no. I mean, yes. But it was a long time ago.' I hooked my arm through hers and kept walking. We were on borrowed time. 'Right after we first got here. I knew Opie was going to struggle to fit in, and I didn't think I had the power to truly help anyway.'

She let out a sniff, and frowned, still looking unsure. 'Well, what about now? Would you wish yourself away now if you could?'

I considered that and realized with a start that I wasn't so sure anymore. At some point, I'd started to wonder if I didn't need to be here. At least for now. Until I was sure that my friends had a fighting chance against Nocta, and I found out what the hell had happened to poor Lucy, it didn't matter where I was. Thoughts of Neverthorn would consume me.

'No. I would stay.'

I think?

I would get Opie the hell out of here if I could, but that wasn't the question Fable had asked.

Fable managed a tiny smile and nodded. 'Good.'

'We just need to focus on getting past the well without being detected, and finding the others before anyone else does.'

At least one thing was for certain now. If any of us were anywhere near Calypso, lives were definitely in danger, so my promise to Typhon was still very much intact.

We were still about a hundred yards from where I'd first met the sea hag when I paused and called my little battalion to a halt along with me.

'I'm pretty sure that Calypso can't just snatch us from the grounds walking by. I think bad things are only set into motion by throwing an offering in the well. Still, let's each toss a shielding rune over ourselves just to be on the safe side. Sound good?'

Fable nodded and quickly fashioned the required rune. It flickered for a second and then filled with energy. A second later, she all but disappeared from view, leaving behind just the merest hint of herself, like a translucent image with the lowest possible saturation.

'Nice!' I hissed with a silent clap.

I sucked in a breath and did the same hand motions.

'I can still see you,' Fable murmured.

'Yeah. I don't think I'm doing it right.' I tried again, and Fable shook her head.

'You're mixing up the last two motions. It's swipe *then* curl to close.'

I almost snapped at her that I *had* done it that way, but as I repeated the process, the rune filled with energy, and I could sense a haze around me and Bandit.

'It worked?'

'Yup! Great job.'

Super frustrating that I was still getting mixed up, but I was relieved it was done.

'Let's go.'

To my everlasting relief, we crept up to and past the wishing well without incident. I led us in silence due west, and it wasn't long before Fable spoke again.

'All clear?'

'Yup.'

We let our shielding runes fall away.

'I had a feeling we'd be alright but she's a tricky one, so better safe than sorry.'

'Should be pretty close now,' Fable said, her steps quickening. 'Zeed said it should only be a twenty-minute walk from the school to the fairy circle.'

I scanned the grass for signs that they'd passed through this way but noticed nothing out of the ordinary.

'Probably better off sniffing the air to see if you can catch wind of Gary,' Fable said with a nervous chuckle. Bandit thought that was hilarious and let out a chuffle, and even I cracked a smile. But no matter how relieved I was that Calypso hadn't shown herself, there was still something nerve-wracking about being out on the Eve of Samhain. The Horned King himself could have made an appearance to demand a sacrifice, and I wouldn't have been surprised. Especially on the grounds of Neverthorn, where one bad thing after another had happened since I got here. No way was I letting my guard down, no matter how quaint and sweet a frucking fairy circle sounded.

'I swear, it has to be right here,' Fable said as we came upon a copse of trees glimmering in the moonlight. 'Zeed said something about silver birches. But I don't see any mushrooms. He said there would be a ring of giant mushrooms, and that if we stepped inside, and said some silly poem he'd found, the fairies would come out to greet us.'

These were definitely silver birch trees, but I didn't see any mushrooms either. I bit back a snarl of frustration and leaned against a nearby stump for a think.

'Maybe they kept going when they didn't see –' I broke off and let out a grunt as the stump shifted beneath my ass cheek.

'What the fruck?'

As the tree stump shifted, so did the landscape around us. One second, there was nothing but birch trees around us. The next, twenty-foot-high stone walls rose from the ground, massive mushrooms sprouted from the dewy grass, and Fable and I both clapped a hand over our mouths to keep from screeching in shock.

'Whoa,' Bandit whispered as he scuttled behind me, weaving between my legs. 'That's so cool!'

'You guys found it! How? These walls totally weren't here when we came by!' Ross called, laughing. He and the others were to the left of us, appearing out of the trees like ghosts on the wind.

'Good job,' Zeed said, rushing forward and spinning around to take it all in.

The others followed and soon enough they were all chattering excitedly, seemingly unbothered by the fact that Fable and I beat them to it, and unaware that we'd come to rain on their parade.

'Who wants some brandy?' Gary asked, waving the half-empty bottle in my direction and laughing as Marina snagged it and took a long pull.

'How did you make the circle show itself?' Zeed was asking Fable.

But I barely heard all the talk. All my attention was zoned in on the wall farthest from me. My feet carried me toward it as if of their own accord. At first glance, it was a wall like all the rest. Roughly hewn of stone, dirt and vines clinging to its surface in spots. But it was the crimson smears peeking out from behind the flora and fauna that had caught my attention.

Stop.

I was five feet away when the voice inside me snapped the command. But now that I'd gotten that close, there was no denying what I was looking at.

Blood. So much blood.

I stared at it long and hard, a sense of dread creeping up

the back of my neck. It was old, that much seemed obvious with the depth of the red tones. But so much of it, it could be from nothing short of a massacre. Maybe this had been some sort of hunting ground? Or an ancient holy place where offerings were sacrificed to Hecate and her mate, the Horned King?

'This was a bad idea,' I whispered under my breath.

I didn't want to, but I couldn't stop myself. I just watched like a moviegoer at the drive-in as my hand lifted in front of me and pressed itself against the cold stone.

A memory was trapped in the stone, and now I was living it.

Violence, death, and chaos surrounded me. Screams filled my head. Terrified, tortured pleas that pierced me to my very soul. I turned toward them, feeling like I was stuck in mud. Behind me, my friends were gone. No Fable, or Zeed, or Marina. But other students had taken their places. Younger students, some that I recognized from Phyllis's pictures. Mouths agape, eyes wide with horror as their very souls were sucked from their bodies. And standing before them?

Nicodemus Oliphant, hand extended, literally draining them of their life-force and pouring it into some metal machine with tubes sticking out of it.

I wanted to scream, to make him stop, but no sound would come. A dark figure came up behind him and rested its hand upon his shoulder. Young Nicodemus closed his eyes, and I could've sworn a tear leaked down his cheek . . . or maybe I was just blinded by my own.

'Please,' I whimpered, trembling from head to toe as I tried to pull away from the wall . . . to get to one of the kids – any of them – to help. But when I turned away from their tormentor, I knew it was too late. They were writhing on the grass, empty husks of people with twisted limbs and ruined faces.

'Harlow!'

Zeed's voice penetrated the vision and a second later, I felt his hand on mine. I could sense his terror and heard him howl with the shock of it. Then he yanked me hard and both of us stumbled backward, landing on the grass as we tried to break one another's fall.

Breathe, just breathe.

But I could barely do that. It was like the trap of the memory still had a hold on me, and I could do nothing about it.

Zeed's hand tightened over mine and his eyes locked on me. 'Harlow. What's happening?'

A burst of light suddenly fluttered around his chest, settling over his heart. He stiffened and arched as the light slid through him. And then the world sped back up again, the others were yelling, but through the cacophony was a voice that struck through everything.

'Get back to the school, *now*!' Typhon's voice boomed as I blinked and tried to get my bearings. It was an impossible task as the fairy circle disappeared, giant stone walls sliding back into the ground, mushrooms popping off into thin air.

'Zeed?' Fable's voice called out to him.

The others were bolting back toward the school, but Zeed remained motionless on the grass beside me. The glow gone. His hand limp in mine.

'You okay?' I managed, barely able to get the sound from my constricted throat as I sat up and squeezed his fingers.

His skin was cold as ice.

'Zeed!'

26

Beep.

Beep.

Beep.

The chirp of hospital equipment and all the wires sticking out of my friend sent me back to another place for the second time that night. It was the soundtrack of my sixteenth year on earth. The soundtrack of my mother dying.

If I thought my legs would hold me, I might have run to the bathroom to vomit.

'We think that the stress of the situation may have triggered Zeed's Quirk, hence the light you saw coming off him,' the nurse said softly. 'Doyen O'Connor is on his way to confirm that. Sometimes, the power of one's Quirk can overwhelm the nervous system. That's what we're hoping for Zeed. It's probably best if we limit visitors so he can get the rest his mind so clearly needs.'

'I'll stay with him,' Fable was saying. 'You guys go.'

'The rest of us can hang in the waiting room, at least until we hear some test results and what Liam has to say . . .' Ellie turned her attention to Typhon. 'Maybe you can take Harlow back to your quarters and get some hot soup into her. She's still shivering and in shock herself.'

I pressed a shaky hand to my mouth. 'I'm not leaving.'

'As soon as we know anything, I'll come tell you. Please let Doyen Moreno take care of you . . . I can't be worried about you both right now,' Fable whispered, eyes glued to Zeed's pale cheeks even as she gripped my hand.

She was right. I was nothing but a distraction from what really mattered right now. The fact that Zeed had a pulse, was breathing, had no sign of injury, and was still catatonic and unresponsive was . . . not good, Quirk or no.

'I'll see you in a little while,' I managed, my stomach cramping and sending a rush of bile to my throat. I rushed from the room and into the bathroom across the hall, barely making it. I gripped the bowl with both hands, hanging on for dear life.

Typhon crouched beside me, put one hand on my forehead and one hand on my lower back.

He could have said a thousand things, but instead he let me lean on him.

He held my hair and put a gentle pressure on my back as I dry-heaved into the bowl.

Five minutes turned to ten before the cramping finally ceased. Spent, I leaned against the wall and swiped the sweat from my brow.

His eyes flicked over me, but I couldn't meet his gaze.

Typhon helped me up. He walked me to the sink, holding me up as I rinsed my mouth out with water. Then he swept me into his arms like a child, and I let him, unable to speak to so much as utter a protest. Burying my face into his neck, breathing in the scent of him, letting it soothe the chaos in my mind.

By the time we got to Typhon's room, and he set me down, I had gotten some control back.

'Thank you,' I managed, crossing my arms over my chest with a shiver. His body had been so warm . . . so right, that now, I felt oddly bereft.

'Okay now?' he asked, searching my face for signs to the contrary.

'Yes. Much better.'

'I'm going to get you some soup from the kitchen. Can I trust you to stay put for five minutes?'

I winced and shook my head. 'I can't eat. I'll drink some tea later, but I won't be able to keep food down.'

He wheeled around and busied himself at the small kitchen in the corner, throwing a rune to heat me up a mint tea. He passed the steaming cup to me, and I took a deep drink, letting it warm me to the bones.

'Thank you, that's perfect.'

'You sure you're alright? You don't want to go back to the infirmary yourself?'

'No.' So long as I kept what I'd seen tucked in the furthest part of my brain, for a little while longer. 'I'm good,' I said, setting the tea down on the countertop. 'Just worried about Zeed.'

'Great. So can you tell me what the fuck you were thinking?' Typhon said, scowling down at me. 'You promised me that you wouldn't —'

'I promised that I wouldn't sneak off unless one of our lives depended on it,' I shot back, ignoring the stab of guilt. 'And it did. You know it did.'

'You took your whole damn house with you and almost got yourself and Zeed killed,' he growled. 'How is that keeping anyone safe, Harlow?'

'They were going whether I went or not.' I wasn't going to tell him they'd literally left without me. Typhon was already furious enough.

I eyed him closer . . . saw the shaking hands, the wild eyes. It was only then that it hit me for real. He wasn't furious.

He was terrified.

He jerked me closer, so we were nearly touching. 'Why didn't you just forbid them to go, or tell me? I could've stepped in and forced everyone to —'

'No. NO! That is not the way it goes, Typhon, even if you'd been here!' The urge to slap his face was so hot I clenched my fist to keep my hand still. 'Unlike you and those in charge here, my solution to every problem isn't to force people to bend to my will whenever they make a choice I don't like!'

He winced as if I'd followed through on the slap.

'And what if that is the only way I can protect them, Harlow? What if forcing them to stay safe, and bending their will, is the only option I have? It's easy for you, because you are not the one who has to bear the weight of your choices.'

His eyes were . . . haunted, the green of them so dark that I could have fallen into them.

We were both breathing hard and in a split second his lips were on mine, angry, demanding. I kissed him back, biting his lower lip, just as angry. I couldn't help the little whimper that slid out of me as he held me there, the urge to wrap my legs around his waist ripping through me.

He jerked back, cutting off the kiss and letting me go at the same time. I struggled to stay upright, my legs wobbly and my breath coming in gasps.

Typhon took another step back and I was glad to see he was struggling to breathe normally too. 'What was that out there tonight, Typhon? What did he do to those poor kids? And what was that awful machine? It was helping him suck the life out of them.'

He turned away and raked a hand through his hair with a growl. 'You know there are things I cannot discuss with you, Harlow.'

'Keep your secrets, Typhon. And I'll keep mine.'

I turned on my heel and yanked open the door. Then I ran like the hounds of hell were chasing me. When I got to my dorm room, it was blessedly empty except for Bandit, who was curled on the end of my bed.

'I'm so sorry, buddy,' he murmured, instantly climbing onto my lap as I collapsed onto the bed. 'That must've been awful . . . can you tell me . . . what did you see out there tonight?'

I finally let myself think about what I'd witnessed. All those kids, in the prime of their lives, here to learn and grow and make friends and mistakes and have their first kiss . . .

I snuggled Bandit closer, breathing in his musky fur as I let my eyes drift shut, and dreamed of vengeance.

27

'What do you mean you're not coming down for lunch?'

I looked up from the little desk in the corner of our dorm room to find Fable staring at me, eyes narrowed.

'Marina said you were staying in the room. Are you sick again or something, do we need to go to the infirmary?' she demanded.

'No.' Not unless you counted heartsick. The guilt seemed to be growing inside me like a virus. Between Zeed winding up in the infirmary, and me not being able to save Lucy from whatever fate it was that she'd feared, my innards were in knots. 'I'm just not hungry.'

Fable blinked. 'That's not a thing. You're always hungry.' She stepped closer and I quickly closed the notepad I'd been scribbling in. I was trying to make sense of what I'd seen the night before.

Nicodemus Oliphant had murdered his classmates in cold blood.

I'd told the others everything I'd seen, except the very end. That there was something about his expression . . . A moment I couldn't stop replaying in my mind. Was it grief etched on his face? And who or what was the dark figure behind him?

Maybe it was time to tell her who my father was, before we grew any closer. Before my betrayal could cut any deeper.

I took a steadying breath. 'Fable . . . I need to tell you something.'

She nodded. 'Sure. Can I tell you something first though?'

'Okay . . .'

'I know you don't like mushy stuff, so I'll make it quick. I know you feel bad about what happened last night, but no one blames you. You have to know that.'

I let out a bark of laughter.

'No one that matters, anyway,' Fable replied with a half-grin. 'I don't have a sister, and while I loved him with all my heart, my brother and I had grown apart and were very different people when he died. I guess what I'm saying is, you're awesome. You took one for the team by coming with me even when you didn't want to. If you hadn't, Zeed might be dead right now. So . . . thank you. And I love you.'

Frucking hell.

I squirmed for about ten seconds and then mumbled the same back to her, which had her throwing her head back with laughter.

'Not exactly a marriage proposal, but I'll take it. Now, what did you want to tell me?'

I sighed. I couldn't make myself say the words now. Before Fable, I could count on one finger the number of people who loved me. Right or wrong, I just couldn't watch that love turn to hate right before my eyes. Not today, at least.

'That girl who jumped out the window . . . Lucy?' I cleared my throat before continuing. 'She said some things to me that I can't seem to let go of. She was terrified of what would happen to her if Tarquinius sent her back to wherever she'd come from. He's trying to act like she's another acolyte of Nocta, but I'm not so sure.'

'Zeed wondered that too. We even went to the library to check it out while you were in the infirmary.'

My eyebrows shot up. 'Really?' At least they didn't think I was crazy.

'Yeah. Zeed thought it was strange that she could sneak

in without being detected beforehand. We were looking for blueprints or maps to see if maybe there was some sort of underground network of tunnels leading to various parts of the island. I hate to say it, but that's how he found out where the fairy circle was. I can't tell you how much I wish I'd just told you at the time instead of waiting.'

She let out a miserable sigh and I reached out to give her hand a squeeze.

'You thought you could convince them not to go. It's not your fault, Fable. And it's definitely not as bad as it could've been. Once he's back from the infirmary, he can help us figure out who Lucy was and how she got here.'

And tell us what the hell his Quirk was.

She brightened at the thought and nodded. 'Okay. So why don't we go grab you something small to eat, and then hit the library to get a head start. We can look up info about Lucy, but also find out more about whatever the hell you saw last night.'

Fable *was* good at research, and I couldn't just sit here and wallow, no matter how much I wanted to. Resigned to the plan, I pushed away from the desk to stand.

'Let's check on Zeed first.'

'Definitely,' she said with a relieved smile. 'I was down there this morning, but I wasn't allowed in.'

Weird.

'Was he still unconscious when you saw him last?'

Fable gave a slow nod, her eyes pinched at the edges. 'He was. But they said they think he was just in shock and that he should come around soon.'

Together, we made our way to the infirmary. I stopped in front of the nurse's station and rang the little bell at the corner of the desk.

'Yes?' A pretty young nurse I hadn't seen before stepped

through the door behind her and smiled. 'What can I do for you?'

'We're here to visit Zeed.'

She cocked her head and *snick*ed her tongue in disappointment. 'I'm so sorry, girls . . . no one told you?'

My vision blurred.

'Told us what?' Fable demanded, her voice shrill.

'He was released early this morning.'

I grabbed onto the wall for support.

Fable stared at her, blinking back tears. 'You made it sound like he was dead!'

'Oh, I'm so sorry!' the nurse said, drawing back in surprise. 'I didn't mean it that way. I've only been here a few weeks. I'm good with the patients, and I've got some healing skills, but I'm not so great with the rest of it.'

'It's okay,' I shot a glance at her name tag, 'Cara. You just gave us a little scare.' And I, for one, was still pretty scared. 'So just to clarify, Zeed is in the clear?'

'Not exactly. He went back to his family to heal in peace and quiet. Whatever happened last night definitely shook him deeply, and sometimes that makes our bodies and minds shut down to protect us.' She shook her head. 'It's hard to say for sure how long it will take him to get back to normal but when he left, he was awake, he knew his name, and remembered mine, but not the incident that brought him here. I don't want to give you false hope, but I wouldn't be surprised to see him back at school after the holidays.'

Fable and I let out long, relieved sighs at the same time.

'That's good news, then,' I said, tugging at Fable's elbow. 'Thanks for filling us in.'

As we turned to leave, Liam was walking toward the infirmary. 'Ah, ladies. How is Zeed today?'

'They sent him home,' Fable said.

Liam's eyes narrowed. 'Sorry, what the fuck?'

Fable clenched her hands tight, flicking a glance to me and then back to Liam.

'Right, of course. It just caught me off guard. If you'll excuse me.'

And with that he turned and strode away from us with far more vigor than he'd started with.

'I don't like that at all,' Fable whispered.

I didn't either. 'Liam will find out what's going on. I'm sure of it. Come on, let's get that food.' I tugged Fable along now, drawing her away from the infirmary.

The two of us headed for the dining hall. I was still feeling far from a hundred percent but hearing that Zeed was likely to make a full recovery helped a lot.

'I wish we'd been able to say goodbye to him at least,' Fable said, her expression troubled. 'I'm going to miss him.'

'Me too. But he'll be back. And one thing is for sure. The way things have been going, home is definitely safer than this place. It's probably for the best.'

Despite my reassurances, the crease of worry didn't leave Fable's brow. She was silent, caught up in her own thoughts as we each grabbed a sandwich, and I wrapped a trio of cookies in a napkin and shoved them into my bra for later.

By the time we'd scarfed down our lunch and got past Doyenne Portencia at the library front desk, I had almost talked myself into skipping the whole library idea. I was great at playing a persona when working a mark and had a poker face to rival the best of them. But seeing more of my father's reign of terror was sure to elicit some knee-jerk reactions, and Fable wasn't a mark.

She was a friend.

Maybe even my best friend.

So, after we collected all the research books and newspapers we could carry I decided that she deserved as much of the truth as I could give her. Starting with Phyllis.

'I went into Phyllis's room to try to get some information a few nights ago, and I think she's hiding something. She and Nocta weren't just classmates. Based on a bunch of pictures I saw, they were really close friends. And the people I saw Nocta . . . kill in the vision? I know I saw some of them in those images.'

'What?' Fable said, eyes popping wide. 'Surely, she must know him pretty well, then. Why aren't the powers-that-be using her for information that might help defeat him?'

'She's still here, so I'm guessing maybe they know? But she didn't say one way or the other, and Typhon didn't know. She either doesn't have enough info to help more than she already has, or they just keep her around because they don't trust her away from the school. Who knows? I got the sense that there were things she couldn't tell me – I think she is rune gagged. If we go to her with some well-researched theories and facts, maybe she'll crack.'

Unfortunately, facts were hard to come by at Neverthorn, even in the library – at least about Nocta.

Fable paused and looked off at the far wall, her eyes distant. 'I can't help but wonder if it wasn't so much a memory as it was a booby-trap or nightmare you got sucked into? Surely, the mass murder of a bunch of students by one of their own would've been something we'd have heard of?'

I shrugged. 'You'd think.' But I knew better than anyone that this place had more than its share of secrets. Just because we hadn't heard about it didn't mean it hadn't happened. 'If that wasn't real, it was the most powerful bit of magic I've ever encountered. It was so . . . visceral.'

But the more we dug, the more I couldn't help but wonder . . . and hope. Maybe it was just some evil little fairy trick.

Two hours passed, and we made no progress. Frustrated, and desperate for a win of some sort, we moved on to trying to find out more about Lucy.

'And how old did you say she was?' Fable asked as she stacked the yearbooks we had selected by date, newest on top.

'Hard to pinpoint. She had this . . . sort of ethereal quality. In fact, if I hadn't touched her with my own two hands, I might have been able to convince myself that she was a ghost. Early twenties, maybe?'

'So, she graduated a few years ago, then. I mean, if she really was a student here, she should be in one of these books.' She tugged two from the pile and handed me one. 'Let's start here.'

I cracked open the book and began leafing through, seeing with my eyes, but my thoughts wandering.

They wandered all the way back to Typhon and that kiss, the heat of his lips, the taste of his mouth . . .

Fable looked up. 'What? Did you find something?'

I hadn't realized I'd made a sound. I cleared my throat. 'Nope, not yet.'

She went back to her search and so did I. It took three false starts – Lucys who weren't my Lucy – before we stumbled on something promising.

'Could this be her? The name is close. I remember her a bit! She left early, kinda like you, and just never came back,' Fable asked dubiously as she held up the book and tapped one image with her fingertip.

I squinted my weary eyes, leaning closer. 'No, I don't –' but I broke off before I could finish that thought. The more I stared at it, the more it looked like her. Albeit with plump, round cheeks, a glorious, gleaming mane of dark-blonde hair, and a wide, dimpled grin.

'If so, she's almost unrecognizable,' I admitted softly,

reaching for the book. 'When I saw her, she was painfully thin and so pale.' Like the health and joy had been leached from her body.

Lucinda Azalea Maura.

I glanced at the age of the yearbook and winced. The girl that I'd seen in the hall was barely twenty? Whatever she'd suffered had aged her.

I shoved down the emotions threatening to choke me and forced myself to look at Fable again.

'It's her. I'm almost sure of it.'

'So, she went to school here . . . what does it mean?'

I had no idea. 'Let's put a pin in it for now.'

And by 'put a pin in it', I meant 'track down Typhon at some point and grill him about it'. And if not Typhon, then Liam, or both. One of them knew the truth, and I was going to get it out of them if it killed me.

'And while we're at it, Phyllis is sixty-five, which means she would've been . . .' Fable trailed off and frowned. 'That's weird. There's a two-year gap here. So where are those yearbooks?'

She snagged the next one in date sequence order and pulled it open. A second later, her face drained of color as she laid it on the table between us.

'Look familiar?'

I stared down at a two-page spread, all black with white lettering standing out in stark relief.

'November 9th, 1965. In Memoriam of the Neverthorn Nine, gone but never forgotten,' I mumbled through numb lips. 'That's it. That's what I saw last night.'

'How could we never have heard of this before?'

'I don't know, but I know who does.'

Fable nodded as we said it in unison.

'Phyllis.'

28

Fable and I prepared ourselves as best we could to win Phyllis over. Raiding the pantry was first on the list, but better than that . . .

'You can't be serious?' Fable whispered as I stood with my back to Typhon's door, my fingers working a thin piece of metal into the lock. I was worried about using a rune. One, in case it failed, and two, in case it worked. It would definitely be traceable, and he would definitely know who'd broken in.

I could sense him three levels below, so I knew I had time.

'We want to win her over, getting her drunk is going to help. Or at least getting her tipsy should loosen her lips.' I frowned, as the stubborn lock refused to give in to me easily.

Fable waved at a few students who walked by.

'House Phoenix,' one of them muttered. 'They should've named it House Pigeon Shit.'

'Idiots,' Fable whispered. 'They all hate us now, largely thanks to stupid Mortan, Julius and their cronies in Draconell.'

I shrugged. 'Nothing new for me.'

The lock gave way, and I grinned. 'Wait for me here.' I took a quick look up and down the hall and slid backward into Typhon's room.

His smell enveloped me first and, for a split second, I just stood there and breathed it in.

No. Bad Harlow!

I made my way quickly to the cupboard where he stashed his whiskey and pulled an empty plastic container from under my shirt. It wasn't huge, but only Phyllis would really be drinking.

I poured a bunch in, noticed the change in the fill line.

'Not water to wine. But how about we just water it down.' I tucked the bottle under his tap and filled it until it was close to the previous line. Perfect.

I tapped the door and Fable let me out, and I locked it behind me.

'He'll notice,' Fable whispered as we hurried down the hall, headed to Phyllis's room.

'Nah, I filled it back up with water. Swished it around.' I grinned.

'He's going to kill you.' She chuckled but sounded nervous.

'Maybe.' I let myself feel him through the bond and slid to a stop. He was coming toward us, like just around the corner. 'Fruck.'

I pressed my hands over the plastic container in my hand. The color was . . . brownish. Golden.

I cleared my throat. 'You know, Fable, I don't know if this urine sample is going to be enough? You think that Phyllis will be able to tell if you're low on – oh, Doyen Moreno.'

Fable was staring at me like I'd sprouted horns, and Typhon's face was screwed into a grimace. He glanced at the 'sample' and kept moving without a word, his face tight, almost as if he barely saw us.

The bond between us gave me nothing.

Preoccupied for sure.

Fable's eyebrows shot up. I shook my head, and we picked up our pace.

'He'll know if he goes for the whiskey,' she whispered.

'We'll just have to hope he doesn't have a drink tonight.'

Less than a minute later we were knocking on Phyllis's door. She opened it and narrowed her eyes.

'What are you two doing out and about?'

I held up the container and sloshed it around. 'Drinks on me.'

She stared at me long and hard and then shrugged.

'It's been a shit few days. Come on in.'

The thing about whiskey is you don't even really know you're drunk until it's too late, and that was as true for a Dwimmer as a plain old human. I poured Phyllis a heavy-handed drink, and she tossed it back.

'Oh, it's been too long since I've had a decent whiskey. Where did you get it?'

'Doyen Moreno.'

'I'm sure he didn't hand it over, but I'm not telling.' She held her cup tight. 'Drink it fast, ladies. Hide the evidence of your theft.'

Laughing, I snapped my shot back, refilled Phyllis and let her have her second drink, and another half before I pretended to refill Fable's and mine.

'Good, so good,' Phyllis sighed and sank into her chair.

'I need every drop. After that girl jumped to her death, and then the frucking fairy circle . . . I could drink for a week straight.' I fake sipped at my drink and watched over the rim as Fable mimicked me.

'Poor girl, she didn't have many friends when she was here. Not a very strong Dwimmer from what I remember. I think she was in House Unicorna.'

Fable shot me a stunned look and then set her cup on the side table. 'You knew her?'

My heart beat faster.

'She never even graduated. I thought she'd gone back home, but I guess not, poor girl, poor, poor girl . . .' Phyllis stared into the cup as if the answers would be found at the bottom, written in the tea leaves, as Doyenne Storm would say.

'There have been lots of mysteries in this place,' Fable said. 'One in particular we've been trying to figure out since the other night.'

I took a breath. 'What can you tell us about the Neverthorn Nine?'

I was watching Phyllis closely, so I saw her flinch.

Then she sighed and poured some whiskey into her teacup. 'You two . . . why didn't any of you tell me you were going to the fairy ring? I would have told you it was a bad idea.'

Fable winced. 'The others were determined to go. They didn't even tell Harlow.'

Phyllis looked over her teacup at me. 'You mean you didn't go willingly?'

I didn't fake the next sip, instead let it burn the anxiety a little as it went down my throat. 'No. I went to bring them back, with Fable. But what we saw there . . . it freaked me out, Phyllis. Tell me it wasn't real.'

She gave a low *harumph* and ignored my question. 'And then Zeed . . . his Quirk was triggered?'

'Yes.' A hint of a smile tugged at Fable's lips before it disappeared. 'But he didn't even get to enjoy it before he was sent home.'

Phyllis nodded slowly, seemingly digesting that nugget.

When it was clear she wasn't going to speak without some more prodding, I leaned in.

'That place,' I shook my head, memories of that dark, terrible night tugging at me. 'Phyllis. Please. We need to know about the Neverthorn Nine.'

'I . . . it happened when I was enrolled,' she whispered, holding her spiked tea closer to her lips but not drinking. 'Terrible, so very terrible what happened. Nine lives, families torn apart. That place absorbed all that fear, all the terror . . . it was magical before they died, but their blood

293

did something to the ring. Made it more than just a fairy ring.'

'Phyllis, when we were there, in the ring, I thought I saw . . .' I swallowed hard again. 'I know you and Nicodemus were friends. He must've been a good person at one time. How did he change so quickly? Did something terrible happen to him?'

A tear slid down her cheek and plunked into her tea. Then another, and another.

Fable opened her mouth to speak but I held my hand up, stopping her.

Patience was not a strong suit of mine, but it came in handy here and there.

And this time, it paid off in spades.

'I don't know what happened to him, and I don't care, Harlow. I refuse to make excuses for that monster. I watched him do it. I got there at the edge of the ring as . . . he sucked the life out of them all . . . my friends. My housemates. I watched my first and only love die that night.' Phyllis was shaking, her drink sloshing but she seemed unaware. 'They were everything to me. It's why I wear black, even now, in mourning. The least I could do after . . . everything . . .' A hiccupping sob rolled through her and her fingers slipped on the teacup.

I grabbed at it, flashing a rune that would clean up the mess.

I placed my hands over hers, holding her tight. 'You aren't alone now, Phyllis.'

She bowed her head forward, her tears dripping in hot splashes, onto my hands. 'You . . . you have no idea what that means, Harlow. I've been here all these years . . .'

'Why?' Fable whispered.

'Because I am afraid.' Phyllis whispered back. 'I'm the only survivor. The only remaining witness to the beginning of Nocta's reign of terror.'

'I thought I saw someone else there. Behind Nicodemus. A shadowy figure.'

'No. Tarquinius came, but he was too late to save any of them. I know you don't trust him, but he protects me. Just as he is trying to protect you all, too.'

Tarquinius may have muted our magic and done some pretty sheety things in the name of finding the new Heronius, but Phyllis had been here under his care for a long time, and she was still alive.

'He'll help you find your Quirks.' Phyllis nodded to herself. 'Tarquinius wants that for everyone.'

'How?' I blurted, not able to disguise my outrage. 'How can he want that, but then put bracers on us,' I held up my right arm, 'that block us from our magic? How is that helping us find our Quirks?'

Phyllis shook her head. 'I'm sure he has his reasons.'

I leaned forward. 'Are you? Because the only person that actually seems to want that is Liam. Not even Typhon is trying to –'

Mother goddess Hecate. I hadn't realized how angry I was about that until I'd said it out loud. He'd kissed me, held my hair while I dry-heaved into the toilet, and of course, helped us with the bracers, but since then . . . nothing. It was like he'd backed off completely since that night weeks ago. No field trips. No extra rune-crafting classes. No answers.

No help at all.

Fable held perfectly still as Phyllis and I faced off. 'You think the Irish doyen will help you, then?' Phyllis asked, one brow raised dubiously.

'I'm sure of it. But I'm hamstrung. Still pair bonded to Typhon. I can't do anything without him knowing.' I slumped back in my plush chair and tipped the last of the whiskey into my mouth. I broke my own rule and poured myself some more, held it out to Phyllis and she nodded.

'They kept you bonded to him? Odd.' Phyllis frowned, staring into her tea. 'I suppose if someone had a temporary blocking for a bonding like that . . . you'd be interested?'

I blinked a few times. 'Is that a real thing? Can you –'

'I've been around the block a time or two, Harlow Daygon,' Phyllis nodded. 'I'll have something put together for you. If you want. Seeing as we are family now.' Her smile was wobbly and I felt the olive branch extended toward me.

A way to block the bond. I didn't like how that rib below my heart twanged, but I gave her a thumbs-up. 'Yes. I want. When?'

'A few days. Saturday should be good. If you take it in the afternoon, you'd have most of that night before the dulling wears off.'

Most of the night, hot damn.

My thoughts were already swirling. I could get Liam, we could go out to maybe the Dark Wood, off school grounds, and then maybe he could help me find my Quirk?

'Thank you, Phyll.' I grinned across at her, which was why I saw her face go white, her eyes wide.

'No.' Her eyes shot to mine. 'I told you not to call me that, ever. You need to go now. Please.'

I stood; Fable was already at the door. Still, I hesitated.

'I'm so sorry, I didn't mean to –'

'Just go, Harlow.'

I glanced toward the pile of materials that had covered the photo of her and Nocta. 'I'm sorry I upset you, Phyllis. I truly am.'

'Everyone's always sorry, but it doesn't change a thing. I'm done talking,' she whispered, and then collapsed into a heap on her chair, her eyes closing.

Fable and I shared a look. I'd pushed her too far.

We made for the door, closing it behind us.

I blew out a slow breath and looked at Fable.

'Damn. She came unglued. Did you know that was going to happen?'

I shook my head and then winced and shrugged. 'She reacted strongly before, too. I think . . . I think one of her friends, or maybe even her boyfriend who died, used to call her Phyll.'

I wouldn't make that mistake again.

Fable ticked her fingers as she spoke. 'Okay. So, we learned a little more about Lucy. And we learned that Phyllis has some serious demons. And she's going to help you out of your sticky situation. And . . . well, that's about it.'

'You sound disappointed. That was a lot for a single interrogation!'

'I just feel like there's more,' Fable said. 'Like there is so much more she could have said.'

We made our way to one of the few spots that was quiet and not quite as public. An alcove in the center of the third floor that allowed you to see both ends of the hall. We ducked into it.

'Maybe she has a journal or a diary.' I frowned.

'Did you see one?' Fable asked.

'No, I'm just taking a leap that after being stuck here for like a hundred years, she might have kept some sort of record.'

'Good point,' Fable said. 'And if not, maybe something else. More pictures, letters from loved ones . . .'

'If she won't give us the info, I'll take it,' I said, reiterating the promise I'd made to myself earlier, only this time, out loud.

Fable wrinkled her nose. 'I don't know. I mean, it's one thing to steal a little whiskey, but that's not personal. A journal is private. Or really anything you find in there. Not to mention entering her room without consent. She won't be your friend ever again or make you that bond-blocker stuff.'

I hadn't thought of that. But being bonded to Typhon, as irritating as it was, would end at some point. It had to. 'I'll take the chance.'

'And I'm right in assuming you want me to stand guard?'

I sighed. 'Yes, and yes. As much as I hate it, it's a price I'm willing to pay to get to the truth that's hidden in the past. This school has so many secrets, and all of them seem to be wrapped around Nocta.'

Fable nodded, her eyes tight. 'We are doomed to repeat the past, if we don't understand it.'

I pointed a finger at her. 'Exactly how I would have said it. We need whatever information we can find. The sooner the better. Let's do it tonight. At dinner, she'll be out of her room.'

Fable chewed her bottom lip. 'It will be noticed. You don't miss meals.'

She made a good point. 'You'll have to go then and tell them I'm not feeling well; they'll believe it after the other night. I can handle the rest on my own.'

'I don't know, Harlow. This makes me seriously nervous.' Fable shook her head.

'I did this for a living.' I winked at her. 'I'll get in, get what I need, and get out. No one will be the wiser. Trust me, I've got this.'

But most assuredly, I did not have it.

I waited until I saw Phyllis leave her room an hour later, still a little more unsteady than usual after the drinks. Fable met her just a few feet from her doorway.

'I'm sorry about earlier,' Fable said, her voice pitched softly.

'Where's Harlow?'

'Lying down, too much . . . tea.'

'Hmm.'

Once they were gone, I waited for another five minutes before I made my way to Phyllis's door and put my back to it. Her lock was not as sticky as Typhon's.

Not by a long shot. I was through the door in under thirty seconds. Flicking the lock open, I let it settle in place so that the door wasn't fully shut. I'd hopefully hear if someone was coming along.

I let myself feel the bond to Typhon. He was several floors down, irritation flowing from him to me. Something was bothering him, keeping his attention.

Good enough.

The room was dim, all the lights turned way down. I held up my hand, flicking two fingers with a simple rune to bloom a light over my palm.

I went straight to the pile of books and papers, rifling through until I found the picture of Nocta, Phyllis, and the other kids I'd seen die at his hand.

My guts clenched and I made myself breathe in through my nose, out through my mouth. I picked up the picture and made myself look at just Nocta. I didn't have any pictures of my father, but in that dimly lit room, I could see my face in his. The line of his cheekbones, the arch of one eyebrow, the intensity in his eyes. Phyllis was a couple of people away from him in the picture, laughing. Happy.

They were all smiling, all except my father. Shaking slightly, I turned the picture over.

November 8, 1965.

Exactly one day before the Neverthorn Nine were killed.

'Fruck.' Chills rippled through me. I slid the picture back.

If I were hunting for something hidden, what better spell

to cast than 'Finders Keepers?' It was an oldie but goodie. I just had to figure out the proper way to do it instead of relying on my shorthand version. It took me ten tries to get it right, but then the rune outlines finally formed. I did a little shimmy of excitement and filled it with energy.

'Journal,' I whispered.

I fully expected the spell to take me to a specific place in the stack. The spell had other ideas, hovering in the air, sparking tiny little bolts like red lightning, leading me to the cupboards where the teacups were. The sparks shot up to the top shelf, well above my head.

I pulled myself up onto the counter and stood, opening the cupboard.

The top shelf was covered in dust. I leaned closer. What looked like two journals were tied together with a thin string. As I reached my hand in, I felt the magic over them.

Protective, and it sparked a burning sensation on my skin. There would be no grab and dash on this. I would have to figure out how to break the spell if I had any hopes of taking it.

I paused. Going up onto my toes, I looked in at the journal cover, the one on top.

Nicodemus Oliphant
Fall Semester, 1965

Fruckfruckfruckfruckfruckfruckfruckfruckfruck

I couldn't breathe.

It wasn't her journal. *It was my father's.*

The urge to grab it and damn the consequences had my hand moving again. But the patter of footsteps changed my plan. I dropped soundlessly to the floor even while my heart beat a rhythm that I wasn't sure was even possible without it stopping soon.

I slipped over to the door and paused, as did the foot-steps. The bond between me and Typhon spiked just before he spoke, his tone sharp. 'We can't take risks like this again, Tarquinius. Someone could have been killed.'

Tarquinius snorted. 'I will decide what risks will and will not be taken. That is not your job, Doyen Moreno. Or would you rather find a new one? How much luck do you think you'd have with that? If anyone knew . . .'

Typhon's rage and fear shot through me as Tarquinius kept on blabbering.

'And while we are discussing risks, you need to get a handle on these House of Phoenix students. Off to the fairy circle, no less. No more leaving the school for them. And you will not take a single one of the House of Phoenix on any of your little field trips again. I know you want to help, but I'm sure that Harlow Daygon used a slew of bastardized magic while she was out there. I am certain that her cavalier use of unsanctioned runes is what released Lucinda in the first place. That would make her – and by association *you* – responsible for how things . . . ended.'

A stab to the heart, for both myself, and for Typhon. But he did not back down.

'Nocta himself is getting closer to breaking through the weave into Everdark every single day,' Typhon replied, his voice low and tight. 'The weavers can't keep up. It's not a matter of *if* anymore. It's a matter of *when*. House Phoenix is our only hope against him. We've been pushing them hard in their classes, and they are learning. Faster than I would have thought. But they need us to give them the tools owed to them. We either allow them to flourish or the Dwimmer world will be forever lost to the dark side. Is that what you want?'

Holy. Sheet. Everdark . . . the closest thing to Hell that the Dwimmer world had.

I held my breath.

There was the not so quiet grinding of teeth.

'We need to control this. Look at Zeed. Useless now, because his Quirk was triggered out in the wild, without me there to help guide him. Magic without rules and boundaries is nothing but chaos. How do you think we got here in the first place? We cannot have history repeating itself. I will request more volunteers from the Senate. Ones that aren't as nosy as that damn O'Connor. Until then, any work with the House of Phoenix students will go through me. That's an order.'

A single set of heavy footfalls sounded down the hallway. A moment later, I carefully reached for the bond I had to Typhon. Though it was quiet outside Phyllis's door, I knew he was still standing there. His attention was not on me.

He was royally pissed.

'Fucking prick,' Typhon muttered and then started away, down the hall.

I waited until I felt him drop down a level, before I slipped out of Phyllis's place and headed to the seventh floor.

As I reached the dorm, I saw a figure waiting for me outside my door. I didn't have to force my smile. 'Opie!'

'Hey, Harlow.' Her blue eyes were shadowed, glittering with unshed tears. 'Can I talk to you?'

My own face fell. 'What's wrong?'

'I think . . . I think the boy I like has a crush on Phoebe.' And she promptly burst into tears. Patting her back as I pulled her into a hug, I dragged her with me into the room.

What I wouldn't give for my only problem to be that of an unrequited crush.

I grimaced and tucked her under my arm. 'Boys lie and kind of stink, Opie. That is a truth that will never fade.'

She hiccupped a laugh. 'Really?'

'Even when they are all grown up. So . . . my best piece of advice? Act like you don't give a sheet about him. He'll either come around or he won't. But you don't need to stress about him.' The words were good advice, and even as I said it, I knew I had to follow through on it.

'Why are you laughing, Harlow?' Opie sniffed up at me.

'Because sometimes I'm stupid about boys too. You'll still want one when you're grown up, even if he's all wrong for you.'

The laughter kept bubbling out of me, a combination of nerves and understanding. Because I knew that whatever it was between Typhon and me . . . it was far from over, and the puzzle pieces I kept finding did nothing to drive me away from him.

29

Luckily, the next couple days sped by. And, despite Typhon's aloof behavior in class and his and Liam's inability to give us any more lessons themselves, our little group seemed to be more determined than ever to step it up.

For ourselves.

For the Neverthorn Nine.

But mostly, for Zeed.

And we were actually killing it. Sure, rune crafting was still super labor intensive for me. It took me twice as long to learn them as it did the others. But once I got it down the resulting magic was typically the strongest of all of ours. Even Nikita was having a hard time finding fault with us. For the first time since I'd gotten here, I was starting to wonder if maybe we did have even the slimmest chance . . .

'You'll need to gather all your ingredients and prepare them at your table.' Doyenne Parunah's voice droned on like a hive of honeybees. It was hard enough to concentrate when I couldn't wait for this last class to end. Phyllis had told me the night before that the potion should be ready by the end of classes today, and I'd already made a plan to meet up with Liam that evening so he could help me trigger my Quirk. I was champing at the bit to see if her potion worked.

'Every item needs to stay completely separate until the right moment, or the poison you are creating will be nulled,' Doyenne Parunah continued.

I did as I was told and gathered up the ingredients, making sure nothing touched.

'That's a hell of a lot harder than she made it sound,' Ross muttered from his circular table across from me. He was balancing a large chunk of a dark-brown root – heart of pine – and the sap was dripping everywhere. This class was specifically for us, teaching us poisons we might be able to use in fighting Nocta and his army. Not exactly something you'd teach the average teenager.

I took the smallest piece of root that I could and put it down on the edge of my table, away from the other ingredients and from my heated cast-iron frying pan.

From behind me I heard Marina snicker. 'We look like we're a bunch of Dims out in the woods trying to whip up a meal.'

Her assessment wasn't far off. 'We're missing marshmallows,' I said.

'Quiet! This is a test, you hooligans!' Doyenne Parunah snapped.

Ross chuckled. 'Hooligans?'

To my left, Fable raised her hand.

Doyenne Parunah smiled thinly at her. 'Yes, student?'

Student. She still didn't know any of our names after three months of teaching us.

'Does the bergamot seed have to be intact? Mine's cracked.'

Doyenne Parunah let out a sigh and gestured to Phyllis, who was closest to Fable.

'Can you take care of this? My gout is giving me fits today and I don't want to get up.'

Phyllis leaned over to inspect Fable's table full of ingredients as I turned my attention back to my own.

'So long as more than half the seed remains, you're fine,' Phyllis explained patiently.

I met her gaze and raised my brow in question as she moved back behind her own station.

She pursed her lips, but then tipped her head in a little nod. It was ready. Score!

For the next forty minutes, I managed to put my thoughts about Phyllis and the coming evening on hold while I did my damnedest to produce a poison that would make my enemy's tongue swell like a balloon and block off their airway just long enough to finish them off.

The only way to tell if it was going to work? My least favorite part of potions class . . .

'Check, please,' I called, raising my hand.

'With ten minutes to spare, hmm?' Doyenne Parunah stood with a harrumph and hobbled her way over, wincing as she moved. She was a bit crotchety, but I still liked her well enough. I couldn't help but wonder if there wasn't any Dwimmer who could help with her pain.

'Go on, then,' she said with a wave, squinting at me through her oval specs.

'Down the hatch,' I muttered, before downing the thimble-ful of thick, black liquid.

I stood there, face scrunched, waiting for the inevitable, but nothing happened. I slumped in disappointment.

'Damn. I must've mixed up the – *glerg*!'

I dropped the vial in my hand and clutched at my throat as my neck expanded like a threatened pufferfish.

Dimly, I heard the murmurs of my classmates over the rush of blood in my ears.

I must've looked as terrified as I felt, because Fable lurched toward me, her expression panicked. 'Holy sheet balls!'

Doyenne Parunah held up a staying hand and I caught sight of an approving nod before my vision started to go dark.

A *pfffthppp* sound echoed through the room, and then suddenly, the pressure was gone.

As I swiped at my watering eyes, I could see the others

exchanging nervous looks, but Doyenne Parunah was beaming.

'Well done . . .' she eyed me expectantly.

'H-Harlow. Harlow Daygon,' I croaked.

'Well done, Ms. Daygon. That was a real cracker of a poison. Keep up the good work.'

How silly was it that her words had my throat aching almost as much as the poison I'd mixed? How I'd longed to hear those words from someone my first time here at Neverthorn . . .

'Good job, Harlow,' Ellie called as Fable blew out a relieved sigh.

'Yes, Harlow, congrats. That said, I, for one, will not be drinking mine,' Phyllis added with a sniff.

Doyenne Parunah managed a smile for her.

'That's fine by me, Phyllis, I know your skillset in this arena and you're exempt. But the rest of you finish up. Time's a ticking.'

The others all completed their poisons before the bell, and every one of them worked to varying degrees. Even Phyllis's, as Ross offered to take one for the team and get poisoned twice.

When class finally ended, we were all on a high.

'I'm starving. I heard Mrs. Wickersham is making a low country boil tonight,' Gary said, smacking his lips as we all made our way to the door. 'Sausage, shrimp, potatoes . . . I've been thinking about it all day.'

I chewed at my lip, realizing I was going to miss out.

'Can one of you guys make me a doggie bag?' I asked, slowing to wait for Phyllis as the others went ahead.

'Sure,' Fable said, shooting me a wide-eyed look. She was the only one other than Phyllis who knew what I was up to, and her poker face was trash. 'Have fun studying alone at the library,' she called, tossing a wave over her shoulder.

Phyllis shook her head and smiled. 'That one is a peach, isn't she? I hope to hell the enemy never catches her. I don't think she could keep a secret for long.'

I didn't correct the older woman, despite knowing first-hand that she thought wrong. I just nodded and eagerly held out both hands. 'So, it's ready, then?'

'It is,' she said, drawing a tiny, satin bag from the pocket of her dress. 'But remember, it's not a permanent fix. The second you can tug on the connection between you again, so can he. I'd say you've got three hours before you should start testing it every few minutes. Best be back in your dorm before the fourth. And if you get caught –'

'I made it myself,' I vowed, crossing my heart with my fingertip.

'Good luck. I hope you find what you're looking for,' she said softly as she pressed the bag into my hand. 'I hope . . . that it's just been waiting for you to be ready.'

Her words tugged at me – a Quirk wasn't a living thing, and yet perhaps there was something in what she said. Maybe we both – me and my Quirk – had to be ready.

She headed toward the dining hall, and I went the other direction, toward my dorm. Phyllis had explained that my attachment to Typhon would remain wherever I was when I took the potion. He hadn't seemed too interested in finding me the past couple of days, but in the event he came look-ing, he would assume I was napping if I didn't answer when he knocked.

By the time I'd closed the door behind me, my hands were shaking with a mix of nerves and excitement.

'You look weird,' Bandit murmured.

I clutched at my pounding heart and wheeled around to

find him directly behind me. 'You scared the sheet out of me! What are you doing here so early? Shouldn't you be trolling the forest looking for a lady trash panda?'

'The ladies are going to have to wait.' He licked his paw and ran it over his face. 'I smelled the seafood cooking all day. Fable promised to bring me a plate. Speaking of which, where are you going again?'

'I have to meet with Liam about something. But first . . .'

I untied the pouch and peered inside, surprised to find what looked like a purple, oblong pill. I'd assumed it would be liquid in a vial like the poison from today's lesson . . .

'So, am I supposed to chew it or swallow?'

Bandit blinked up at me. 'How would I know?'

It was pretty large, so I went with chew, a choice I regretted instantly. It tasted like the bowels of hell, bitter, chalky, and oddly sour.

'That's awful,' I muttered at my reflection. A second later, my mouth and tongue turned purple and started to foam.

Okay, so apparently chewing was a no-no. Had I ruined it, then? But my fears faded as a strange sensation rolled through me, like someone was running the tip of a knife up my arm, to my shoulder, across my throat and then lower, to my heart.

Snip.

I dropped to my knees as a shooting pain lanced through my ribs.

'Frucking fruck!'

I clutched at my chest, as the pain faded almost as quickly as it had come, leaving behind a deep, aching sense of loneliness.

What was this fresh hell?

'You okay?' Bandit asked, circling me.

'Yup. Just . . . yeah, I'm good.' I knelt there for a long moment, waiting for the feeling to subside, but it persisted.

Instinctively, I reached for my connection to Typhon, only to find . . . nothing in its place. My skin prickled with unrest as I tried again.

Again, nothing.

Was this how I was going to feel for the next few hours? And what happened when I finally broke free for good?

I forced myself to stand. This time was precious, and I couldn't waste a second of it.

I swished with some mouthwash, ran a brush through my hair and then headed out with a quick wave to Bandit.

Liam and I had agreed to meet in his quarters, which, as luck would have it, were on the same wing as my dorm, but on the first floor. While he wasn't happy about the idea of me taking a potion from Phyllis, he'd agreed it was the best way to block Typhon. I made my way down the stairs and, after a quick check of the hallway, scooted down to the first door and tapped on it lightly.

It swung open almost immediately and Liam tugged me inside.

'Do you think anyone saw you?'

I shook my head.

'Everyone is basically at dinner, the halls were empty. Phyllis's potion worked.' Maybe too well, I thought as the ache in my chest flared again. 'I think we're in the clear.'

He frowned and then leaned closer, swiping a thumb over my bottom lip. 'Were you drinking red wine?'

'I wish,' I said with a snort, trying to ignore the little zing that shot through me at his touch. 'I was supposed to swallow, and I chewed instead. It's fine. I have so many questions to ask you,' I said, rushing to take a seat in the postage-stamp-sized living room of the studio-like apartment.

He grabbed my hand and dragged me over to his window. 'This way.'

I almost laughed at the ridiculousness of sneaking out his window. 'Don't the kids normally sneak into bedrooms these days?'

Liam chuckled and just threw his leg over the windowsill. I followed, knowing we had very little time. We needed to be outside of Neverthorn's grounds so that Tarquinius didn't figure out what we were up to.

Without a word we both broke into a jog as we headed to the west of the school, toward the Dark Wood.

Of course, all that silence left my mind to wander. To consider what it would mean to have a Quirk. Would it help me keep Opie and my friends safe? That was the goal of course but what if . . . what if it was something dark and terrible? Bile swelled up from my belly and I had to work to push it down, breathing carefully.

The massive trees of the Dark Wood rose up in front of us, shadows and fear lurking beneath the ferns and leaves. I shook my head at the direction my thoughts went.

'Here,' Liam said. 'We don't have to be far over the line.'

He stepped behind a couple of trees and held out his hand to me. Of course, there were only two of us, we didn't have to hide the entire House of Phoenix like Typhon had done.

Thoughts of him did nothing to calm my nerves. But I had time. We had time. I couldn't feel a single twinge of Typhon's bond to me.

I put my hand in Liam's and let him tug me forward. And I found myself stalling.

'When we saw you the other day, you seemed surprised Zeed had gone home. Why?'

His dimple flashed as he stood across from me.

'You are too sharp for your own good, Harlow.'

'Exactly, so don't bullsheet me. Is Zeed okay? Fable has

already started sending him letters, but I'm sure it will take a week or so to hear back. If you know anything –'

'I know that I have a gut feeling that something isn't right here at Neverthorn.'

His expression was stark, his dark eyes full of worry, and my stomach did a flip.

'Agree.'

'As for Zeed, I get the sense that he's alright, but again, I can't say for sure. It's all just intuition, which, given my Quirk, tends to be pretty good. It's possible that what they're saying is true. Gaining a Quirk through something traumatic the way he did can definitely take a toll. What bothers me is that Tarquinius knows he has an expert at his disposal in me. Why did he send Zeed home before I could even speak with him?' He tossed his hands in the air. 'Makes no sense, unless of course he really doesn't trust me. I *do* know he doesn't see eye to eye with the Senate, so my being here at their behest makes us wary colleagues at best. I have some feelers out with friends in the Senate that have agreed to send word once they have confirmation that Zeed is, indeed, home and safe.'

I released a pent-up breath. One more thing. The conversation between Typhon and Tarquinius about Lucinda had been rolling around in my head.

'That's . . . that's great. That will definitely help all of us feel more settled. Do you think you could ask your contacts about a Lucy? Lucinda Azalea Maura? The wraith that was supposedly haunting the school. She was a student here for a short time, but I also overheard some things that make me think she might have come through the weave between Neverthorn and Everdark. Is . . . is that possible?'

It was the only explanation I could come up with, when thinking about how Tarquinius said she'd been freed, and they'd been talking about the weave.

He scrubbed at his jaw and then nodded slowly. 'It's definitely possible. But typically, dark Dwimmers from the other side would be considered interlopers and dangerous. She certainly wouldn't have been sent a letter to attend Neverthorn. I will definitely look into it.'

I bit my lip and looked away.

'Look, I know it's hard not knowing, but I'm going to get answers for you. It's just going to take a little time.'

'And I appreciate it.' I took a breath and looked up at the underside of the trees. 'I don't mean to be ungrateful. It's just been a lot.' Even more than I could tell him . . .

He took my hand and gave it a squeeze. 'If we want the best shot at getting to your Quirk, we've got to get started. I don't know if you're aware, but you've got a stubborn streak a mile wide that makes mining for yours kind of like trying to chip away at a wall made of diamonds using a spork.'

I almost laughed.

'I don't doubt it. So go on. Do your best.'

I leaned back and he held my hand a second longer, brushing the tips of his fingers along my wrist.

The zing was back.

Sheet.

'What do you need me to do?' I said in a rush, relieved my voice wasn't husky. 'Close my eyes, right?'

'Exactly.'

He snapped a rune quickly, and the dirt swelled as a stump shoved up from underneath the heavy underbrush. 'Sit and shut your eyes.'

I did as he asked, then he made a second stump chair for himself, so close that our legs were interlocked. Close enough that I could see the tiny gold flecks in his eyes.

'They're not shut,' he said, the corner of his mouth tipping as he held my gaze.

'Right. Sorry. Go.' I squeezed my eyes shut and held my breath.

'The best thing you can do to help things along is relax. Let the tension drain from your body.'

I could sense as I had before that he was moving his fingers close to me, swiping the mental cobwebs and worries away. After a minute or two, even the deep ache in my chest faded some.

'That's . . . nice,' I whispered.

'What is it you love most in this world, Harlow?'

Part of me wanted to say in that moment, his minty fresh breath, but instead, I answered honestly as I had before.

'My sister, Opie.'

'And what is it that you want most, in your heart of hearts?'

I swallowed hard and paused for a long moment. 'To find out that I have a fanfruckingamazing Quirk that will help me defeat Nocta so I can save my friends and get me and Opie the fruck out of here for good.'

I could almost feel the warmth of his grin and couldn't help but smile back.

Two hours later, though, no one was smiling. All I had to show for my time was a pounding headache, a purple tongue, and most disturbing of all, the deep and overwhelming sense that I'd lost something I couldn't identify.

If I didn't find a Quirk, and soon, it would have all been for nothing. At best we had maybe another hour.

'If you don't let your guard down this is never, ever going to work, Harlow.'

Liam paced in front of me, his stump chair gone and a line where his feet had pressed the moss down. I couldn't help but notice that sweat had made his T-shirt cling to his lean muscles in a way that had me struggling not to stare.

'Last time at least we got you to the lever. Now it's like a vault in there. What's different?'

'Yeah, well last time I hadn't seen a girl leap to her death, the murder of nine innocents, and one of my friends go all catatonic.' I scratched at my gritty eyes and let out a groan. 'Stuff's gotten pretty real here, in case you didn't know, and it's hard to trust.'

His voice was not unkind, but hard. 'You came to me, Harlow. Not the other way around. If you don't want to do this, that's fine. But if you do, you better get serious because we're running out of time. Trust me or don't.'

I wanted to. Hell, if you'd asked, I'd have said I *did* trust him. But as it stood, deep down . . .

I guessed not, even though he'd given me no reason to doubt him.

'Old habits die hard,' I whispered, knowing that trust was something I'd always struggled to give.

'Cast a rune,' I said before I could talk myself out of it. 'There's got to be something that can help. Like a magical Valium.' I closed my eyes and leaned back, clenching my fists. 'Hit me with it.'

'You can't be serious. That's not something I would do, Harlow. It goes against every code of ethics I teach. And besides, it might not even work. We could get to the same place we got to last time.'

I opened one eye and glared at him.

'It will work if my resistance is the only issue. When I was more open to this, you said it yourself . . . we both saw the lever. We just need to get rid of this block. So do it. I'm giving you permission. Come on. Hit me with it.'

I'd spent the past two months fighting tooth and nail for people to stop trying to control me and now I was begging for him to take control.

If that wasn't trust, I didn't know what was.

He stared at the trees again and mumbled something under his breath that sounded like a prayer. Then, he hung his head in defeat.

'Fine. We'll try it. If you're sure . . .'

'I'm sure.'

I leaned back again and crossed my hands over my chest like a corpse, trying not to let the beginning nigglings of a panic attack take hold.

I kept my eyes shut tight. 'Do it quick.'

Liam was nothing if not a good listener. What felt like seconds later, a warm sensation closed over me, and I was floating . . .

'Ohhhh, that's niiice,' I whispered, sinking deeper into my stump chair. 'That's . . .' I let out a sigh and my stiff body went slack. 'I could really go for a hot chocolate right now.'

'I'll get you one as soon as we're done. For now, though, just focus on the sound of my voice.'

'Not a problem. Your voice is like warm syrup.' I cracked my eyes open and *boop*ed his nose with my fingertip. 'Mmm, syrup. On pancakes.'

'Which I will also get for you. But first . . .'

I got the sense of his fingers tracing shapes close to my forehead again, a mere whisper of a touch.

'We're going to try one more time, my friend. What is it you fear most?'

In that moment, I almost said nothing. But an image of Nocta shimmered to the forefront of my mind. Not Nocta. Young Nicodemus Oliphant, draining the life from those who cared for him most.

'My father,' I murmured, my pulse pounding in my ears as a long, winding road appeared in my mind. I followed it slowly, cautiously, and then stopped short. There was no lever or rope to pull at the end of it. This time, there was nothing but a fork in the road. A choice to be made.

What did it mean?

'Do you see it, Harlow? The two paths you can take. Choose one.'

I was about to reply when a strange sensation washed over me. Like I was suddenly being watched, even as the pain in my ribs faded and the emptiness began to subside.

Typhon knew I was off grounds. His anger snapped through me and fruck me, he was close.

This . . . this was not going to go well.

'We're in deep sheet,' I whispered.

30

I wish I could say I scrambled to my feet, that we somehow got back to Neverthorn before Typhon realized that we'd even stepped foot off the grounds, but my luck, well, we all know how much luck I have. Not a lot.

And none of it good.

'What's wrong?' Liam crouched in front of me. 'Harlow? The paths are gone, and you've blocked me out again. I need you to pay attention and try to find the path.'

I wanted to reply, but I couldn't form the words. Typhon's emotions were slamming into me, dizzying me. Fear and rage were at the front. And I was still gorked on whatever rune Liam had cast. The sensation in my chest, the way my rib ached, Typhon's emotions, they were all too much when my guard was so far down from the relaxation rune. It was like Typhon had reached through the bond and kicked Liam out of my head altogether.

'Harlow,' Liam's voice was insistent, and I stared into his eyes as he cupped my face, holding me close enough that our noses nearly touched. 'Harlow, dig deep my friend, you need to get to your Quirk. Do you understand?'

I did understand, but we were out of time. I had to find the words to warn him. 'Typhon,' I whispered.

Saying his name was like whispering a prayer in that moment, and he answered as if I were in danger.

Liam was in front of me one moment, and the next he was just gone, thrown from my view as the blur of a black cloak took his place in a swirl of magic.

'Damn you, O'Connor! What the fuck are you doing?'

'Trying to find her Quirk!' Liam snarled back. 'It's not like you and Tarquinius are doing anything about it. You realize she could wind up dead without it.'

I stumbled to my feet, wobbled and ended up leaning against a tree. They circled around one another, and I knew what was coming.

'Stop it!' My voice was weak. I shook my head and tried again, pushing through the fog that made me want to lay down and sleep. 'STOP!'

Neither of them looked at me. They were too focused on each other. Runes flashed in the air as they threw their magic at one another. Faster and faster, body binders, bone breakers, runes to knock each other out at the least, and then the defensive runes, blocking one another as fast as they were trying to hurt one another.

It was a display of speed and power that had the trees around us trembling. In another situation I would have been in awe of what I was seeing.

But I didn't want either of them to die, one was my friend, and the other was my . . . I didn't know what Typhon was . . . so I did the only logical thing that my addled brain could come up with. I shoved off the tree and flung myself between the two men.

My timing, as always, was impeccable. I fell between them just as one of Liam's runes left his hand. I saw it, closed my eyes and took a deep breath. I was going to need it if I read the rune right, because there was no time to block it.

The magic slammed into me, wrapping itself around my throat, cutting off my air supply. I pitched forward, gurgling, fingers going to my neck. Strangulation rune, a particularly nasty one that reeked of vileness. I crafted a counter rune, but even as I tried casting it, I knew it was wrong.

319

Backwards. I tried again, scrambling now as I fought to get the strangling rune off me.

But the rune tightened around my throat, cutting off more than just air. It cut off the blood, and the yelling around me faded. I flopped onto the ground, face down, everything going dark, the world around me disappearing.

There was a moment of sheer panic that I was going to die, but then I wasn't alone. I knew it in my bones.

Typhon will save me.

I don't fully understand what happened next. I was in the Dark Wood one moment, strangling to death, and the next I was in a bed, staring up at a painted ceiling. The deep-blue velvet looked like the night sky with stars painted on it, and that was interesting.

Warmth surrounded me, the heaviness of a soft comforter, the smell of a wood fire and the musk of a man sinking into my bones. I could just go to sleep, but I knew I shouldn't.

Something had happened, hadn't it?

It all came back to me in a rush.

I blinked. 'Where am I?' The words scratched out of my throat, and I winced. Between Doyenne Parunah's poison and this, my throat had taken a beating today.

Typhon stepped into view, bruises on his chin, shirt partially torn, his hair completely mussed. 'Drink this, it will ease the pain.'

He pressed a flask to my mouth and a honeyed mead poured into me. There was a bite of ginger that lingered, sharp and distinct against my tongue. I pushed the flask away and sat up, grimacing.

'What happened?'

'You mean after O'Connor tried to kill you?' Typhon stared down at me. 'Or before, when you blocked the bond between us?'

I scrunched up my face. 'The former.'

'I reversed the strangulation rune, and carried you back here, but you were still out of it. The combination of the two runes he laid into you . . . left you babbling all sorts of stuff at first. Then, you got violent.' He touched his chin. 'You have a wicked right hook.'

My eyes just about bugged out of my head. 'I . . . hit you?'

He grunted. 'I've had worse.'

Pushing to a sitting position I realized I was in his room and subsequently . . . in his bed. 'Why didn't you take me to the infirmary?'

He didn't sit on the bed, he just stood there staring down at me. 'You think things would go well for you if the Sage knew you were outside school grounds? With O'Connor?'

I couldn't help but flinch. 'Point taken.'

Typhon took a step closer and the bond between us seemed to shiver, giving me a quick insight into the fact that he was . . . afraid.

'I'm sorry,' I whispered.

The frown pulled at his scar, making him seem far fiercer than the bond was telling me in the moment. 'For what?'

'For scaring you.' I shrugged. 'I could feel that once the bond snapped back into place. I was just . . . I want to find my Quirk, Typhon. I'm still slower than everyone else with the rune casting and can't stop Nocta with my bare hands. I can't protect anyone if I can't dig into what I've got, and you've been stonewalling me. I had to do something. I would do anything, break any rules, to keep Opie and my friends safe. If that makes me a bad guy in your book, so be it!'

Might have been yelling that last bit. But it didn't seem to bother him.

He looked away from me, then back, the bond carefully

contained again. 'Do you understand what rune O'Connor used on you? He said you asked him to use it. And I need to know that he isn't lying.'

'It was a relaxing rune. Like a Valium,' I explained. 'I asked him to use something on me, so that I could find my way to my Quirk.'

His silence hung over us, and the words that broke it did nothing to ease me. 'Yeah, well, I left him in the Dark Wood, with a full body bind on him, for what he did.'

In the Dark Wood where there were predators a plenty. Like that massive wolf that had found us, even behind Typhon's protective runes.

'Typhon! He could be killed!' I pushed the covers off and got to my feet only to have my knees crumple under me.

He caught me, and held me there against his chest, and I didn't need to feel the bond to know his heart was pounding.

'Harlow . . . it's the equivalent of a date-rape drug,' he bit out, his one hand at my lower back, the other cupping my head. 'That's what I could sense when the bond snapped into place. I thought . . .'

He truly thought Liam was going to hurt me. And he'd left him to die.

His fingers softened against my cheek, so damn gentle I couldn't help but melt against them.

'Don't let him die, Typhon. He was trying to help me. At my request.'

He let out a heavy sigh, his head lowering. For a second, I thought he might kiss me. Hoped, maybe. But he just pressed his chin to my forehead.

'I'll go get him. Go back to your dorm and stay there, Harlow.' He paused. 'Please.'

'Okay.' I couldn't say anything else.

He let me go and I grieved the loss, my body aching to find my way back into his arms. He shut the door behind him, and I just stared at it for a long time.

There had been no questions about how I'd blocked our bond.

And that made me wonder just what I'd said when I'd been incoherent and fighting in his arms . . .

31

'If something was really wrong, would you tell me?'

I jerked back and blinked over at Opie, who was staring at me, face full of worry.

'It depends,' I answered honestly. She was sharp as a tack. She knew I wasn't myself, same as I knew she wasn't exactly jumping for joy lately, either.

'On what?'

I shrugged and popped a cherry tomato in my mouth before replying.

'On whether I thought it was something you needed to know.'

She glared at me, but I ignored her and continued.

'Sometimes, grown-up problems are exactly that. For grown-ups. Kids should be able to focus on being kids. Learning, having fun, navigating friendships,' I added with a pointed look. 'Sheet like that.'

For the past two days, she'd been eating lunch with me and House Phoenix instead of with Phoebe and Krishna after the whole debacle with the boy she liked. No great loss as far as I was concerned, but she was clearly upset.

'Fine,' Opie said, pushing her lunch tray away. 'Have your secrets. But don't be surprised when I have mine, too.'

Refusing to take the bait from a moody child, I dragged the tray close again and nudged at her uneaten sandwich. 'It's testing day for Hand-to-Hand Combat,' I reminded her gently. 'You should eat something. You might need your strength.'

She snorted. 'Yeah, right. Like I'm going to get picked to fight anyway.'

Hand-to-Hand Combat Day was second only to the Solstice Games as far as events the students most looked forward to. It was a fight to submission, zero magic allowed. First up was determined by the roll of a die. Whichever house crest was cast got to select a single fighter to represent them, and that fighter would select their opponent. As a first year with average non-magical combat skills, there was almost no chance Opie was getting picked by her own team. But another team might pick her as a weaker fighter.

'What do I always say, Opie?'

She cocked her head and shrugged. 'Never pass up a free meal?'

'The other thing.'

She thought a moment longer. 'Mmmmm . . . Screw the Golden Rule? Treat people how they treat you?'

I sighed and pressed two fingers to my temples.

'No. I say that it's better to hope for the best and prepare for the worst.'

She scowled at me. 'So even you think picking me to represent House Unicorna would be the worst.'

'Don't twist my words. You know exactly what I'm –'

'Sorry I'm late,' Fable said breathlessly as she took the empty seat next to me. 'I wanted to get another letter off to Zeed.'

I raised my brows at her, grateful for the change in topic. 'What's that, like number four? He hasn't been gone that long.'

'Yeah, but regular mail must be moving super slow right now because he still hasn't responded to my first one.' She glanced around and leaned in close, dropping her voice to a whisper. 'I tucked this one in with the second half of the year's tuition request letters. I'm sure those will go out high priority.'

I let out a low whistle of approval. 'Pretty slick.'

I wasn't sure if her cheeks were pink at the compliment, or because we were talking about Zeed.

Zeed. Fruck, it had been awful seeing him like that – even if he had gained his Quirk.

A wave of guilt, fresh and hot, rolled over me and I pushed it away. *Nope. What's done is done.* There was nothing I could do about that now. I just hoped he was the same old Zeed when he returned to Neverthorn as when he'd left.

Plus, a new skillset, whatever it was he'd gained.

'Are you going to eat that?' Fable asked Opie, poking at her sandwich.

'Help yourself.'

'I'm only going to eat half, though.' Fable snatched up one of the triangles stuffed with meat, cheese and veggies. 'I'm saving room for cake.'

Opie's lips twitched and she rolled her eyes. 'Feeling pretty confident, huh?'

She grinned. 'We have a ringer, kid. Harlow fights dirty.'

I snorted. 'I survive. There's a difference.'

Mind you, fighting for cake was a new one, even for me. But the added incentive only made me want it more.

Aida Wickersham had announced an additional prize to the Hand-to-Hand Combat Day.

'You need more than glory to get you through a battle.' She'd stood at the front of the dining hall, flour dusted across her cheeks. 'You need good food. So, I have decided that I will make cakes for the victors of each battle in a flavor of their choice. They will be big enough to share with every member of the winning houses. You may put in your requests after breakfast.'

And when I say cheers went up from most of the students? It was deafening.

326

Tarquinius had stood after she left. 'For the losers? No dessert, and certainly no cake.'

'What flavor did you request from the list she gave us?' Fable asked Opie, eyes lit with excitement.

'Banana peanut butter,' Opie admitted, her mood seeming to lift a little. 'You?'

'Dark chocolate cake with a blood-orange curd.'

'Blueberry and lavender sponge with lemon buttercream,' I replied.

'Oooh, that sounds sooo good. Let's pinky swear on Hecate's heart that we share if either of our houses wins. Deal?' Fable asked.

Opie looked the most hopeful I'd seen her in days as she nodded and extended her little finger. 'Deal.'

'What are we swearing to?' Bandit interjected as he leapt onto my lap and snatched a crust of bread from my tray.

'That we will share if we win the big cake.'

'In.' He lifted his paw, and we all interlaced fingers.

Solemn vow made, I gently lifted the trash panda from my lap and set him on the floor.

'I'm going to head out to the courtyard now. I want to get there a couple minutes early in case any of the teams are openly discussing strategy. We need every advantage we can get.'

'Yes! Good idea. I'll come with,' Fable said, pausing to polish off the last of Opie's lunch. 'I don't want to brag, but I've got pretty good lip-reading skills.'

'Guess I'll see you guys there,' Opie said, shooting a wistful glance at the table where the rest of her housemates sat.

It took everything I had not to walk over and threaten Krishna and Phoebe with dismemberment. There was no leaving now, that dream had fled. With Zeed gone, I could feel Tarquinius's eyes on me at every turn.

Typhon's words . . . *You are the strongest Dwimmer in your house.'* I had more than an inkling that he'd shared his thoughts with Tarquinius.

Which meant that until I saw this through to whatever end waited, I just had to remind myself that Opie wasn't special when it came to this type of thing. Teenage girls were capable of cruelty beyond measure. If she could learn to navigate these shark-infested waters, she would only be stronger for it.

But damn, I hated every second of sitting back and letting her figure it out on her own.

'Come with us,' I said, already knowing what her response would be.

'I'm never going to make any of my own friends if I spend all my time following you and yours around. Just go. I'll be okay.'

She looked less than sure on that front.

'Fine, but Bandit will hang here with you so you can walk over together, if that's alright?'

He waddled over toward Opie and climbed into her lap as she shot me a wobbly smile.

'Thanks.'

When Fable and I got to the courtyard a few minutes later, there were only a handful of other students present, all from House Kirinash. While they were a force when it came to casting runes, they weren't known for their combat prowess.

They looked up when we walked in and pressed closer together, dropping their voices to a murmur.

'Good call,' Fable said with a curt nod. 'They are definitely here early strategizing.' She squinted hard, her face a mask of concentration. 'Okay, so Renata is talking now.'

I whipped off a quick sound amplifying rune, but it fizzled into nothing but a shower of golden sparks. With a frown, I tried it again.

Nada.

What the hell?

'We've placed wards to prevent the students from using magic throughout the courtyard until our winners are declared,' a low voice intoned from behind me.

Don't think about kissing him. Don't think about kissing him.

I'd been avoiding him as best I could since *the incident*, but that didn't mean I'd stopped thinking about him. In fact, since our bond had been reestablished, I couldn't get him off my mind. I turned to face him and forced a tight smile to my lips.

'Perfect. That shouldn't affect House Phoenix at all, since that's pretty much how we lived the first three months here due to Tarquinius's muting runes.'

He shook his head in a subtle warning as several of the other professors came to stand beside him.

'Moreno,' Liam murmured, flicking an icy glance Typhon's way.

'O'Connor,' Typhon replied, jaw flexed so tight, I wondered if we might hear a tooth crack.

Whatever happened when Typhon went back to free him the other night, it clearly hadn't included kissing and making up. I guess anything short of murder was a win, though. There was and never would be love lost between these two, I feared.

Still, I couldn't shake the gut-deep feeling that I needed both of them if I was going to give myself and my house-mates the best possible chance of defeating Nocta. The question was, how did I convince them of that?

Because as it stood, I was still Quirkless and bound.

'Let's take our seats on the dais while the students work out their strategies, shall we, gentlemen?' Nikita said, slipping between the men and hooking her arms through theirs.

She leaned in close and pulled them away as Fable and I looked on.

I was still staring holes through her retreating back when

the rest of my housemates poured into the courtyard led by a pale-faced Phyllis.

'What's wrong?' Fable asked, eyeing the others. 'Did something else happen?'

Marina shrugged helplessly over Phyllis's shoulder.

'Phyllis thinks that, given the heightened threat coming from Nocta this year, we shouldn't be –'

'I can speak for myself, child,' Phyllis snapped, cutting Marina off mid-sentence. 'And it isn't a matter of opinion. It's just common sense. What's the point of this silly game? To make students believe that throwing a good punch here or there can actually save them against the likes of Nocta and his acolytes?' Her laugh was bitter and harsh, but her eyes were filled with anguish. 'It's *ludicrous*. And not only that, it's also dangerous. Who among you all will succeed today, have your celebration and your cake, full of pride, only to find yourself in a situation where you stand toe to toe and battle against evil itself when you should have run?' Her voice broke and she turned to me, nearly pleading in a whisper, 'Why didn't they just run?'

I could hear my own heartbeat as the others broke into an argument, most scoffing at the matriarch's worries, but a couple taking it to heart. Ellie stood with her. 'You know me. I hate fighting unless there's no other choice.'

As for me and Fable, we were both struck dumb, because we knew the truth. She wasn't talking about some future hypothetical. Phyllis was talking about the past. The Neverthorn Nine. And what had they gotten for their efforts? No annual day of remembrance. No memorial gardens with headstones to shower with flowers. In fact, they had been basically erased from Neverthorn history. All that remained was a page in some yearbook that someone forgot to purge from existence while those in power cleaned up the unsavory mess, probably using dirty tactics like memory wipes, silencing spells and rune gags.

And Phyllis. Who had remained here ever since, under the watchful eye of our Sage.

The chill that settled over me had nothing to do with the bite in the air and everything to do with the stark realization that, while Nocta was definitely the bad guy in this story, he certainly wasn't the only one. Neverthorn was run by a team of soulless ghouls who cared more about public relations than they did its students.

Never forget that.

Second on the list? I needed to get my hands on that frucking journal again. And this time, electricity or no, I wasn't letting go.

I reached for Phyllis and was about to pull her aside when Tarquinius stepped up to the podium and lifted a hand to silence the chatter. The courtyard had filled up quickly and all houses were present, looking toward the Sage expectantly.

'Good afternoon, students of Neverthorn. As you all know, it's a big day. An important day. One that will determine who among you can claim to be the strongest. The fastest. Maybe even the smartest when it comes to non-magical disciplines. This might seem a small thing but mark me. There are times in battle where magic is . . . inaccessible. It is in those times you will need to dig deep and find the strength in your humanity and your body.'

I could feel Phyllis stiffen beside me and I gave her hand a pat. I wished there was something I could do to spare her having to sit through an event that was clearly triggering for her.

'We will roll the die to see which team will select its opponent first,' Tarquinius continued, waving his hand with a flourish and producing a palm-sized, multi-sided die. 'Make some space, will you?'

The students directly in front of him stepped back, leaving a large empty swath of grass.

'Annnd, off we go!'

He tossed the die high in the air and it hit the ground with a *thunk*, sticking the landing.

We all leaned in, craning our necks to see. A black cat with orange wings.

'The first house to select its opponent . . . Felinita!' he boomed, rubbing his hands together in anticipation.

House Felinita exploded into chatter, forming a circle as they discussed who would represent them and what house they would challenge. Strategy was one of their strong points.

'I bet they select Big Benji Meadows as their representative and challenge someone from Unicorna,' Marina murmured as we all looked on in interest. 'I would.'

Unicorna was Opie's house. They were one of the weaker teams when it came to magic, maybe just a step above Felinita, and most of their members were on the smaller side physically. That all said, it was still possible that House Felinita wanted to flex and show some strength by picking a strong house with a strong opponent.

Or not.

'We choose Benji Meadows, and challenge Aiden Quimbly of House Unicorna!' a grinning young woman shouted, sweeping a hand in front of her.

A massive teenager wrapped in the body of a full-grown linebacker stepped forward. I glanced over to find House Unicorna gathered together, clearly stressed as their discussion grew heated. Opie and the rest of the underclassmen stood to the side looking worried, and I was glad to see Bandit pressed against her ankles. Gladder yet that they hadn't challenged Opie.

Good looking out for her, little buddy.

332

A short, lean young man from Unicorna stepped forward and swallowed hard. 'Um . . . Aiden Quimbly. I will be representing House Unicorna.'

I could feel Opie's panicked gaze locked on me and barely managed to keep myself from wincing. This was going to be a bloodbath.

Tarquinius nodded. 'Here we have it. Our first match. Clear the square, everyone. You all know the rules. If you are knocked clear of the border, your team is automatically disqualified. You have two minutes to force your opponent to submit. To the winner go the spoils. If there is a draw, there are no spoils.'

Which meant no cake. Damn, he was being extra dicky today.

There were some grumbles at that, but Tarquinius waved them off.

'Both boys, please enter the field of play!'

Big Benji and not-so-big Aiden stepped into the marked-off square and faced one another.

As much as I wished I could report that Aiden used his speed and agility to win that battle, it didn't pan out that way. Although I had to admit, he did better than I'd expected. Sure, Big Benji tenderized his breadbasket for a few seconds before lifting him overhead and tossing him bodily out of the square into a heap long before the time bell rang, but Aiden was still alive, and in one piece when they carted him off, aside from the collapsed lung. If I was Unicorna, I'd be calling that a win.

'Way to go, Aiden!' Opie called, clapping loudly, Bandit joining in. 'So brave!'

Krishna and Phoebe both shot her dirty looks and moved further away.

If no one challenged me, I had half a mind to pick one of those little witches to fight.

'Don't even think about it.' I looked to my right to find Liam there, smiling at me.

'Think about what?' I asked, with an innocent shrug.

'You're not fighting thirteen-year-olds,' he added, shooting them a glance. 'You're House Phoenix. You're going to do this the right way and select a worthy adversary if you get the chance.'

'I know . . .'

His dimple faded and he leaned closer. 'We haven't had the chance to talk since . . . Are you okay, Harlow?'

I resisted the urge to fidget, realizing he was trying to have a heart to heart I wasn't ready for.

'You know. Just out here fighting a bunch of teenagers for cake. Living the dream.'

His lips quirked and he bumped his shoulder lightly into mine. 'Got it. We won't speak of it for now. Just know that I would never . . . ever . . .'

I glanced up at him and nodded. 'I know that. And I'm sorry I dragged you into my . . . mess with Typhon.'

There was a sudden flash of rage in my gut, and I struggled to understand where it had come from. A tug on the bond, and I was looking across the ring at Typhon. His eyes were narrowed on me and Liam.

I struggled to breathe around the anger that snapped through me. Anger that was not my own.

'Are you okay?' Liam put a hand to my back. 'You went kinda pale there.'

I cleared my throat and nodded. 'Maybe a bit of nerves after all.'

'I'll get you something to drink,' he slipped away from me, and the anger blazing from Typhon faded. Thank the gods. I wasn't sure I could fight with that sudden emotional surge from him.

The next two fights were at least somewhat even. A scrappy-looking dude from House Wolven challenged and lost to a muscular third-year Kelpish girl who, unbeknownst to anyone, was the daughter of a professional wrestler in the Unlit world. When she got her opponent to tap out, he had the grace to let out a rueful chuckle. She even helped him up afterward and they exchanged a quick handshake and, if I wasn't mistaken, some googly eyes.

It almost renewed my faith in humanity for a hot second. Until Tarquinius rolled Kirinash, and they pitted their strongest fighter against Draconell's weakest at *Nikita's* insistence. If our illustrious Sage had been hoping for blood, he got it in spades this time. Even Typhon looked disgusted by the time they wheeled the poor boy to the infirmary so they could try to mend the compound fracture he'd sustained in his left arm — his spellcasting arm. It was a dick move for sure.

Then again, Neverthorn was not known for being gentle when it came to training young Dwimmers. How did you get to be the strongest school, without the most brutal tests?

You didn't.

'I can't watch for another second,' Phyllis murmured, swaying on her feet. Her face was devoid of color, and she looked like she was about to be sick.

'Last but not least, the only team remaining and unchallenged . . . House Phoenix! Choose your opponent.'

'Maybe we should just forfeit,' Fable whispered, looking a little green around the gills herself. 'Who cares about cake anyway?'

Who cares about cake!? I damned well did. But more than that, even . . .

'We can't forfeit. Even if Tarquinius let us, which he probably wouldn't, it will show weakness to the other houses. They still doubt us. We're supposed to produce the next

Heronius. We're finally getting up to snuff with the runes. We need to show them we can fight too. We need them to respect us if we want to be able to lead them in times of war. We have to fight. You guys trust me, right?' I turned away from Fable and met the eyes of each one of my housemates, who, to their credit, nodded. 'Then let's do this. Let's get the damn cake.'

I lifted my hand and turned. 'I'll be representing House Phoenix.'

Tarquinius looked pleased at the notion. 'Excellent. And your opponent?'

Liam's words though had given me an idea. He was right, I shouldn't be fighting a child, even if they were in their teens. Which left only the most obvious choice.

'And we choose to challenge Doyenne Nikita Elmwood, of House Kirinash.'

That bombshell was met with dead silence.

'She can't do that!' Doyenne Parunah snapped.

'You can't challenge a professor!' Doyenne Storm added her voice to the fray.

Even Doyen Bob spoke up. 'What in the world is she thinking?'

But there was only one opinion that mattered.

I locked my gaze on Tarquinius, who stared down at me, his eyes thoughtful.

'It's not against the rules you set forth, correct? You said we can challenge anyone present . . . and I think that a grown adult fighting children is rather . . . despicable.'

'A student, is a student, is a student,' he said, his voice deeper than usual. 'We've never needed to spell it out before under the assumption that you would all use common sense.'

'The way *she* did when her choice nearly sent that poor boy from Draconell home in a body bag?' I shot back in disgust.

'Spare me your version of common sense and let's abide by the rules of the challenge, shall we? I choose Doyenne Elmwood as my opponent.'

'She's within her rights. A fight between an adult and a child hardly seems fair,' Liam called, and several of the other professors chimed in their agreement.

Including Typhon. 'It will make a better showcase for her skills, Sage.'

Tarquinius looked to Typhon and nodded. 'You make an excellent point, Doyen Moreno. I will allow this fight.'

Nice.

I turned to face Nikita, who sat on the dais with the other professors as she glared holes through me. 'Well. Do you accept my challenge?'

She bristled and patted her long, luxurious ringlets.

'I'm hardly dressed for a fight. I didn't sleep well, and this is highly irregular . . .'

'Bock.'

She opened her mouth and then snapped it shut.

'Bock,' I said again, this time a little louder.

'Bock.'

'Bock, bock, bock!'

A few voices blossomed into a dozen and soon enough, it seemed like most of the courtyard was *bock*ing like a flock of chickens at a flummoxed Nikita.

Her expression went steely, and she stood.

'Fine. You've wanted a piece of me since we were in school. Let's go, then.'

She flounced off the dais and made a beeline for the square, fingers flashing as her hair tied itself into a knot on the top of her head and she kicked off her high heels. The skirt she wore was long and she used another rune to tie it between her legs in some semblance of a harem pant. With her aquamarine eyes flashing fury and her impromptu outfit, even I had to admit, she looked kind of like a bad beech.

Then again, she'd never faced a beech as bad as me.

'Bring it, *Nikita*,' I muttered, rolling my shoulders as I moved to join her in the square.

'Be careful, Harlow,' Phyllis called. 'She won't play fair.'

Just how I liked it. Because no one knew better than me. Real life was rarely fair.

'Rules are the same,' Tarquinius boomed. 'Two minutes starts in three . . . two . . . one . . .'

Nikita and I began to circle one another, each staying at the outer edge of the square. She was solidly built, clearly spending a good amount of time in the gym, and she had a mean streak a mile long. But did she know how to fight?

I was about to find out.

I feinted forward, and threw an exploratory jab, which she dodged pretty handily before waggling a brow at me.

Okay. So, she had at least some skills. That made this even better.

I was still contemplating my next move when the stiletto she had kicked off moments before came flying at me, warp speed.

'Sheet!'

I dodged a scant second before the wicked heel took my eye out, and nearly stumbled.

My housemates cried foul, but as I met Nikita's triumphant grin, I knew there was no point in complaining. There was no mention of weapons in the rules even if it was common sense that they weren't to be used. She'd turned my own strategy against me.

Touché, Keeks.

We danced around one another, and it felt like I was moving through thick mud. What the fruckery was this? Her hand at her side twitched, just the pinky. The lightest glow around it.

Just like . . . Typhon had done in class when we'd been talking about Quirks. His pinky had twitched as he'd said . . .

'Slowing time, a Stall, is a less commonly known Quirk.'

Fruck me upside down, she was slowing the passage of time, but just enough to block me. Apparently, the dulling runes had only applied to the students, which made sense. No one expected the professors to be fighting. But she knew the rules . . .

That cheating beech.

'Rethinking your choice? I won every hand-to-hand challenge through school. Not that you'd know that,' Nikita breathed out as she snapped a quick jab, catching me only because she slowed things down, her pinky finger working overtime.

A burst of stars crossed my vision, but I cleared my head quickly. 'Pathetic cheater,' I murmured, just loud enough for her to hear me. It wouldn't matter how fast I was, if I didn't come up with something, she was going to win.

'Ready to lose?' Nikita smirked, her pinky finger twitching. The magic wrapping around her.

It felt like my feet were in cement now. But that didn't slow my mouth down, not a bit. It was one weapon she couldn't take from me.

'I'm actually flattered you've had to stoop to using magic. I guess that means both of us know I'm tougher than you . . .'

Fury lit her features, and she rushed me, stepping into my reach.

I worked to try and grab hold of her. If I could get hold of her hands, I could also stop the flow of her spell, by breaking that pinky finger.

I dropped low and grabbed at her feet. Clamping my arms around her legs, I twisted hard to the left, slamming her face-first into the ground. The air whooshed out of her, and she lay there stunned. Still under the slow effects of her spell, I crawled up her body, and wrapped my legs around her waist from behind. And the cherry on top? I clamped a choke hold on her.

She squawked, and immediately went limp, because I was a monster when it came to choke holds.

There was no tapping out, no yielding, she just stopped fighting. I let her go and stood up, the Quirk she'd used on me, gone.

'The winner is Harlow Daygon, of House Phoenix!' Tarquinius shouted, his expression both solemn and thoughtful. 'That ends the Hand-to-Hand Combat Day.'

House Phoenix ran to me, squealing and shouting in glee. Even Phyllis joined in, although I imagined she was just relieved it was over and we'd all survived.

Horns blew, confetti exploded in the sky above us, and best of all, four cakes so large they needed to be dragged out on wheels were set before us. Wickersham was right there, winking at me. 'I knew you'd win it, Shortbread.'

The losing teams looked on with envy, most clapping in recognition of our accomplishments, some silent, contemplating their own defeat as their opponents' houses each got a cake of their own.

'Winning houses, enjoy your rewards!' Mrs. Wickersham shouted. 'They were a joy to make!'

'Losers, make your way back inside post haste,' Tarquinius added.

'Wait!' I said, waving my arms as the students made their way to the double doors. 'Wait! House Phoenix wants to share ours. There is plenty for everyone!'

Tarquinius looked like he was about to argue, but then the girl who won for Kelpish joined in.

'Us too!'

Felinita conferred and then pointed at their cake. 'We will also share.'

Tarquinius threw up his hands in defeat. 'Fine. Do what you will. O'Connor, with me. I'd like to speak with you.' He was gone in a swirl of robes as the courtyard broke out into cheers.

Liam sighed. 'I'd better go. See you later, Harlow. That was a solid win.' He leaned in almost as if to hug me, but then stopped short and turned away.

I stared after him a moment.

'That was foolhardy,' Typhon muttered as he made his way toward me and handed over the first slice of cake.

I bent low and breathed in the heavenly scent. Blueberry, lavender, and lemon.

'She will hate you even more now,' he added as his eyes drifted to Nikita dragging herself out of the vicinity.

'You say that like I had a chance of winning her over. Which we both know I didn't. And I'll be honest, that only makes my win sweeter,' I admitted, plugging a forkful of cake into my mouth with a blissful sigh. With my eyes half closed, I watched him, watching me. His eyes dipping to my lips, then sliding further down my body, like a caress.

The intensity of his gaze had cake sticking in my throat and pressure pooling low in my belly.

Pathetic.

'You did it!' Opie crowed a second before hurling herself at me and nearly upending my cake.

'Awesome, right?'

'So cool. Totally badass.'

'Yeah, that was really cool, Harlow,' a reedy voice chimed in. I pulled away from Opie to find Krishna standing there with Phoebe at her side, an apologetic smile on her face. 'Opie, you want to sit by the fountain and do a tasting of all the different flavors of cake with us?'

Opie beamed, nodding. 'Sure. See you later, Lo-lo!'

I tried not to roll my eyes as they ran off.

'They're kids,' Typhon muttered. 'Go easy on them.'

'And kids like that grow up to be adults like Nikita. Mark my words.'

His eyes drifted over me again. 'I'd like to talk to you about –'

But he was cut short as a chant broke out around us. My friends were ready to celebrate.

'Har-low! Har-low! Har-low!'

Bodies swarmed toward me, and I even lost my cake in the bustle as I was swept up high in the air by my housemates. I couldn't lie. It felt really nice to be appreciated.

All in all, it had been a good day.

No. A *great* day.

Had I figured out what my Quirk was?

Decidedly not.

Had I managed to turn off the spigot of lustful thoughts aimed at one super sexy, infuriating doyen?

I peered down at Typhon beneath my lashes only to find him staring at me, barely disguised hunger still lingering in his eyes.

That was a big fat negatory.

But tomorrow was another day. For now, House Phoenix was happy and united, Nikita was awash in humiliation, my Opie was smiling, and there was still cake.

Lots and lots of cake.

And nobody could take that away from me.

32

The cake was delicious. But the flavors didn't outlast the stressors that came with living in Neverthorn.

As the earth continued to turn, the threat of Nocta's attack grew.

The Solstice Games would be held in just a couple of weeks, and we'd be able to flex a little. It would be held miles from the school, off grounds, which meant the dulling effects we were all still grappling with would disappear.

In theory, at least.

But would our time at the games be enough to prepare us for what was to come? To prepare for Nocta himself? I still felt like we were missing something important. Something that was being kept from us.

I blew out a breath and looked at the date hung on the wall. Two days before the Feast of Abundance.

'Bandit . . .' I rolled over and pulled the covers over both our heads early on a Sunday morning, quickly spinning a rune of silence over us so we couldn't be overheard. 'I need to find an inexpensive gift for Opie, and one for Fable. I've got like two days, and I'd like to get them each something, and I don't have time to search on my own with all the home-work I've got.'

Traditionally, small gifts were traded between yourself and those you were most grateful for in your life. It was a day to thank Mother Hecate for the gifts of her magic and thank the Horned King for not frucking about in your life too much.

The date had snuck up on me, and now I needed to get

something together quickly. And, in truth, I hadn't thought I'd still be here by the time the Feast of Abundance rolled around.

'Didn't you all agree not to do gifts?'

He was not wrong. House Phoenix had decided on the whole not to exchange gifts on the Feast of Abundance. Simply because we'd all kind of forgotten about it until last minute. Like me, they'd been swamped with classes, home-work, and worry.

I shrugged, hating how this was going to sound, like I was playing favorites, but it was the truth. 'I know, but they . . . the two of them mean a lot to me, and the gifts . . . I think I can find a way to make the gifts more than just gifts.'

'How about a chicken?' Bandit slapped his hands together. 'You could let them pull their heads off themselves.'

I grimaced. 'They aren't raccoons,' I reminded him.

'Right, right. Okay, what are you thinking?'

'Something Opie can wear, like a bracelet or a ring so she knows she's never alone. She's . . . she's going to need it.' I felt terrible even saying the words, but I knew that one day she'd realize, truly realize, that there was no magic in her and she would feel very much alone. I had to admit, the gift was partly for me. If she wore it, I'd mark it so I would always be able to find her in case anyone ever tried to separate us again. 'Check the Nevershoppes. See if you can find any-thing good, and then I can go back and pay.'

'And for Fable?' He cocked a brow. 'You going to produce Zeed for her to kiss under Hecate's flowers?'

I laughed softly and shook my head. 'She'd love me for-ever if I could do that. But no, I'll leave that to the two of them to decide when he comes back.'

If he came back. He still hadn't answered any of Fable's letters. Liam still hadn't gotten any info from the family, which was weird. Fable had thought maybe he was mad at her for telling me that they'd gone to the fairy ring . . .

What could Fable possibly need that I could get for her on a limited budget? 'I think a pair of small throwing knives would be good. I can start teaching her. That way if anyone tries to dull her magic, she has a way to protect herself.'

Bandit saluted me and then he was springing out of the bed and rushing out of the massive dormitory.

I pulled the sheet back to see Fable staring at me. 'What was that all about?'

'Secrets abound,' I said with a wink.

She laughed and slid her runners on. None of us slept in pj's anymore; we all slept in some variation of being fully clothed now that we all shared one big room.

'Come on, let's go check out the library. We have some time before remedial runes with Doyen Moreno.' Fable grabbed my arm and dragged me to my feet. We hit the kitchens first, snagging coffee and breakfast sandwiches from Mrs. Wickersham.

The library didn't give up any of its secrets, not a single one. Or at least, no secrets that would do me or Fable any good. There was nothing on Nocta we hadn't already read in another book or article. There was nothing in the legends section that was new. But we kept at it.

Because there was no other choice.

The next morning, I found myself negotiating with a giant of a man over his handmade knives.

'They be worth more than what you are offering,' his low growl rumbled against my skin.

I tapped the knives, knowing that they would fit Fable perfectly. They were balanced, light, and in their sheaths, they would lay flat against her inner forearms so that even with a shirt on you'd not notice she had knives strapped to her.

'I know that.' I rubbed a hand over the back of my neck. I didn't have much to offer. I paused. 'Can I put it on an account?'

His dark eyebrows arched upward over blue eyes flecked with silver. 'I don't do accounts.'

Damn.

I ran my fingers over the two blades and their arm sheaths. 'I'll be back.'

I needed enough money to pay for the necklace Bandit had found for Opie too. Neither of these things were negotiable in my mind. Both gifts would protect them in different ways.

I let myself out the door and stood in the street. The Never-shoppes hadn't changed in a hundred years as far as I knew. They were rustic, with thatched roofs, some had rounded doors, other large square ones. Big windows were in place in some of the shops, allowing people to peek in at the wares before actually committing.

The Black Bear pub still called to me, but I didn't have time or the extra funds to actually visit the place with the amazing food.

The cobblestone lane that ran through the middle of the shops was full of students hurrying between the stores. Everyone was looking for last-minute gifts.

And that gave me an idea. There was an option to get the funds I needed. I blew out a slow breath and let my eyes drift over the kids who were in and out of multiple shops, those with the biggest packages.

If I was going to do it, now was the time. I tucked my hands in the pockets of my jacket and lowered my head into the wind as I walked straight toward a girl from Draconell – Misty Lillentia. She was from one of the wealthiest Dwimmer families around. A snob who talked down to the staff at school, she loved to brag about how much money she and her family had.

Maybe it was time to separate her from a tiny bit of it.

I plowed right into her, gasped as we kind of danced around one another, my hand going into her pocket and snagging an entire bundle of coins, sliding it into my own pocket as the parcels and bags went in the air.

'Oh, sheet, I'm sorry!' I was yelping as I grabbed at the bags, helping her gain her feet. 'Sorry, totally in my own world there.'

Misty shook her head. 'Whatever, loser.'

I handed her the last bag that she'd dropped, and she and her friends carried on back toward Neverthorn.

Bandit tugged at my leg. 'That was slick.'

'Yeah.' I felt lower than dog poo stuck in the treads of a shoe, but for Opie and Fable, I'd do worse if I had to.

Back into the blacksmith's shop I went. I opened up the coin purse and counted out the agreed price for the two blades and their sheaths.

'Managed to find that money awfully fast, lassie,' he said as I dropped the coins into his open palm.

I shrugged. 'Playing hardball wasn't getting me anywhere. I had the money all along.'

Lies, lies, lies.

I had a feeling the big blacksmith knew it. Even so, he wrapped up the blades. 'Fae-made, they won't break, and they'll find their way back to her should she lose them.'

I nodded. 'Thanks.'

He winked and a tiny flush of heat made me look away. The man was good looking, and if he was part Fae then I was right to avoid his full gaze.

Leaving, I headed down the street to the junk house. Yes, you read that right, junk house. Apparently, Bandit had found the perfect pendant in all the junk that was lying around.

Boxes upon boxes were stacked to the ceiling, teetering as I brushed by. The store clerk was nowhere to be found. But that didn't mean he or she wasn't there. I probably just couldn't see them. I edged through the spaces sideways, following Bandit.

'Come on,' he whispered, motioning for me to keep up with him as he raced through the store.

A teardrop ruby he'd said – I wasn't sure if it was fake or not, but he led me straight to it, at the back of the store, which smelled like mothballs and unwashed bodies, not a great combination.

I held my breath as best I could as I dug down and through the box he indicated. The box was labeled as knickknacks. My fingers brushed against the smooth gem, and there it was. I tugged it out of the pile of assorted items. A ruby necklace that caught the light, throwing color like flames around. Whoever had put it in here had no idea what they were throwing out.

'Nice! Thank you for finding it.' I kept my voice low.

I motioned for Bandit to move and searched the area until I found what else I was looking for: something to hide it in.

A teapot.

'This is perfect! Phyllis will love it!' I held it up and slipped the ruby pendant into it. I had no doubt that the pendant was real now that I'd seen it, and I wasn't about to pay full price for it – not when I was certain that even if I still had my entire pouch of money from Misty that it wouldn't be enough. Was the teapot actually for Phyllis? No, of course not. It was cracked and stained, not a real gift. But the shop owner didn't know that.

I made my way back to the front desk – or what I assumed was the front desk. The barest space with a chair behind it.

'Hello?'

'You found something? A treasure?'

'A teapot, for my friend.' I held the teapot up.

'A silver piece will do for that.'

I snorted. 'Half a silver piece at best. It's chipped!'

I pointed out the chip on the base.

'Fine!' the voice answered, though I still couldn't see a face. 'Three quarters of a piece.'

I put the teapot down. 'Come on, Bandit, let's go.'

His eyes were wide, and I shook my head at him. We were almost to the door when the voice called out.

'Wait! Half a silver piece then. You don't negotiate like the others from the school.'

I plopped the silver piece on the counter and cut it in half with a quick rune that mercifully worked on the first go. 'I'm too old to be stupid about negotiating.'

I picked up the teapot and held it tight as I slipped out the door.

'Hey, we gotta hurry, dinner bell!' Bandit yelled and then he was bounding away from me toward the gates of Neverthorn. I ignored him, turning back to the shops. I still had more than enough coins left to find a few more items . . . there were, after all, five others in my dorm, and a real gift for Phyllis. Did we agree not to do gifts? Sure, but after all we'd been through . . . we deserved a little joy and abundance.

Though I was looking forward to giving something to each of my friends the next day, the night had been like every other for me. Restless, struggling to sleep, sweating at intervals when my mind raced too hot. Counting my breaths.

Itemizing things in the room.

Fighting to keep the anxiety at bay.

In spite of that, I was still excited to take my present to Opie, first thing.

'Don't take it off, and, if you're ever lost, I'll always be able to find you.'

'It's beautiful! Thank you!' She lifted her hair so I could put it on for her. 'But once my magic really kicks in, I won't need it. I'll always be able to find my way to you too!'

I cleared my throat and nodded. 'And . . . I got you these too.' I held out a second package that held a Unicorna statue that glowed at night, and a set of watercolors. Her squeal was enough for me.

'You did such a great job with my presents! Here, I made this for you.' Opie pressed her gift for me into my hands. A small package. I opened it up to find a bracelet made of all sorts of items. Pebbles, wood, bone, glass. 'I made it myself, found all the little pieces. See this one, it reminds me of your eyes. And this one for that time you took me to the beach and the sunset was all purple and orange . . .' her words slid over me. A bracelet made up of her memories and her view of me. It was beautiful, more so because she didn't have a single dark piece in the lot, not one black chunk of stone to mar it.

I shoved back the rush of guilt as I thought of all my ill-gotten gifts . . .

'I love it,' I whispered around a rather tight throat as I put the bracelet on. I hugged her tight to me, longer than she wanted, if her squirming was any indication.

'I'll see you at breakfast, okay? Me and my friends are exchanging gifts soon.' She grinned up at me, gathering up her stuff.

Bandit followed me as I made my way back to my dorm. 'How did it go?'

'Good. But I worry about her . . .'

He sniffed. 'Because she doesn't have any magic.'

I choked on what I was going to say. 'Shush your mouth.'

350

'It's the truth. I can't smell a lick of it on her. I mean, I guess someone could have muted her too, but she'd have a little magic smell even then, wouldn't she?'

'Bandit,' I growled his name.

He shrugged. 'You're trying to protect her. That's good. She's lucky you love her so much.'

I was trying to protect Fable too, and was looking forward to giving her the knives, but when I got back to the House of Phoenix dorm, it was empty. I was about to turn around and leave but caught sight of a tiny box on my bed. It wasn't wrapped, just bound shut with a gold string. No name, no card. I turned it over, hearing something rattle softly inside of it.

Bandit grabbed it from me and sniffed it all over, finally licking an edge. 'Smells like Typhon.'

I pulled the string loose and the box fell open. A round, yellowish piece of glass sat inside, set in an ornate gold frame. Like a mini picture frame, only there was no picture inside of it. I rolled the piece in my hand. It fit nicely in my palm.

A piece of paper fell out. Directions?

Hold the glass over a spell book.

I pulled the spell book out from under my bed that I'd brought back from the library weeks ago and had never returned.

Holding the piece of glass over the first line, I couldn't help the gasp.

The words under the yellow glow of the glass . . . made *sense.*

'It's . . . is this for real?'

I scanned the first page, and the words not only made sense, I retained them.

My heart was beating stupidly fast for a gift that was as nerdy as they came. A gift that meant Typhon had been paying attention to me and my struggles. I put a hand over my eyes, pinching the corners. I would not cry, damn it.

But I couldn't help but think . . . when was the last time a gift had been given to me that had meant someone was actually seeing me, the real me?

I wasn't sure I'd *ever* received one.

'Hey, are you coming down for breakfast?' Fable stepped into the room, her voice pulling me out of the emotions that were threatening to choke me.

I wiped at my face and nodded. 'Yeah, I . . . I wanted to get your gift for you.'

Fable grinned. 'Ha! So much for not getting each other anything! I have something for you, too!'

She handed me a soft package. I tore the paper and found a pair of hand-knit gloves. 'I left the fingertips open, so you could still cast runes,' she said, her cheeks pink.

'I love them.' I pulled the gloves on. They fit like . . . well, like a pair of gloves meant for me. The material was very thin, and I could feel the magic woven into them. 'What else is in them?'

Fable winked. 'You'll have to find out.'

I laughed. 'I like a good surprise. Now you open yours.' I pushed the smaller box into her hands.

She opened it and gasped when she saw the knives. 'Harlow! Where did you get these? They're amazing.'

'They're handmade, with Fae magic. Think of them as back-up should anyone ever try to dull your magic again. You strap them to your forearms, and I'll teach you how to throw them.'

Her hug shouldn't have caught me off guard, and yet it did. I squeezed her back. 'May only abundance flow to you, Fable.'

'And to you, Harlow.'

Breakfast was a mess of food, people were happy, light-hearted, and there were none of the shadows that had been lingering.

I had found small gifts for everyone in House Phoenix with the last of the coins I'd taken from Misty. A teacup for Phyllis. A new journal for Caterina etched with a dark forest, little fireflies littering the cover. For Ellie I'd tracked down a tiny first-aid kit that I'd shrunk with my nicking notions. Marina got a book about the history of the Runecoats. Gary had a thing for puzzles, and I'd gone back to the blacksmith and had him fashion a puzzle made of iron rings that needed to be separated. And Ross . . . I couldn't resist a pair of sleeping pants patterned with trees.

He held them up. 'Sick of seeing me in my holey boxers, I guess?'

I pointed a finger at him. 'You got it.'

'You didn't have to get us anything,' Caterina said. 'You've done so much for us already.'

I ducked my head and shrugged, my throat tighter than I would have liked. It had started with the exchange with Opie, then Fable and now this.

'We each made a little something for you.' Ross grinned.

Made. They'd made something for me? I looked around but it was Phyllis who caught my eye. She smiled and nodded. 'We look to you, Harlow.'

My heart was beating way too hard as each of the others came up to me and pressed something into my palm. Stones. Smooth flat stones, all of different colors.

'They're worry stones,' Ellie said. 'We each cast a rune into the back, with our initials.'

'And I suggested we put a sword on the front,' Gary added. 'You know, swearing fealty to you, with our swords.'

'We made one for Zeed too,' Fable said, handing me a

353

second stone. 'He can imbue it with a rune and his aura signature when he gets back.'

'And,' Marina said, 'we made sure that they wouldn't make noise. A little rune on the velvet bag and voilà. Silent!'

I shook my head. 'No, I can't, you don't want to swear –'

Fable closed my fingers around the stones. 'We do. We are in this fight together and these stones, they are connected to each of us.'

They'd done the same thing that I'd done for Opie. So I could find her anywhere.

And now I could find them too.

I looked at the matron of the group who gave me a wobbly smile. I took note that she hadn't given me a stone. 'Why?'

Ross ran a hand over his head, ruffling his thick hair. 'Because. From the beginning you've fought for us. You're the leader. The big cheese. The man. The boss. We wouldn't have gotten this far without you.'

Caterina pulled out a black velvet bag and held it under my fingers. Each of the stones fell from my palm, one at a time. No sound came from the clink of stone on stone. She smiled up at me. 'Friends to the end.'

The group descended on me in a hug to end all hugs. There might have been tears, I don't know. I just know that my friends were turning into something far more to me.

They were turning into family.

Love and joy seemed to have dispelled the worries about Nocta from everyone's minds.

Well, not everyone's . . .

Fable grabbed at my hand, dragging me from breakfast. 'Come on, we have a full free day, and with the gift you got from your secret admirer, you can really help me dig into the Dwimmer books.'

I rolled my eyes but didn't protest. As I stood to leave with Fable, I caught Typhon's eye.

There was no gift from me to him, which made me feel like a sheet. Worse, he gave me a nod like he knew there would be nothing left for him on his bed from me.

As we reached the library I put a hand on Fable's arm. 'Wait, I have to do one thing first. I forgot a gift.'

I turned and bolted back toward our dorm before she could protest. Skidding into the room, I dug under my bed for the only other thing I had to give.

The teapot I'd smuggled Opie's necklace out with.

I ran a hand over it, and then took it back with me to the library.

Fable's eyes went wide. 'Um. What is that for?'

'A last-minute gift,' I muttered. 'Now help me find a spell on transposing liquids that I can make work.'

Fable tipped her head back and laughed. 'Freaking genius. Okay, it'll be over here.'

It took us less than fifteen minutes to find the rune combination that would turn water into wine. Only I didn't want wine, I wanted it to be whiskey.

Adjusting the runes in my head, I glanced back at the page, able to see how they should look at least. Not shorthand, just . . . meshing the two runes together. That wouldn't hurt the weave. Would it?

I was banking on not.

'If I turn my hand that way, and then give it an extra flick there, that should do it,' I muttered. I put my hands on the teapot, tracing the runes directly into the fine bone china.

'That's a good idea. I bet my brother would have loved it,' Fable said softly and then her eyes started to well up, tears sliding down her cheeks.

The runes settled into the teapot, fading from my fingers with a warm amber glow, not unlike the color of whiskey.

'I'm so sorry about your brother.' I turned to face her, feeling slightly nauseous. 'I wish I could fix it for you. I wish I could bring him back.'

'It's not your fault.' Fable's tears were streaming now. 'It's Nocta's fault. And you are helping. We're going to stop him. Me and you.'

I felt the truth bubbling up in me and knew that it was time.

'I hate Nocta too. For what he did to my family. To my mom.'

She nodded. 'I know.'

I sucked in a breath. 'But also, because a girl wants her dad to be her hero, and not a monster waiting to kill her and her friends.'

She stared at me for a long moment, and then her eyes widened.

'Fable . . . Nocta is my father.'

33

I waited, stomach churning, for her fury. For accusations, more tears, or worse, silence. But when I gathered the courage to meet her gaze again, I found her soft eyes full of sympathy.

'Promise me you won't breathe a word to anyone else.'

'Fable, I –'

'Promise me!'

I drew back, startled by her intensity. Gentle, sweet Fable meant business.

'Okay! I promise.'

'Good.' She nodded slowly and let out a breath, seeming to gather her thoughts. 'Harlow, the others care about you, and respect you, and they just trusted you with their fealty. But they don't know you like I do. And they are also finally finding their feet. We need morale high going into the games. We need to feel like a true team. I think this news would be a lot to digest, and we don't have that kind of time.'

I swallowed hard. 'I hated lying to you guys.'

'I get that. And it doesn't have to be secret forever. Just a couple more weeks, until after the games. They don't need the distraction. Alright?'

'Yes. Of course. I don't want them wasting energy on me when they need to focus.' I bit my lip and reached out to grab her hand, still sort of reeling that she hadn't just slapped me and walked away. 'So . . . You don't hate me?'

'I wish you'd told me sooner, but I understand why you didn't. And you're still the best friend I've ever had.'

Her eyes were full of tears again, which only made my own well up.

She wrapped her arms around me and squeezed. I hugged her back and for just a moment let the world be okay. I had finally laid my darkest secret bare, and Fable loved me anyway.

If that wasn't family, I didn't know what was.

'Hey,' Fable said, pulling away to shoot me a look. 'You still have that teapot. Maybe we should try it out?'

'Yes,' I laughed through a sob. 'Hell yes.'

Which was how we ended up in the House of Phoenix common room, drinking out of the teapot I'd meant to give to Typhon. But damn, it made a real fine whiskey – a rather strong whiskey with a hint of magic. I poured out a few more cups for Marina, Ross, Phyllis, Gary, Caterina, and Ellie. Anyone who wanted a drink on the Feast of Abundance got one.

More than a few slurred. 'May abundance find you,' popped out of mouths before taking their shot.

It was close to midnight before everyone was finally in their own beds, the two boys snoring. Everyone out cold with the amount of whiskey we'd imbibed.

I realized with a start that I was running out of time to give Typhon his gift before the day was over. Hugging it to my chest, I left a snoring Bandit on my pillow and slipped out of the room.

I started down the stairs and then headed east to the stairway that led down to the Draconell wing. As I passed their house sitting room, a male voice called out a soft 'Hello?' Freezing in place, I tried to pretend I wasn't there. Maybe if I closed my eyes, whoever it was wouldn't see me . . .

'Harlow?'

I opened one eye and sighed.

Busted. But by who?

I stepped to the open doorway and craned my neck to see

into the room. It took a few seconds to catch sight of Liam seated on a massive leather chair bathed in the light of a cheery fire crackling in the hearth.

I let out a long, relieved breath, my heartbeat slowing.

'You're up late,' I mused, weaving my way into the room unsteadily.

'I am. Lot on my mind, I guess.'

I squinted hard until he came into full focus, and then plopped down on the sofa across from him, clutching the teapot close to my chest. Now that he mentioned it, Liam did look more solemn than I'd seen him in the past. No hint of a smile tugging at one corner of his firm lips. No glint in his eye.

'Is everything okay?'

'That's the problem, Harlow. I'm not sure.'

This sounded serious. I scuttled back against the cushions and folded my legs to sit criss-cross applesauce.

'Talk to me. I'm a good listener.'

'I imagine you are. And, even better, you'll likely forget everything we talked about by morning.'

'Don't let the drunk sorority girl bit fool you. It's a steel trap up here, buddy.' I tapped my noggin for good measure.

He nodded slowly, steepling his fingers beneath his chin. 'Don't I know it. It's one of the things I really lo – like about you. But the things I'm thinking right now . . . they're not for sharing.'

Liam eyed me in a way that made me want to look some-place else. I uncrossed my legs, suddenly desperate to get away from the crackling fire that had somehow ramped up inside me to a seventh-level-of-hell inferno.

'Okay, well, it was really good to see you. We have to catch up at some point. Maybe after the holidays! We can have that drink I owe you at the pub.'

In public. With people around so I didn't feel so suddenly

and utterly exposed. On that note, I wheeled around and basically sprinted for the door.

'By the way,' Liam called after me softly, 'if you're looking for Moreno, he's not in his room. He walked past the door, headed the other way about an hour ago.'

I refused to contemplate how he'd known where I was headed. Instead, I closed my eyes and focused on the bond that connected me to Typhon while I still was full of liquid courage. It took a bit, but then, there it was. Calling to me . . .

Up and up it took me, all the way to the rooftop of the school. I had to climb several sets of stairs, cursing the burn in my muscles all the way, and finally up a rickety-ass ladder, one-handed no less.

Whatever that weirdness was with Liam, it was surely just a product of too many drinks, not enough sleep, and an unintentional midnight meetup.

He was just a friend. A very cute, funny, warm friend.

It was all so easy with Liam.

As for Typhon, on the other hand, things were never easy. Were we even friends? Who the fruck knew anymore. All I knew was that, in that moment, I needed to see him more than I'd ever needed anything in my whole life.

Surely that was the whiskey.

I pushed the teapot out onto the roof first then climbed out after it, staying on my knees. 'I sure hope you appreciate that I made it here before the day was over,' I mumbled under my breath as I grabbed the handle of the teapot and stood.

What I hadn't counted on was Typhon not being alone.

He and the other person – the woman – stepped back from each other as if I'd interrupted something.

I stood there, staring at him, his shirt opened and flapping in the wind.

At Nikita, her face flush.

360

Tucking the teapot back under my arm, I turned and went back down the ladder. 'Nope, nope, nope.'

I could feel Typhon heading my way.

I made it down the ladder without falling, and down the first two sets of stairs before he caught me by the arm.

'It's not what it looks like,' he growled. 'I –'

'Screw you, Typhon. I'm not a child to be told it's not what it looks like, when it is exactly what it looks like.'

His eyes darkened. 'You don't understand –'

I glared at him and shoved the teapot in his hands. 'Happy Feast of Abundance.'

I spun – sloppily – on my heel and stalked – stomped wobbly – off toward my dorm. I was done, so done with him. I hoped he choked on the whiskey.

Throwing myself into my bed, I lay there as the room spun and all I could feel was Typhon's emotions.

I'd not been paying attention to his emotions before, so I had no idea what had been going through his head when he'd been with Nikita.

But now? Sorrow, so much sorrow.

I hated that his emotions made me hate him less.

I growled under my breath and Bandit mimicked me.

'Who we growling at?'

'Typhon,' I whispered. 'He was hanging out with Nikita. It . . . didn't look good, I'll just say that.'

'Worm food!' he hissed. 'You want me to bite him in the ass?'

I snorted and pulled him tight to me, hanging onto him for comfort. 'I just want to sleep and pretend none of it happened.'

Bandit patted my cheek. 'Good idea. Tomorrow will be better, chickie!'

But like a lot of days here, tomorrow was, in fact, not better.

34

The next morning, I woke up with a thick tongue, a pounding headache, and a furry raccoon pressed against my face.

'Ugh, get off,' I muttered, shoving Bandit off and onto the pillow beside me. He didn't even wake up. He just let out a snuffle and curled back up before starting to snore again.

'Here, drink this.'

I looked up to find a clear-eyed Fable looking down at me, her gaze full of pity as she handed me a mug.

'Bless you, my friend.' I took the offering and tossed back its contents in one open-throated gulp. My belly heaved instantly as the taste of whiskey filled my mouth. 'Blerg.'

I barely made it to the trash can beside my bed before I wretched, chucking up the contents of my stomach.

'Gods, what the hell was that?' I swiped a hand over my mouth as I blinked back a hot rush of tears that had come along with the heaving.

'The hair of the dog that bit you. Plus, some clamato juice.'

I stared at her like she'd grown a second head.

She shrugged and held up both hands. 'Look, I'm a newb when it comes to partying. Maybe next time just drink one or two, and we won't have this problem, hmmm?'

For a second, our eyes locked, and a memory of the night before passed between us.

'Harlow, it doesn't change anything . . .' she whispered, taking the empty mug from my unresisting fingers.

'Good morning, sunshines!' Marina crowed as she rushed through the door balancing two coffee cups in one hand and a heaping bowl of oatmeal topped with fruit in the other. 'You two better get down and eat before they clear breakfast away. I'm carbing up big for the next two weeks. If we can't find our Quirks, at least we'll have our strength.'

My head had its own pulse, and I grimaced. 'What time is it?'

'Nine fifteen. You're just sleeping the day away,' Marina replied.

'Weirdly, your hangover concoction may have actually worked. I was super nauseous before, but now I'm just hungry. Some food, couple of aspirin, and I'll be right as rain.'

Once I'd washed my face and brushed my teeth, I was already feeling marginally better. Until I walked into the dining hall to find Typhon in deep conversation with Nikita, their heads pressed close together. To my surprise, though, the second we made eye contact, he excused himself and made his way toward me.

'I can't believe I have to say this out loud, but I am not sleeping with Nikita.'

I wanted to be furious, but weirdly, the more I looked at his anguished face, the less angry I felt. 'Tell me why I should believe you? Better yet, tell me why you care if I do?'

'Because it matters. I . . . I am not a good guy, Harlow, but – forget it.'

He turned to walk away, but I couldn't let him go. I needed answers.

'Was she trying to sleep with you?' I asked, bracing myself for the lie.

'Yes. Ever since she came here. It's never worked.'

Fruck me, I believed him.

'Are you feeling unwell?' he asked, studying me through narrowed, dark eyes. 'You're looking feverish.'

Part of me wanted to snap back and say the same to him,

but it would've been a lie. Even tired and strained, he looked amazing and smelled even better.

'Rough night's sleep,' I conceded with a tight smile. 'Look, I . . . um, the whole reason I tracked you down last night was that I wanted to thank you. For the gift.' He was dead silent and, for a second, I wanted to crawl into a hole. 'I mean . . . I assumed – did you leave something on my bed, or . . .'

'I did,' he replied with a nod.

The relief left me feeling a little dizzy.

'Oh, good. Okay then, well thanks.' I forced a smile, 'I, um, really appreciate you thinking of me. It really helped a lot. It was like someone turning a light on in a dark room. If I'd known, maybe . . .'

Maybe things here at Neverthorn would've been different for me the first time around.

'Anyways,' I said, forging on. 'Thanks.'

Again, no reply.

I resisted the urge to start fidgeting under the heat of his gaze.

'I got you a teapot full of whiskey, but I drank it. Hence the chipped teapot. The rune on it should still work, though. It will make you more once it's recharged.'

His lips twitched but the hint of a smile was gone before it ever fully materialized.

'I didn't give you something because I expected something in return, Harlow. And it wasn't even really meant to be an Abundance gift. I just so happened to finally get it exactly right only yesterday morning.' He stepped close enough that his woodsy fire smoke scent filled my senses, and I nearly got lost in those deep-green eyes. 'The reason I made the glass of lucidity was so I could right a wrong.'

'Oh?' I croaked.

'We failed you the first time around. Someone should have

noticed sooner. It's our job to make sure we connect the dots for the students who rely on us. Those dots never connected for you, even more than the others, and no one stopped to ask why.'

'You were just a student teacher yourself. And I didn't exactly make it easy for you or anyone else to ask me anything. I wanted to be home with my mom, and I know I was a pain in the asterisk –'

'You were a kid and there was a whole team of adults tasked with your care. Facts are facts. The school dropped the ball, and it had a lasting effect on you and your life.'

Having someone acknowledge and validate a piece of my childhood trauma knocked the breath out of me. My eyes stung, filling with unshed tears, and I blinked hard.

'Anyway, on behalf of Neverthorn Academy and for myself personally, I wanted to . . . apologize.'

'I accept your apology,' I said. 'And I thank you again for your very thoughtful gift.'

'On that note, there's one other thing I'd like to give you. Once you've finished your breakfast, can you stop by my chambers?'

I blinked at him, my imagination running wild.

His lips twitched like he could read my mind, and I launched into a nervous chuckle.

'Uhm, yeah. Sure thing. About a half hour, sound good?'

'That's fine, yes.'

The clanging of trays and dishes was a welcome distraction from his unrelenting gaze, and I whipped my head around to see the staff clearing away the breakfast spread.

'I've got to make a plate,' I mumbled, giving him one last glance through my lashes.

'See you shortly.' He turned on his heels and headed out of the room, taking a piece of my heart as he went.

A thoughtful, kind, and apologetic Typhon? One who still looked like he might pull my hair and smack my asterisk in bed?

That Typhon was positively lethal.

Stop thinking about it. He probably just wants to show you some rune trick or something.

And for that alone, I should be grateful. I'd missed our field trips, and our team needed every leg up we could get going into the games.

I'd just finished up making a plate and was looking around for Opie when Fable rolled up beside me.

'I've got a great idea,' she murmured in a low voice as she all but dragged me back toward our dorm. 'We are going to be stuck with crap rations at the Games, which got me to thinking, what if we start squirreling food away now, and then the morning of, someone hit all this with a nicking notions, shrinking rune . . .'

I snicked my tongue at her in mock disdain. 'Fable, you naughty girl. Where is this coming from? Don't you want to play fair?'

'I learned from the best. And no. We aren't even supposed to play fair. It's guerrilla warfare, isn't it? That's why we're going to win, because you know how to survive better than any of us. So, are you going to do it, or do I have to try to figure out how to stuff all this into my bra and explain my suddenly bodacious boobies?'

We reached the dorm, and I pushed the door open, chuckling. 'Of course I'll do it. I'm just busting your chops. I've just got to get the proper rune for it. You're turning into a real baddie, and I have to admit, I like it.'

'You got some mail, Fable.' Marina handed her a red envelope before flitting out of the room again, calling over her shoulder.

Fable set her plate down on the desk near my bed and

tore open the envelope. Her excitement drained away almost instantly, and she lowered her hand.

'It's from my mom and dad. Abundance card and the promise of a shopping spree whenever I come home next.'

'And you're worried you might not be able to go home for a long time?' I asked gently.

'Nah. No offense, but I'm looking forward to kicking Nocta's ass now. I was just hoping . . .'

Zeed.

He'd been gone for weeks now, and still hadn't written back to her or anyone else. We got reports from Tarquinius every once in a while, and he told us that he was on the mend, but it wasn't the same as hearing from Zeed himself.

Especially not for Fable.

'I have a meeting with Typhon in a few minutes, but after I'm done, I'm going to track Liam down, come hell or high water. See if he's heard anything from his sources at the Senate. He at least will talk to me, and give me answers when I ask.' I squeezed her arm gently and offered an encouraging smile. 'Maybe he can even see if they will agree to bend the rules a little and let us have a video call with him or something.'

She let out a big breath and nodded. 'Yeah. Yeah, I like that idea.'

And if that didn't work?

I'd figure out another frucking way. Because that's what real friends did. They were ride or die. They stuck by each other through thick and thin.

35

A short while later, I found myself in front of Typhon's door, fist poised to knock. He'd been in a good mood. A giving mood. Maybe it was time to broach the subject of getting us off school grounds again. At least once more before the games.

Or maybe this wasn't about magic or school at all.

Maybe . . .

The door swung open before I even knocked, and Typhon's big frame filled the doorway. 'Right on time.'

I expected him to move to the side and wave me in. Instead, he stepped into the hall and closed the door behind him.

'Are we meeting out here, then?'

'No. In fact, I won't be joining you at all. I've got to go to my own meeting with Tarquinius. I expect it to take a long time. At least an hour or two.' His eyes captured mine and held them. 'Don't waste it.'

With that, he strode away without a backward glance.

I stared at the doorknob and then down the hall again.

'What the actual fruck . . .'

I turned the knob, half-expecting some alarm to go off or to get zapped by a protection ward. Instead, it swung open freely and quietly.

I poked my head inside. And there, on the living room sofa, sat Liam O'Connor, watching me with a bemused expression.

I stepped into the room and closed the door, the click echoing through the silent room.

'Hiya.'

'Hey?' I replied, a confused bubble of laughter escaping my lips. 'Am I dreaming, or did Typhon Moreno just invite me to his quarters and leave me here alone with his nemesis?'

Liam stood and shrugged. 'Seems as if. I'm as shocked as you, but here we are.'

It was a weird sensation being in Typhon's room, surrounded by his things, his musky scent still filling my nose, while I was looking at Liam's handsome face. He wore a cable-knit sweater the color of mushed peas that should've looked awful but instead made him look like the sexiest boy next door ever who also happened to be a fisherman.

I cleared my throat, willing the heat in my cheeks to flee.

Liam waved toward the seat across from him. 'Apparently, Typhon has come around to our way of thinking as far as the Quirks are concerned. The moons are passing fast, and if you want to activate your Quirks and have any time at all to learn how to wield them, it has to be now. He's decided to bend around Tarquinius and help us by getting me some time with each of you before the games. He's keeping him occupied now.'

I almost couldn't believe my ears.

'And you put aside your differences, even after he bound you and left you for dead?'

Liam's dimple made an appearance as I took the offered seat.

'We've come to an uneasy truce on this matter and this matter alone. You and your housemates will be safer if you have your Quirks. That satisfies us both as we both have a . . .' his chocolatey eyes locked onto mine, smile fading, 'let's call it a vested interest.'

I folded my hands on my lap and looked away.

'Right. Well, whatever the reason, I'm relieved. Speaking

of the others, though, have you heard anything from your contacts at the Senate about Zeed?'

He retook his seat on the sofa and shook his head, brows caving into a frown. 'They were pretty tight-lipped about Zeed, which I'm not thrilled about. They said they'd get back to me. I do have news about your Lucinda, though. Apparently, she was a student here at Neverthorn for a short time. She left due to some mental health issues. I reached out to a PI in the Unlit world who agreed to search for her family and get some answers, as well as pay a visit to Zeed's home and check in.'

I blew out a sigh. 'Okay. At least it's something.' Hopefully, it would ease Fable's mind that there were wheels in motion to check on him.

'We'd better get started. We might not get another chance.'

He leaned forward, hand extended, and nerves jangled in my belly.

'Wait. There's got to be something I can do to help. Something that will make this time different than the others.' I speared a hand through my hair and slumped back. 'I have so many people counting on me . . . this needs to work.'

Liam lowered his hand. 'Maybe that's what you need to think about when we're inside your head. Instead of focusing on the sense of violation or loss of control, you can focus on taking charge of this process yourself because of all the people counting on you.'

I swallowed hard and nodded. 'Okay. I can try.'

So I did.

Liam stuck his fingers into my brain and started poking around. And, this time, instead of thinking about that and worrying about whether I was going to fail again or the questions he would ask me and how they would leave me feeling vulnerable, I reached a hand in my pocket and ran my fingers over the worry stones.

'What do you fear most, Harlow?'

'Failing my team and one of the people I care about getting hurt as a result.'

Like both other times, I could sense him swiping away the cobwebs of anxiety and delving deeper. This time, though, I forced my muscles to stay slack and invited him in.

'Good. Less resistance this time.'

The dirt road I'd seen before shimmered to the surface of my mind, but this time, the sky around me wasn't dark. I moved with a sense of purpose, knowing that, soon, I would come to the fork.

'Stay with me here, Harlow. We've got this.'

His voice was low and soothing, and I clung to it even as I ran my thumb over one of the stones.

F. For Fable.

'Yes.'

When I reached the spot where my paths parted, I paused, looking down one, and then the other. Now, with an ethereal light illuminating my way, I could see where they led.

One path opened to a meadow surrounded by trees. Fat, succulent fruits weighed the bows down. The grass was green and lush, the sky periwinkle blue and inviting.

The other was wild. Craggy cliffs that dropped off to choppy seas. The winds howled, and the sky was a stormy gray.

'Choose.'

I didn't so much hear the word as sense it in my bones. Which way?

I ran my fingers over the little mound of stones one last time, took a deep breath, and then sprinted forward . . .

36

'I still can't believe it. You're a frucking Boost. The first of its kind,' Caterina said, shaking her head.

Ten days later, I was still getting used to the fact myself. Who would've thought that I, Harlow Daygon, who, up until very recently, couldn't throw a proper rune to save my life, would be able to take my magic, let it build until it almost split me in two, and then release it into an incredibly powerful super-rune, boosting my magic tenfold.

On the flip side?

Ten days later and I was still the only one with a new Quirk, despite Liam having had a chance to meet privately with the others. He'd advised me to keep it from Tarquinius for now. If he knew the strength of my Quirk, Liam feared I would be sent to the front lines with the Runecoats immediately. We both knew I wasn't ready. I was barely able to wield the power even now. Me and the others agreed that no matter what or when our Quirks developed, we'd keep it quiet. None of us trusted this place, or those who ran it.

'I think it's just too much pressure,' Ross grumbled.

He was curled up on a bean-bag chair in the corner of the common room, tossing miniature pretzels into his downturned mouth.

'And we only had like an hour,' Fable added. She sat on the floor with her back to Marina, who was perched on the couch braiding Fable's hair.

'I don't mean to sound ungrateful, but it really would've

been nice to have had access to Liam this whole time,' Marina said with a sniff.

'I get it. I'm pissed too. If Tarquinius wasn't such a frucking tool, we'd have all had a chance to work with Liam by now.'

'And at least you got yours, Harlow. As our leader –'

'Stop with that.'

'And as our leader,' Fable said again, more forcefully this time, 'I'm really glad if only one of us could get our Quirk that it was you. It puts us in a way better position going into the games tomorrow.'

The others murmured their agreement.

'I have a really sick feeling that mine is going to be like Doyenne Parunah's damp Quirk. Watch, I bet I'll be like an Amplifier or something and be able to make quiet noises slightly louder,' Gary said with a snort.

The others chuckled and began teasing one another with their possible potential Quirks.

'What if you can control the temperature, but you can only make things lukewarm?' Ellie said to Marina.

Marina howled with laughter and tugged Fable's head back. 'And yours is going to be that you have this uncanny knack of going to a store and picking out the fruit that's per-fectly ripe.'

'Whoa,' I chimed in, laughing along with them now. 'That is an amazing Quirk, actually. Perfect fruit, every time!'

We continued bantering back and forth until the mood that had been weighing on us lifted. This was what I had been missing my first time around here in Neverthorn. The friendship. The camaraderie. Feeling like I belonged . . .

'Guys, I just want to say –'

'If you're listening to this, it's because you need to hear it,' a disembodied voice boomed, cutting me short.

'What the fruck?' Ross murmured as we all sat up and looked around in confusion.

The air at the center of the room crackled, and then an image the size of a movie theater screen came to life. At the center of it was Nocta himself standing at a dais, dressed in black, looming.

He spoke again, and I was glued to my seat, unable to look away.

'If you're listening to this . . . if you can see me, it's because you need to hear what I have to say.' His teeth clenched and the fury in his eyes bordered on madness. 'I am the Lord of the Night. And we're going to blow the weave to bits, destroy anyone who tries to stop us, and let magic do what magic does. We will be free again. Archaic, barbaric rules meant to chain us be damned.'

As much as his words terrified me, they also struck a tiny chord. And that scared me. But that's what master manipulators did, wasn't it? That was how dictators came into their own. The power of passion and charisma, a cheerily painted view of a terrible idea. If the people were ready for change, they became easily swayed.

'So, I call on you now, to stop fighting me and join me. Time is almost up. The people you put your trust in –'

The picture suddenly flickered and Nocta went in and out of focus before disappearing altogether.

'Students,' Tarquinius's voice interrupted as his own face flickered into place. 'Please do not be alarmed. Nocta and his men are far away, and the school is a fortress of safety. This was a breach of airwaves only. We've now regained control. Please head to your dorm rooms. You'll need a good night's sleep in preparation for tomorrow's games.'

The image grew wavy and then disappeared altogether, leaving us staring at nothing, shocked into silence.

Hard to get into Solstice Games mode when a magical killer had just declared that he planned to tear open the weave that protected us from dark magic users and murder anyone who tried to stop him.

But after we'd all gone to bed a short while later, I couldn't help but recall that strange feeling in my chest when Nocta had been talking about freedom. Control.

Part of me wanted to rail along with him at that. Enough to murder a bunch of people? Definitely not. But enough to . . . I don't know, understand where the germ of his madness had started.

Yes, I could understand that much.

And the realization terrified me.

37

Runecoats stood all around the top edge of the arena. They wore long, deep-red coats with vertical black stripes. Masks covered the lower half of their faces, to keep their anonymity. I found myself counting them, then realizing there were more tucked in the crevices and nooks of the massive structure.

Six a.m., the morning of the solstice, and we stood on the Isle of Thanatos, awaiting instructions on how the games would go.

The arena itself was three times the size of the actual Roman Coliseum, with walls that reached over two hundred feet, complete even with stands for the teachers and the rest of the school who would be cheering us on. The center of the arena was built up like a maze, with walls and doorways, and low-hung ceilings.

Apparently, those who sat in the stands could see down into the hidden parts of the arena, watching us all like we were some sort of reality TV show.

My eyes drifted back to the Runecoats. 'Is it normal for this many Runecoats to be in attendance?'

The others shrugged, and I found myself looking for Liam. Typhon was with his team already and Liam . . . well, Liam was at least someone I trusted.

He stood with the other teachers not participating, while everyone arrived and got settled. I hurried over to him.

Liam nodded at me. 'Yeah, I see them too. I imagine the prophecy, the attack on Central Park, and Nocta's crazed speech have them being extra careful. He's clearly escalating.' He shrugged. 'But I'm not unhappy they've sent in the Runecoats. If this keeps you all safe, then so be it.' He reached over and tucked a strand of hair behind my ear. 'Be careful in there, Harlow. I have . . . a bad feeling about these games, but Tarquinius won't back down from holding them.'

A gong sounded and I swallowed hard. 'Thanks?'

The gong boomed again, and I had no choice but to turn and go back to my team.

I was nothing if not a bundle of anxiety and nerves. I found myself reaching for the small velvet bag in my pocket, rolling two of the smooth stones between my fingers.

Marina and Ellie's emotions rumbled back to me, and it did not help calm me. I all but yanked my hand away from the anxiety that bounced back to me. Nope, I did not need more of that.

Tarquinius stood on a small platform in front of us, his wiry body enveloped in a deep-green robe. He really needed a good meal or two.

'And, last but not least, to ensure each team has what I like to think of as some extra "skin in the game" this year,' Tarquinius said, his voice carried to us on the rune he cast, 'as a team or player is eliminated, they will be spirited topside. If a team loses their flag, or a player is grievously injured, that will constitute a loss. We will then be sending eliminated teams back into the fray after a waiting period of one hour. They will not be allowed to win this portion of the games; however, they will make it more difficult for the remaining teams.' His eyes swept over the crowd, resting on each of the houses. 'The winners of the Solstice Games will of course have the traditional choice of feast, and one thousand dollars of credits for the Nevershoppes.'

Tarquinius waited for the din of excited voices to calm. 'Any questions?'

Only, like, a hundred of them, but I wasn't about to call undue attention to myself by asking any out loud. Not when I'd managed to bypass the fanny pack check for smuggled rations or unapproved weapons on the way into the venue. Still, my mind was racing – which it had been doing since we'd made the trek as one massive unit all the way to the southernmost tip of the island. From there we were boated to an island another five miles from Neverthorn.

Isle of Thanatos. Yup, Island of the Dead. Not ominous at all.

Students from every house, youngest to oldest, were practically vibrating with excitement. Even though the event was held every year, it was still a big deal. Tales of Coliseums past and all the best Solstice Games had been flying between students the whole trip over.

'Then, Heronius himself took a broadsword and lopped the swamp-thing's head clean off. I heard it still haunts the murky waters, even now!'

'By the time Maribel got back to base, she was struck mute. Whatever she saw out there was so terrible, the poor thing never spoke again.'

'Peter Polanko was so hungry, he stuffed his face full of what he thought were blackberries and turned out to be belly-buster berries and wound up with a case of the squirts so bad, he sharted himself.'

Even the professors seemed caught up in the excitement. All except for one.

While Tarquinius fielded questions from various students, I peered over my shoulder and caught sight of Typhon standing at the very back of the crowd, looking around like he expected someone to ambush us from behind or something.

'He can't understand why they would still do it this year. I overheard him speaking to Tarquinius,' Phyllis said, following my gaze. 'He feels like the arena has us all corralled together. He's concerned that Nocta will use the opportunity to stage an attack. Nikita has been supportive of Tarquinius, saying that it will help test all the students, and prepare them for battle. Besides, with the prophecy, we already know when the true war will be waged.'

I didn't think Typhon was wrong. We were, essentially, in a massive, stone pen that appeared to only have one entrance or exit.

'Are you worried?' I asked, eyeing Phyllis for signs of worry. In truth, she seemed much calmer than she had been during the team hand-to-hand combat battle.

She cocked her head as she considered the question. 'I'm always worried when it comes to the students, but I think Tarquinius, and perhaps even the Senate, feel the ends justify the means, and I trust him. I always have. The Runecoats are here to help, and truly, this test is needed. Especially since you'll all have access to your full powers here. We need to see the cream rising to the top and in order to do so, you need to be challenged in all ways. Hand-to-hand fighting has the potential to be a bloodbath. This is more a battle of wits, and magical abilities which I much prefer. So, I'm cautious, but I think it's going to be alright.'

I wasn't sure if the swamp-thing or poor Peter Polanko would necessarily agree with that assessment, but I wasn't about to stress her calm. Besides, I had my Quirk now.

A Quirk no one else had. At least, as far as Liam or Typhon knew.

I gathered my team around me. 'Okay, our primary objective for the first part of the challenge is to capture the "flags" of any opposing teams. The flag being the head of each house. So, for Kirinash, it's Nikita. For us, it's you, Phyllis, and so on. If our house "flag" is captured, we're yanked out of the game for a period of time, and we lose points. On the last day, there will be a final showdown of sorts between any of the participants who haven't lost their flag. And then it's just an all-out, head-to-head magic battle at the center of the Coliseum. Points to the winners, and at the end the tally is taken. Team with the most points wins. Is that right?'

'Yes.' Simple and yet not.

'And remember, the heads of house can only assist with team strategy,' Fable piped in as she and Ross made their way to stand beside us. 'They're not to engage in battle magic at any time. But Phyllis is an exception because she's not a teacher. Because we have fewer on our team than the other houses, they are allowing her to participate.'

A key point that was definitely to our advantage. I was pretty sure Typhon could wreck us single-handedly, and Nikita would relish the chance to turn me into a frog if she was allowed. Phyllis, on the other hand? As much as I'd grown to respect and care for her, what she'd witnessed all those years ago had scarred her and made watching violence difficult, so I doubted she'd be of all that much help on that front. Still, something was better than nothing, given that all the other houses had been allowed to handpick thirteen students to represent them, and we had to work with what we had.

'The arena will shift, literally changing shape to confuse or corner us,' Phyllis said. 'After major battles usually, but also sometimes at random moments. We need to be ready as soon as we hear the gears grinding, to move quickly.'

Tarquinius clapped his hands, and everyone turned to him again.

'Two final things before we are ready to start. There will be *no lethal runes* used. It will mean immediate expulsion if you so much as start to cast one. And finally, you will all be sent into the Coliseum through different doorways, at the same time. There will be extra lead time for everyone except House Phoenix. They will wait a full minute before entering the Coliseum.'

The grumbling was instantaneous from our house. 'What the hell?' Ross snapped.

'That's not fair!' Marina added.

'Dog piss,' Ellie said under her breath.

I wasn't surprised, though. Not one bit.

'Settle down,' Tarquinius shouted over the complaints. 'I realize this seems unfair, but war isn't concerned with fair. We need the strongest houses to stretch themselves for the good of us all. Not another word about it, understood?'

'The strongest houses? Shouldn't House Phoenix go back to the school and sit this whole thing out, then?'

I turned to find Julius standing behind me, a wide grin on his face.

Doyenne Storm clapped her hands and thunder rolled above our heads. 'You'll treat one another with respect, or you'll leave the competition. Is that understood, Mr. Rendimion?'

Julius's smile dimmed as he shuffled in place. 'Yes, ma'am.'

I couldn't wait to see his stupid face when he got a load of House Phoenix without the magical cuffs on.

'If that's all?' Tarquinius swept the now-silent crowd with a scathing look and then nodded in satisfaction.

'Head to the stone overhang with your flag in front of it and wait for my call to begin. Good luck.'

'We're going to kill it, I can feel my magic better even than before,' Ross said, rubbing his hands together gleefully as we made our way to the far-right corner of the Coliseum.

'Yup. We just have to stick to the plan,' Caterina agreed, falling into step next to me.

I was about to go over the strategies we'd discussed in the

days leading up to the event, when a firm hand gripped my elbow, tugging me to a stop.

I turned to find Typhon eyeing me expectantly.

'Can I help you?' I asked, immediately on guard.

'Be careful.'

I frowned and shook my head.

'It's just a game.'

He held my gaze.

'Typhon . . . Isn't it?'

He waved a hand as he let out a long-suffering sigh. 'It's never just a game, there are too many people who want to make a name for themselves. So just be careful.' His eyes were fathomless, giving away nothing. 'Get your bracers off, as soon as you're in there.' He took my hand and traced a quick rune against my palm.

He let my hand go as Tarquinius approached our group, a smile dusted by his mustache. 'House of Phoenix. I truly wish you the best of luck. You have come a long way, in a short time.'

Damn, praise from the man himself. The group shifted, no one smiled though.

'However, I do detect some magic that is not allowed.' His eyes landed on me. 'You have something in your satchel.'

My heart stopped. 'I don't know what you mean.'

'The satchel. Give it to me.'

Without a word, I handed my pack over. When he was done rifling through and confiscating all my miniature eggs, rolls, and even the bacon – gods, the bacon – he tossed it back to me with a tight smile. 'Your team just lost twenty points for contraband.'

Twenty down, before we even started. 'That's not fair!' Fable said.

Typhon's face was tight. 'Sir, is that –'

'No. They will do this my way, or they will not do it at all.' Tarquinius shook his head. So much for praise. 'May the best team win.'

'Don't worry. We will,' I shot back with a wink.

'Well that sucks the big one,' Marina mumbled.

I tried not to think about the food we'd lost. We had rations spaced out through the arena, which meant we wouldn't starve. But man, I'd gone hungry a lot in my late teens. More times than I'd cared to count.

And I hated being hungry.

Don't think about it.

'Tarquinius is a real donkeyhole,' Ross added.

By the time we reached our designated starting spot, my mind was already onto other things as stone rumbled and cracked around us. I stared across the massive Coliseum, barely able to make out the figures of Typhon and team Draconell in the distance. Maybe I wasn't classically trained like all the Draconells and Kirinashes, but this would be different. All of the tutors and fancy prep schools money could buy couldn't prepare them for what was about to come their way.

'Ready team? This one is for Zeed!' I held out my fist and bumped my way through the group, knocking knuckles.

'For Zeed!' they echoed with gusto.

Fable sidled closer to me as slabs of magic-infused granite rose from the ground, consuming us in ever-increasing darkness. The roof closed in shortly after, and Tarquinius's voice rang through the cavern a final time, as if coming from the stone itself.

We watched as the other teams got the go-ahead. I counted down from sixty, my skin prickling with the need to move.

Tarquinius lifted his hand and pointed at us. 'House Phoenix . . . Begin!'

All the hours of practicing runes that wouldn't work for us finally came into play. I wove a quick lighting rune on instinct, feeling it work even before it lit up, glancing at the forked hallway ahead of us. The whole place buzzed with subtle magic, and there was nothing obvious making one path more attractive than the other.

In the first hall we stopped. 'Wait. Typhon said to get the bracers off.'

'What?' Marina crowded close. 'The muting should be off here. Shouldn't it?'

'It should be, but I'm willing to trust him on this.'

'How do we do it?' Fable asked.

I scrunched up my face and traced the rune Typhon had set in my palm over Fable's bracer. It flung itself off her arm, like it had a life of its own.

'Whoa, me next!' Ross pushed forward. I wove the rune over each of their bracers, then held my arm out and Marina wove the rune over my arm.

The Phoenix bracers littered the floor.

I took a deep breath. 'Let's do this.'

We slipped into the Coliseum; the walls around us were solid sandstone, a dusty light brown.

I turned toward the rest of House Phoenix only to find seven sets of eyes staring right back at me with varying degrees of anxiety in their expressions.

Fable was the first to speak. 'Which way are you thinking? Should we check out both?'

'I can't sense anything pulling us either way,' I said, feeling the weight of their expectations as I glanced at Phyllis.

'I think we should just pick one path and stick together, no point in dwelling on which way we go, though,' said the older woman, shrugging. 'Your call, Harlow.'

I exhaled sharply, nodding as I strode into the left corridor.

I had always been more of a loner, only looking out for Opie and myself and the occasional runaway, but now that the other members of the house had given me their fealty, I was determined not to fail them. 'Gary and Marina, you two watch our backs. Use the rune Doyenne Parunah taught us to sense magic. There'll be traps all over and we don't want to get sandwiched.'

Fable and I took up the front, relying on the same sensing spell that we'd been taught in class a few weeks earlier. It sent a ripple of magic ahead through the ground, moving a few dozen feet ahead before returning with a report of any irregularities or magic, almost like a magical radar system.

There was a pitfall just ahead, and we avoided it easily, triggering it then covering it with a magical barrier and stepping right over it.

We were less than half an hour into our otherwise uneventful trek when we reached a bend in the corridor, and a soft light became visible ahead. I probed cautiously toward it with my radar spell, but nothing seemed amiss.

The sandstone walls were still smooth, and there were no offshoots, meaning we'd had no choice but to take this path. But that wasn't what caught my eye. For the first time there was a deviation in the stone – small, but it was there.

The numbers two, twelve, and thirty-six were carved into the wall above a doorway. I wrote them quickly onto the back of my left hand with magic.

'What's the point of starting us off in a labyrinth if we're just gonna end up outside a few minutes in?' Ross asked from behind.

'Perhaps we got lucky with our choice of path at the start,' Phyllis said.

I nodded, even though I doubted we'd made it through already. The light was just a short way away now, around another bend in the corridor, and there didn't seem to be anything amiss. 'Wait here a second,' I said, poking my head around the corner.

An enormous, stalagmite-studded cavern came into view, with a chandelier hanging from the ceiling that would've looked significantly more at home in a palace than a cave but was the obvious source of light. So much for making it out quickly.

I waved the others on, stepping forward cautiously as I probed the room with magic.

We made our way into the room, and the locked door on the other side came into view. Magic of all the elements danced inside it, vaguely similar to the one at the entrance to the school, albeit much less impressive.

I was still surveying the room when a thunderous crack rang out from behind, and I whirled to see Gary, Ellie, and Marina diving forward as a granite slab slammed downward, sealing off the path we'd used to enter the room. I cursed under my breath and leapt into action. 'We need to check that door out,' I said. 'It'll be locked somehow, and we have to figure out how to open it.'

Phyllis nodded, leading Gary, Marina, and Ellie, toward it. 'You three with me.'

'The rest of us should spread out and search the room,' I said. 'There's some test for us here, though I'm not sure what it is yet. Look out for traps and let someone else know before you touch anything that seems off.' I wiped a droplet of sweat off my forehead, a wave of irritation rushing through me. This leadership stuff was stressful.

I glanced up at the chandelier, which was spinning slowly in place, and found myself chewing at my lip as I mulled the situation over. Whatever the key to leaving the room was, it was definitely going to play a role.

It was too out of place not to be a part of this puzzle.

I strode over to a small pool of water on one side of the cavern, staring at the way the reflection of the light danced across its surface. Stalagmites lined the edge of the cave, shading parts of the wall in darkness. They had little holes and crannies in them like Swiss cheese. I leapt over the pool and examined one more closely, but nothing seemed off about them.

'We think the door opens with some kind of spell,' Phyllis called from the far side of the room. 'We haven't found the right one yet but we're going to keep trying.'

'Sounds good,' I called back, continuing my search.

'Over here,' Fable called, and I strode over. She jabbed her finger toward the ground. 'Watch this.' She wove a tiny rune, one to create a small light, through the floor, and a spot in front of her lit up with a bluish light, revealing the number ten inscribed on the ground below. 'When I touched it with a rune it lit up, but it isn't visible otherwise.'

I nodded quickly, shouting out a quick explanation of what she'd discovered to the others. 'We'll search the room with magic light pulses, there should be more of these.' I glanced at my hand and the numbers etched there – numbers that the Coliseum had already given us. 'I think we're looking for the numbers two, twelve, and thirty-six.'

The minutes stretched on, and my annoyance grew with each passing one. I'd circled the room a dozen times, as had the others, and we'd found numbers one through thirty-five, but still not thirty-six. I wiped my forehead clean of sweat for the dozenth time, then cast a probing rune for what felt like the thousandth.

The magic felt somehow sluggish, and I groaned, seeing nothing. Were we muted again?

'Let's grab a snack and do a little brainstorming,' Gary called, making his way to the packs.

387

My stomach growled, and I found myself agreeing.

'Something's off about this room,' Phyllis said as she approached. 'It feels like it's draining us of our energy or something.'

I cursed softly, nodding. That made perfect sense, what with the magic feeling so slow and difficult – not unlike what we dealt with at Neverthorn to be fair – and it meant we didn't have much more time at this rate of drainage.

Ellie slumped against a wall, and Caterina hurried to catch her. 'Harlow!'

'I see!' I yelled. The problem was I didn't see the solution on how to get out of here. And we were running out of time.

38

I glanced around the space, forcing down my own nerves as I saw the discouraged faces all around me.

'Come on, team. We've dealt with being muted our whole lives. We got this. Think hard about where the last number could be. Have we been checking the stalagmites themselves?'

'Yes,' said one very annoyed Marina. 'Assuming that's even what we need.'

'Even if we can find the last spot, we still don't know what they do,' Ross muttered.

I clenched a fist. 'We need to rally here, guys. We can figure this out. It's the draining that's making us so miserable, and we can rest once we're out of here. Now brainstorm. Is there *anywhere* we haven't been? Let's go through the whole room methodically again, maybe we missed something last time.'

'Maybe there's some kind of trick to it?' Fable suggested.

I nodded, 'Brainstorm on that, but let's take another pass at the same time.'

'Hurry,' Caterina said. 'Ellie's almost out cold.'

'The spell will drain her,' Phyllis said, 'Then move to another of us until we are all out cold.'

Crap.

I had only taken a few steps when Ross caught me on the arm, his previously dark expression lit up. 'The wall-walking spell Doyen Moreno taught us last week,' he blurted.

'Right!' I shouted, pulling quickly away from him. 'We need to check the walls and ceiling,' I called.

We each spun a rune — literal walking fingers pointed at

our legs – then dashed up the walls with newfound vigor, and it didn't take long before I found the number. It was positioned directly above the chandelier itself, where it connected to the ceiling, which was, counter-intuitively, beneath my feet.

'Got it,' I called out, glancing down at the others, and was suddenly struck with a strange sense of awe. The walls were covered in a brilliant display of color, dozens of tiny orbs shone all around from the Swiss-cheesy stalagmites, shimmering beautifully in the light of the slowly spinning chandelier.

I ignored the others as I stared at it a moment longer, and realized, with a start, that a few of the lights on the walls weren't just orbs. They were *runes*. Archaic ones I'd never seen, but runes, nonetheless. My hand went quickly to my pocket, and I tore Typhon's gift free from it, bringing the yellow glass to my eye, and I was suddenly able to read them.

It was a strange sensation, as if their meaning and how to use them were being transmitted directly and instantaneously to my brain. I kicked off from the ceiling, releasing the wall-walking spell and casting one to cushion my fall in a single flourish. 'I figured out what to do with them. They each represent a piece of the rune we need in order to open the door. Now for the two and the twelve,' I said.

The other two went just as easily, and I clapped Ross on the shoulder on my way over to the door. 'Good work.'

I swung my fingers in lengthy strokes, feeling the power from the magic as I drew the rune triumphantly onto the door. It disappeared into mist rather than opening, revealing a golden pedestal that shone in the sunlight coming from the stairway behind it. As soon as it opened, the draining spell eased off.

A shimmering, sleeveless coat sat atop the pedestal, draped over a stone replica of a human torso. I held out my arm, probing warily at it, and Ellie popped up next to Caterina.

'Is that a ward-vest?' she marveled, her voice a whisper.

'A what?' I asked, cocking my head.

'The Runecoats wear them for their toughest jobs,' Phyllis explained. 'The wards woven into it absorb attacks made against the wearer.'

Ellie nodded eagerly. 'They eat a certain amount of magic before being destroyed, and it takes a team of experts months to weave each one. Incredibly valuable.'

I nodded slowly, glancing toward Phyllis. 'Sounds like the perfect thing to protect our flag,' I said.

Phyllis opened her mouth to answer, but a reptilian screech pierced the air, coming from the cavern behind us, and I snatched the vest from the pedestal. 'Fable, block the door with me,' I called, waving everyone else up the stairs.

I panted as we wove a series of barriers, then darted up the stairs behind the others. Whatever it was coming from behind us, it'd be bad to fight it in our current state, drained of magic as we were. The stairway opened into a rustic-looking town, and Gary slammed the cellar door shut behind us as we emerged, then began to tie it off with a piece of magically imbued rope from his bag.

'That should hold back whatever that was,' Phyllis said, 'but we should get a bit further away before finding somewhere to rest.'

Before long, we circled around a well in the middle of town and spent the next hour eating and recovering from our draining time at the cave.

'So, what's the plan?' Fable asked, sipping from one of the water canteens making the rounds between our group.

'The longer we can rest before fighting the better,' Phyllis answered. 'Worst case is that we run into other teams while drained of magic like this.'

I nodded, sending a probe of magic outward. We'd recovered a fair bit of energy in our short break, and the spell wasn't particularly draining, but we were taking turns on watch, nonetheless. If Draconell or Kirinash or any of the other teams came within a few hundred feet or used magic from a few thousand, we'd know. 'We should be prepared to fight them by tomorrow – I can't imagine we'd be able to avoid them any longer than that. Any ideas for how we should approach things?'

The question had been directed at Phyllis, but Ross was the one who answered first.

'I used to play capture the flag when I was a kid, and we would always leave a few people around the flag as defenders, usually the slower runners, and send the others out on attack.'

I nodded slowly, 'I doubt running speed matters much for this, but we can definitely play to our strengths. Who is confident in their warding spells?' Gary and Ellie raised their hands. I nodded. 'You two can be our defenders, then. You can support us from the back and make sure they can't capture Phyllis.' I was confident enough in my warding, too, but the prospect of capturing Typhon or Nikita was too enticing to turn down.

'The rest of us will be on the attack.' We'd each been given a set of magical handcuffs, which served as a win condition if we managed to get them onto the wrist of the enemy team's 'flag'. 'Now let's talk about the weapons we brought. Maybe that'll give us some idea for our plan of attack,' I said.

'Can you pass that canteen?' Caterina asked.

I turned to do so, but a flicker of light caught my eye, coming from the roof of a barn a dozen feet to our left.

'Get down!' I hissed.

Six members of House Draconell were staring down at us, all drawing a series of runes to create a single, terrible, spell. Not unlike how me, Gary, Ross, Marina, and Caterina had woven that single spell in the hall, deflecting Mortan's fire.

The difference? Our spell had come together smooth and fast, as if we'd been working together for years. Theirs was slow enough that I could see it coming and prep.

A little.

The fireball about to shoot toward us was like nothing I'd ever seen. The warmth drained my lips and eyes of moisture before the spell had even begun to move, and it was blindingly bright. Pulling my eyes into a thin squint, I leapt to my feet.

I searched deep within myself for the right rune to create a ward that could counter something like this. My mind raced with a dozen thoughts at once. How had they snuck up on us? How many of us would be hit by the attack? Were things really going to end this quickly for us?

Fable, who was closest to the barn, flailed wildly in a futile attempt to block it, and I came back to my senses in a rush. My eyes flitted to the ward-vest on Phyllis.

'The vest!' I yelled at her as I ran in her direction. She tossed it to me as I ran by, and I caught it in one hand.

Bingo.

I sprinted forward, vest in my left hand, as I drew up a rune to increase my speed. I had to make it to Fable in time.

Here goes nothing.

I raised the vest in front of myself like a shield and slammed my eyes shut. The smell of burning hair filled my nostrils and the vest dissolved in my hands, heat washing over me like a wave. I gasped, dropping to my knees, and opened my eyes back up, fully expecting to have been killed.

But I wasn't dead. Pain shot through my hands and arms, and my clothes were singed but here I was, watching as House Draconell leapt from the barn's roof, charging directly at us.

'Protect Harlow!' Phyllis shouted from behind me, barely audible over the horrible thrumming of my heartbeat.

I forced myself to my feet a few moments later, taking deep breaths in an attempt to center myself. 'Be careful from the flanks,' I croaked. 'Don't forget your positions.'

The battle exploded into action as spells crashed into our barriers, and I forced myself to the front lines, standing side by side with Fable.

My fingers were singed, but I could still cast runes.

Typhon stood in the back, behind his team, and he spared me a quick glance between shouted orders to his students. The bond between us flared with concern, worry, and a fair bit of anger. I got the feeling he didn't like how the Draconells were playing the game.

'On the right!' Phyllis shouted from behind.

I moved to draw a rune, but a warding from Gary buzzed into existence, blocking a lightning bolt before I could react. Blocking out the connection to the bond, so I could focus on keeping my team together. We could not lose Phyllis.

'Leave them, get Moreno,' Fable called, dashing forward.

She was right. We were already behind in points, we needed to capture a flag. I fired off a quick door-busting rune at the nearest enemy. It smacked through his warding spell, still doing significant damage, but three others jumped to his aid, whipping off runes at Fable.

I rushed toward them, slamming the door buster into the shield of one and blocking a spell from the other as Ross came to our aid.

A massive bolt of lightning cracked from the sky above our head, and, for a half second, I almost thought Typhon had joined the battle. Then I caught sight of Julius Rendimion, which was almost as bad. I let out a curse, straining my limited energy reserves to block his attack.

I sent a long-range lightning rune right back at him, but my opponent's fingers blurred with textbook precision, not only blocking the spell, but blasting it back at me with nearly the same strength.

I growled, barely getting a ward up in time.

Marina and Caterina were working as a team on the left, handling two others on the opposing team, and they looked to be holding their own. The other Draconells came forward, targeting Fable at close range, and she narrowly avoided the swing of a magic-infused sword. I moved to blast at one but was sent sprawling as a rune slammed into my side before I could.

'You don't have time to worry about anything else, except me, loser,' Julius called, laughing harshly as gouts of flame sprang from his fingertips, ripping through a hastily created ward.

'We'll handle these three,' Fable said. 'Take him, Harlow.'

I rolled sideways, dodging a blast as I flung myself toward Julius. I took a risk and threw a rune I'd never used before; one I'd seen in the books Fable and I had been scouring. Roots sprang from the ground, grasping at Julius's legs. He burned through them in a single motion, but I had already fired off my next rune. Lightning arced toward him, with me following just behind it.

Thank you, Doyenne Storm, for your magical weather defense classes.

Tempo was important in a magical duel, and the person who had to focus on defending from the other person's attacks was at a serious disadvantage. I fired off a quick slicing rune at his legs, dropping into a roll beneath the fireball he'd managed to send my way a moment earlier, then blasted another attack at his chest. I had always been confident in my close-quarters combat, and was even more so after my fight with Nikita, and if I could just get close, I could –

He leapt over the slashing attack, and he moved to ward against the blast at his chest with his left hand as expected, but his right hand whirred into motion simultaneously. At the exact same time as my spell fizzled into nothing, a rock slammed directly into my torso.

I flew backward, my body screaming in pain as I rolled back to my feet, preparing to block his next attack. I'd seen the two-handed carnival tricks in class, but to be able to do it at this level was astonishing and frankly, it scared the sheet out of me.

He grinned wickedly, and I was forced to watch helplessly as his next attack slammed into Ross's side as he was about to strike one of the Draconells.

'You really thought you could challenge me all by yourself, dropout?' he jeered, both hands casting spells at blinding speed.

I spared a quick glance at Ross in between blocking spells. He rebounded and came running, but Julius threw a screamer of a rune above head, the blast sending a stalactite plummeting down straight for Ross.

I scrambled to throw a rune, but it was Phyllis who saved him.

'No! I won't stand aside! Not again!' She threw Ross to the ground and erected a protective shield over the two of them a split second before the rocks struck. The sound was like a cannon, and I covered my ears as dust obscured my view. The fighting came to a momentary standstill, no one could see through the dust.

By the time it cleared, Ross was flat on his face, out cold, but still alive, thank the gods . . . and Phyllis. She stood over him, her hands flashing runes at a speed I'd never seen her capable of. Judging by the astonished look on her face, she'd never seen it either.

There was no time to celebrate, though, as the Draconells unleashed a fresh attack on Fable in the three-on-one melee, and she let out a yelp, barely dodging a follow-up that would've ended it.

I let out a roar, leaping forward to close the distance, even more desperate – we were down a man, we had to end this, and quickly.

My fingers moved faster than I had thought possible, blocking a dozen spells in between throwing out attacks of my own in my mad dash. Julius's expression darkened, just a hint of anxiety working into his haughty expression as I closed in on him.

I had to move like our lives depended on this. It was no longer a game.

This was survival.

I'd seen this rune used . . . by Nocta in Central Park. Fruck it, all was fair in love and war.

I let the energy build inside of me, prepping to flatten them all. The rune, if it worked, was going to literally send bodies flying, but how to get my friends clear of it?

The rune storm was everything the weather gods could ever imagine, driving winds, lashing rain, and as I cast it, I opened myself up to my Quirk.

A rush of adrenaline poured through me.

I had a Quirk. I had an amazing, awesome, sweet frucking Quirk, and I was going to use it to save my friends. It was just going to take me a minute.

A gout of flame sprang from the ground in front of me at the same time as Julius fired a blast at me from the side, but I never let my momentum stop, throwing up a shield as I surged directly through the flames, casting a rune with my left hand to add weight to my foot as I lashed out to kick at his leg.

Shock and fury warred on his face as he drew a rune to block the attack, but I pulled back at the last second, tugging a throwing knife from my belt with my right hand and aiming it directly at his chest. He whipped his arm up in time to block it, but my fist was just behind, catching him in the shoulder.

It was almost like watching myself from above, as if I were playing a video game and had just unlocked a secret skillset. Speed.

Speed and more speed. It was frucking awesome because behind that speed was coming the super punch that would deal with Draconell in one blow.

Fire surged to life beneath my feet, and I rolled forward rather than back to dodge, keeping up my flurry of attacks, this time with a magical slicing attack. He warded it off, firing a hasty lightning bolt at me with his other hand at the same time.

My Quirk hummed inside of me, like a tone going off to let me know it was ready.

'Quack!' I yelled at my team. Quack. Duck. I hoped they got the message. Surprise flitted through the bond between Typhon and I, and then a flood of what could only be understanding. He got the message.

I spun the rune I'd seen Nocta use, drawing power through my Quirk and then unleashing the storm inside the cavern.

As it left my fingers the world around us slowed, my friends dropped to the ground, as did Typhon.

Smart guy.

The rune rippled out as if I were the center of an atomic

bomb, the air itself shaking as the storm absolutely demolished the entire Draconell team.

Rocks fell, the walls shuddered as if they'd come down, but there wasn't a single Draconell member left.

They faded as they slammed into the walls furthest from us. Was this how they got pulled out for their reset, before they were sent back in?

I didn't understand what had just happened there, why they had disappeared. But I didn't have time to stand around.

Typhon had been just behind Julius, he was flat on his belly, his eyes wide.

'Harlow. What the fuck was that?'

I walked over to him, bent and locked the magical handcuffs around his wrists. 'A rune, Typhon. Backed up by my Quirk.'

He stared up at me. 'The bond between us . . . I sensed you had more in you. Were you holding back?'

I thought about it. 'Yeah. Yeah, I was.'

'Fuck me,' he whispered. I could have said yes please, or only if you ask nicely, but I was all out of quips.

There were no more sounds of fighting. The rune I'd borrowed from Nocta had done exactly what I'd seen him do to all the trees in Central Park.

Flattened them.

One by one my friends stood up, staring at me. Would they remember the rune that Nocta had used? I wasn't sure. But when I looked at Phyllis, I knew she understood where I'd gotten it from. The shame was hot, but I fought it back. 'I would do anything to save you all.'

Phyllis tipped her head at me. 'I know.'

Fable stood across from me, panting, looking at where her attackers had been just a moment before. 'Holy sheet balls. We frucking did it. We got their flag!'

39

'There is no time to celebrate, certainly not here.' Phyllis cut through the cheering with those simple words.

Much as I wished she was wrong, I knew we had two major problems. One, we weren't out of the Coliseum yet, and two . . . I wrapped an arm around my middle, my fingers reaching to the side where the lightning from Draconell had struck. Warm, wet . . . nope, that was not good.

'I need to lay down, I think.'

'Harlow!' Fable yelled. 'You're bleeding!'

I grimaced. 'I'm not going to die, I just need to lie down and get this fixed up. Some stitches, I think.'

She slid her arm around my waist, and I leaned on her as Phyllis took the lead. 'This way. Everyone, get in line, follow me.'

Marina helped Ross to his feet, Ellie, Caterina, and Gary stayed close to Phyllis, and we were moving. No one was in the mood to argue after that battle.

I paused where Julius had been spirited away for his mandatory hour holdover, and scooped up a cylindrical tube with my foot, popping it into the air. As I snatched it out of the air, a buzz of *something* rippled from the item to me. What was this? A clue? A tool? I wasn't going to leave it behind, maybe it would help us. I tucked it into my pocket.

'Put Typhon in the middle,' I said, forcing myself to speak through the growing pain in my side. Seeing as he wasn't allowed to fight, he hadn't had much to do during the fight. He was, however, our way to winning. 'He's the prize, we can't lose him.'

Gary and Marina maneuvered him to the middle of our group. He opened his mouth to speak, and Gary slapped a rune over his mouth, gagging him.

'Hurry,' Phyllis called. 'The arena is shifting, and we need to take advantage of it.'

I didn't remember at first, then it clicked. After every battle, the arena walls shifted, changing the setting and prepping us to get lost again. The walls began to slide sideways, breaking apart and then some slid into the floor, opening up a narrow cut in the wall.

'Quickly!' Phyllis stood at the top of the cut and counted us as we went down the tight staircase ahead of her. Fable went right in front of me, and I put a hand on her shoulder, using her for balance as we hurried down the steps.

'Faster!' Caterina yelled from the back of the group. 'It's closing behind us!'

A yelp from her and then we were all running, full speed down the stairs which ended with Gary tripping and taking us all out. We slid down like we were bobsledding the last twenty feet of stairs.

At the bottom, we all sat up, groaning. But the walls had ceased moving, so we were in the clear.

Phyllis did another head count. 'Good, we didn't lose any of you.'

I pressed my fingers to my side. Yeah, I was still injured. But for the moment, my adrenaline was keeping the worst of the pain at bay.

Phyllis leaned against the wall. 'I've been here a long time. This is not my first foray into the Coliseum. After every major battle there is a rest period of six hours. Six hours where you have a chance to heal your wounded and strategize your next steps. Most people don't realize that there are foxholes like this all through the Coliseum. They don't tell you about these things in the beginning. You're meant to figure it out on your own. It's all a challenge.' She circled around a fire pit and with a few quick runes had a flame going in no time. 'You can recognize them by this symbol.' A tree with wide spreading branches was etched into the wall. It glowed lightly, green, soothing.

'Why didn't you tell us this before?' Fable said.

Phyllis sighed and slumped to the ground. 'I meant to once we got in here. No one can speak about this outside of the Solstice Games. It's a minor rune gag to keep students from knowing just what they will face.'

Typhon grunted as Gary sat him down by the fire.

'Take his gag off, Gary,' I said as I lowered myself to the floor, doing my best not to wince, breathing carefully.

Now that we'd slowed down, the pain was hitting me, and it was no small thing. Damn it, this was not going in my favor.

Ellie made her way over to me. Her amber eyes narrowed as she looked at my side. 'We need to see how deep it is, but I need you to take your hands off, chica.'

I grimaced. 'It's going to bleed.'

'Something tells me it's not going to stop just because your hand is there.' She tugged my fingers away and gasped. 'That is a lot of blood.'

A rune flashed from her fingers, one I'd never seen before, but I understood it, even if I wasn't sure I could ever duplicate it.

'That's like an X-ray vision rune,' I muttered, my tongue feeling thick as the room started to go fuzzy.

'It is, and lucky for you my mama taught it to me, before she died. She was the best at it,' she said.

I gritted my teeth. With my hand off the wound, it was

bleeding more freely. Regardless of what Ellie thought, my fingers and compression had been holding it together. 'Ellie . . .'

'You know,' she was moving quickly now, runes flashing faster and faster, 'my mother once said that in order to truly heal, you have to be willing to lose a little part of yourself. I think she was right, and that's why I've been so scared to find my Quirk. But what if, in the losing of yourself . . . you gain something more?'

Her voice was a line to consciousness, and as soon as she stopped talking . . .

I could feel the darkness closing in on me as I slumped backward, suddenly cold.

'Free me, right now. I can at least staunch the blood,' Typhon snapped, but his voice seemed so far away.

'Harlow? Harlow!' Fable shouted.

Her voice was the last thing I heard, and then I was somewhere else, floating, floating. The face of my mother flashed before me. A moment later, she came into full view. She beckoned me toward her, smiling. Her hair was like mine, a bright white blonde, and her eyes were a bright blue.

'Come on in, the water's fine.'

The beach. We were at Old Orchard Beach, just like when I was a kid. The seagulls were squawking, the waves were crashing, and I could feel the salty spray on my lips. I wondered if this was what death looked like. Was I dead?

'I miss you so much, Ma,' I whispered, my heart full as I reached for her.

She took my hand and squeezed my fingers. Warm, comforting, she wasn't skeletal as she'd been before she died. But more like the vibrant, kind woman she'd been when I was young.

I tried to grab her with both my hands, but she stepped back, the water up to the back of her knees.

'I miss you too, my sweet girl. More than you know. But you've still got work to do . . . it isn't your time yet.'

'I'm scared, Mom.' I took a step into the water, following her. 'I don't want to face him.'

Tears slipped down her cheeks as she took another step back, the water to her thighs now. 'I know. But you must trust your heart, Harlow. You have a good heart. The heart of a lion beats inside your chest and I know you will do the right thing, no matter how hard it is.'

'Mom!' I reached for her as a wave rolled forward, stealing her from my view. 'MOM!'

The summer sky flickered, and the sounds of the sea faded, giving way to shouts.

'Holy sheet, it worked. Ellie did it! She has a pulse!'

'Keep going, Ellie! See if you can staunch the bleeding and heal the wound.'

'No!' I instantly recognized Typhon's voice. 'Concede the battle and let's get her spirited back to the infirmary where they can do proper surgery,' he demanded, his voice hoarse. 'Ellie hasn't been trained.'

I sucked in a shuddering breath and forced my eyes open to find Ellie hunched over me, her hand splayed over my heart. 'As you said before, these aren't just games. There's more at play than we know,' I said, somehow knowing it was true. As much as I missed my mother, she was right. I wasn't done here yet, not in the Solstice Games, and not with Nocta. My hand went to the velvet pouch that held the worry stones.

'Do it, Ellie. I trust you. We aren't losing because of me.'

She gave a tight nod as her hands flashed runes that I only partially saw. Her fingers were as fast as any of ours – only instead of inflicting damage, they mended it. Magic flickered along my skin, light-green colored sparks that were so beautiful, my eyes welled up with tears. They broke free and slid down my cheeks as the pain came in waves. I watched in

404

stunned silence as my flesh knit back together, the wound closing until there was nothing more than a simple white scar.

Ellie sat back on her heels and swallowed hard. 'I guess I found my Quirk.'

It made perfect sense, now that I thought about it. She hated fighting and was always the first to try to help. But given the rarity of a true healer, it was nothing short of a miracle.

'Amazing,' I said, reaching for her wrist and giving it a squeeze. 'Thank you, Ellie. Is this . . . is this why you don't like fighting?'

Her lips split into probably the widest smile I'd seen out of her since . . . well maybe since the start of school. 'Yeah, I think maybe. Is . . . is there anyone else in need of help?' Her cheeks went pink, as if she was maybe expecting to be made fun of. But the others who had injuries lined up. Gary was first, and then Ross and Marina. Caterina had only a few bruises, but Ellie insisted it would help.

And she wasn't wrong.

'That was impressive,' Typhon admitted as we all sat around the fire a short time later, healed and doing better than probably most other teams. 'Stupid, but impressive. Thing is . . . you should have been spirited away. Same with Ross. You two should have been pulled out. You would have lost some points, but you would have been sent back in once your injuries were tended to.'

I snorted. 'Unless someone is trying to kill us. You know, like that "non-lethal" fireball your boys used.'

His jaw ticked and our eyes locked.

Fable cleared her throat. 'Doyen Moreno . . . is it possible that someone could have done something to make sure we all got stuck here, unable to be removed even if we were hurt?'

We all looked at him, and I thought he'd clam up, but he answered.

'Anything is possible, I suppose. But I don't know who would do such a thing.'

'One of the other houses, maybe? Just look at how hard Julius and his crew from House Draconell came at us. They don't want to be replaced. Certainly not by people they consider losers,' Caterina said.

Gary grunted. 'Who'd want to be replaced by a bunch of nobodies?'

Typhon shook his head. 'You aren't nobodies. You've all done amazing things today.'

Ellie blushed again, and Caterina patted her on the shoulder. '*You* are amazing, don't for a second believe you aren't.'

He surprised me and went on. 'You all did incredibly well.' He tipped his head at each of us. 'You work as a unit, better than I would have thought. The hours of practicing to get the runes exact, the struggles you've faced . . . the improvisations you've made. All of it. Especially against those that had a distinct advantage. Removing the bracers, I think that was the last key.'

I stiffened and felt the others from my house mimic me. 'What kind of advantage?' Did he mean because they were better than us?

He sighed. 'None of you read the rules, did you?'

'We didn't break any rules!' I said, feeling the heat from the fire in my veins now.

'There was nothing against you bringing in one item each – a single item from your dorm. That's why Mortan had the flaming sword. Julius had a power booster. The others all had something to aid them in defense or offense. Any magical item would have counted.'

As the de facto leader, that was on me one hundred percent. I'd wasted time breaking the rules and bringing food when I could've – and should've – been *reading* the rules and bringing a frucking weapon. But instead I'd inadvertently brought Typhon's gift with me – the enchanted glass. And it had saved us. So maybe I wasn't such a sheet loser after all. Still, I couldn't help but mourn the fact that we could've been armed with Fable's Fae knives and my still-untested magic gloves.

'And Julius,' Phyllis said. 'What exactly is his item, you said a power booster?'

'An object of great power that has been in the Rendimion family for generations. It comes to Neverthorn with any of their bloodline, specifically to help with any fights or duels. Because they would not want to lose face.'

I pulled the cylindrical item out of my pocket. 'This it?'

Typhon nodded. 'That's it.'

The item was about six inches long, smooth, I realized that it was stone. The colors just seemed so unreal. Deep red swirled with black and gray, tiny flecks of iridescent sparkles danced through the item as I rolled it, changing each time it did a full roll in my palm.

'What does it do?' Fable asked. 'I've been studying magical items. I've never come across it in all my reading.'

'You wouldn't have found it anywhere. It's not well known outside of the Rendimion family, never mind outside of Draconell,' Typhon said.

Was he trying to help us? I shot him a look, but he was staring at the fire, avoiding my eyes.

'You didn't tell us what it does.' Gary frowned. 'Or are you forbidden from telling us?'

I winced and wanted to yell at Gary not to give Typhon an out, but he surprised me again. 'I am not forbidden. It dulls the scent and sensation of magic so people will be less likely to pick up on their presence, or the building of a rune spell. That was how they ambushed you. It can amplify magic too, at least

of the person holding it – making Julius that much stronger.'
He looked at me and this time I could all but read his mind.

He couldn't figure out how I'd beaten Julius when he'd
been holding the stone cylinder.

Me either, big boy, me either.

Because even with a Quirk like mine, that allowed me to
throw my weight around like a supernova, it was new and
largely untested. Julius, with his experience, still should have
been that much stronger and faster than me. Those moments
had been a blur of instinct and rune magic.

'That explains the fireball,' Phyllis said, her voice dry as a
crisp white wine. 'We can use it now. Any items taken from
the fallen become a part of our stash of weaponry or tools.'

Fable held out her hand and I let her take the . . .

'Does it have a name?' I asked with a frown.

Typhon shook his head. 'It's not got a name. Or at least
not one that I know.'

'Caterina,' I looked over at her, noticing and trying not to
notice that she'd been holding Ellie's hand, 'Can you set up the
outer wards? Everyone needs to do a layer, follow her lead.'

No one argued.

Typhon was staring at me again.

I rolled my shoulders and tipped my head side to side
as I began my own ward, weaving the runes with my fingers, seeing the magic of my friends sliding around us. Reds,
orange, yellow, white, even a whisper of blue and green.
Colors of the House of Phoenix. The colors of the flames
that made up each of us.

'Harlow, explain why you're each doing a ward,' Typhon
said, pulling my gaze from the colors of the magic.

'Because each of us will wake up when our ward is disturbed,' I said. 'We won't have to wake each other up, we will
all be woken at the same time. Caterina is the strongest at

hiding things, so she goes first. The rest of us pile on behind her, buoying up her rune casting as an added bonus.'

His smile was swift and gone like a bird on the wing. 'Smart.'

'It was Harlow's idea,' Fable muttered as she ran her fingers over the cylinder. 'She's a survivor. Here. I think I can set this up now too. I can make it so our magical signatures are harder to trace.' She cast a rune that slid into the magical item we'd taken from Julius. It glowed for a moment and then a pulse of energy rolled out of it, casting us all in a coating of silvery mist that settled into our hair and clothing, resting on our skin.

'That will do it,' Typhon said. 'I'd say you have about five hours of sleep ahead of you, if you're lucky.'

No one needed prompting.

One by one they curled around the fire, sleep overtaking them quickly if the sound of their even breathing was any indication.

I found myself staring wide awake at the ceiling of the cavern. It didn't take me long to give up and scoot so that my back was against the wall. Typhon was to my left, his head tipped back against the wall as well, his eyes closed.

His stomach growled.

I snorted. 'Bet you're wishing Tarquinius hadn't taken all that food.'

'Indeed,' he muttered. 'He has a strange sense of fairness.'

Another snort out of me, this one with some serious weight to it. 'Since when has Neverthorn played fair?'

He opened his eyes and looked at me, and there was none of the irritation or ire I expected. He looked . . . worried.

'Typhon,' I shimmied closer to him as I lowered my voice. 'What's going on? Like, what's really going on?'

His eyes seemed to search my face. 'House Phoenix has

far more at risk in the Solstice Games than any other house. I think the fact that neither you nor Ross was pulled out when you were so badly injured is an indicator that there is more at play even than I know. I think you're right.'

I stared at him. 'You think someone . . . might be trying to kill us? I was just speculating earlier.'

His eyes were thoughtful. 'I didn't want to panic the others, but there is no reason you two shouldn't have been pulled out. Not with injuries like that.'

I frowned and rubbed at my face. 'I know, it's a training exercise, making sure we weed out the weakest, like Tarquinius said.'

'There's more.' Typhon lowered his chin, and his voice. 'This isn't just about weeding out the weak.'

I leaned closer to him to hear. 'What then?'

'Heronius was killed because he wasn't strong enough, despite being the best we had. Not just to face Nocta. But because he couldn't wield even a single piece of the Grym Dunaras.'

I laughed; I couldn't help it. 'That's a fairy tale.'

I sat there, my mind whirling. The Grym Dunaras was a myth of a myth. Part magic, part weapon, all powerful. The story went that it was created by the Morrigan when she felt that Arthur was becoming too powerful with Excalibur at his side. She wanted something to offset the human king's power.

Only . . . Typhon wasn't laughing. My jaw dropped, I stared at him, and whisper yelled. 'Are you frucking serious?'

'A piece only – we had a shard of the weapon and set it into the blade of a sword. And it was stolen by Nocta after he killed Heronius.'

The Grym Dunaras had been the Morrigan's answer but it was *too* powerful. A battle between Arthur and the Morrigan had ensued, one not spoken of by the Dims' history books.

This one had rocked the foundations of the world and had resulted in Excalibur being banished, and the Grym Dunaras being shattered into four pieces and spread out across the world.

No one even knew what kind of weapon the Grym Dunaras was – that's how dangerous it had been. Every mention of it wiped out of books, out of everything but oral lore.

'It's not real.' I knew I sounded naive, but it terrified me. Not only because the Grym Dunaras had been used as a threat, almost like a boogie man, but the thought of Nocta holding even a piece of it . . .

'We're frucked if he has it.' I grimaced when he was dead silent. 'You're not arguing.'

'Nothing to argue,' he said, which scared me even more.

I closed my eyes and tried to think of something – anything else. Maybe my heart rate was up, maybe I was hyperventilating . . . whatever the case was, Typhon noticed.

He took one of my hands in his, and held on tight, locking our fingers together. And then he did something I didn't know he had in him.

He broke the rules. 'Sleep, Harlow. You need to sleep.'

He traced a rune across my hand with the hand that wasn't clenching mine, and sleep crashed over me.

40

The smell of *bacon* pulled me out of a deep sleep. I groaned and stretched, my face tucked in tight to the crook of . . . Typhon's neck.

I jerked away from him, feeling our hands separate as I stood, my legs shaky. 'Why do you smell like bacon?'

He grimaced and pushed to a crouch. 'I don't. Someone found a stash.'

Stashes were exactly what they sounded like. Little boxes of goodies stuffed all over the place and if you were brave and smart, you could find them.

'I found it!' Marina crowed as she flipped the bacon over in the frying pan. She had scrambled eggs going, and Phyllis had a pot of coffee on the fire too.

'Oh, my gods, I could marry you.' I stuffed my fists to my belly to stop the growling.

In a few short minutes, we all had a plate of food – yup, all the plates and utensils were a part of the stash – there was even enough for Typhon because our team was smaller than everyone else's.

Bellies full, spirits high, everyone was excited to tackle the day.

Everyone except for Phyllis. She grabbed at my hand and squeezed my fingers – hard. 'Listen.'

I tipped my head but couldn't hear anything, at least not right away. 'Everyone, shut it!'

They went silent at the same time the sound grew louder. A grinding of stone, a plunk of . . . water?

I looked up as the ceiling groaned, a crack shot in four directions, water spilling out of it like a shower head. 'We gotta move!'

'What happened?' Ellie yelled.

'The stash,' Typhon said. 'It might have had a tracer on it.'

'Oh no!' Marina yelped. 'I'm sorry . . .'

'Let's head out, then. Phyllis, you got a suggestion?'

She bobbed her head. 'This way.'

I thought there was only one way in and out and was about to say so when the wall opened up to reveal a hole.

I hurried the group through, counting, putting Typhon in the middle again. We couldn't lose our flag, and I wasn't going to lose anyone to whoever was trying to off us.

We needed each other. We'd get through this, and then . . . we'd find a way to keep our house together.

We were stronger together.

Phyllis led the way deeper and deeper into the tunnels. 'This isn't right! The symbols aren't leading us out!' she yelled back.

We were in water up to our knees now. I didn't think we were going to drown – I mean, I had a rune spell I could use to keep breathing underwater, but I wasn't sure everyone else could cast it. Fruck that one up and your lungs would explode.

The water rose rapidly, panic was kicking in fast . . . and then it just stopped.

'Marina?' Fable's voice quavered. 'You're glowing.'

I whipped around to see the center of Marina's chest indeed glowing with a soft blue. She held her hands out to the side and the water circled up and around her wrists. 'I can . . . water . . . my Quirk is controlling water.'

Her lips trembled, the tough girl act cracking as she came into her own power. 'Bad beech!' I pumped a fist in the air.

She laughed, rolled her wrists in tandem. The water flowed around her. 'This is so dang cool.'

It was cool, but we were still stuck.

I spun around, water sloshing as the way behind us flattened, stairs and walls rearranging so that we were looking out across a swamp the size of a football field. All around it bushes and plants shot up, things stirred in the depths. Here and there were small islands that looked like they would give some hope, but I could see things moving on them.

A door on the far side flashed a simple sign.

Exit.

'Typhon, is that *really* the way out of this room?'

'Yes. Tarquinius's idea of a joke.'

I grimaced. 'Okay, so we have to go through the swamp. No problem.'

Exactly. No problem. There weren't sharks in swamps.

Right?

'I can't swim,' Ellie said.

'Me either,' Gary added. 'If it's deep, we're screwed.'

'I got you,' Marina said. 'I think I can lower the water at the very least.'

She stepped forward and put her palms together, then swung them to her sides. The water level lowered a significant amount. 'There's nowhere for me to put it, so that's the best I can do,' she said with a grimace.

I patted her on the shoulder, wishing that I could have mastered my Quirk as fast as her, but knowing we all had our own journey with our new powers. 'It's awesome. This is so much better than swimming. I'll go in first, test the depth. If it gets above my chin, we'll work around that. Maybe you can maneuver the water around us?'

'And what about the ... things in the water?' Fable whispered.

I'd never heard her so afraid and that snapped something through me. I did a slow turn.

'You ever see *The NeverEnding Story*?'

Two nods, one from Marina and one from Phyllis, the rest of them shook their heads. Gods, no one watched the classics anymore.

'Look, here's the deal. There was a swamp, a swamp of sadness. And if you let the sadness get to you, you sank. I think this is the same idea, only it's fear. It's infecting us with fear and we have to just . . . we have to be brave. Okay? We've got this.'

Don't think about sharks, don't think about sharks, don't think about sharks.

I turned and forced myself to step into the water, sinking up to my waist. I let out a hiss as the cold hit me.

There was a bit of nervous laughter as they followed me in.

Things brushed up against our legs. Things moved in the distance. But nothing erupted out of the water, and it didn't get that deep, thanks to Marina.

In fact, I thought we'd made it. I really did.

The creatures waited until we were about as far in as we could be before they struck.

The water exploded around us, vines and weeds wrapping around limbs and waists, yanking us up and out of the water until every one of us was dangling twenty feet up. Everyone was flinging runes, but none of them were working.

I tried a slashing rune, and it bounced off the vine wrapped around me as if it was titanium and not a plant. Snarling, I tried three more runes, each one more aggressive than the last before I stopped.

'Anyone got something that works?'

We were pulled by the vines, up higher yet, deep into the overhead recesses of the cavern. We were dangling, wrapped up in vines, and none of our runes were working. I looked at Typhon and he shrugged. 'I can't help you.'

'I know that,' I snapped.

'Why so high?' Caterina moaned. 'I hate heights.'

'Look,' Phyllis said, pointing below.

Way, way below us was another group sloshing through the water – I could just make out the movement, a few voices carried, high-pitched and fearful. They got to the middle of the swamp, the same as us.

The plants were faster than any person, moving like lightning as they wrapped themselves around their victims and yanked them up out of the water. They didn't even look our way. They were too busy throwing runes, trying to get loose, the same as we had.

A light above the exit sign lit up. A literal countdown.

I groaned. 'We got three minutes, guys, we gotta get out of this or we're toast.'

And by toast, I had no doubt that we would be killed.

'I have an idea,' Fable said.

'All ears, girl.' I tried to wiggle my way out of the vines.

'Plants have been known to react to song positively. There is a rune that makes music so that you hear it inside your head, or you can broadcast it elsewhere, say, into the head of a child to soothe them at night. I'm going to show you, and then I'm going to use it. If it works, we should be able to get them to release us.'

I managed to twist around to see Fable flash the rune at us. 'Someone grab Typhon if it works,' I said. 'We aren't losing our captured flag.'

A familiar screech from below made me grin. Nikita had been caught in the vines along with House Kirinash. If Fable's rune worked, we were going to have two flags by the end of this.

The rune looked like a musical note hovering in the air, Fable's magic powering it. But there was no sound. She pressed her hand against the plant stalk that held her tight, and it began to lower her to the ground.

One by one, the House of Phoenix fumbled through the musical note rune, copying Fable. Phyllis was the one to grab Typhon, and I watched as they slid down. The other team saw us dropping from the ceiling above them and began yelling, begging us to help them.

I cast the rune, not once but twice, one in each hand so that it settled into both of my palms, and pressed my right hand against the thick plant that was wrapped around me. It began to lower me, and I swayed side to side, swinging the body of it until I was lowering right through the midst of the team below us.

'Hurry, Harlow!' Fable yelled from below.

'Get to the door!' I called back. I wasn't going to leave without another flag and all the points it would gain us.

Especially if that flag was the reason we were on the chopping block. Did I know that Nikita was behind us being blocked from being taken out of the games when we were injured? No. But she was as good a suspect as any at this point, given how much she hated me, and how poorly she'd treated House Phoenix.

I wrapped my legs around the vine that had Nikita bound up and pressed my left hand against the vine.

'Don't you dare!' she screamed.

'I wouldn't dare.' I winked and cast a quick rune to cover her mouth, then caught the edge of her vine with a toe and spun her so that her back was to me. Putting on the handcuffs we were given couldn't have been sweeter.

No. Not true.

The plants dropped us at about the ten-foot mark and

417

Nikita landed in a pile of soft black mud that smelled like sheet. She opened her mouth to scream, but while no sound came *out*, the mud . . . it splashed *in*, which left her gagging.

I grabbed her around the arm, dragging her with me all the way to the exit door where my team waited.

'One more day after this,' Marina said as we stepped through, the doorway behind us buzzing as time ran out. 'We're going to win the whole frucking thing.'

I grinned, but my heart was only half in it. Because I had no doubt the worst was to come.

The final day was going to be hell.

41

After the swamp, we ran a literal gauntlet of things trying to kill us. In no particular order there was:

A cavern of spiders.

Gas that caused hallucinations – Gary totally saved us on that one, seeing the gas before anyone else did.

Potions we had to create in order to open a door to safety while we were being rushed by rabid lions.

Poison arrows. One came straight for me, and I ducked but I knew I wasn't going to be fast enough.

A rune was cast from behind me, deflecting it. The only person behind me was Typhon.

'Doyen Moreno,' I said. 'You breaking rules?'

'No.' But I knew the feel of his magic, and the bond between us thrummed. He surely had deflected the arrow, but he wasn't going to admit it. Fine. I wasn't about to tattle on him.

And that was just the highlights. We spent the rest of the day and half the night running, fighting, throwing runes, and using everything we'd learned up to that point, and a few things we learned on the fly.

Finally, sometime in the middle of the night, Phyllis found us another foxhole, the tree etched into the wall, and I had never been so happy to stand still. This foxhole was open to the sky, and it was raining lightly. I tipped my face upward and let the rain wash some of the dirt, sweat, and blood away.

The color of the sky though . . . the Northern Lights were

more red than any other color and that caused more than a little fear to drive through me.

Typhon had stayed far quieter with Nikita around, barely speaking, all his emotions through the bond clamped down, quiet.

Nikita was still blessedly gagged. We'd tried taking it off, but she just screeched like a banshee, trying to bring down the other teams on us.

We had no idea how many of the other teams had been removed, and then put back in. Who had stolen other flags? Had anyone gotten through to the center of the Coliseum?

House Felinita we'd only seen in passing. They hadn't even tried to fight it out with us and we couldn't catch them to take their flag – Doyenne Parunah, and Doyenne Storm who had previously belonged to House Wolven. I silently cheered for them, knowing that they'd outsmarted House Wolven in order to take their flag.

House Wolven, who we'd beaten, but barely, had come after us a second time – they'd already lost Doyenne Storm at that point. Houses Unicorna and Kelpish still had their own flags when we crossed paths. They'd both run from us.

Then there was Draconell. They'd come after us with a vengeance. Awesome.

So far, we'd kept everyone at bay. Draconell without their little magic boosting item were not as strong as us.

Our two captured 'flags' were put over against the wall, as far from the only entrance into the cavern, and as far from our team as possible as we pulled a huddle together. We probably looked like the most ragged football team in the world. But we were still standing. We still had everyone.

Fable was on my left, Phyllis on my right. I looked at the people I'd grown to care for, no matter how hard I'd tried not to. I made eye contact with each of them as I spoke.

'The last fight is coming. They told us the third day was like a massive showdown of abilities. That means we will be fighting one on one. Taking turns, right Phyllis?'

Phyllis nodded. 'Correct. It will go down to the last man standing on each team. That's how we gain the most points.'

Ellie paled. 'I hate fighting.'

'I know. You're going to go last. From behind the lines, you are going to cast your healing runes on our team. Okay? That's your job. Keep us as strong as you can. If you end up in the ring, or fight, or frucking octagon, whatever they have, you yield. Okay?'

Her back stiffened. 'I won't yield.'

'But —'

'I hate it, but I can do it. This is my family I'm fighting for.' Her hand was wrapped up in Caterina's. 'Right? We're a family.'

My throat got tight. I nodded and tried to clear the tension in my neck. 'Yes. We are. Fable, you have the rod?'

Gary snickered and I rolled my eyes. 'Unless you have a better name for it? Tube of death maybe?'

'Does it need a name?' Ellie asked.

'Maybe a Latin name?' Fable offered.

I looked at my friends. 'I don't think —'

'Regardless of what you call it, it can be taken from you if you lose it when holding it.' Typhon said. We all looked at him. 'And if you lose it, another team has that advantage.'

I held up my hands. 'Fine. We can't use it, because if one of us loses, it will go to the other team. So, we leave it with Phyllis. Agreed?'

Everyone nodded.

What I didn't tell them was that I'd been using the gift Typhon had given me to scour through rune books in the short time I'd had it before the games. And I'd found a rune that, if I could cast it well . . . I could give them some of my own strength. If I was next to Phyllis, I might even be able to pull some power through the still unnamed tube of death.

Yeah, that was stupid. But I was too tired to come up with anything better.

I was crossing my fingers on that last one. 'We set wards. Get some sleep if you can. Tomorrow will come fast and it's going to be a beech. No snooping for food. Just stick close.'

Marina winced a little but other than that, everyone settled down. I thought there would be no sleep for me, but again, Typhon turned his back to the others, and cast a rune that settled my mind, and I slept for the few hours we had.

The next morning, I jerked awake, smelling *bacon*. 'You frucking well didn't!' I yelled as I scrambled to my feet.

Marina held her hands up. 'I had some bacon and toast left, I kept it in my pocket and, don't gross out, I was able to duplicate it this morning. There's enough for a BLT, no L and no T, for everyone.'

I let out a breath. 'Good job. Sorry I freaked.' I took the bacon sandwich and had a bite. It was a bit soggy and tasted faintly of the swamp, but it was food. And we needed fuel to get through this.

Nikita refused the sandwich, but Typhon let me feed him his. We'd put his cuffs back on him, once we had Nikita under wraps. You know, keeping things fair.

The familiar grinding of the walls stilled everyone.

The Coliseum opened up in front of us, the walls peeling back and revealing a literal coliseum – yes, just like the one in Rome.

'Welcome and well done to you all, so far!' Tarquinius's voice boomed through the air. 'Now, to the final fights. One on one, it will be a single winner take all, giving their team an additional one hundred points.'

I turned to face the others. 'Caterina, you still good with starting us off?'

She rolled her shoulders, flexed her fingers, cracking each knuckle. She was one of our better hand-to-hand fighters, and she was quick, even if she didn't have a Quirk yet. 'Hell yeah, let's show them who they're messing with.'

I looked back at Phyllis who was pale again. 'What's wrong?'

She shot a look at me. 'The skies are dark, Harlow.'

I looked up. There was not a cloud in sight. 'The sky is blue . . . Are you okay?'

'No,' she whispered.

What was up with her? I didn't have time to ask. We stepped out of the shadow of the foxhole and into the Coliseum proper. There were few cheers for us. Opie screamed my name louder than anyone, Krishna next to her, bouncing and cheering.

I took note that the Runecoats were still there, spread out around as before. None of them were cheering.

But as a whole, the students of Neverthorn cheered for the other teams.

I scanned the remaining competitors and winced.

There were a lot of them and only seven of us left, eight if we counted Phyllis.

'Fruuuuuck,' Gary breathed. 'That is not good math.'

Tarquinius strolled out into the middle of the arena. 'Ah, extra points for the House of Phoenix for capturing not one, but two flags. Well done. Perhaps you will live up to all of our expectations after all. You didn't lose a single teammate, nor did your team ever need a restart. A slight adjustment to the next challenge, the final one today. You will face everyone over seventeen from the other teams, regardless of their losses. One on one, House Phoenix against the combined might of the other houses. This is necessary to prove your strength in battle. To prove you can face Nocta when the time comes.'

The crowd sucked in a collective breath, and I felt my friends behind me do the same.

'That is unfair!' Liam shouted. 'You can't be serious?'

Tarquinius didn't take his eyes from us. 'We must test them fully, Doyen O'Connor. Would you have them fail when they face Nocta?'

I mean . . . how did you say no to that? You didn't.

'Sir,' Typhon took a step. 'I agree with O'Connor, this seems unnecessary.'

Tarquinius ignored him completely and snapped his fingers – both Typhon and Nikita were flown through the air to him, their handcuffs disappearing, and the mud and dirt scrubbed from their bodies.

Mother goddess Hecate . . . we were facing all of the others. Not just another team. No quarter finals. All of them.

'What do the extra points do for us?' I yelled at him.

He smiled in my direction. 'You can have two losses and still continue – one for each flag – and then that fighter can continue later, or another in their place.' Essentially that gave us two extra fighters if we were careful. And we had Ellie to heal them up, a little piece of information that Tarquinius had no clue about.

I grinned. 'Works for us.'

My grin seemed to unnerve him, and his smile faltered. Which only made me grin wider.

I motioned for my team, already strategizing. 'Caterina you still go in first, but when you get hurt, I'm pulling you. Then we'll get you healed up and put you back in later. Okay? We can do it twice, but if we don't have to lose anyone, we aren't going to.'

Ellie nodded. 'I can heal you easier if you come off the mats.'

'Who's going to be the other sub?' Ross asked, looking hopeful.

'Let's see how it pans out,' I said. 'Could be you, maybe me.'

The group nodded and Caterina moved to step up to the ring.

'Wait,' Phyllis said. 'I'd like to go first.'

We all turned to the matriarch of the group. It would help our numbers for sure, but . . .

'You sure you want to fight?'

'They won't expect it.' She shrugged. 'And if I can take one or two down, it will help. The fact that someone has been trying to kill us . . . I want a piece of them.'

She was still super pale. I stared at her. 'You got it. Phyllis first, then Caterina.'

I wasn't sure at all, but I trusted Phyllis.

I put my palm out and slapped hands with each of my teammates . . . with each of my new family.

'Let's kick some asterisks!'

It took about ten minutes for the other teams to decide who was going first. I took note that Julius was way down the line. Fine by me. I was going to go second to last, which meant that however many idiots were left . . . that was how many I had to handle.

In the center of the arena was a circle set in stones. We had to stay within that circle and not disturb a single stone or we were out.

To win, we had to knock our opponent out, make them submit, or toss them out of the circle. Similar to the hand-to-hand combat, only this was no holds barred. Magic. Fists. Weapons.

When Phyllis stepped up first, the other team – cause let's be honest, it was a single team now – they laughed so hard someone in the back fell over. Her shoulders sunk a little. She needed to have fight in her, she needed to be pissed off . . .

'You got this Phyll,' I said, knowing exactly how touchy the nickname was for her. I needed her to be full of fire for this.

'Stop calling me that,' she snapped over her shoulder.

'Okay, soon as you knock a half a dozen out.' I grinned at her, and she glared right back.

'Just like Nico,' she said. 'You know how to push me.'

The wind swept out of me, and I just about went to my knees.

Did she know he was my father?

But the fight was on, and my eyes were trained on Phyllis. She was about a quarter of the way inside the circle now. Her opponent was a young woman from Kirinash.

The girl sniffed at Phyllis as she stepped over the ring of stones.

Phyllis didn't give her a chance. She used a quick rune of air and pushed the girl right back out, so she landed on her butt outside of the ring.

'One point to House Phoenix.' A voice boomed. I didn't know the voice, but it tickled at my memory banks. Deep, resonant. One of the older students maybe? Someone from Draconell?

We cheered and I watched with absolute frucking glee as Phyllis straightened and rolled up her sleeves.

She took the next three opponents out so fast they barely had time to cast a single rune. I'd known she was fast, and of course she'd been in school for years longer than anyone else . . . I just hadn't thought she had the fire in her. Not with what had happened to her all those years ago.

I grabbed a hold of Fable's hand. We were going to win this, and Phyllis was going to take them all out. I could just see it in my mind now. A sixty-year-old taking out the best of the best, over and over again.

We'd all be drinking from the whiskey teapot tonight! There was no way Tarquinius could send half of us home if Phyllis cleaned house all on her own.

There was a shuffle in the ranks and the students that were at the back of the line . . . they moved up.

Ramusan 'Ram' Wintreck stepped into the ring, a brute of a Wolven. House Wolven was known for their violent tendencies, and him more than the others. And we'd already locked horns with him — we knew just how mean he was.

'Oh, my gods,' Ellie breathed out. 'He'll kill her.'

'No, he won't.'

I stepped up to the edge of the circle and flicked my fingers against my thigh. A rune for bravery that my mother had traced on my cheek how often? At least once a week when I'd been a child afraid of the dark.

'This rune carries my love, and gives you strength, Harlow. Don't forget it.'

And I hadn't. I just hadn't needed to remember it until now.

I connected to it, drawing my own energy and strength, imbuing the rune with them both, then finally casting it toward Phyllis. Her back straightened and a shiver ran through her spine.

Ram had a blocking rune up before he even stepped into the rune circle, and the fight was on.

Phyllis moved like water around the ring, her hands flashing as she avoided the physical blows.

I fed her my energy, eyes focused on their every move, ready to jump in if I had to.

Ram flung a rune at her feet, tripping her and sending her to the ground. Behind me a gasp went up through our group.

'Get up, Phyllis!' I shouted, but she stayed down on her hands and knees as Ram strolled toward her.

'You shouldn't be here. You're weak, useless.'

Phyllis looked up at him, and I'd never seen such rage in her. 'I am not weak.'

She'd been spinning a rune with the hand furthest from him, her off hand. She rocked back and flung the rune with a scream, the colors and shape of it telling me everything.

A tornado spun around Ram, twisting him off his feet and flinging him out of the circle, slamming him into the far wall of the Coliseum.

'Point to House Phoenix. Well done, Phyllis. Well done.'

That same voice. Who the hell was commentating?

'I am out.' Phyllis hobbled to the edge of the circle. I caught her around the waist, and she looked at me. 'You aren't like him; *he* never would have done that, I felt the boost from you.'

Shared power, that's what she meant. I squeezed her around the waist. 'You are a damn rockstar, Phyllis.'

Her smile wavered and then the rest of the team were there, lifting her toward Ellie to heal her hands and knees.

'That counts as a loss. You cannot leave the ring unless you are beaten, or forfeit your match,' Tarquinius said.

I shrugged. I would take it, Phyllis had done more than her part. One of us would go another round in her stead. 'Caterina, you ready?'

She bobbed her head, and I saw her weave a rune for bravery behind her back, letting it sink into her skin before she stepped into the circle.

The fights were brutal. There was no holding back on any side.

Caterina dropped six fighters before she went down. Gary managed three. Marina had four before she was thrown clear of the ring.

Fable also wove the bravery rune before she went in, and she took out another five. On her sixth fight, my spine tingled, like someone had walked over my grave.

I looked around the Coliseum to see dark clouds – the ones that Phyllis had claimed to have seen – wrapped around the space. The sky began to crackle with lightning, deep booms of thunder reverberating in my chest.

Fable backed up and I put a hand on her shoulder, giving her a boost of strength. My own reserves were low, but I didn't care. We were winning.

My friends were killing it. 'You got this.'

Fable grinned and put her hand on mine, squeezing it back. '*We* got this.'

We both turned to face her next opponent. As he stepped toward Fable, he flicked something overhand toward our friends behind me. I turned with it but didn't understand what the tiny blinking red light was until it was too late.

It landed in the huddle where Ellie was tending to Gary's wounds.

And exploded.

Students were flung everywhere.

Screams rent the air, and the team across from us cheered. Not that I could hear them, but I could see them high fiving one another, faces plastered with grins.

The blast was meant to disorient us, to shake us up. Because, if it had been meant to kill us, it would have carried a bigger punch. It wasn't even on par with the fireball that Draconell had flung at us.

I was on the ground, flat on my belly. As I stood up, Fable was outside the ring, and I went to her first.

I put a hand on her and felt her breathing. I touched the velvet pouch with all the stones my friends had etched their auras on, and that connection to them lit up like a beacon in the night. My friends were hurt, and scared, but they were okay. Not unlike the bond to Typhon, I could just pick them out at the edges of my senses.

Across the ring stood the biggest monster of House Draconell. The one who'd thrown the bomb.

Mortan Blackstone.

'Full circle,' I growled. 'It's about time we dealt with you.'

'Continue!' Tarquinius bellowed. I glanced at the headmaster, and the encouragement on his face. He tipped his head in my direction. Because this was what it might look like, facing Nocta – facing someone who had no conscience.

'This is war, Ms. Daygon. And real war is messy and full of surprises.'

Mortan flicked his wrist, his runes prepared as I moved toward the ring. Someone was yelling at me, but the words were fuzzed as I focused in on the prick in front of me.

He wanted to do more than beat us.

Every line of his body was set to do damage that wasn't supposed to happen. Call me crazy, but I would have bet money in that moment he'd been behind the flaming rune the Draconell team had cast.

I didn't prep a single rune as I stepped over the threshold of the ring.

'Take her out, Mort!' Julius yelled.

Mort smiled, greasy, confident.

He kept spinning runes and I didn't so much as twitch. 'You aren't going to fight now? Going to just stand there and let me level you?'

I knew the rune I wanted. Bone shattering, I would make him hurt for what he did to my friends. I could feel their injuries – could feel the broken ribs and the gasps for air, could feel the open wound across Caterina's side and the blow to Phyllis's head.

He was a monster.

My fingers itched to spin the rune and cast it at him, but the timing had to be right.

Mort rushed me, a rune flying. I spun to the left, dropped down and kicked out at his knee, catching it hard with the heel of my boot. The bone snapped and I swept upward, jump-kicking and snapping my other foot into the bottom of his jaw.

His eyes rolled, but he stayed on his feet.

He swung a fist, catching me in the ribs, driving me back, but I dodged his other hand as he tossed a splicing rune at me. Meant to cut me in half.

'No deadly runes!' Typhon bellowed from somewhere over by my friends. I couldn't look, but I could sense him near them. Helping them.

'Ooops,' Mort laughed. 'Forgot.' He spat to the side, blood gobbing at his feet. 'You think you can take top spot? You gotta come through me first.'

I smiled and circled him. 'I'll go through all of you to take that spot.'

He arched a brow. 'All of us? You can't beat eight in a row. Eight that are all ready to graduate?'

'You don't have a healer, do you?' I asked.

'Hasn't been one of those born in forty years. But I won't need one.' Mort threw a rune and followed it with a fist. Again, I ducked and dodged, keeping him moving, I needed him to line up perfectly.

I needed to set the bait so he took it, and I could sink their entire ship.

I drove in close, fists driving toward his face, ribs and upper thigh, making him dance like the monkey he was.

He sidestepped so that he was directly in front of the remainder of those I'd face. All seven were bunched together, hanging onto each other, cheering him on.

Julius was in that bunch.

I brought my hands up and spun the rune fast, but not as fast I could have. Mortan saw me and dove to the side as I released the rune that soared out of the ring, and right into the remainder of their teammates.

The sound of bones snapping filled the air, the students screamed as they went down all at once and I turned to face Mort.

'Ooops. Missed.' Maybe another day I would have felt bad. I might have felt guilty if they'd been younger. But these were the oldest ones – eighteen and nineteen years old, in their last years at Neverthorn. The ones who damn well knew right from wrong. And they'd cheered as my friends were hit by a rune bomb.

His face purpled with rage, and he rushed me, the splicing rune on his fingertips again.

There was no more pulling punches, no more being careful.

We clashed, fighting for blood. Runes, fists and feet, I danced around him as if I hadn't been giving my energy over to the others.

As if this was indeed a fight to the death.

Mort stumbled and I didn't hesitate, I went straight for his head, snapping a rune of sleep into his face.

He went straight down, face into the sand.

'House Phoenix, you have won,' the commentator said, and even gave us a slow clap by the sounds of it. 'But that is no surprise.'

My house, though, they were hurt.

I didn't care that we'd won. I could *feel* the injuries of my friends. Ellie was pulling them together, but gods, they were hurt. I ran off the mats and went to help Ellie. I used the rune to draw energy from me, and I gave it to her.

'They will be okay,' Ellie said. 'No one is injured too badly.'

'Well done!' Tarquinius said, as he approached us, with a half glance over his shoulder. Looking toward the upper levels. 'Very good.'

The commentator spoke again, his voice deepening with each word, booming all around us. As if he'd been hiding his true voice before – of course he had. Tarquinius would have recognized him – he'd been his star pupil all those years ago.

'They are not yours to congratulate, Sage. You did not test them. You did not train them. You used them, didn't you? True to form, as always.'

'No.' Tarquinius paled, slowly turning. 'No, it cannot be.'

That *voice* . . . a chill cut through to the core of me.

He spoke and my memories took me back to the one day I'd met him as a child.

'You thought you were so clever. Don't you see? No matter how many soldiers. No matter who you think to train. I will never stop coming for you.'

I turned to see the clouds darken and familiar figures seemingly dropping from the sky. Creatures of someone's twisted mind, bodies that had been pulled apart and then put back together with bits and pieces of animals.

Lion heads.

Bear claws.

Snake mouths.

I was sure I'd seen one of them in particular at the Nevershoppes all those months ago. I thought he'd been killed.

433

The voice sounded familiar, because I had a memory of it, from when I'd been a little girl hiding in the closet. I put my hand out to my team.

'Get behind me!'

Nocta's men leapt from behind the Runecoats, taking them out with a speed that seemed impossible.

Screams rent the air.

And then he stepped out from the upper part of the arena, from the announcer's area. He was as I remembered him as he cast a rune effortlessly and floated himself to the floor of the Coliseum.

His voice was magnified, shaking the air and sending students scattering.

'Run and hide, children. I am the Lord of the Night. And I have come to free you from this life.'

The sky went from a stormy day to a pitch-black night in a split second. More of the franken-creatures erupted around us from the ground as if they'd lain in wait under the loose sand.

The world seemed to pause in that moment, the air stilling, even the breath in our lungs unmoving. The Runecoats were fighting back now, slowing the onslaught of Nocta's men.

He continued to float down toward the ground.

'Heronius, even with his team and his amazing Quirk, wasn't enough. You think any of these children have what it takes to face me?'

Nocta continued, his voice smooth, and seemingly calm despite the words. 'Tarquinius, you bested me once. You didn't truly think I'd let you do it again?'

From the corner of my eye, I saw Tarquinius, Typhon and Nikita face Nocta together.

My heart clenched, thinking about what Nocta could do

to Typhon. No . . . I had to trust that he'd be okay. That he was strong enough.

House of Phoenix was fighting injured, but they joined the fray and began fighting off Nocta's men as they launched into an attack. Stepping up next to the Runecoats left, giving the younger kids a chance to flee.

A high-pitched scream spun me around.

'Harlow!'

Opie dangled from the edge of the stands. Her friends were trying to pull her back up over the railing, but one of Nocta's men was below, and had grabbed her ankle. His mouth was open wide, sharp teeth gnashing as he yanked on her, dragging her from the safety of her friends.

'No!' I ran, bolting around the bodies that were everywhere, flinging runes where I could but focused on my sister.

Opie lay crumpled on the dirt with her attacker hulking over her, hand lifted. Krishna leapt over the edge and used a rune to send a franken-critter skittering back several feet. Anger flashed across her features.

'Get away from my friend!' she screamed, her hands spinning another rune.

I wouldn't reach Opie fast enough; I was too far away to stop what was happening. The monster lifted two swords over his head, as if he'd take Krishna's head off. I flung a rune in desperation, shrinking the blades with my nicking notions.

If it meant saving the girls, I'd destroy the very weave itself.

The shorthand rune hit the blades as they swept toward Krishna, turning them into weapons the size of pens.

The beast – part gorilla, part goat – spun toward me and lowered his head. There was a flash of blue eyes, and then he was charging me.

I leapt sideways, pushing off the side of the Coliseum as I rolled over the creature's back and onto the other side, so I was between him and the girls. Three more creatures stepped up.

A whip lashed out around me, binding my hands to my sides.

I tried to form a rune to free myself, but in the panic and exhaustion of the past three days, it was a mix of gobbledygook in my head.

'Run! Opie, you gotta run!'

Two Runecoats appeared, they took out two of the three creatures. But the gorilla-goat hybrid was enraged. He charged the Runecoats, slamming into them and then flinging them over his head.

One of the Runecoats pulled a weapon. A broadsword that glowed as if it had flames inside of it. He swept his sword toward the gorilla-goat, who ducked out of the way. I screamed in horror as I realized Krishna and Opie were behind him, directly in the path of the blade as it swung fast and hard. They clung to each other, and all I could do was try to throw myself in front of them.

I breathed out. Felt the tip of the sword start its path through the meat of my upper arm, headed toward my neck.

The world seemed to stop – no, it *had* stopped. I was frozen in mid jump – the blade no longer moving.

Darkness suffused the space around us – sudden and absolute.

From the darkness, Nocta appeared in front of me, his hand held out toward the Runecoat.

A flick of his wrist using a rune I didn't know – but I could see it was shorthand, like the ones I used to craft – and he snapped the Runecoat's neck.

The whip unraveled from around me and I dropped to

my feet, standing there in the darkness, staring at my father. There was no noise, no sound of a battle, it was as if we were in a vacuum.

He turned slowly to face me. 'Things are not as they seem, Harlow.'

His voice was . . . sad?

'There are some you trust who do not deserve it. Their lies are poison. You must flee.'

Flee.

I should have been fighting him, I should have been throwing rune after rune, but all I could do was stare at the man who was my father.

'Forgive me if I opt not to take the word of a monster. No matter who he is.'

'Monster?' His smile was as sad as his voice. 'Even now, I'm only here as a distraction so my soldiers can free those in chains. And to see you one last time.'

I blinked up at him, not understanding. 'What does that even mean? Who is chained? Where are they chained?' My thoughts rapid-fired, for some reason, to Lucy. She'd been so afraid to be captured again . . . was she one of his people after all?

He dipped his head in my direction and took a step back.

'I will take my men and leave. You are strong. And brave. Everything I could want for you to have grown into. It is a boon that the Horned King has given me, to see you fight for those you love. Perhaps one day, you will fight for me.'

'Never,' I growled the word and once more he dipped his head in my direction.

'We shall see, daughter of mine.'

A flash of light blinded me, and the darkness fled as fast as it had descended.

I looked all around the stadium.

Nocta was gone. The franken-creatures were gone. The Runecoats were flattened.

The light around us had shifted to something close to normal. Not cloudy. Not stormy.

I turned and something slammed into me. At first, I thought it was a punch. Until the blinding agony roared through me.

Knife.

Blinking, I looked up as Mort grinned down at me. Looked like Julius wasn't bluffing. Mort was more than just a dangerous Draconell, he was a psychopath.

He yanked the knife out and moved to slam it in again when a rune hit him from the back, crumpling him, his eyes rolling back in his head.

I put my hands to my middle and stared down at the blood flowing from me. Two wounds. Too much blood. This was bad. I looked up as Typhon ran toward me, as Opie screamed my name and the last thing I thought as I fell to the ground was . . . *at least we won the match.*

Even if it had killed me.

42

A cool sensation on my forehead had my eyelids fluttering open and I winced at the bright light.

'Sorry about that,' a soft voice said.

The lights dimmed and my pupils adjusted; I realized it was Ellie standing over my bed in the infirmary, concern written all over her pretty face.

'Man, have I got a headache,' I muttered. Then I jerked upright. 'Is everyone okay?'

'Everyone is okay. As the rune bomb landed, Gary and Ross managed to shield us from the worst of it. I mean, it still hit us, but no one was killed.'

I sat back. 'Thank fruck.'

Her lips tipped into a smile, and she let out a sigh.

'You lost a ton of blood but not an ounce of that winning personality, I see.'

It took a few seconds to process her words but when I did, my stomach bottomed out as I struggled to sit up and looked around.

Where was everyone else?

Oh, gods –

'Did we . . . is anyone . . . ?' The rest of that sentence stuck in my throat, but she was already shaking her head.

'No. I sent them all away once they knew you would be okay. It was a zoo in here, and you needed to sleep. Everyone else fared alright. We were very lucky. We've got some broken bones in House Felinita that the administration has opted to handle with potions and plaster. I kept everything I did quiet, like we talked about. They just think the people I was working on weren't injured that badly to begin with . . . they don't know I was using healing runes . . .' she trailed off with a shrug.

'And Opie?'

'She's fine. As soon as I stemmed your bleeding, I treated her first in spite of Tarquinius's objections. I just –' she chewed nervously on her lower lip, 'well, that was what I thought you'd have wanted me to do. She's family too. It doesn't matter what house she's in.'

A fresh rush of affection for the quietest, most unassuming member of our crew swamped me and I reached out to squeeze her hand.

'You did exactly right.' The truth was my world would be nothing without Opie in it. But Ellie wasn't the only one with a hand in saving my little sis. 'Did . . . did anyone see Nocta flee?'

Her brow knitted as she lowered herself to sit on the bed beside me. 'No. And frankly, I'm not even sure why he did. It seemed like he and his creatures were putting up a pretty good fight. The outcome was still very much up in the air when the arena went dark. And then next thing I saw, he was calling them off, retreating into the shadows again. Do you remember what happened behind the shadow shield he put up? Did you fight him?'

As much as I hated lying to her, I sure as hell couldn't tell her the truth. How did I explain that he'd saved me, and told me that I needed to flee? I swallowed hard, trying to push down the pulse of anxiety as it spread through me. 'I didn't. I think I took a pretty big knock on the head, and things are sort of scrambled.'

She shrugged and then stood. 'Completely normal. And I guess it doesn't really matter why he aborted his mission. I'm just glad he did. It could've been so, so much worse. All the Runecoats were in trouble. Very few of them were left standing.'

I knew she was right, but somehow I couldn't seem to shake the building dread inside me.

There are some you trust who do not deserve it. Their lies are poison. You must flee.

My father's words replayed in my mind on a loop, but I couldn't dwell on them right now. My head already ached, and I needed to see the rest of my team with my own eyes.

I glanced out the window beside my bed and frowned at how dark it was.

'How long was I out?'

'About six hours, give or take. We kept you sedated so your body could finish healing. I think after a couple aspirin and a good meal, you'll feel a lot better. If you want to try to stand up, make sure you keep a hand on the wall, for balance. Maybe take a hot shower before you head back to our dorm, you've got a lot of blood on you.'

I looked down under the sheet. She was not wrong. I was coated in blood.

Ellie stood and stretched. 'They've canceled classes for the next two days so everyone can recover from the scare, and the doyens can focus on shoring up the wards around the school.'

Typhon would be busy all day. Which meant if I wanted to talk to him in private – and I did – I would need to do it tonight.

A sense of urgency pulsed through me, and I stood, probably a little too quickly.

'Easy, I got you.' Ellie grabbed my forearms and steadied me. 'You lost a lot of blood so let's take it easy until you've eaten, alright?'

I nodded and thanked her. 'You really are a gem. I don't

know what we would've done without you the past couple of days.'

She let out a low chuckle. 'I guess that means I'd better stay close then. You and trouble seem to find each other on the regular, don't you?'

'You have no idea,' I grumbled.

But as I took a quick shower in the infirmary bathroom to get the blood off, my whole body started buzzing with adrenaline, and my headache faded. Despite how difficult and scary the games were, we'd learned a lot that we didn't know before. But some new mysteries had also come to light . . .

I needed to talk to Fable, stat. Maybe she could help me decode my father's cryptic words and warnings.

Flee.

Refreshed and healed thanks to Ellie, I was just about to open the infirmary door and head out when it swung open.

Fable stood there, pale as a ghost on laundry day. 'Harlow . . . bad sheet . . . we gotta hurry.'

She reached out and took my hand, her fingers cold.

'Tarquinius is coming to speak with us all.'

'Why?'

'I don't know. But . . . I have a bad feeling, Harlow. Worse than usual.'

She dragged me to the seventh floor where the others were waiting for us in the dorm. Fable shut the door behind us and leaned against it.

'He'll be here in a few minutes,' Marina said quietly. She had a bruise on her cheek, her eyes looked as fatigued as I felt.

I pushed off the door and went to my bed, where Bandit lay curled on the pillow. He reached for me with grabby hands, and I scooped him up.

'Hey kid, you made it.' He butted his head under my chin. 'I never doubted you for a minute.'

The silence was heavy, and Phyllis cleared her throat.

'Maybe he is just coming to congratulate you all. You did well.'

'We all did.' I tipped my head at her.

Behind us the door opened, and I turned to see Tarquinius step through the doorway, Typhon on his left, looking pale and furious as the door shut with a resounding click.

Tarquinius folded his hands at his back and smiled at us.

Okay, so maybe it wasn't going to be so bad . . .

'House Phoenix, you have outdone yourselves this day. Not only in the games, which you won, but on the field of battle. You moved without hesitation to protect the students from Nocta's men. You have our thanks.'

Whatever fear Fable had handed out to us, started to fade. He was just here to thank us, that was it.

The Sage cleared his throat.

'Harlow, I do apologize for not seeing how serious Mortan Blackstone's issues had gotten. His jealousy had built to an obsession, and he did his best to sabotage you anyway he could. He's been sent to a mental health facility and will be punished for his crimes. I hope you trust that something like that will never happen again.'

I wasn't sure 'trust' was the right word, but I was glad to have him out of Neverthorn.

Tarquinius wasn't big on apologies and swept a hand in the air as if to delete it from his memory.

'Now, final order of business. I was very pleased to find that several of you have been shown to have Quirks of considerable strength. Marina, with your control of the water, Ellie with your healing abilities, and of course, Harlow with the power of ten Dwimmers at your fingertips.'

I had to fight not to look at the others.

The jig was up.

I'd hoped to keep some of our Quirks under our hats for a little longer, but clearly, we'd outed ourselves in the Coliseum and Tarquinius knew them all.

Still, despite this new information, none of us spoke, and Tarquinius seemed encouraged by our silence. 'With abilities like those you've displayed, you will each be deployed to a Runecoat division to work directly with a cadre of fighters. By spreading you out, there will be less chance of Nocta attacking you all at once.'

'That . . . that is a terrible idea.' I barely managed to get the words out through clenched teeth. 'We work as a team.'

The others murmured their agreement.

His smile was tight. 'And you will again . . . when we see fit. You need to trust that we know what's best.'

Too bad I was fresh out of trust.

'When will you be sending us out?' Ross asked, his Adam's apple bobbing.

When would he split up the family we'd created, the bonds we'd made . . .

'First thing tomorrow morning.'

43

Two hours later, Phyllis handed me a steaming mug of cocoa, and I raised one brow, my heart still aching at what Tarquinius had told us.

We were being separated, after everything we'd been through.

'What, no marshmallows?'

'Forgot them. My apologies.' Without hesitating, she whipped off a rune that summoned a trio of three fat marshmallows and set them bobbing merrily in my cocoa. Then, she pinned me with that eerily perceptive gaze. 'Anything else?'

It took everything I had not to fidget like a five-year-old.

'Sorry. I'm feeling super anxious and stressed, and sometimes I use humor as a defense mechanism.'

Cripes on a frucking cracker, where had that even come from?

Shaking my head in awe, I let out a low whistle. 'You'd have made one hell of an interrogator, Phyll.'

I winced, realizing my slip up, and was about to apologize for the second time in less than thirty seconds, but she held up a hand as she settled into the purple velvet chair across from me.

'It's fine. I've come to terms with you calling me that. It was just a bit of a shock, initially. Only one person ever called me that.'

And we both knew who that was. I took a sip of my cocoa.

'Which brings me to why I wanted to talk with you tonight,

at least in part,' Phyllis said softly. 'What I'm about to say might sound cruel, but you need to hear it from someone who cares about you.' Her eyes filled with despair and just the hint of tears before she blinked them away and stiffened her jaw. 'You're a liability here, Harlow. Now that he's made contact, your father will never stop coming for you – I know him. Everyone around you will be at risk. Including your housemates.' She pursed her lips. 'Including Opie.'

When Phyllis fired shots, she went straight for the heart.

I put my mug on the table between us. Then I wrapped my arms around myself and sank deeper into the sofa.

'Here's the thing,' I said after a while. 'He could have taken me. At the arena. But he didn't. He . . .' She immediately started to protest, but I waved her off. 'No, I mean, I realize people did get hurt. I just . . .' I scuttled to the edge of the cushion and leaned forward, almost afraid to say what I had to say too loud. 'When we were out of sight . . . when one of the Runecoats was fighting with one of his men, Opie and Krishna were in the line of fire. I got between them, I would have died, Phyllis. He came and –' I broke off and raked a hand through my hair, wondering how much to say. Because now that Tarquinius was sending us to the Runecoat divisions, separating us, Nocta's message seemed all that much more real.

'There's no other way to put it. He saved her and Krishna. And me. Then he spoke to me directly. He said that I was trusting the wrong people, and that things weren't as they seemed – that I needed to flee.'

Unspoken were the questions I kept to myself . . .

Had he said all that to recruit me and gain my sympathy? Or had he changed?

She set her own untouched cocoa down and then stood, leaving the room without speaking. For the next five minutes, I could hear her voluminous skirts rustling and the opening and closing of drawers in the next room. I was starting to wonder if I'd been summarily dismissed and shunned in one fell swoop and just didn't know it yet, but before I could call out and ask her, she was back. In her hands, she held a small pile of items.

She settled herself back onto the chair and laid the items between us.

'I'm going to tell you about your father because it's imperative that you know, but it brings me great pain to do so. After today, we'll never speak about this again. Is that understood?'

I swallowed hard and nodded, half tempted to walk out but knowing that wouldn't change anything.

'I loved him. Nico.' A soft smile spread across her lips as she gazed down at the photo on the top of the pile. 'He was my first – my only love, you know. And I knew it the second I laid eyes on him. He wasn't just gorgeous and charismatic, much like you, Harlow. He was also brilliant. His mind was the thirstiest of sponges, soaking in every drop of knowledge and immediately on the hunt for more. Even Tarquinius saw it in him. He became his mentor, teaching him, molding him into his own image. Despite being the housemaster's pet and some petty jealousy from a few of the other boys, your father was very popular. Everyone wanted to be his friend or his girlfriend . . . bathe in the light he gave off. We kept it a secret from the others, but he loved only me.'

She handed me the picture and I took it hesitantly.

'I know you've seen it already but look again.'

I stared down at the face that haunted me.

'That was springtime . . . before the darkness. Before he changed. He'd just found out he had a Quirk. A Splice, if you can believe it. One of only two Splices ever born. He could meld mundane items together, which was amazing in itself, but he could also meld magics together. He was just scratching the surface of what he could do, and we were so optimistic about our future. So in love, and heartsick that we would have to spend our six-week summer break apart. I don't know exactly what happened during that time. Although we sent letters, his quickly grew short and cryptic. He'd been asked to stay at Neverthorn for special training with Tarquinius. I thought he was just too busy to write much, but when I came back that September, I knew it was more than that. Something was different. He seemed . . . troubled. His zest for life was tarnished. And when we spoke of the future, he seemed bleak. Depressed. I tried to get him to talk to me, but the harder I pushed, the more he withdrew. I shouldn't have let that stop me, though. If only I'd told someone that I was worried, maybe they could've —'

She started to rock almost imperceptibly, wringing her hands.

'In any case, I did as he asked and gave him some space. And every couple of weeks or so, he would come to me. Usually exhausted, always distraught. But he would lay his head on my lap, and we would talk. Sometimes I could even make him laugh. It gave me hope. The last time he came to my room was on November second. He was even more upset than usual. He started ranting about power, and how corrupt it could be. It was a time of political unrest in both the Dwimmer and Unlit worlds. Lots of protests happening, and that type of talk, especially for our generation, was fairly common. He said he felt helpless . . . he didn't even know who he was anymore. It finally had a name, this demon dogging my Nico. He was having an existential crisis. And I remember feeling almost relieved. Less than a week later, he murdered nine of our housemates in cold blood.'

My head was spinning, and I took a long gulp of the cocoa to dislodge the stone wedged there. I regretted it instantly as the cloying sweetness of the marshmallows set my stomach churning.

'Why did he do it? He was brilliant. Surely, he'd have seen that his actions would achieve nothing good?' I asked, desperate to make sense of it. 'And you said yourself that Tarquinius was mentoring him. They spent the whole summer together. Surely, he would've seen the changes in Nicodemus, same as you?'

She shrugged. 'Maybe. And maybe not. Your father was very good at playing the part. When he was in class or out and about around school, he seemed almost normal. Maybe a bit more reserved, but everyone chalked it up to his rigorous study schedule. He was only his true self with me.'

'And at that time, did you believe his true self was capable of mass murder?'

Until that moment, I didn't realize how much of me desperately wanted her to say no, despite what I'd seen in those bloodied walls of the fairy circle. For the one person who loved and knew him best to tell me that I wasn't the fruit of a poisoned tree . . .

'I don't think it, Harlow. I *know* it.' Her eyes filled with tears and her lips began to tremble. 'I saw it with my own two eyes as he used a siphoning machine to suck the magic out of our classmates, leaving them dead. Nothing but empty shells. Skin and bones for their parents to bury.'

Same as what the fairy circle had shown me. Why was I being so stubborn when I'd seen it with my own eyes?

The same eyes you saw him save Opie with, a little voice reminded me.

She tugged a scrapbook out of her pile and slid it over toward me. 'That's them, Harlow. All the children your father killed.'

I'd seen them before, but there were more images. Some

449

looked like Polaroids. Others were from newspaper articles or yearbooks. All pictures of young teens smiling, not a care in the world. No hint that their days were numbered. That their lives would be brutally cut short by one of their own. I stared at each one in turn, committing their faces to memory.

Mary Wood with teeth that her face hadn't grown into yet but would've been the envy of all a few years down the road.

Angela King with hair the color of a shiny penny and a hint of mischief in her eyes that reminded me of myself at that age.

Jennifer Rhodes, Lisa Richardson, Rick Butler, Eric Gomez, Randall Martinez, John Rahl, Michael Carolinus. Their names blurred with their young faces, so full of hope for a future that was not meant to be. Not for them.

Phyllis leaned in and closed the book with a snap, jarring me back to the present.

'Do you understand now, Harlow?' she whispered urgently, her face full of an anguish I couldn't even hope to understand. 'I will always love the boy your father used to be, but something broke inside him. My Nico and the monster known as Nocta are not the same person. You need to forget everything he told you, and you need to leave – not because he told you to, but because you and I both know that the others look to you. Take them far away and train until, together, you have the strength to defeat him. And don't come back until you do.'

I shook my head furiously.

'No. No, there's got to be another way,' I said, my brain churning so hard I could almost hear it sizzling. 'Opie won't want to leave, and –'

'Nor should she. She'll be far safer here, away from you. I'll stay behind to watch over her. Tarquinius will protect this place to his last breath.'

She wanted me to leave Opie behind. I shot to my feet.

'No frucking way. I'm not doing it. Sorry, Phyllis. I like you, and if there was anyone I would trust with her, it would be you.'

'Don't you understand?' she asked again, her face so grieved it twisted something inside of me. 'She has no magic, Harlow. If he thinks you are still here . . . if he comes to Neverthorn again and wants to punish you once he realizes you won't turn to him, she's a sitting duck.'

'Nope.'

She stepped forward and grabbed my shirt, dragging my face down to hers. 'Until you and the rest of House Phoenix are strong enough, no one can protect her or any of the rest of us from him. He is that powerful. You all need to grow stronger and *then* come back to face him.'

'But he didn't kill her. He could've and he chose not to.'

'For *now*. Who knows why? To gain your trust? To twist your mind into thinking he's the hero and not the villain?' She let out a low snort. 'He's good, so very good at manipulating people. He almost had you. But surely you see it now. He's the game master and we're just all pieces on the board. He proved the prophecy a lie and shows up, blasting through every ward we have, to get to the Coliseum. He wants you on his side, so he tries to convince you he's someone else. Someone who cares for you and wants to do the right thing. It's all lies to bring about whatever his end game is.'

But her words echoed his. *Perhaps one day, you will fight for me.*

She pursed her lips and then shook her head.

'Until you and the others have everything you need to defeat him, we are at his mercy. So again, I tell you. You need to gather your housemates and leave this place before you're separated. Use your powers, your skills, your resources, whatever it takes to hide so he can't find you for long enough that one of you is strong enough to find and wield the Grym Dunaras. Liam can go with you. He can help draw out the rest of your Quirks without interference. He knows something is amiss here at Neverthorn. He is in full agreement that House Phoenix will be unable to flourish separately, and he agrees that it's best you all go. He's ready and awaiting your decision.' Tears streamed down her cheeks now, unchecked. 'Then, once you're all as powerful as your destinies meant you to be, you can come back and protect the innocents at this school . . . like I never could.'

I knew she was right. But . . .

'I literally can't.' I pulled back and threw my hands up in the air. 'Even if I wanted to, I can't. I'm still bonded to Typhon, remember?'

I was angry at him for not speaking up when Tarquinius had delivered his edict about House Phoenix leaving and splitting up, but part of me still felt connected to him, because I was. And I feared and hoped in equal measure that I always would be.

Phyllis leveled me with a hard stare. 'I can help you break it – the potion I gave you before was just to numb it – we couldn't have cut it when you were still in the school. He would have known. This one . . . this one will cut all the bonds.'

I hesitated, heartsick.

'I will guard Opie with my life.' The way she said it – solemn, truth ringing in her voice – I knew she would.

'We have to do it now. Tonight.'

'I know. Before the wards are done being fortified. Before Tarquinius has made it official that House Phoenix is going to be split.'

Barely time to do the job, never mind say my goodbyes.

But right was right. I had to do it, and just pray to every god that I didn't fruck this whole thing up. Which, given my track record, seemed unlikely.

'Okay. I'll do it.'

'Good.' She nodded and let out a shaky breath. 'Good.'

She leaned over and grabbed another book from the pile. This one, I recognized.

'Your father's journal. So far, I've never been able to open it. It's rune-locked. Somehow, I feel like if anyone can find a way, it will be you. You're good at getting into things you aren't supposed to,' she said with a sad smile.

I accepted it gingerly and nodded. 'Thanks.'

She stared at me for a long while and then cleared her throat. 'Now the last thing to do . . . break the bond with Typhon.'

I squinted at her, not loving the apprehension on her face. 'Okay?'

'But you're not going to like it . . .'

44

'You're going back to the wishing well?' Fable demanded. 'Are you out of your frucking mind?'

Part of me had wondered the same thing when Phyllis suggested it, but the more we'd talked, the more I knew she was right. There truly was no other way . . .

Explaining that to my housemates was a whole other ball of wax though.

'Calypso already tried to kill you once. And this is a good idea, why?' Ellie's eyes filled with concern.

'We could fight her instead. Do you need me to go fight her?' Gary asked, flexing his muscles.

'No fighting. I just have to hope that if I make her an offer she can't refuse, she'll make the deal. And I'm going to take back up. I'm going to ask Liam to come with me, as Phyllis suggested.'

In case I couldn't convince Calypso to make a deal, Liam would – hopefully – be able to pull me out.

Phyllis and I had come up with a doozy of an offer. Everything in my being told me so, and even considering my Quirk and all I'd learned here at Neverthorn this time around, my gut was still my greatest strength.

But even a victory here would surely ring hollow. Leaving Neverthorn was going to be the most painful sacrifice I'd ever been asked to make. I'd already broken the news to Bandit and had given him a letter for Opie. If I saw her face to face and had to explain what was about to happen, it'd break my resolve. Even seeing Bandit's big, sad eyes had been bad enough.

'I don't love it,' Fable said with a sniff. 'But I get it.'

I'd already explained everything to them. Why we had to go, what was at stake if we stayed and let them separate us. Everything except Nocta being my father. Fable already knew, of course, but I needed everyone to be fully committed and given all that he had done to cause harm over the years, it definitely wouldn't help my case. As much as I hated keeping secrets from them after all we'd been through, this was the only way for us to get strong enough to protect ourselves and the rest of the students at Neverthorn.

I'd do what needed to be done and beg their forgiveness later. Assuming we all made it out of this mess alive.

By the time their interrogation was over, and everyone was on board, it was nighttime, and I was mentally drained. And there was still one more thing I had to do before I left the building.

My eyes flitted this way and that as I made my way down the hall.

To Typhon's door.

I rapped on the door and called his name in a low voice. 'Typhon?' Silence reigned, and I knocked again, harder. Hard enough to make my knuckles sting. 'Typhon, it's Harlow. Open the door.'

Again, silence.

I reached for the door handle and tried to turn it, but it was locked. I jiggled and banged on the door with the heel of my palm. 'Typhon, if you don't open this door, I'm gonna open it myself.'

'Tarquinius is misguided.' His voice was gruff, as he spoke through the door, like he'd swallowed glass. 'I'm going to the Senate before morning light and won't leave until they've agreed to intervene. But I need you to go. We'll talk about it tomorrow when I get back.'

Knowing he was ready to stand up to Tarquinius and fight for me only made the stab of guilt for what I was about to do even sharper. But if I told him we were all leaving tonight, he might feel he had no choice but to try and stop me. And if by some miracle he trusted Liam enough to protect us and did let us go, he would no longer have plausible deniability.

If he didn't know we were leaving, he couldn't be blamed for not stopping us.

There was no other way.

'Typhon . . .'

'Go, damn you!'

It was like he didn't know me at all. I whipped off a quick rune, and the door handle gave way. I pushed my way inside, blinking as my eyes attempted to adjust to the darkness.

'Get out!' a voice snarled from the corner of the room.

He sounded like a monster.

I stepped inside and closed the door behind me. As I padded across the room, his form slowly began to take shape by the moonlight filtered in through the shutters covering the window. He stood in front of a roughly hewn wooden desk. I realized with a start that he was shirtless, his hair was almost as wild as his eyes, and blood was running in a stream from the crook of his arm, down his hands and into a plain, iron chalice.

What the –

'Typhon, please talk to me. I can't leave you here like this. I don't know what's wrong, and until I do, I'm going to be worried sick. Please –'

His laugh was harsh and humorless. 'I knew it was a mistake to have you come back. You just don't know when to fucking quit, do you? And I don't know who it's going to kill first, Harlow: you or me.'

I rushed closer and grabbed his arm, peering down at the

wound there. The gash was deep, and the blood was flowing heavily.

'Gods, what happened?'

He yanked away as I registered just how hot his flesh was.

'Typhon –' I broke off as my gaze lowered to the desk to see a large blade lying next to the chalice. It was wet with fresh blood.

Typhon's blood.

I swayed on my feet, suddenly dizzy. 'Did you – did you do this to yourself?' I demanded, grabbing him by his shoulder and yanking him to face me. The answer was in his eyes, along with a slew of other emotions that I couldn't even begin to decipher. 'Gods, Typhon, why?'

There was a white cloth on the desk as well, and I picked it up and moved to staunch his wound, wrapping it as tightly as I could. He didn't fight me, and for that I was grateful. It was only when I got my own feet under me that I realized he was swaying too.

'Sit before you fall down,' I said gently, pulling him toward the edge of the bed.

I lowered myself to the mattress, and he followed suit. He leaned in heavily, and with a broken sigh that made it seem like all the energy had been drained out of him in one fell swoop.

'Don't bother asking. This isn't something I will speak of. Not now, not ever.'

'Because you're rune gagged?'

He stared at me long and hard and then shook his head. 'Because I choose not to tell you.'

'Okay, but a few weeks ago, when Lucy was wandering the halls and you came out covered in blood, was it this too? And that night on the roof with Nikita?'

His non-response was answer enough.

'Save your pity. Whatever my struggles, they're less than I deserve, I promise you that.'

'Someone recently told me that the people I trust do not deserve it,' I admitted softly as I moved closer. 'And I instantly thought of you. But I know you aren't as bad as you pretend to be. In fact, I think you're the only person with any power here that isn't a monster.'

His jaw went so tight it could've cut glass, and I resisted the urge to trace my finger over the pulse pounding in his neck. Then he let out a harsh laugh, but it sounded forced.

'How quickly we forget.' He reached out to splay his big palm over my heart, which thudded hard in reply. 'I nearly killed you once, Harlow. What makes you think I've changed?'

I stared at him long and hard as the blood rushed in my ears. 'Maybe you haven't. But maybe you weren't a monster then either. Tell me the truth, Typhon. Did you want to hurt me that day?'

The words hung between us for so long, I almost asked the question again, but then he broke the silence.

'I fired a killing rune straight at your chest, Harlow. You do the math.'

But the longer I stared at him, the surer I became. And the truth rocked me to my core.

Holy sheet.

'It was an accident, wasn't it?' I demanded, thinking back to that day. Thinking of how furious I was that he'd lorded his power over a kid who was so much weaker than him. Alvin Prisby. 'Why did you have him in that stranglehold? The truth, Typhon.'

He winced and shook his head. 'That kid was a prick. He'd tried to create a potion that would make a girl he liked more agreeable to his advances. He put it in her drink at dinner. I was dealing with him when you walked in.'

My stomach did a nosedive even as the pain in my ribs throbbed.

'And I intervened. Knocked you off him with some half-baked rune,' I continued, pressing. I could still see the expression on his face when he'd lifted a finger to send off the first rune. Pure shock. And then panic as I continued to fire my sloppy magic at him . . . 'Something I did startled you. Sent you reeling and confused you enough that you made a terrible mistake.'

'Stop.'

I shook my head furiously. 'You can keep lying if you want to Typhon, but I can feel it in my bones. You didn't mean to do it.'

'You just can't accept that you were annoying enough that I did it on purpose.' But again, the words rang hollow and when he tried to move his hand away, I grabbed it and held it tight to my chest.

'I forgive you.'

'I don't forgive me!'

His face was tight with remembered pain, his eyes full of regret even as he shook his head.

'Please, just let it go, Harlow.'

'I forgive you, Typhon,' I said again, hoping he could hear the truth ringing in my voice.

'I don't deserve your forgiveness.' He was shaking his head furiously now, but I found myself leaning into him anyway, until I could feel the heat rolling off him.

'Typhon . . . please let me help you.'

'Gods damn it. You don't know what you're asking for. Last chance, Harlow,' he muttered, a growl reverberating deep in his throat. 'Go while you still can.'

He was right. This was a terrible idea. I should do what I came to do, and walk away . . .

'No.'

The second the word left my mouth, I was on him, closing the distance between us, my lips slanted over his. And, as if he'd never considered otherwise, he wrapped one hand in my hair, his wound forgotten.

Stars exploded behind my eyelids as his tongue danced with mine. He was everything dark and delicious, but there was an edge of desperation . . . of a shared suffering that made it painfully beautiful.

I wrapped my arms around his broad shoulders, and he slanted his body over mine, pressing me against the mattress with a groan so guttural that it could've been pleasure or pain. Maybe both.

He tore his mouth from mine, peppering my jaw with kisses before nipping me sharply.

'Gods, I dream about this every night.'

Heat flared in my stomach as I gripped him tighter and rolled my hips against his. He was a massive wall of a man, and that didn't stop at the waist. In fact, he was so thick and hard against my belly, it felt like a length of steel.

More.

This wasn't part of the plan, damn it, but what if I never had the chance again? What if I left Neverthorn a second time, and we never found our way back to one another?

I reached between us to yank my shirt open. Buttons flew, pinging off the floor, as he made short work of my bra.

I closed my eyes as the cool night air hit my overheated, bare skin.

'If this was the last sight I ever saw, I could die a happy man.'

I let my lashes flutter open and found him staring down at me, one knee on either side of my hips, naked hunger on his face.

'You are so fucking beautiful. You don't deserve –'

He let out a groan as he rolled away, springing to his feet like a tiger, looking every bit as dangerous as he stared down at me, eyes still wild with need.

I sat up, tugging my shirt to cover myself. 'Typhon –'

'It can't happen. I shouldn't have even let it get this far. There's too much you don't know. Go!' he snarled. 'Before I do something we both regret.'

I scooted to the end of the bed to stand in front of him, then laid a gentle hand on his cheek. For a second, it felt like he leaned into my touch before grabbing my wrist roughly and yanking it away.

'Goodnight, Harlow.'

I yanked my arm away, tears stinging my eyes as I pushed my way blindly into the hall before letting the door close behind me.

'Goodbye, Typhon,' I murmured under my breath, heart aching like it had been torn in two.

Hopefully, Typhon would fall into a deep, exhausted sleep after whatever he'd been through tonight, and by the time he figured it out, it'd be too late. But just in case . . .

I drew in a breath and crafted a blocking rune in front of his door. Then I breathed as much power into it as I could, letting the magic expand and fill me before filling the rune to bursting. Steeling myself, I pushed away from the door and rushed down the hallway.

I'd bought myself a twenty-minute head start. Maybe a little more if he didn't discover the rune right away.

Another wave of guilt rolled over me, but it was just one more piece of kindling to add to the fire. I couldn't let it sway me from what I knew was right.

No matter how much it was killing me.

45

My legs were still shaking twenty minutes later as we crept toward the well.

'Remember the rune I showed you if there's trouble,' Liam said for the third time. He'd agreed immediately to help me. No questions asked.

'Got it.'

'And remind me once more why I can't go down with you?'

So much for no questions.

I shook my head. 'She doesn't trust people. The fewer the better. Besides, I need you out here to fish me out if it goes tits up.'

'I've been studying all sorts of new healing runes. I won't fail you, Harlow,' Ellie said, gaze solemn as she stared at me like she was trying to commit my face to memory one last time, which wasn't exactly confidence-boosting.

I stopped a few yards short of our target and then turned to face them.

'I'll go on my own from here. See you shortly.'

Every single one of them looked like they were attending a funeral, but I hadn't come this far to fail them now. The storm that had been threatening all night chose that moment to break, and the rain didn't start with a gentle patter. Nope, it opened up like someone was emptying out their eternal bucket on our heads. If I believed in omens, this would not be a great one.

I muttered as I slogged toward the nature-made wall of thorns and vines where Calypso's well was hidden. Only now, a fresh and more complex shielding spell helped conceal it, likely courtesy of Tarquinius after my last adventure. We'd prepared for that, though. I closed my eyes and traced the rune Liam had taught me, shuddering with a mix of relief and dread as the cobbled stones of the well shimmered into view.

Only this time, I didn't need to dive in. There was a heavy splash and then Calypso pulled herself up to sit on the edge.

My jaw dropped as I took in her face and form. She was as terrifying as the last time. Her lower body was a thickly muscled tail, the scales catching the faint light around us, flashing iridescent green and silver. Her upper body was bare, her ribs clearly visible, and her breasts covered by the bones of someone's hands. Her long dark hair clung to her shoulders, falling all the way to her waist. Yellow, predatory orbs narrowed on me. She flashed a wide smile at me, all her teeth on display.

Only at least now, she was on my turf and my friends were –

'They can't hear or see either one of us behind my own shielding spell, so don't make the mistake of thinking you're safe, child. But I have to admit, I'm curious. You have ten seconds to tell me why you're here . . . a second time.'

I wet my lips and reeled off my request as I pulled out a sack of gold coins that Liam had given me for just this purpose. 'I would like to give you this offering of gold. In exchange, I would ask that you break a binding spell for me.'

Her expression didn't change as she studied me in silence. The rain continued to pelt at me and streamed down my face as I waited.

'Who are you bound to?' she asked, cocking her head.

'Doyen Typhon Moreno.'

Her yellow eyes widened and she drew back in surprise. 'Now that is interesting . . . What will you do once the bond is broken? And don't lie, child, or I'll know it.'

'I will leave Neverthorn with the rest of my house and grow our magic so we can defeat Nocta.'

Calypso laughed, her head thrown back as a sharp snap of lightning cut across the sky, right above us. 'Pity. That Typhon is a looker, so I can hardly blame you. All dark and broody. I'd have laid with him too, but I surely would not have let my heart get tangled up. He's basically a fucking vampire, isn't he?'

The boom of thunder that hit next felt like it was right inside my chest. 'What . . . do you mean?'

Calypso leaned forward, laying across the top of the well, propped up on her elbows like we were girlfriends dishing at a party.

'He's a Draw. A natural siphon. He sucks the magic out of other Dwimmers. The only one of his kind.'

I was already shaking my head. 'No. He would never do that.' The cold of the rain and wind seemed to strike me to the core as I remembered the look on his face earlier. How he'd all but admitted he'd done terrible, terrible things . . .

'Nocta used his little tool to suck his classmates dry. Moreno is no different, only he doesn't need a machine. He can do it all on his own.'

I wanted to argue, but everything suddenly clicked into place with a *snap* as memory after memory flitted through my mind. All those times my housemates and I had failed. Felt weak and ineffectual. It wasn't a spell that had kept us muted, it wasn't a ward that Tarquinius had created.

It was Typhon skimming off our magic.

What better way to keep us from seeing the truth of it. Pretend to help us while he sucked us dry. Gave us just enough to keep us in line, while draining us on the other side. I had to swallow hard against the nausea that rose through me.

Those you trust do not deserve it.

'Ah, love hurts, doesn't it, child?'

'I don't love him,' I spat at her, struggling to pull myself together as I remembered how little time I had before the man himself would be free to hunt me down. Suddenly, I was glad for the rain as hot tears joined the icy droplets to streak down my cheeks. 'Please. I need your help, and quickly. Will you accept my offer?'

She moved closer, so my face was right in hers. Her teeth were sharp little daggers, and her wide yellow eyes locked with mine.

'You are brave, Harlow Daygon. I'll give you that,' she murmured, shaking her head. 'Let us negotiate, then. I'll take your gold, of course. But I also want you to retrieve something for me. You found my well, twice. I think you must be very good at finding things.'

I blinked and gave a slow nod. 'I have a knack.'

She lifted a hand and the ethereal image of what looked like a dinner plate coated in gold appeared. 'I need you to find this gold piece and bring it to me.'

The massive galleon turned over in the air so I could see both sides of it. The kraken etched into the tails side; the head of a mermaid etched onto the other. The year on it was 1567.

'I can do that.' I could probably do that. 'Do you have any idea where it was last seen?'

She ignored the question and let the image she'd created shimmer away. 'You have thirty days to retrieve it and get it into my hands. If you fail, you will die, and I will add your bones to create another layer to my well.'

Thirty days was not a lot of time. But it was more than I had now, and I was nothing if not resourceful.

'Done.'

She smiled and then reached around her neck, unfastening the necklace that hung there. She placed it in my hand. 'There is a mirror inside that locket that I can access to watch your progress. It will also allow me to continue to help you.'

'I don't need your help beyond what I've requested.'

Her eyes narrowed and her tail flipped once, like an irritated cat. 'I'm not asking. You will take the locket with you so I can join you on your quest. I don't get out . . . ever, and I find myself intrigued with your life. Once we shake on it, it is set in stone.' She held out her webbed hand, and paused for one, long moment.

Then, I shook it.

The second I did, a pain like I'd never felt exploded through my chest. My vision went black, and I had to grasp the stones to stay on my feet. My heart was shattering against the inside of my chest, that rib Typhon had broken so long ago aching as if it were fresh.

'Do you feel it, child? I've kept my promise, yes?'

Phyllis's dulling pill had hurt, but this was like being hit by a bus. Worse, I got the sense that as my brain caught up with my body, and the loss I'd just suffered, it would only get worse.

'I . . . I have to go,' I whispered, barely managing the words.

'One more thing.'

I scrunched my eyes and slowly turned back to Calypso, chest aching. 'What?'

'A show of good faith.' She tossed me what looked like a string of seaweed.

The long string was indeed seaweed, but it was not by any means brittle or weak. It felt like bands of steel had been woven through it. Little bumps littered the string, like tiny kelp balls.

'Take that. Have your friends each grasp it. It will spirit you away from Neverthorn. A gift. Free of charge. The sooner you go, the better. The prophecy you've been told is right, but there is more you do not know. It's true that a savior will come from Neverthorn who can defeat Nocta. But there are two sides to that coin. Another here with the strength to see Nocta's cause through to the end. You and the others of House Phoenix need to gain enough strength to defeat them both.'

'Who?' I demanded. 'When?'

'That I do not know. You must go now. Time is ticking.'

'W-where will it take us?' I asked and shivered as she smiled at me once more.

'Your journey will begin at the home of the kraken galleon, of course.'

I frowned at her, feeling the trap settling around me, and knowing I'd step willingly into it in order to get out of this place. 'And that is?'

'Heathermoor Academy.'

Opie

Dear Opie,

Hey kid, I know that you are probably freaking out right now. I'm so sorry. No matter what happens, I need you to know that you are my little sister, blood or no blood. And that everything I do, I am doing to keep you safe.

Right now, that means you can't come with me.

I'm going to work with Doyen O'Connor on a project that's going to take me far away. You stay here and learn lots. Go to Phyllis if you need anything at all.

And take care of Bandit for me. He can't come where I'm going.

I love you, Opie, more than you can know. Krishna is a good friend. I'm glad you have her.

I'll write if I can.

Love always.
Harlow

Opie stared down at the letter as the air left her lungs in a *whoosh,* and blood roared in her ears. Crimson and black spots impeded her vision, flickering like fireflies, making the words blur into a mass of black ink. This couldn't possibly be real. Harlow had left her here?

Alone?

'She would never do that. This has to be a trick . . .' Her voice was a whispered plea in the silent room.

But Bandit himself had delivered the note only moments before, and the sharply pointed scrawl was all-too familiar.

Alone.

She tipped her head back and stared out at the moon. It was barely visible through the rain lashing at the windows. A chill rolled through her, and she shuddered as memories came storming back in . . .

'Stop crying, Ophelia. It's unbecoming of a Baumgarten. You'll accept your fate, and land on your feet, or you won't.'

The Rolls-Royce slowed to a smooth stop, and her mother turned to her; the only hint of emotion on her unlined face? Annoyance.

'Now go on with you.'

Opie stared into those steely-gray eyes, knowing that there was no changing her mind. Knowing that, once she stepped out of the car, she would likely never see her family again.

'B-but . . . it's pouring out . . .'

'Which is why you have an umbrella in your suitcase, and enough money to put a roof over your head.' Her mother snapped her fingers twice. 'Get a move on. I have a dinner party to attend.'

'A dinner party to attend,' Opie said with a harsh laugh. 'She dumped me on the street like a stray dog, and she was worried about a dinner party.'

She tried not to let the rest of the memories in. The terror when she realized no one would rent a room to a child. The bone-chilling nights at the shelter as she latched herself onto one woman or another and pretended she belonged. The weeks she spent at a foster home with the Willises, waiting in agony for the night that Mr. Willis finally made good on the menacing promise in his eyes.

And then the sun had come out.

She'd met Harlow, and everything had changed. *She* was going to be forever family. It had taken over a year, but eventually, Opie had let herself believe it. And now . . .

She bit her lip so hard it bled as she balled the letter up in her hand.

'Fuck you, Harlow. Fuck you, and your stupid raccoon, and your promises and your lies. Fuck everyone who has left me alone and disappointed.'

The sensation that flowed through her was white-hot, like a cleansing fire, burning everything in its path. Her whole body began to shake violently, rattling her bones and teeth.

She swallowed a feral scream as her palm lifted of its own accord, fingers splayed wide as the note burst into flames. She stared, almost in a trance . . . the fire danced, growing, spreading up her arm, but never burning her skin. Instinctively, she lifted her other hand. There, in her palm, a yawning void. A black so black it nearly dragged her into it, consuming her whole.

Nocta's words, which had come in the form of a thought when he'd saved her and Krishna – words she'd convinced herself were a figment of her imagination, came back to her in a rush.

'You are more than you know, child. Find me when you find yourself. I will show you the way.'

Was this what he meant? She'd been so afraid to tell anyone, even Harlow, because even if it had been real, surely he was wrong. Surely, it was just evil talking . . . telling her what she wanted to hear.

But as the fire danced and the void pulsed, her fear faded, leaving behind a sensation she'd never felt before.

Power.

Acknowledgements

There are so many people to thank when a book comes together and the truth of the matter is, the list is enormous and so incredibly boring for readers it makes their eyes blur and they usually skip this part.

So let's make it interesting.

Christine Bell, when I was hanging from the sheer rock cliff by two fingers, you know, that time we climbed Mount Everest, you threw me a rope. Mind you, it was too short, and fraying, but the efforts you made were that of a true friend. Sort of. Laughing at me while I screamed and peed my pants, not so much. Maybe next time you could cut that shit out, because then I was laughing, and it was very hard to hold on when I was shaking like a hyena.

Kelly Walker and Erica Collins, the two of you regularly tag-teamed me, and I distinctly remember being clotheslined to the mats more than once. Mind you, I'm sure I needed the rattling of the brain from time to time to shake the cobwebs loose. So . . . thank you? Also, let's get ready to rumble, because we have round two coming up!

Susan Velazquez, you pimped me and *Neverthorn* out, like we were a high-priced escort that had the skills of a two-bit . . . cough, cough . . . nope, that's too far in the gutter. Let me try again. Your ability to pitch a spell, as if you hailed from Neverthorn yourself, and helped us find a place in the hallowed ground of the world of *TradPub* . . . a space few get to stand in; I am grateful for the help finding my way there. Most days. Some days I wonder at your sanity and mine for working in this crazy world.

Stevie Finegan, a battle mage for sure, and when we fought that dragon side by side, I will never forget the fierceness in your eyes, or the knowledge that your sword was next to mine in whatever fight came our way. I am looking forward to fighting more beasties. Something smaller than a dragon though would be lovely if I'm being honest.

To the Knights of the Round Table, the Penguin Michael Joseph Family . . . a team of word assassins (ah, so many sentences cut, bleeding out on the paper, but for the better of course), and polite English suggestions as we sat at the round table and made *Neverthorn* better, and stronger with each pass. My deepest curtsey to you all.

Finally, and not least of all, to all those who see me on a regular basis. Family. Friends. Veterinarians. For putting up with my squirreling around for ideas, thoughts, blurting of said ideas and thoughts, for reminding me to take my Vyvanse, for checking in to see if I'd eaten, or slept, or taken a breath. You all keep me from bouncing too far off track (I mean, I'm going to bounce, we know it, but less when you all are involved). Thank you, for the parts you play in my story. Sometimes as villains, sometimes as mentors, so often as mental health support, I would not be where I am in my own story, without the influences of all of yours.

You have all my love, to the moon and back, through whatever worlds we all step into, real and imagined.